"Are you okay?" a deep male voice asked.

She was covered in sand, grabbing her wrist and whimpering like a baby seal that had lost its mama. Did she look okay?

"I'm fine," she lied. "Just a little spill."

She looked up—way, way up—and somehow wasn't surprised to find the other runner she had spotted a few moments earlier.

Her instincts were right. He was great-looking. She had an impression of dark hair and concerned blue eyes that looked familiar. He wore running shorts and a formfitting performance shirt that molded to powerfully defined muscles.

She swallowed and managed to sit up. What kind of weird karma was this? She had just wished for a man in her life and suddenly a gorgeous one seemed to pop up out of nowhere.

Surely it had to be a coincidence.

* * *

THE WOMEN OF BRAMBLEBERRY HOUSE:
Finding love, one floor at a time

RaeAnne Thayne finds inspiration in the beautiful northern Utah mountains, where the *New York Times* and *USA TODAY* bestselling author lives with her husband and three children. Her books have won numerous honors, including RITA® Award nominations from Romance Writers of America and a Career Achievement Award from *RT Book Reviews*. RaeAnne loves to hear from readers and can be contacted through her website, www.raeannethayne.com.

New York Times and *USA TODAY*
Bestselling Author

RaeAnne Thayne

———

A Soldier's Return &
The Daddy Makeover

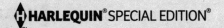

HARLEQUIN® SPECIAL EDITION®

ISBN-13: 978-1-335-98483-8

A Soldier's Return & The Daddy Makeover

Copyright © 2019 by Harlequin Books S.A.

The publisher acknowledges the copyright holder of the individual works as follows:

A Soldier's Return
Copyright © 2019 by RaeAnne Thayne LLC

The Daddy Makeover
Copyright © 2007 by RaeAnne Thayne

Recycling programs for this product may not exist in your area.

Printed in U.S.A.

www.Harlequin.com

CONTENTS

To Jill Shalvis and Marina Adair.
I love our seaside adventures!

A SOLDIER'S RETURN

Chapter One

Some days, a girl reached a point where her best course of action was to run away from her problems.

Melissa Fielding hung up the phone after yet another unproductive discussion with her frustrating ex-husband, drew in a deep, cleansing breath, then threw on her favorite pair of jogging shoes.

Yes, she had a million things to do. The laundry basket spilled over with clothes, she had bills to pay, dirty dishes filled her sink, and she was scheduled to go into the doctor's office where she worked in less than two hours.

None of that mattered right now. She had too much energy seething through her, wave after wave like the sea pounding Cannon Beach during a storm.

Even Brambleberry House, the huge, rambling Victorian where she and her daughter lived in the first-floor apartment, seemed too small right now.

She needed a little good, hard exercise to work some of it off or she would be a stressed, angry mess at work.

She and Cody had been divorced for three years, separated four, but he could still make her more frustrated than anybody else on earth. Fortunately, their seven-year-old daughter, Skye, was at school, so she didn't have to witness her parents arguing yet again.

She yanked open her apartment door to head for the outside door when it opened from the other side. Rosa Galvez, her de facto landlady who ran the three-unit building for her aunt and a friend, walked inside, arms loaded with groceries.

Her friend took one look at Melissa's face and frowned. "Uh-oh. Bad morning?" Rosa asked, her lovely features twisted with concern.

Now that she was off the phone, the heat of Melissa's anger cooled a degree or two, but she could still feel the restless energy spitting and hissing through her like a downed power line.

"You know how it goes. Five minutes on the phone with my ex and I either have to punch something, spend an hour doing yoga or go for a hard run on the beach. I don't have a free hour and punching something would be counterproductive, so a good run is the winner." Melissa took two bags of groceries from Rosa and led the way up the stairs to the other woman's third-floor apartment.

"Run an extra mile or two for me, would you?" Rosa asked.

"Sure thing."

"What does he want this time?"

She sighed. "It's a long story." She didn't want to complain to her friend about Cody. It made her sound bitter and small, and she wasn't, only frustrated at all the broken promises and endless disappointments.

Guilt, an old, unwelcome companion, poked her on the shoulder. Her daughter loved her father despite his failings. Skye couldn't see what Melissa did—that even though Skye was only seven, there was a chance she was more mature than her fun-loving, thrill-chasing father.

She ignored the guilt, reminding herself once more there was nothing she could do about her past mistakes but continue trying to make the best of things for her child's sake.

Rosa opened the door to her wide, window-filled apartment, and Melissa wasn't surprised to find Rosa's much-loved dog, an Irish setter named Fiona, waiting just inside.

"Can I take Fiona on my run?" she asked impulsively, after setting the groceries in the kitchen.

"That would be great!" Rosa exclaimed. "We were going to go on a walk as soon as I put the groceries away, but she would love a run much more. Thank you! Her leash is there on the hook."

At the word *leash*, Fiona loped to the door and did a little circular dance of joy that made more of Melissa's bad mood seep away.

"Let's do this, sweetheart," she said, grabbing the leash from its place by the door and hooking it to Fiona's shamrock-green collar.

"Thank you for this. Have fun." Rosa opened the door for them, and the strong dog just about pulled Melissa toward the stairs. She waved at her friend, then she and the dog hurried outside.

The April morning was one of those rare and precious days along the Oregon Coast when Mother Nature decided it was finally time to get serious about spring. Sunlight gleamed on the water and all the colors seemed saturated and bright from the rains of the preceding few days.

The well-tended gardens of Brambleberry House were overflowing with sweet-smelling flowers—cherry blossoms, magnolia, camellias. It was sheer delight. She inhaled the heavenly aroma, enjoying the undernote of sea and sand and other smells that were inexorable scent-memories of her childhood.

Fiona pulled at the leash, forcing Melissa to pick up her pace. Yes. A good run was exactly the prescription she was writing herself.

As she headed down the path toward the gate that led to the water, she spotted Sonia, the third tenant of Brambleberry House, working in a bed of lavender that hadn't yet burst into bloom.

Sonia was an interesting creature. She wasn't rude, exactly, she simply kept to herself and had done so for the seven months Melissa had lived downstairs from her.

Melissa always felt so guilty when she watched the other woman make her painstaking way up the stairs to her second-floor apartment, often pausing to rest on the landing. She didn't know the nature of Sonia's health issues, but she obviously struggled with something. She walked with a limp, and Rosa had told Melissa once that the other woman had vision issues that precluded driving.

Right after moving in, Melissa had offered to switch apartments with her so Sonia wouldn't have to make the climb, but her offer had been refused.

"I need…the exercise," Sonia had said in her halting, odd cadence. "Going upstairs is good…physical therapy…for me."

Melissa had to admire someone willing to push herself out of her comfort zone, sustained only by the hope that she would grow from the experience.

That was a good life lesson for her. She wasted entirely too much energy dwelling on the painful reality that life hadn't turned out exactly as she planned, that some of her dreams were destined to disappointment.

Like Sonia, maybe it was time she stopped being cranky about things she couldn't control and took any chance that came along to force herself to stretch outside her comfort zone. She needed to learn how to make the best of things, to simply enjoy a gorgeous April day.

"Beautiful morning, isn't it?"

"Lovely," Sonia said with her somewhat lopsided smile. "Hello… Melissa. Hello… Fiona."

She scratched the dog under her chin and was rewarded with one of Fi's doggie grins.

While the Irish setter technically lived with Rosa, the cheerful dog seemed to consider all the occupants of Brambleberry House her particular pack. That shared pet care worked out well for Melissa. Her daughter had been begging for a dog since before the divorce. Skye had been in heaven when they'd moved into Brambleberry House and discovered Rosa had a dog she was more than willing to share. This way, they got the benefits of having a dog without the onus of being responsible for one all the time.

That was yet another thing she had to be grateful for on this beautiful spring day. She had been so blessed to find an open apartment in Brambleberry House when she and Skye returned to Cannon Beach after all those years of wandering. It was almost a little miracle, since the previous tenant had only moved out to get married the week before Melissa returned to her hometown and started looking for a place.

She didn't know if it was fate or kismet or luck or simply somebody watching out for them. She only knew that she and Skye had finally found a place to throw down roots.

She ran hard, accompanied by the sun on her face, the low murmur of the waves, the crunch of sand under her running shoes. All of it helped calm her.

By the time she and Fiona made it the mile and a half to the end of the beach and she'd turned around to head back, the rest of her frustration had abated, and she focused instead on the endorphins from the run and the joy of living in this beautiful place.

She paused for a moment to catch her breath, looking out at the rock formations offshore, the towering haystacks that so defined this part of the Oregon Coast, then the craggy green mountains to the east.

It was so good to be home. She had friends here, connections. Her dad was buried not far from here. Her mom and stepfather were here most of the time, though they had just bought an RV and were spending a few months traveling around the country.

She would have thought being a military wife to Melissa's dad would have cured her mother's wanderlust, but apparently not. They would be back soon.

Melissa didn't envy them. After moving to a new base every few years during her childhood and then following Cody around from continent to continent, she loved being in one place. *This* place. She had missed it more than she even realized, until she finally decided to bring Skye here.

She should have done it years ago instead of trying so

hard to stay close to her ex-husband for Skye's sake. She had enjoyed living on Oahu, his home training location, but the cost of living had been prohibitive. Most of her salary as a nurse had gone to housing and the rest to food.

When he decided to move to South America on a whim, she had finally thrown up her hands and opted not to follow him. Instead, she had packed up her daughter for one last move and come home to Cannon Beach.

She started her run again, not wanting to spend more time than she already had that morning dwelling on her mistakes.

It made her sad, wondering if she should have tried harder to make things work, even though she was fully aware both of them had left the marriage long before they finally divorced.

Now wasn't the time to obsess about her failures or the loneliness that kept her up at night.

He had gotten married again. That was what he called to tell her earlier. It had been a spur-of-the-moment decision and they'd gone to St. Croix for their honeymoon, which had been beautiful but expensive. He'd spent so much on the honeymoon, in fact, that he couldn't make that month's child support payment, but he would make it up to her.

He was coming back to Oregon to stay this time, and was willing to finally step up and be the dad he should have been all along. She'd been hearing that story or versions of it for fifteen years. She hoped it would happen, she really did.

Cody wasn't a bad man. She wouldn't have loved him all those years and followed him from country to country to support his dreams if he were. But with the birth of their child, her priorities had changed, while she was afraid his never would.

Enough about Cody. She was genuinely happy for her ex, even if hearing about his new marriage did make her wish she had someone special in her own life.

She sighed again and gripped Fiona's leash. "Come on, Fi. Let's go home."

An odd wind danced across the sand, warmer than the air around it. She almost thought she could hear laughter rippling around her, though she was virtually alone on the beach.

She was hearing things again. Once in a while at the house, she could swear she heard a woman's laugh when no one was there, and a few times she had smelled roses on the stairwell, for no apparent reason.

Maybe the ghost of Brambleberry House had been in the mood for a run today, too. The thought made her smile and she continued heading home.

Few people were out on the beach on this off-season morning, but she did happen to catch sight of a guy running toward her from the opposite direction. He was too far away for her to really see clearly, but she had the random impression of lean strength and fluid grace.

Ridiculous, she told herself. How could she know that from two hundred yards away?

She continued running, intent now only on finishing so she could go into work.

Fiona trotted along beside her in the same rhythm they had worked out through countless runs like this together. She was aware of the other runner coming closer. He had a dog, too, a small black one who also looked familiar.

They were only fifty feet apart when Fiona, for no apparent reason, suddenly veered in front of Melissa, then stopped stock-still.

With no time to change course or put on the brakes, Melissa toppled over the eighty-pound dog and went flying across the sand. She shoved her hands out to catch her fall instinctively. Her right arm hit sand and she felt a jolt in her shoulder from the impact, but the left one must have made contact with a rock buried beneath the sand, causing a wrenching pain to shoot from her wrist up her arm.

This day just kept getting better and better.

She gasped and flopped over onto her back, cradling the injured wrist as a haze of pain clouded her vision.

Fiona nosed her side as if in apology, and Melissa bit back her instinctive scold. What on earth had gotten into Fiona? They had run together dozens of times. The Irish setter was usually graceful, beautifully trained, and never cut across her path like that.

For about ten seconds, it was all she could do not to writhe around on the ground and howl. She was trying not to cry when she gradually became aware she wasn't alone.

"Are you okay?" a deep male voice asked.

She was covered in sand, grabbing her wrist and whimpering like a baby seal that had lost its mama. Did she *look* okay?

"I'm fine," she lied. "Just a little spill."

She looked up—way, way up—and somehow wasn't surprised to find the other runner she had spotted a few moments earlier.

Her instincts were right. He *was* great-looking. She had an impression of dark hair and concerned blue eyes that looked familiar. He wore running shorts and a formfitting performance shirt that molded to powerfully defined muscles.

She swallowed and managed to sit up. What kind of weird karma was this? She had just wished for a man in her life, and suddenly a gorgeous one seemed to pop up out of nowhere.

Surely it had to be a coincidence.

Anyway, she might like the idea of a man in her life, but she wasn't at all prepared for the reality of it—especially not a dark-haired, blue-eyed runner who still somehow managed to smell delicious.

He also had a little dog on a leash, a small black schnauzer who was sniffing Fiona like they were old friends.

"Can I give you a hand?"

"Um. Sure."

Still cradling her injured wrist, she reached out with her right hand, and he grasped it firmly and tugged her to her feet. For one odd moment, she could swear she smelled roses above the clean, crisp, masculine scent of him, but that made absolutely no sense.

Was she hallucinating? Maybe she had bonked her head in that gloriously graceful free fall.

"You hurt your wrist," he observed. "Need me to take a look at it? I'm a doctor."

What were the odds that she would fall and injure herself in front of a gorgeous tourist who also happened to be a doctor?

"Isn't that convenient?" she muttered, wondering again at the weird little twist of fate.

He gave her an odd look, half curious and half concerned. Again, she had the strange feeling that she knew him somehow, but she had such a lousy memory for faces and names.

"Melissa. Melissa Blake?"

She narrowed her gaze, more embarrassed at her own lousy memory than anything. He knew her so she obviously had met him before.

"Yes. Actually, it's Melissa Fielding now."

"Oh. Right. You married Cody Fielding, Cannon Beach's celebrity."

And divorced him, she wanted to add. *Don't forget that part.*

"I'm sorry. You know me, but I'm afraid I don't remember your name."

He shrugged. "No reason you should. I was a few years older and I've been gone a long time."

She looked closer. There was something about the shape of his mouth. She had seen it recently on someone else...

"Eli?"

"That's right. Hi, Melissa."

She should have known! All the clues came together. The dog, whom she now recognized as Max, the smart little dog who belonged to Eli's father. The fact that he said he was a doctor. Those startling, searching blue eyes that now seemed unforgettable.

How embarrassing!

In her defense, the last time she had seen Eli Sanderson, he had been eighteen and she had been fifteen. He had graduated from high school and was about to take off across the country to college. The Eli she remembered had been studious and serious. He had kept mostly to himself, more interested in leading the academic decathlon than coming to any sporting events or social functions.

She had been the opposite, always down for a party,

as long as it distracted her from the sadness at home in those first years after her father died of brain cancer.

The Eli she remembered had been long and lanky, skinny even. This man, on the other hand, was anything *but* nerdy. He was buff, gorgeous, with lean, masculine features and the kind of shoulders that made a woman want to grab hold and not let go.

Wow. The military had really filled him out.

"I understand you work with my dad," he said.

She worked *for* his father. Melissa was a nurse at Dr. Wendell Sanderson's family medicine clinic. Now she realized why that mouth looked so familiar. She should have picked up on it immediately. His dad's mouth was shaped the same, but somehow that full bottom lip looked very different on Dr. Sanderson Jr.

Her wrist still ached fiercely. "How's your dad?" she asked, trying to divert her attention from it. "I stopped by to see him yesterday after his surgery and was going to call the hospital to check on him today as soon as I finished my run."

"He's good. I was trying to be here before he went under the knife, but my plane was delayed until last night. I did speak to the orthopedic surgeon, who is happy with the outcome so far. Both knee replacements seem to have gone well."

"Oh, good. He won't tolerate being down for long. I guess that's why it made sense for him to do both at the same time."

"You know him well."

After several months of working for the kindly family medicine doctor, she had gained a solid insight into his personality. Wendell was sweet, patient, genuinely concerned about his patients. He was the best boss she'd ever had.

"Let's take a look at this wrist," Eli said now. Unlike his father, Wendell's son could never be described as kindly or avuncular.

"I'm sure it's fine."

"Again, I'm a doctor. Why don't you let me be the judge of how fine it might be? I saw that nasty tumble and could hear the impact of your fall all the way across the sand. You might have broken something, in which case you're going to want to have it looked at sooner rather than later."

She was strangely reluctant to hand over her wrist—or anything else—to the man and fought the urge to hide her hand behind her back, as if she were caught with a fistful of Oreos in front of an empty cookie jar.

"I can have the radiologist at the clinic x-ray it when I go in to work in an hour."

"Or you can let me take a look at it right now."

She frowned at the implacable set of his jaw. He held his hand out and she sighed. "Ugh. You're as stubborn as your father."

"Thank you. Anytime someone compares me to my father, I take it as a compliment."

He gave his outstretched hand a pointed look, and she frowned again and, cornered, held out her wrist. The movement made her hurt all over again, and she flushed at the unwilling tears she could feel gather.

His skin was much warmer than she might have expected on a lovely but still cool April morning. Seductively warm. His hands were long-fingered, masculine, much longer than her own, and he wore a sleek Tag Heuer watch.

Her stomach felt hollow, her nerves tight, but she wasn't sure if that was in reaction to the injury or from the unexpected pleasure of skin against skin. He was a doctor taking a look at an injury, she reminded herself, not a sexy guy wanting to hold her hand.

Melissa aimed a glare at Fiona, who had started the whole thing. The dog had planted her haunches in the sand, tail wagging, and seemed to be watching the whole episode with an expression that appeared strangely like amusement.

"It doesn't feel like anything is broken. You can move it, right?"

He held her hand while she wiggled her fingers, then rotated her wrist. It hurt like the devil, but she didn't feel any structural impingement in movement.

"Yes. I told you it wasn't broken. It's already feeling better."

"You can't be completely sure without an X-ray, but I'm all right waiting forty-eight hours or so to check it. I suspect a sprain, but it might be easier to tell in a few days. Do you have a way to splint it? If you don't, I'm sure my dad has something at the office."

"I've got a wrist brace I've worn before when I had carpal tunnel problems."

"You'll want to put that on and have it checked again in a few days. Meanwhile, ice and elevation are your best friends. At least ten minutes every two hours."

As if she had time for that. "I'll do my best. Thanks."

A sudden thought occurred to her, one she was almost afraid to entertain. "How long will you be in town?"

When he was making arrangements to be gone for his surgery, Wendell had hoped Eli might be able to cover for him at the clinic. The last she had heard, though, Eli's hadn't been able to get leave from his military assignment so his father had arranged a substitute doctor through a service in Portland.

Given that Eli was here, she had a feeling all that was about to change—which meant Eli might be her boss for the foreseeable future.

"I'm not sure how much time I can get," he answered now. "That depends on a few things still in play. I'm hoping for a month but I'll be here for the next two to three weeks, at least."

"I see."

She did see, entirely too clearly. This would obviously not be the last she would see of Eli Sanderson.

"I need to go. Thanks for your help," she said quickly.

"I didn't do anything except take a look at your injury. At least promise me you'll raise it up and put some ice on it."

Considering she was scheduled to work at his father's clinic starting in just over an hour and still needed to shower, she wouldn't have time for much self-pampering. "I'll do my best. Thanks."

"How far do you have to go? I can at least help you walk your dog home."

"Fiona isn't my dog. She belongs to my neighbor. We were just sort of exercising each other. And for the record, she's usually very well behaved. I don't quite know what happened earlier, but we'll be fine to make it home on our own. I don't want to disturb your run more than I already have."

"Are you sure?"

"We don't have far to go. I live at Brambleberry House."

His expression registered his surprise. "Wow. You're practically next door to my dad's place."

They couldn't avoid each other, even if they wanted to. She didn't necessarily want to avoid *him*, but considering she was now bedraggled and covered with sand, she was pretty sure he wouldn't be in a hurry to see her again.

"Thanks again for your help. I'll see you later."

"Remember your RICE."

Right. Rest, Ice, Compression, Elevation. The first-aid prescription for injuries like hers. "I'll do my best. Thanks. See you later."

This time as she headed for the house, Fiona trotted along beside her, docile and well behaved.

Melissa's wrist, on the other hand, complained vociferously all the way back to the house. She did her best to ignore it, focusing instead on the unsettling encounter with Dr. Sanderson's only son.

Eli told himself he was only keeping an eye on Melissa as she made her slow way along the beach toward Brambleberry House because he was concerned about her condition, especially whether she had other injuries from her fall she had chosen not to reveal to him.

He was only being a concerned physician, watching over someone who had been hurt while he was nearby.

The explanation rang hollow. He knew it was more than that.

Melissa Blake Fielding had always been a beautiful girl and had fascinated him more than he had wanted to admit to himself or anyone else when he was eighteen and she was only fifteen.

She had been a pretty cheerleader, popular and well-liked—mostly because she always had a smile for everyone, even geeky science students who weren't the greatest at talking to popular, pretty, well-liked cheerleaders.

He had danced with her once at a school dance toward the end of his senior year. She had been there with her date—and future husband—Cody Fielding, who had been ignoring her, as usual.

While his own date had been dancing with her dad, the high school gym teacher and chaperone, Eli had gathered his nerve to ask Melissa to dance, hating that the nicest girl in school had been stuck sitting alone while her jerk of a boyfriend ignored her.

He remembered she had been everything sweet to him during that memorable dance, asking about his plans after graduation.

Did she know her boyfriend and future husband hadn't taken kindly to Eli's nerve in asking Cody's date to dance and had tried to make him pay? He still had a scar above his eyebrow from their subsequent little altercation.

It had been a long time ago. He was a completely different man than he'd been back then, with wholly different priorities.

He hadn't thought about her in years, at least until his father had mentioned a few months earlier that Melissa was back in town and working for him.

At the time, he had been grieving, lost, more than a little raw. He remembered now that the memory of Melissa had made him smile for the first time in weeks.

Now he had to wonder if that was one of the reasons he had worked hard to arrange things so that he could come home and help his father out during Wendell's recovery from double knee-replacement surgery. On some subconscious level, had he remembered Melissa worked at the clinic and been driven to see her again?

He didn't want to think so. He would be one sorry

idiot if that were the case, especially since he didn't have room in his life right now for that kind of complication.

If he *had* given it any thought at all, on any level, he probably would have assumed it wouldn't matter. He was older, she was older. It had been a long time since he'd felt like that awkward, socially inept nerd he'd been in the days when he lived here in Cannon Beach.

He had been deployed most of the last five years and had been through bombings, genocides, refugee disasters. He had seen things he never expected to, had survived things others hadn't.

He could handle this unexpected reunion with a woman he might have had a crush on. He only had to remember that he was no longer that geeky, awkward kid but a well-respected physician now.

In comparison to everything he had been through in the last few years—and especially the horror of six months ago that he was still trying to process—he expected these few weeks of substituting for his father in Cannon Beach to be a walk in the park.

Chapter Two

"You're late." Carmen Marquez, the clinic's receptionist and office manager, gave an arch look over the top of her readers, and Melissa winced but held up her braced wrist.

"I know. It's been a crazy day. I'm sorry. Blame it on this."

"What did you do? Punch somebody?" Tiffany Lowell, one of their certified nursing assistants, gave her a wide-eyed look—though the college student and part-time band front woman wore so much makeup, she had the same expression most of the time.

"I tripped over a big, goofy Irish setter and sprained my wrist. I'm sorry I'm late, but I was on strict orders to rest and put ice on it."

"That's exactly what you should be doing. In fact, it's what Dr. Sanderson would be telling you to do if he were here," Carmen said.

Dr. Sanderson Jr. *had* been the one to give her the instructions, but she wasn't ready to share that interesting bit of gossip with the other women.

"You look like you're either going to puke or pass out," Tiffany observed.

"We don't have any patients scheduled for another half hour," Carmen said with a great deal more sympathy in her voice. "You should at least sit down."

"I'm fine. I need to get ready for the new doctor. He should be coming in today."

Carmen angled her head in a strange way, her mouth pursed and her eyes twinkling. "He's already here. Oh, honey. Have we got a surprise for you."

The butterflies that had been dancing in her stomach since earlier on the beach seemed to pick up their pace. "The substitute doctor is Dr. Sanderson's son, Eli."

"Whoa! Did your fall make you psychic or something?" Tiffany asked with much more respect than she usually awarded Melissa.

"In a way, I guess you could say that. Sort of. I bumped into him on the beach this morning. He was a firsthand witness when I made my graceful face-plant into the sand, and he ended up kindly helping me up."

The memory of the concern in his blue eyes and of his strong fingers holding her hand, his skin warm against hers, made her nerve endings tingle.

She firmly clamped down on the memory. She would have to work closely with him for at least the next few weeks while Wendell recovered. It would be a disaster if she couldn't manage to keep a lid on her unexpected attraction to the man.

"I keep forgetting you grew up in town," Carmen said. "You must know Eli, then."

While Cannon Beach could swarm with tourists during the summer months, it was really a small town at heart. Most permanent residents knew one another.

"We went to school together. He was older. I was a freshman the year he was a senior. I didn't know he was going to be filling in until I bumped into him this morning. Last I heard, we were getting a temp from the Portland agency."

"That's what I heard, too," Carmen said. "I guess we have to roll with what we get."

"I'm pretty sure plenty of women in Cannon Beach will want to roll with Doc Sanderson's son when they see him." Tiffany smirked.

Melissa turned her shocked laugh into a cough. "He told me he wasn't sure until the last minute whether he'd be able to make it back to fill in."

"You know where he's been, right?" Carmen asked.

"Some kind of war zone," Tiffany said.

Wendell had told her something about what his son was doing, how since finishing his internship in emergency medicine several years earlier, Eli had been on a special assignment from the military to work with aid agencies, setting up medical clinics and providing care to desperate, helpless people whose countries were in turmoil. He had been deployed almost constantly over the last five years.

Wendell had been so proud of his son for stepping up, even though his service put him in harm's way time and again. He had also been worried for him.

"He feels things so deeply," her boss had said. "I can't imagine it's easy, the kinds of things he has to see now."

She remembered feeling great sympathy for Eli and admiration for him, though at the time she had pictured him as the nerdy, scholarly, skinny teenager she remembered, not the buff, gorgeous man she had encountered that morning on the beach.

"One thing I need to ask, though. Maybe you know the answer," Carmen said. "How can he just show up in Cannon Beach and start practicing medicine here? Do I need to check with the licensing board? Doesn't he need an Oregon license or something?"

"Fun and interesting fact. The particular license given to U.S. Army doctors allows them to practice medicine anywhere."

Melissa could feel her vertebrae stiffen and nerves flutter at the deep voice from behind her.

Oh, it was going to be a long two or three weeks if she didn't take control of this ridiculous crush she had suddenly formed for Eli Sanderson.

"I guess that makes sense," Carmen said.

"Yes," he answered. "Think how confusing it would be if an army doc had to go before the licensing board every time he was called to an emergency or had a new assignment."

"That would be a serious pain." Melissa hated the slightly breathless note in her voice. She sounded ridiculous, like the kind of brainless bikini-clad groupies who used to follow the pro surfers on the circuit.

She cleared her throat, wishing she could clear away her nerves as easily.

"Good to know. I'll file that little tidbit away, in case I'm ever on a game show where 'Army Doctors' is a category."

Tiffany snorted, and Eli's mouth quirked up into a little smile, teeth flashing. She had the strangest feeling he hadn't found that many things to smile about lately, though she couldn't have said exactly why she had that impression.

"That would be the most boring game show ever," he said. "Unless you love learning about regulations and protocol."

"I really don't. As long as you can legally see your father's patients, that's all I care about."

"I'll do my best. I know he's been worried about his caseload."

"Your dad is a great doctor, but he worries too much about his patients," Tiffany said.

"Is that possible?" Eli asked.

"He should have worried a little more about himself. He could barely stand up the last few weeks before the surgery."

Tiffany was a bit rough around the edges but like everyone else, she adored Dr. Sanderson and frequently told patients how cool it was that she now worked for the doctor who had delivered her twenty years earlier.

"Your father was so worried about taking time away from his patients he almost didn't have the surgery, though his specialist has been urging him to for months. At least as long as I've been here," Melissa said.

"Longer," Carmen said, her expression exasperated. The older woman liked to mother everyone, even their boss, who was at least two or three years older than the office manager.

"I think he would have continued putting it off and hobbling around if he hadn't injured the right one so badly two weeks ago," Melissa said. "Then the surgery became not only urgent but imperative."

"Everything worked out for the best," Eli said. "I was

able to create a gap in my schedule and here I am, at least for a few weeks."

Yes. Here you are.

She had thought him gorgeous in skintight workout clothes. That was nothing compared to the sight of him in khaki slacks, a white exam coat and a crisply ironed button-down shirt a few shades lighter than his blue eyes.

She had been a nurse for years and had never been particularly drawn to a physician, until right this moment.

"How's the wrist?" he asked.

At his words, the pain she had been staving off seemed to rush back. She held up the brace and wriggled her fingers. "Still aches but it's bearable. I agree with you that I should hold off a day or two before I have it x-rayed."

"Did you have any time to put ice on it?"

"A few minutes. Which is the main reason I'm late."

"Good. That's the best thing you can do."

They lapsed into silence and she tried to keep from gawking at him. She loved her job, working with Wendell Sanderson. The man had been nothing but kind to her since the day she'd come back to Cannon Beach. She hated thinking things would be awkward and uncomfortable with Eli here.

She could handle anything for a few weeks, Melissa reminded herself. Even working for a man for whom she had developed a serious thirst.

"Can you give me the charts of those who have appointments today? I'd like to try familiarizing myself with their files."

His words were directed to Carmen yet still provided Melissa the reminder she needed. He was her boss and she couldn't forget that.

"I've already pulled the charts of those coming in this

morning. They're on your dad's desk, since I figured you would be setting up in there," the office manager replied. "I'll find the rest and bring them in for you."

"Thank you." He gave the woman a polite smile, and Melissa could swear she felt her ovaries melt.

When he walked back down the hallway toward his office, Melissa slumped into one of the chairs in the waiting room.

Oh, this was not good. At all. She might have silently wished for a man this morning, but in truth she didn't have time for that kind of complication. She had Skye and work and friends, not to mention the online classes she was taking to work toward her nurse practitioner license. There was no room left for her to be stupid about Eli.

"Are you okay?" Carmen asked.

"I will be."

Eventually.

"He seems nice, doesn't he?" Tiffany said. "Dr. Sanderson talks about his son like all the time, but I always pictured him different, somehow. Since he's in the army, I thought he'd have a buzz cut and be all harsh and by the book."

She hadn't pictured him at all, hadn't really given Eli Sanderson much thought over the years. Now she was afraid she would be able to think about little else.

Even her throbbing wrist couldn't seem to distract her.

"How did your first day go? Any problems or unique diagnoses you think I need to know about?"

Eli adjusted his dad's pillow, giving him a stern look. "Your only job right now is to focus on healing from this surgery. I can take care of your patients, got it? You don't need to worry about them."

"I have no concerns on that front," Wendell assured him. "You're a better doctor than I ever could have dreamed of being at your age."

Eli knew that was far from true. How could it be? His own dreams were haunted by the ghosts of all those he couldn't save. Miri. Justine. Those ghosts at least had names and faces, but there were scores of others who drifted through, anonymous and lost.

He let out a breath, wondering when the hell the sense of guilt and loss would leave him. It had been six months but still felt like yesterday.

He turned his attention back to his father, instead of that war-battered market town.

"Dad, I could never be half the doctor you are. We both know that. I'll be trying my whole life to catch up."

His father rolled his eyes. "We could be here all day patting each other on the back, but I know what I know. And what I know is that you're a damn fine doctor and I'm proud to call you my son. There's no one else on earth I would trust more than you to fill in for me while I'm laid up. When I ask about my patients, it's only because I'm concerned about them, not because I don't think you can care for them the way I would."

His father had been the best doctor Eli knew. Wendell and his genuine concern for his patients had been the main reason Eli had gone to medical school in the first place. He had wanted to help people, to deliver babies and diagnose illnesses and give little kids their first shots.

He had never expected that his first years of practicing medicine would be in a series of emergency shelters and refugee camps, but that was the path he had chosen and he couldn't regret it.

"If I'm not mistaken, that sweet Julia Garrett was supposed to come in today for a prenatal checkup. She and Will had an early-term miscarriage during her last pregnancy, so I've been watching her closely. How did things look today?"

Though he instinctively wanted to tell his father to put all his patients out of his head, Eli knew that wouldn't happen. Wendell wanted to stay current on all the people he had cared for over thirty-five years of practicing in Cannon Beach. Eli had a feeling that was the only way his father would be able to endure the long recovery from his double knee replacement.

"Everything looked good today. The baby measured exactly where she should be at this stage in the pregnancy, the heartbeat sounded strong and steady, and Julia appears healthy and happy. She didn't report any unusual concerns."

"Oh, that's good. This is her fourth pregnancy—fifth, if you count the baby they lost and sixth if you count the fact that her first were twins—and I wanted her to feel confident and comfortable."

As far as Eli was concerned, his father was the iconic family physician. Wendell was dedicated to his patients, compassionate over their troubles and driven to provide them the best possible care. He had delivered some of his own patients—like Will Garrett—and was now delivering the second generation and providing care over their children.

Those patients had saved his father, plucking him out of the deep depression Wendell had fallen into after Eli's mother died following a short but hard-fought battle against breast cancer when Eli was twelve.

They had both been devastated and had dealt with the blow in different ways. Eli had retreated into books, withdrawing from his friends, from baseball, from social activities. His father had done the same, focusing only on his patients and on his son.

The pain of losing Ada Sanderson had eased over the years but hadn't left completely. Eli suspected it never would.

"And how are you, son? I mean, how are you *really*? You haven't talked about what happened with that friend of yours, but I know it still eats at you."

The question, so intuitive, seemed to knock his own knees out from under him. It had always seemed impossible to conceal his inner struggles from his father's gimlet gaze. Still, Eli did his best. He had never told Wendell how close he had been to Justine, or how her death and Miri's had been his fault.

Somehow he managed to summon an expression he hoped resembled a smile. "I'm good. Why wouldn't I be? It's a beautiful time of year to be home in Oregon. I don't remember the last April I was here. I'm not sure what I'm looking forward to more—watching the spring storms churning across the water or savoring the explosion of flowers."

Wendell saw right through him, as usual. His father gave him a searching look even as he shifted on his hospital bed to find a more comfortable position.

"After all the exotic places the army has sent you, are you sure you won't be bored out of your mind treating cold sores and high blood pressure?"

"No. I'm looking forward to that, too, if you want the truth. It will be a nice, calm change of pace. Just what I need to decompress."

"Maybe this will help you figure out whether you're going to stay in the military or settle down somewhere and open a practice. Or maybe join a practice that's already busy with tourists and locals alike."

Since the day Eli finished his residency, Wendell had been after him to become his partner here.

It had always been in his long-range plan, but how could he walk away now, with this heavy sense of responsibility he carried everywhere? He felt the weight of it even more on his shoulders now, after what happened to Justine. She had been dedicated, compassionate, completely driven to help those in turmoil. Her dedication had been silenced forever and she could no longer carry out her work. He had made a vow to carry on in her place.

"Tell me how they have been treating you here," he said to change the subject. "Have you already charmed all the nurses?"

"Not all of them. A few of these nurses have been coming to my office since they were children. I'm afraid they know all my tricks by now."

Wendell was regaling him with a story about the surgeon who had operated on him when Eli heard a slight knock on the door.

A moment later, it was pushed open, and a delicate-looking girl of about seven held the door open while cradling a huge cellophane-wrapped basket in the other.

"Hi, Dr. Sanderson," she said cheerfully, giving his father a winsome smile.

Wendell beamed back at her. "Well, hello there, my dear. Isn't this a lovely surprise?"

She gave a grin, missing her two front teeth, and held up the basket. "This is for you. My mom was busy talking to her friend at the nurses station and I got tired of waiting for her, so I told her I would come by myself. This thing is *heavy*."

"Eli, help my friend Skye out and take that big basket from her before her arms break right off, will you?"

He dutifully rose so he could take the basket out of the girl's arms and set it on the small table next to his father's bed.

While he was occupied, the girl stole his chair, the one right next to Wendell's bedside.

"That stuff is all for you" she said, pointing to the basket. "Even the candy. My mom and I went shopping in three different stores, trying to find all the things you love."

"That is so sweet of you. Your mother is a treasure and so are you, my dear."

She giggled. "My grandma says I'm a pill and too big for my britches."

"I don't doubt that's true," Wendell said.

The girl turned to Eli with a curious look. "Hi," she said brightly. "I'm Skye Fielding. What's your name?"

When she identified herself, he gave her a closer look. Skye Fielding. This had to be Melissa's daughter. He should have picked up the resemblance before she even identified herself. Now he could see she shared the same vivid green eyes with her mother and the same dimple that appeared and disappeared on one side of her mouth.

"This is my son, Elias Alexander Sanderson."

"Whoa. That's a big name. It's…" She counted on her small fingers. "Ten syllables."

Yes. He was fully aware. Try filling out all those letters on military forms designed for guys named Joe Smith. "You can call me Eli," he said.

"Hi, Eli." She settled deeper into his chair, perfectly at home, which he found more amusing than anything he'd seen in a long time. With nowhere else to sit in the room, he leaned against the sink.

"Mom says you got brand-new knees because your old ones hurt you all the time," she said.

"*Old* is the key word there," Wendell muttered.

His father wasn't that old. He was only in his early sixties and vibrant for his age. Why hadn't Wendell started dating and married someone? His father was still a handsome man. Judging by all the flowers and cards in his room, he was fairly popular around town, too. Maybe Eli could work on that while he was home.

"My mom says you have to stay here for two whole weeks!"

She seemed positively aghast at the idea.

"It's not that bad. They have fun things to do all day long. Games and movies and music time. Plus, they serve good food and have free popcorn in the cafeteria."

Eli had a feeling Wendell was trying to convince himself as much as he was the little girl. His father wasn't thrilled about the time that loomed ahead of him in the rehabilitation center, but that was the price for his impatience and desire to do both knees at the same time, when he needed daily therapy and his house wasn't fully accessible.

"Free popcorn! You're lucky. I love popcorn."

"So do I, but if I eat all the free popcorn, I might have a tough time getting back on my feet."

"I guess." She appeared to consider that. "Do you think I could have some now?"

Wendell laughed. "Maybe. You'll have to ask your mom. Where do you think she is?"

"Probably still talking to her friend," Skye said.

A moment later, as if to prove her daughter wrong, Melissa appeared in the doorway, looking slightly frazzled.

He had seen her three times that day, in three different wardrobe changes.

This morning on the beach, she had been wearing running clothes—leggings and a comfortable-looking hoodie, with her hair up in a ponytail. All day he had been aware of her moving around the office in burgundy-colored scrubs and a black cardigan. Tonight, Melissa had changed into jeans and a soft coral sweater and had let her hair down to curl around her shoulders.

He wasn't sure which version he found more attractive. It was a little like being asked to choose among his favorite ice cream flavors.

"Oh," she exclaimed, slightly breathless, with a stern look to her daughter. "Here you are. I didn't know where you went. I was busy talking to Jan and when I turned around, you had completely disappeared."

He could still see the shadows of unease in her expression and felt a wave of sympathy. He didn't have children, but he knew that panicked feeling of not being able to find someone you cared for deeply. He had a flashback of running through a panicked crowd, everyone else screaming and trying to escape the market center while he ran toward the chaos and fear. He closed his eyes, trying to scrub it away and return to the moment.

"I told you two times I was going to carry the basket to room forty-one," Skye informed her mother. "I guess you just didn't hear me."

More of Melissa's fear seemed to seep away and she hugged her child. "I'm sorry, honey. Jan is an old friend of mine from nursing school. I didn't know she was working here. I'm afraid I got a little distracted, catching up with her."

"My arms were too tired to keep holding the basket, so I found the room and gave it myself to Dr. Sanderson."

"I see that. Thanks, kiddo." She ran a hand over her daughter's hair and the sweet, tender familiarity of the gesture sent an odd lump rising in his throat.

The unexpected emotions intensified when she leaned forward and kissed Wendell on the cheek.

"And how are you? How are the new knees?"

His father shrugged, clearly pleased at the visit from Melissa and her daughter. "I can't complain. Though I'm not ready to dance the salsa yet, I can tell they're already less painful than the old ones. They'll be even better once I break them in."

"Don't be in too big of a rush. How many times have I heard you tell your patients that true healing takes time?"

His father made a face. "Do you know how annoying it is to have your own words thrown back in your face?"

She laughed. "It's for your own good."

"I know." He gestured to the brace she wore. "What happened to your wrist?"

Her gaze shifted to Eli, and he thought he saw a soft brush of color soak her cheeks. "It's a long story. Let's just say Fiona was in a strange mood this morning and I fell. But it's feeling much better. Your son checked it out for me."

Whether she had wanted him to or not. She didn't say the words, but he had a feeling she was thinking them.

"That's good to hear. He's a good boy and an excellent doctor. I've been waiting for him to come back so he can meet you."

Oh, no. That sounded entirely too much like matchmaking. He had to cut that off before Wendell got any inappropriate ideas.

"We've met, Dad. You remember. Melissa and I went to high school together for a year, though I'm older. I knew her ex-husband, too."

"My dad got married again and his wife is going to have a baby."

Melissa gave her daughter an exasperated look, and Eli had the feeling she wasn't thrilled with Skye for sharing that particular nugget of information.

"Yes," she said. "We're very happy for them both."

"Sounds like you've got a lot on your plate," Wendell said. "That makes your visit mean even more. A visit would have been enough, you know. You didn't have to bring along a huge care package, so heavy your strong seven-year-old daughter could barely carry it."

"It's only a few things, I promise. The fancy packaging always makes baskets look bigger than they are."

Except for that fleeting glance, she seemed to be avoiding looking at him directly. Why? Had he done something wrong that day in the office? There had been a little awkwardness early on, but Eli had thought by the end of the day they had started to establish a bit of a comfortable rhythm.

Skye nudged the basket closer to Wendell. "Open it. I want to see if you like the stuff we picked out."

"I'm sure I will love everything. It came from you, so of course I will." He smiled at the girl, who beamed back at him.

His father's rapport with both Melissa and her daughter didn't surprise him. Wendell loved people, one reason his staff adored him and his patients returned to him for generations.

"Go on," Skye pressed. "Open it."

He helped his father out by setting the basket on Wendell's lap, then watched as his father went through the contents. There was nothing elaborate, but all the gifts seemed thoughtful and sweet—a paperback mystery he knew Wendell would adore, a book of crossword puzzles, a box of chocolates and a bag of lemon drops, a journal, a soft-looking knit throw that would feel perfect on chilly spring mornings.

His father was delighted with all of it.

"Thank you so very much," he said after he had unearthed each new delight. "How did I ever get so lucky to have you both in my life?"

"We're the lucky ones," Melissa said with a smile.

"I don't have a grandpa and he doesn't have a grandkid, so Dr. Wendell said we can both pretend we belong to each other," Skye informed Eli.

It warmed his heart that Melissa appeared to watch out for his father. She struck him as someone who couldn't help caring about others. He had witnessed it all day. Even with her own injured wrist, she had been kind and caring to each patient they had seen.

"What are you two up to tonight, besides coming here and making my day?" Wendell asked them.

"We're going to have pizza," Skye informed him. "It's Friday and we always have pizza on Friday. Sometimes we make it ourselves and sometimes we order it from a pizza place and sometimes we go out. Tonight we're going out."

"Nice. Where are you heading?"

"We're going to A Slice of Heaven."

"Oh, good choice," Wendell said. "It's one of my favorites. Have you been there yet, son?"

Considering Eli had only been back in town for thirty-six hours and had been working or sleeping for most of that time—or visiting his father—hitting all the local hot spots hadn't exactly been on his priority list. "Not yet."

"You can't miss it. Trust me," his father said.

"You could come with us," Skye offered with that charmer of a smile. "Mom says maybe we can even get cheesy bread. They have the *best* cheesy bread."

"It's been a long day," Melissa said, a trace of defiance in her voice. "I need a few carbs to the rescue."

He wanted to suggest she also might need to rest and ice her wrist, but he didn't want to stand in the way of a girl and her carbs.

His father shifted on the bed and yawned, his mouth drawn and his eyes clouding with exhaustion.

"We should go," Melissa said, picking up the hint. "Come on, Skye."

"Do you have to?" Wendell said, though Eli heard the exhaustion in his voice.

"I should go, too, so you can get some rest. That's the best thing for you, in case your doctor hasn't mentioned it."

"He has," Wendell said glumly. "I hate being in this hospital bed."

"You know what they say about doctors making the worst patients. Try to behave yourself. I'll stop by tomorrow."

"Thanks."

His father rolled over, and Eli could tell he was already dozing off. He followed Melissa and her daughter out of the room.

"That was thoughtful of you, bringing a care package

to my father," he said when they were out in the hallway. "It obviously touched him."

"Dr. Sanderson has been nothing but kind to us since we moved back to town. It's the very least we can do, giving him a few things to help him pass the time while he's laid up. He's a wonderful man, your father."

"He is."

"Seriously. I've worked with a lot of jerk doctors in my day and your father is a breath of fresh air, as compassionate to his staff as he is to his patients."

"It's always good to hear my own opinion confirmed by those who work closely with him."

"Not gonna lie. He's my favorite of all the doctors I've ever worked with. You have big shoes to fill."

"My feet will never fit in those shoes. Why do you think I haven't come home before now to try? I just have to do my best to stumble along as best I can while I'm here."

That was probably more revealing than he intended, at least judging by the probing look Melissa sent his way. He opted to change the subject. "So you're off to have pizza?"

"Yep. Like I said, we always have pizza on Friday night," Skye told him. "Pizza on Friday, Tacos on Tuesday. The rest of the time, we like to mix things up."

He found it charming that she included herself in the meal-planning process. As precocious as the girl seemed, he wouldn't be surprised if she could fix a gourmet meal all by herself, given the chance.

"That's good. You wouldn't want to be too predictable."

"What are you having for dinner?" Skye asked him.

"I don't know. I haven't crossed that bridge yet. Unfortunately, I do *not* have a pizza-on-Friday tradition, but it sounds good."

More than likely, he would head back to his father's house and make a sandwich or heat up a TV dinner—neither of which sounded very appetizing compared to the carbtastic wonders of A Slice of Heaven.

"You could come with us," Skye suggested.

He glanced at Melissa, who looked taken aback by the invitation. She didn't seem crazy about the idea, yet Eli was surprised at how very much he wanted to accept. The idea of eating alone again at his father's house held no appeal.

"I don't want to impose on your night out together."

"We eat together every night," Skye said. "Besides, pizza always tastes better when it's shared. It's a scientific fact. Anyway, that's what my mom says."

"Funny. I don't remember learning about that in school."

He sent a sidelong look to Melissa, who shrugged and blushed at the same time.

"You must have missed the breakthrough study. Plus, when you share a pizza, the calories don't count."

"Good to know. I wasn't aware."

"But you've probably had a long day," she said. "Don't let us pressure you into it."

He should gracefully back out of it. She didn't want him there anyway. But he found he wasn't willing to do it. He wanted pizza and he wanted to spend more time with her. Neither craving was necessarily good for him, but that didn't seem to matter.

"I haven't had pizza from A Slice of Heaven in years. Now that you've planted that seed, I'm afraid nothing else will do except that. Thank you for inviting me."

She paused, then gave a smile that seemed only a little forced. "Great. Do you remember where the pizza parlor is?"

"I could probably find it in my sleep. I'll meet you there."

"See you." Skye tugged on her mom's hand. "Let's go. I'm starving!"

She followed her daughter out of the rehab center, and he watched them go for a moment before following closely behind.

As delicious as the wood-fired pizza was at the beloved seaside pizzeria, he found Melissa and her daughter even more appealing.

Chapter Three

In her long and illustrious history of bad ideas, inviting Dr. Eli Sanderson out to grab pizza with them had to rank right up there with the lousy perm she got in seventh grade and losing her virginity to Cody Fielding after the prom her junior year.

Technically, Skye had invited Eli, but Melissa should have figured out a polite way to wiggle out of it, for all of their sakes.

Why *had* Skye invited him along? Her daughter did love Dr. Sanderson Sr., but she usually wasn't so spontaneously open to strangers.

Maybe her daughter had responded, as Melissa did, to that air of loneliness about Eli. She couldn't put her finger on it, but there was just something *sad* about him. A shadow in his eye, a particular set to his mouth.

She had tried hard to teach Skye how important it

was to be kind to others. Okay, maybe she tried to over-compensate a little on her end, knowing her daughter wouldn't receive similar lessons on the rare occasions she was with her dad. Maybe she had tried *too* hard, if Skye was going to go around inviting random gorgeous men to share their Friday-night tradition.

So much for her lectures all day about keeping her head on straight around him. That was fine advice in a professional setting when he was her boss but might be harder to remember in social situations.

It was no big deal. They were only sharing pizza. A Slice of Heaven had notoriously fast service, even on the weekend. With any luck, they could be seated, served and out of there within an hour. Surely she could manage to control her hormones for sixty lousy minutes.

"I like the second Dr. Sanderson," Skye said from the back seat as they drove to the restaurant. "He seems nice…maybe not quite as nice as the first Dr. Sanderson, but better than Dr. Wu or Dr. Charles. Whenever they used to talk to me, they never even looked at me. It's like they didn't think a kid could have anything important to say."

How did a seven-year-old girl become so very perceptive? The doctors in the clinic where Melissa worked in Honolulu before coming back to Cannon Beach had treated *her* that way, too, as if her opinions didn't matter.

"They were very good doctors," she said.

"But are they nice humans?"

That was an excellent question. She hadn't been sorry to leave, though her coworkers had only been one of the reasons she had moved from Honolulu back to Oregon. Her mother was here, for one thing, and she found she missed being close to Sharon.

And the cost of living had been prohibitive. She had stayed in Hawaii for the last few years mostly because Cody had lived there and she wanted to do all she could to keep Skye's father in her daughter's life. His visitations had become so few and far between as he traveled around on the professional surfer circuit that her efforts had begun to seem laughable. When he had told her the previous summer he was moving again, she had given up trying.

Skye needed a stable home base. Melissa couldn't keep dragging her from town to town, hoping Cody would eventually start paying attention to their child. She had tried for years after the divorce, then decided being closer to her own mother would provide more benefit to her child than infrequent, disappointing visits with her immature father.

Melissa would have loved four or five children, but life hadn't worked out the way she planned. Good thing the one daughter she had was so amazing. Skye was smart and kind and amazingly intuitive for a child.

"Can I play pool tonight at A Slice of Heaven?"

And persistent. Once an idea took root in her head, she could never let it go.

"If there's an empty table, maybe. Otherwise, nope," Melissa said as she pulled into the pizzeria's restaurant, the same answer she gave every time they came.

The people who hung out at the popular restaurant and played at the three tables in the back were serious about the game. They were probably good humans, but they weren't at all patient with a seven-year-old girl just learning how to wield a cue.

Skye sighed as they parked and walked toward the restaurant but she didn't argue, to Melissa's relief. Her wrist was throbbing, and she really wanted to go home and rest it. She would definitely break out the ice pack after her daughter was in bed.

A wave of garlic and the delicious scent of the pizzeria's wood-fired crusts hit the moment Melissa opened the door. Oh, yeah, she suddenly remembered. She was starving. She'd kind of forgotten that while she was talking to Wendell and Eli. Now her stomach growled and she had a fleeting wish that the wisecrack she had made to Eli was true, that none of the calories or carbs of the delicious Slice of Heaven pies counted when they were shared.

Somehow Eli had made it there before they did. He was inside talking to the hostess and daughter of the owner, Gina Salvaticci, who had been a year or two ahead of Melissa. She had never liked her much, she remembered now. Gina had been friends with Cody before Melissa and her family moved to Cannon Beach, and always acted as if she thought Melissa wasn't good enough for him. Since the divorce and Melissa's return to town, she hadn't necessarily warmed to her.

If her father's restaurant didn't serve such good pizza, Melissa would do whatever she could to avoid her. Fortunately, Gina usually wasn't here on Fridays.

But she was here *this Friday*, *and* Gina looked as shocked by the changes in quiet, nerdy Eli Sanderson as Melissa had been and she was obviously flirting with him. She touched his arm as she spoke to him and looked at him from under her half-closed lids, her body facing him and her mouth slightly open.

Melissa felt a sharp kick in her gut, a weird tension, and realized with chagrin that she was jealous of the other woman, even though Eli seemed completely oblivious to any interested body language.

He looked up when they approached. "Here's the rest of my party. You said you had a table ready for us?"

Gina turned and Melissa knew the moment she spotted her. Her gaze narrowed and her hand slid away from Eli. Gina didn't look at all pleased to see another woman joining him.

Melissa couldn't really blame her. A hot doctor coming back to town, even temporarily, was bound to stir up all the single women.

Not *her*. She was willing to entertain a friendship with the man but that was all she could give him. She had no room in her life for anything more, especially not a wandering doctor who would be heading off to the next hot spot on the globe the moment his dad had his knees under him again. Been there, done that, with a man whose career was far more important than his family. She would never even consider it again.

Her priority had to be Skye, and providing her daughter the most stable home life possible, after the chaos of her daughter's earlier years.

She smiled to let the other woman know she wasn't a threat. If Gina was interested in Eli, she should go for it.

"Right this way," Gina said coolly.

She led them back to a fairly good table with a nice view of the sunset.

"Will this be okay for you?" Gina asked. She looked only at Eli when she asked the question. He in turn deferred to Melissa.

"Does this work for you and Skye?" he asked.

"Looks great," she answered. "Thanks."

He reached for the back of a chair and pulled it back.

Nobody had held a chair out for her in such a long time, it took Melissa an awkward moment to realize he meant for her to sit there.

"Uh. Thanks."

She *really* needed to get out more.

She sat down and Skye plopped into the seat next to her.

"Can I get a root beer?" she asked.

They had a pretty strict no-soda/low-sugar rule 95 percent of the time, but Melissa tended to relax a bit on pizza night. "One. A small."

"I'll let your server know," Gina said. "Here's a couple of menus," Gina said. "Our special tonight is the arugula and prosciutto with our house-pulled mozzarella."

"Sounds delicious," Eli said. "Thanks."

The next few minutes were spent perusing the menu. Skye ordered her favorite, half cheese, half pepperoni, while Melissa and Eli both ordered the special, along with salads with the house dressing on the side and, of course, an order of their cheesy bread.

"If I can't play pool, can I at least go play the pinball machine?" Skye asked. "I brought all my own quarters."

"All of them? I thought you were saving up for a new scooter like your friend Alice has."

"I am. But Sonia gave me two dollars for helping her pull weeds yesterday, so I put that in my piggy bank and took out six quarters."

Skye reached into her pocket and pulled out change that jingled as she set it on the table. "I want to see if I can do better than last time we came."

"It's your money. If that's the way you want to spend it, go for it."

"Thanks."

She shoved her chair back and hurried to the row of gaming machines along one wall of the pizzeria. This was an ideal setup, where she could keep an eye on her daughter but didn't have to stand right over her shoulder.

"She seems like a sweet kid," Eli said. "I know my dad thinks so, anyway."

Melissa had made plenty of mistakes in her life—including a disastrous marriage—but her daughter was not among them.

"She's amazing. Kind, compassionate, funny. I won the kid lottery."

He smiled at that and sipped at the beer their server had brought him. "Does she see her father very often?"

All her frustrations from earlier in the day rushed back, and Melissa did her best not to tense.

"Not as often as she'd like. It's been tough to have a relationship when he's always heading to the next beach with the pro surf circuit."

"Must have made it tough on a marriage."

"You could say that."

"How long have you and Cody been divorced?"

"We split up when Skye was three and officially divorced a year later."

"And she's, what, seven now?"

"Yes."

The sense of failure never quite left Melissa, even after four years. She knew she had no reason to feel guilty, but somehow she couldn't seem to help it.

She didn't tell Eli how hard she had tried to salvage the marriage for her child or how even after it became clear that Cody wouldn't stop cheating, she had chosen to stay in Hawaii, Cody's surfing home base, so her daughter could still see her father.

"Where is he these days?"

"He's coming back to Oregon. His new wife is expecting a baby, and he wants to be closer to his family in Portland so they can help her out."

She wouldn't let herself be bitter about that. When *Melissa* had been pregnant with Skye, Cody hadn't been nearly as solicitous about her needs. He'd been training for a big wave competition, totally focused on it, and couldn't take time away. Instead, they had lived in a crappy studio apartment on the North Shore. He had refused to come back to Oregon, even for her to deliver the baby close to her mom.

Maybe the fact that he was putting his new wife and unborn baby first for once was proof that her ex was finally growing up. She hoped so, but she didn't think anyone could blame her for being skeptical.

"And how long have you been back in Cannon Beach?"

"About seven months. For the past few years, Cody's home base has been Oahu. Last year he moved overseas, so I decided it was time Skye and I came back to be closer to family."

"That's nice. And you live in Brambleberry House."

"For now. We love it there, but I'm saving up to buy a house."

"And going to school, I understand. Carmen or Tiffany mentioned it today."

"I'm working to become a family nurse practitioner," she said as their server set down salads in front of the two of them.

"How's that going?"

"Not going to lie, it's been tough while juggling a full-time job and a child. I still have two years to go. I can do most of the work online, which helps."

"That's terrific. There's such a need for well-trained nurse practitioners right now. Good for you."

The approving look in his eyes sent warmth seeping through her. Going to school and working was tough work, and she had sacrificed sleep and a social life for it, but she was trying to build a solid future for her and her child. All the sacrifices were worthwhile, an investment toward security for Skye.

"What about you? I'm surprised you haven't done the whole family thing yet."

He shrugged, a hint of a shadow in his eyes. "You know how it is. Some guys can handle starting a family while they're in med school, but I wasn't one of them."

"You've been out of med school—what?—five or six years now? There hasn't been a chance in all those years to find somebody you want to make Mrs. Dr. Elias Sanderson?"

"No," he said quickly. Too quickly. The shadows seemed to intensify. Eli Sanderson had secrets. What were they? She had the feeling he had lost someone close to him. Was it a woman?

She wanted to probe, but Skye came back before she could ask a follow-up question.

She was relieved, she told herself. Eli's secrets were none of her business. He was her employer, at least for the next few weeks. Okay, he might also be becoming a friend. That didn't mean she needed to know everything that had happened to him since the day he had left Cannon Beach for college.

"Your quarters are gone already?" she asked her daughter.

"Pinball is *hard*," Skye complained. "Simon made it look so easy."

Simon was the son of her friends Will and Julia Garrett, twin to Maddie, a girl who sometimes babysat Skye for her. The last time they had come to A Slice of Heaven, their family had been there, too, and Skye had been fascinated, watching the older boy.

"Simon is a teenager, honey. Almost eighteen. He's probably had a lot of practice at it."

She pouted but didn't have time to fret more as their server fortuitously came by just then with their pizzas, fragrant and hot.

They were all too busy the next few moments savoring their meal, which didn't leave a lot of room for talking.

In between bites, Skye kept looking back toward the billiards tables with a wistful look.

"You look like you're wanting to try your hand at pool," Eli said.

"Mom says I can't. It's too busy here on Friday nights. There are people waiting their turn to play."

"My dad has a billiards table in the sunroom," Eli said. "You're welcome to come over and practice a little there before you try to play in the big leagues over here at A Slice of Heaven."

"Thanks," Skye said, eyes wide with excitement.

Melissa tried to hide her frown. She really wished he hadn't said that. Eli would forget he made the offer, but Skye wouldn't.

Her daughter had spent entirely too much time being disappointed by empty promises. She didn't need more.

Maybe she was being too cynical. Maybe he wouldn't forget.

She distracted Skye with their favorite game of I Spy for the rest of the meal, and Eli joined in willingly. He had a unique eye and stumped both her and Skye more than once with the things he observed.

"I'm totally stuffed now," Skye said after two slices. She eased back in her chair and placed her hands over her belly.

Eli chuckled. "That was delicious, wasn't it? The best pizza I've had in a long time. I forgot how delicious the crust here is."

"They have a magic recipe," Melissa said.

"They must, especially if they can make it calorie-free."

His smile made her hormones sigh. Seriously, this was becoming ridiculous.

After they boxed up their leftover pizza, Eli insisted on paying the tab. She would have argued, but her friend Sage and her husband, Eben, part owners of Bramble-berry House, came in at that moment and distracted her. By the time she waved goodbye to her friends, the server had already completed the bill.

"Next time is my treat," she said.

"I'll look forward to it," he answered. His words had a ring of sincerity that again warmed her far more than they should.

They walked outside into a lovely April night, rich with the scent of the ocean, with flowers, with new life.

She could hear the low murmur of the waves along with the constant coastal wind that rustled the new leaves of the trees next to the restaurant.

Oh, she had missed it here. She had lived in many beautiful, exotic places since she'd left Cannon Beach, but none of them had been the same. She had lived here longer than anywhere, from the age of thirteen to eighteen. It was home to her.

"That was lovely," he said when they reached their respective vehicles in the parking lot. "The most enjoyable meal I've had in a long time. Thank you for inviting me."

"You're welcome. Thank you for insisting on paying for it."

"Yeah. Thanks," Skye said cheerfully. "It was fun."

Melissa couldn't make a habit of it. She was far too drawn to him.

"Have a good evening, Eli."

Their gazes met, and those shadows prompted her to do something completely uncharacteristic. She stood on tiptoe and kissed his cheek, intending it only as a warm, friendly, welcome-home kind of gesture.

He smelled delicious, of soap and male skin, and it was all she could do not to stand there and inhale.

She forced herself to ease away, regretting the impulse with every passing moment.

"Good night, Melissa. Skye, it was a pleasure. Persuade your mom to take you to my dad's place sometime soon so you can practice your pool game."

"I will! Thanks."

"See you Monday," she said.

"Put some ice on that wrist," he answered, his voice gruff.

She nodded and ushered her daughter to her vehicle. Though her wrist still ached, the injury seemed a lifetime ago.

Chapter Four

Melissa managed to make it through the rest of the weekend without obsessing too much about Eli, mainly because she and Skye spent Saturday running errands, then drove to Portland for the day on Sunday. By Sunday night, the prospect of going back to the clinic and spending the day in his company filled her with nerves.

She managed to push it away by baking strawberry shortcake Sunday evening and texting the other tenants of Brambleberry House, inviting them down to share after Skye was in bed.

Both Rosa and Sonia arrived at the same time, moments after her text went out. The three of them sat out in her screened porch, enjoying the evening breeze and the promise of rain.

"This is…delicious," Sonia said in her slow, halting voice. She gave one of her rare smiles. "Thank you for inviting me."

"You're welcome."

"What brought on your frenzy of baking?" Rosa asked. "Not that I would be complaining, only curious."

Melissa couldn't tell them she had been restless for two days, since leaving Eli at A Slice of Heaven. "We went to the farmers market in Portland yesterday, and the strawberries were so luscious I couldn't resist buying four quarts of them. I have to do something with all those berries."

"Shortcake...was a great choice," Sonia said.

When Melissa offered the invitation, she hadn't really thought their second-floor neighbor would join them, but every once in a while Sonia did the unexpected.

The woman was such a mystery to her. Melissa had tried to gently probe about what medical conditions she had, but Sonia was apparently an expert at the art of deflecting conversation away from herself.

Why did she keep to herself? What secrets lurked beneath her pretty features? Had she been abused? Was she in hiding?

Melissa didn't feel darkness in Sonia's past, only... sadness. She couldn't explain it rationally, it was just a sense. There was a deep sorrow in Sonia. She wished she could get to the bottom of it.

Sometimes she thought becoming a nurse had heightened her compassion for others, giving her instincts she didn't fully understand. Her hunches had been proved right too many times for her to question them any longer, though. Now she simply listened to them.

Fiona, who had trotted down from the third floor with Rosa, lifted her head at that moment and seemed to stare off at nothing in the corner, head cocked as if listening to something only she could hear.

A faint hint of roses seemed to stir in the air, subtle and sly, but that might have been her imagination.

She followed the dog's gaze, then turned back to the other two women. "Do you ever get the feeling we're not the only ones in this house?" she asked impulsively.

"What do you mean?" Sonia asked, brows furrowed. For one brief instant, she looked so panicked that Melissa regretted bringing it up.

"Just... I sometimes feel like the house is alive with memories of the past."

"I know what you mean," Rosa said with her slight Spanish accent. "I never feel like it is malicious or scary."

"No," Melissa said. "I find it comforting, actually. Like somebody is watching over the house and those who live here."

"I don't believe in guardian angels," Sonia said flatly. "I wish I did. At times in my life, I could have used...a guardian angel...or two or twenty."

Her eyes looked haunted, and Melissa wanted to hug her, but she sensed Sonia wouldn't welcome the gesture.

"My grandmother used to say our family is always watching over you, whether you want them to or not."

"Don't you find that a little disturbing?" Melissa asked Rosa.

The other woman laughed and ate more of her strawberry shortcake. "Maybe. My mama's Tio Juan Carlos was crazy. I don't want him anywhere watching over me."

"It's not your crazy great-uncle. I get the feeling it's someone kind. Does that make me as crazy as Juan Carlos?"

Rosa smiled. "A little. But I am crazy, too. Maybe Abigail, the woman who lived here all her life and died when she was in her nineties, didn't want to leave. She's the one who left the house to my aunt Anna and to Sage

Spencer. It could be she's sticking around to keep an eye on things."

"I remember Abigail a little from when we first moved to Cannon Beach," Melissa said. "I like the idea of a sweet older lady keeping watch over the house she loves."

"I do, too," Sonia said. "It's comforting, somehow."

While they finished their strawberry shortcake, they talked about the house and its history, what little Rosa knew from her aunt anyway. Eventually, the conversation drifted to men.

"How are things with the ex-husband?" Rosa asked. "Any updates after your frustration the other day?"

"No. I haven't heard from him."

At Sonia's questioning look, she explained the situation with Cody to the other woman.

"Who was that...good-looking guy I saw you with... yesterday?"

So much for keeping Eli out of her head for five minutes. She fought down a sigh. "That's my new boss. Dr. Sanderson's son, Eli."

"Oh! That's Eli! Wendell...said he might be coming home."

Melissa hadn't realized her neighbor was such good friends with the elder Dr. Sanderson. As far as she knew, Sonia had only visited Dr. Sanderson once since she had been working there. It made sense, though, since he was the best doctor in town.

"If he's that cute, maybe I need to schedule a physical or something," Rosa teased.

"I think... I might be due for a follow-up appointment too," Sonia said.

It was the first joke she had ever heard the other woman make. Rosa looked just as surprised, then grinned. "Maybe we should just drop by the clinic this week to take Melissa out to lunch. We can check him out then."

"Good idea," Sonia said with what could almost be considered a smile.

"You're both terrible. Here. Have some more short-cake."

The conversation drifted to Rosa's work managing her aunt Anna's gift store in town and then to Sonia's plans for the garden.

"This was fun," Rosa said a short time later, stifling a yawn. "But I have to run down to Lincoln City first thing tomorrow to pick up some pottery from one of our suppliers. I had better get to bed."

"Same here," Sonia said. "Thank you for the dessert... and the...conversation."

She rose in her wobbly way.

"It was fun," Melissa said. "We should get together more often. Maybe you two could come for pizza night on Friday. Skye would love hosting a dinner party."

Sonia took on that secretive look she had sometimes. "I won't be here this weekend. But maybe the week after that."

Where do you go? she wanted to ask her secretive neighbor. *And why are you so sad when you return?*

"I'll be gone, too," Rosa said with regret in her eyes. "Fiona and I are going hiking with some friends next weekend."

"No problem. We'll do it another time. Maybe the week after that, then. Put it on your calendars."

"Done," Rosa said with a smile.

"I'll have to look at my...schedule," Sonia said.

She said goodbye to them both, then made her slow

way out of the screened porch and to the entryway that led upstairs to her own apartment.

"I hate watching her make that climb," Melissa said. "Why wouldn't she take the ground-floor apartment? It would be so much easier."

"I do not think that one wants the easy," Rosa said, her Spanish accent more pronounced. She stood up, and her dog rose, as well.

"And you don't know anything more about her...issues?" Melissa asked.

"No. She has been in town longer than I have, about four years. Anna said she showed up in town one day and started coming into the gift shop, mainly to pet Conan. That was the dog my aunt and Sage inherited from Abigail, who left them the house. Fiona's sire. One day she asked if Anna knew of any place in town she could rent, and it happened the apartment she lives in now was available. My aunt said she knew of one but it was on the second floor of an old house, and Sonia said it would be perfect. She has been here ever since."

One day Melissa wanted to get to the bottom of Sonia's mystery, though she knew it really wasn't any of her business.

After she said goodbye to Rosa and her dog, she straightened the kitchen, prepped a few things for breakfast in the morning, then headed to her solitary bedroom.

The apartment seemed too quiet and her mind was a tangle, wondering about Cody's plans, about Sonia's secrets, and about the disturbing knowledge that when she awoke, she faced an entire day of working in close proximity to Eli.

She dreamed that night that she was trapped on one of the rock formations off Cannon Beach in the middle of a storm. She was hanging on by her fingernails as waves pounded against the rock and a heavy rain stung her face. She was doing all she could to hold tight, to survive. And then suddenly Eli was there, shirtless but in a white lab coat with a stethoscope around his neck, like something off a sexy doctor calendar.

She might have laughed at her own wild imagination if she hadn't been so into the dream. "I've got you," he murmured in a throaty bedroom voice, and then he lifted her up with those astonishing muscles he had developed since leaving town. A moment later, she was in his arms and he was holding her tightly.

"I won't let you go," he promised gruffly, then his mouth descended and he kissed her fiercely, protectively.

Her alarm went off before she could ask him how they were going to get off the rock and why he needed a stethoscope but not a shirt.

She awoke aroused and restless to a fierce rain pounding the window, as if she had conjured it with her dream.

It took her a moment to figure out where her dream ended and where reality began. What was wrong with her? She had been divorced for three years, separated for longer, and had told herself she was doing just fine putting that part of her life away for now while she devoted her energies to raising Skye.

Since the divorce, she had dated here and there but nothing serious, only for company and a little adult conversation. She hadn't been out at all since she came back to Cannon Beach.

She was lying to herself if she said she didn't miss certain things about having a man in her life. Topping the list would probably be having big, warm muscles to curl up against on a cool, rainy morning when she didn't have to get out of bed for another half hour. She sat up, wrapping her blanket around her, trying to push away the remnants of the dream.

Her wrist inside the brace ached, but it was more a steady ache than the ragged pain she had experienced over the weekend, further proof that it was only a sprain and not a break.

She looked up at the ceiling, listening to the rain click against the window. She didn't have to get Skye up for another hour, so she decided to stretch out some of the kinks in her back and the tumult lingering from that dream with her favorite yoga routine, making concessions to work around her sore wrist.

It did the trick. By the time her alarm went off, signaling it was time to wake up Skye and start their day, she felt much more calm and centered, and that unwanted dream and the feelings it had stirred up inside her mostly subsided.

She would simply ignore whatever was left, she told herself, just as she planned to ignore this inconvenient attraction to Eli.

The word *ignore* became her watchword over the next week. She managed to put aside her growing attraction to Eli, focusing instead on work and her online coursework and Skye.

She wouldn't exactly call this a good thing, but it helped that the area had been hit with an onslaught of fast-spreading spring viruses and a nasty case of food poisoning from bad potato salad at a spring church potluck.

They were insanely busy all week. Most of her time away from work was spent studying for final exams in the two online classes she had been struggling with, which left her little time to think about anything else.

Her relationship with Eli around the office was cordial and even friendly, but she tried hard not to let the ridiculous crush she was developing on him filter through.

By Friday morning, her wrist was almost completely back to normal except for a few twinges, and Melissa was more than ready for the weekend. It was her late day to go into the office and she decided to again take a quick run after she saw Skye off on the school bus.

She called Rosa to ask if she minded her taking Fiona.

"No!" Her friend said. "You will be doing me a huge favor. My day is shaping up to be a crazy one and I don't know when I will find the time to walk her."

A moment later, she and Fiona were heading out through the beach gate on the edge of the Brambleberry House garden, then running across the sand.

The water was rough this morning, the waves churning with drama. Clouds hung heavy and mist swirled around the haystacks offshore. She wanted to sit on the beach and watch the storm come in, but she had to finish her run in order to make it back for work.

As she and Fiona trotted down the beach, she spotted a few beachcombers and other joggers out. A couple holding hands stopped every once in a while to take selfies of each other and she had to smile. They were in their sixties and acting like newlyweds. For all she knew, they were.

She and Fiona made it to the end of the beach. As she neared home, she spotted a familiar figure running in the opposite direction with a little black schnauzer.

Eli.

This time, she gave him a friendly wave as she approached him, ignoring the nerves suddenly dancing in her stomach. His usually serious expression seemed to ease a little when he spotted her, but she wasn't sure if that was her imagination or not.

He slowed and Max and Fiona sniffed each other happily. "Looks like we're on the same running schedule."

"At least on Fridays. I don't get out as often as I like. The later opening for the office helps since I can go after Skye catches the bus."

"That must make it tough, trying to work out around her schedule."

"It wouldn't be as tough except I'm a wimp and only run when the sun is shining, which hasn't been very often this week."

She didn't want to talk about her sketchy workout habits. She'd done yoga twice. Counting that and her run a week ago when she'd met him on this very beach and today, that made four days in a week. That had to count for something, didn't it? Especially when she had an injury.

"How is your dad?" she asked to change the subject. "When do the doctors say he can go home?"

"He's doing great. The orthopedic doctor says maybe this weekend, but for sure by the middle of the week."

"That's terrific. I can only imagine how tough it must be to have double knee replacements, but I'm sure he'll be happy he did it."

"He already says it's less pain than he was in before."

The sun peeked through the steely clouds to pick up highlights in his hair. She ignored that, too—or at least she tried to tell herself she did.

"How's your wrist?" he asked. "I've been meaning to ask, but things have been so crazy this week as I try to settle in that I keep forgetting."

"It's been a wild week, you're right. You are getting a baptism by fire. We haven't been this busy in a long time."

"How did I get so lucky?"

She smiled. "Maybe all the women in town just want to meet the young, handsome new doctor."

He made a face. "Nice theory. It doesn't explain the food poisoning or the stomach bugs."

"Good point," she said.

Before he could respond, a cry rang out across the beach.

"Help! Please, somebody, help!"

For a split second, Eli went instantly on alert, muscles taut as he scanned the area.

An instant later, he took off at a dead run toward the older couple Melissa had seen earlier. Max wanted to chase after him, thinking it was a game, but Melissa took a moment to secure both dog leashes. As she sprinted after Eli, she saw the woman was kneeling beside the prone figure of her male companion, who was lying just at the spot where the baby breakers licked at the sand.

"What happened?" Eli was asking as he turned the man over to keep his mouth and nose out of the sand and the incoming tide.

"He was just standing there and then he fell over, unconscious. Please. What's happening?"

The man didn't appear to be breathing and his features had a gray cast to them. Melissa suspected a heart attack, but she didn't say so to the woman.

"What can I do?" she asked Eli.

"Help me move him up the beach, out of the water," Eli said urgently. The two of them tugged the unresponsive man six or seven feet up, just far enough that he wouldn't continue being splashed by the incoming breakers.

"Call 911," Eli instructed to Melissa as he started doing a quick first-aid assessment.

Adrenaline pumping, Melissa pulled out her phone and did as he asked.

"Does your husband have any history of heart trouble?" she asked while waiting for the dispatcher to answer.

"No. None," she said.

"Nine-one-one. What's your emergency?"

"We've got a nonresponsive male approximately sixty-five years old…"

"Sixty-seven," the woman said, her gaze fixed on Eli and her husband.

"Sixty-seven. He has no history of heart trouble but apparently collapsed about one to two minutes ago. Dr. Eli Sanderson is here attending to the patient, currently starting CPR. We are on Cannon Beach, near the water's edge about three hundred yards south of the access point near Gower Street. We're going to need emergency assistance and transport to the hospital."

"Okay. Please stay on the line. I'm going to contact paramedics. We'll get them to your location as soon as we can."

"Thank you."

"He's a doctor?" The man's wife was staring at Eli with astonishment filtering through her shock and terror.

"He is. And I'm a nurse. It's lucky we were here."

"Not luck," the woman said faintly. "It's a miracle. We were going to go up to Ecola State Park this morning beachcombing, but when we were in the car, something told me to come here instead."

They hadn't saved the man yet. She wasn't willing to go that far. "My name is Melissa and this is Eli." Though that adrenaline was still pumping through her, she spoke as patiently as she could manage. The woman would have plenty of time to break down later, after the paramedics took over the situation, but right now it was important to keep her as calm as possible under the circumstances.

"Ma'am, what's your name and what is your husband's name?"

"Carol," she said faintly. "Carol Stewart. This is my husband Jim. We're from Idaho. The Lewiston area. We've been here for three days and are supposed to go home tomorrow. Today is our w-wedding anniversary."

Oh, she really hoped Eli and the paramedics could resuscitate the man. It would be utterly tragic for Carol to lose her husband on their anniversary.

"How long have you been married?"

"Th-three years. Three amazing years. It's a second marriage for both of us. We were high school sweethearts but went our separate ways after graduation. I got divorced ten years ago and his first wife died about five years ago, and we reconnected on social media."

"Is your husband on any medication?"

"High blood pressure and reflux medication. I can't remember which one, but I have the information on my phone."

"You can give it to the paramedics when they arrive."

Carol gave a distracted nod, her hands over her mouth as she watched Eli continue compressions without any visible response. "Oh, what's happening?"

Before she could answer, the dispatcher returned to the line. "Okay. I have paramedics on the way. They should be there shortly. I'll stay on the line with you until they arrive."

"Thank you. I'm going to hand you over to the patient's wife so she can answer any questions about his medical history for you to pass on to the emergency department at the hospital."

She turned to the other woman and handed over her phone. "Carol, take a deep breath, okay? I need to help Dr. Sanderson right now and someone has to stay on the line with the dispatcher until the paramedics get here. Will you do that for your husband?"

Melissa could see shock and panic were beginning to take over as the reality of the situation seemed to be becoming more clear. The other woman had turned as pale as the clouds, and her breathing seemed shallow and rapid. Carol took one deep, shuddering breath and then another, and appeared to regain some of her composure.

"I… Yes. I think so. Hello?"

When she was certain Carol wasn't going to fall over, offering them an additional patient to deal with, Melissa knelt beside Eli, who was giving rescue breaths.

"Any response?" she asked quietly.

He returned to his chest compressions without pause. "Not yet," he said, his voice grim.

"Do you need me to take over and give you a break?"

"Not with your bad wrist. I'll continue compressions, but it would help if you handle the respirations."

She moved to the man's head and the two of them worked together, with Eli counting out his compressions, then pausing for her to give two breaths.

She wasn't sure how long they worked together. It seemed like forever but was probably only five or six minutes before she spotted paramedics racing toward them across the sand.

In the summertime, this beach would have had lifeguards who could have helped with the emergency rescue, but the lifeguard stations had personnel only during the weekends in May, then daily from June to August.

She knew both the paramedics, she realized as they approached. One, Tim Cortez, had gone to high school with both her and Eli and the other was a newcomer to town but someone she had actually socialized with a few times at gatherings, Tyler Howell.

She had found him entirely too much like her ex-husband, with that same reckless edge, and had declined his invitation to go out. Fortunately, he hadn't been offended and they had remained friends.

Two more paramedics she didn't know were close behind them.

"Hey, Melissa. Hey, Eli," Tim said as they rolled up. "What's going on?"

Eli was still counting compressions so Melissa spoke up to give the situation report. "We've got a sixty-seven-year-old man, Jim Stewart, with no history of heart trouble, on blood pressure and reflux medication. He collapsed about seven minutes ago and has been unresponsive since then but has been receiving CPR since about a minute or so after he fell over."

"Lucky for this guy, you two were close by," Tim said. "We've got the AED now. You want to do the honors, Eli?"

"I'll keep doing CPR while you set it up," Eli said.

A moment later, the paramedics had the automated external defibrillator ready. Eli stopped compressions while they unbuttoned the man's shirt and attached the leads.

Seconds later, Eli turned on the machine and followed the voice commands. A medical degree wasn't at all necessary to run an AED, but Melissa was glad she didn't have to do it.

The man shook a little when the electrical pulse went through him, shocking his heart.

When it was safe, the machine ordered them to check his pulse, and Eli felt for it. He grabbed a stethoscope that one of the paramedics handed over and listened for a heartbeat.

"Nothing," he said grimly. "We're going to have to do another round."

He resumed compressions while waiting for the machine to power up again, then stood back to allow the paramedics to reattach the leads and went through the process again.

Again, Jim's body shook, and Carol let out a little moan. Melissa went to her and put her arm around her as Eli again searched for a pulse.

"I've got something," he said, his voice containing more emotion than Melissa had heard since they had rushed to the man.

He listened with the stethoscope. "Yeah. It's getting stronger."

Both paramedics looked stunned, and Melissa couldn't blame them. She hadn't expected Jim to survive, either. Not really. If she were honest, she had suspected a massive heart attack, possibly even the kind they called the widow-maker.

"Nice work, Doc," Tyler said. He fastened an oxygen mask over Jim's mouth and nose.

Eli stood out of their way and let the two paramedics load Jim onto a gurney. Beside her, Carol was shaking.

"That's good, isn't it? That his heart is working again?"

She didn't want to give the woman false hope. Her husband wasn't out of the woods yet, not by a long shot, though he was starting to regain consciousness.

"Yes. So far, so good. The nearest hospital is up the coast in Seaside, about a fifteen-minute drive from here. That's where the paramedics will take him first. From there, they may decide he will need to go to Portland."

"Can I ride in the ambulance with him?"

She looked at Tyler, who nodded.

"I'm going to give you my contact info," Melissa said. "Where is your phone? I can enter it in for you. When you need a ride back to Cannon Beach, either to go to your hotel or to get your vehicle or whatever, you call me. I'll come pick you up and bring you back here."

The other woman burst into tears and hugged first Melissa and then Eli. "You've been so kind," she said as she quickly handed over her phone to Melissa. "Thank you. Thank you so much for what you've done. You're a miracle. Both of you. A miracle!"

Melissa was typing the last number of her contact info into Carol's phone when the paramedics started carrying the gurney since the usual wheels wouldn't work well on the sand.

"Let us know how things go with you."

"I will. Thank you."

A moment later, she and Eli stood alone.

"You didn't ride with him," she observed, a little surprised.

"The paramedics had things under control, and I would have just been in the way while they do their thing. I can put my ego aside enough to be sure that the cardiac specialist at the hospital is in a better position to treat Jim than I would be right now."

They both walked to where the dogs were tied up, and Melissa could feel her knees tremble in reaction.

"That was a little more excitement than you probably bargained for this morning," Eli said as he gripped Max's leash.

She patted Fiona's soft fur, wishing she could kneel right there in the sand and bury her face in it for a moment while she regained her composure.

"I would say the same to you. Way to step up, Dr. Sanderson."

"Part of the job description. You help where you can."

"It's more than that for you, isn't it? Even if you weren't a doctor, you're the kind of guy who would jump in and help in any emergency. You must get that from your dad."

He looked surprised by her words and, she wanted to think, pleased, as well. "I don't know about that. I do know that was probably enough of a workout for me today. I'm going to be buzzed on endorphins for at least another hour or two."

"Same here. I need to go." She smiled a little. "I'm supposed to be at work in an hour, and my boss won't be happy if I'm late."

"Sounds like a jerk."

"He's okay," she said.

There was far more she wanted to say, but she didn't trust herself. She had just watched him work tirelessly to save a man's life and she wasn't sure she had the words to convey how much that had moved her.

Chapter Five

His hands were shaking.

Eli gripped Max's leash with one hand and shoved the other in his pocket, hoping to hell Melissa didn't notice.

They had just saved a man's life, and the reaction to that overwhelmed and humbled him.

This wasn't the first time he had saved someone's life. He had been a combat physician and had worked in some nasty hot spots all over the world. For several years, his focus had been refugee camps and providing help and education in war-torn villages, where his patients were usually light on hope and heavy on physical ills from all they had endured.

His efforts weren't always successful.

Too often, there was nothing he could do.

He knew that was the reason for his physical reaction now that the crisis had passed.

Somehow he had traveled back in his memory to the last time he had performed CPR on someone. When he had desperately tried to revive Justine even as he watched her life seep away.

He hadn't really expected Jim to survive. CPR didn't always work and even AED machines couldn't always shock a person's heart back after it had sustained significant damage.

He didn't know what Jim's chances were for long-term recovery, but at least his heart was beating on its own now. Eli had to be grateful for that.

He tried to blink away the image of Justine, of Miri, of those others who had been injured in that suicide bombing, but they remained burned in his mind.

That time, the outcome had been far different. Miri had died instantly. He had known the moment he had raced onto the scene. Justine had survived only moments, conscious and in agony for perhaps thirty seconds after he arrived, until she stopped breathing.

Despite all his efforts, despite the full hour of compressions he had done as they transported her to the makeshift refugee-center hospital. He had done CPR long after his arms started to burn with agony and his back muscles cramped.

The hell of it was, he had known almost from the beginning that she would not survive, and still he had tried. How could he have done anything else?

He let out a slow breath, aware of the cold, hollow ache in his stomach.

"You okay?" Melissa asked as they approached Brambleberry House, her forehead wrinkling with concern as she studied him.

"Fine."

She gave him a searching look but didn't call him on his short answer, which she had to know was a lie. "I'm glad you are, because I'm a wreck," she said instead, with a ragged-sounding little laugh.

"Why?"

"I only wanted to take my favorite dog out for a run. I never expected to play a small part in saving someone's life."

"Not a small part," he corrected. "You were fantastic. You kept Carol calm, focused the dispatcher and helped with rescue breathing when I needed it. We made an excellent team."

She looked surprised and pleased at the completely warranted praise. "Thanks. I'm just glad I was there so I could help. I think the remainder of today is going to seem a little anticlimactic, don't you?

"Probably."

"If only I could persuade my ogre of a boss to give me the rest the day off."

"If only he wasn't such a jerk and you didn't have a full caseload of patients today, he probably would have been happy to give you some time off."

"I guess we'll never know," she said as they reached the beach-access gate leading into the Brambleberry House gardens.

Her humor made him smile. For some reason he didn't quite understand, that made him feel guilty about Justine and Miri all over again. It didn't seem right that he could smile and joke with a beautiful woman who made him desperately want to forget.

Some of his emotional turmoil must have shown on his features.

"Are you sure you're okay? You don't seem as happy

as I might have expected, considering a very fortunate man is alive because of you."

He didn't speak for a long moment, unable to articulate the morass of emotions inside him. He should make some excuse and be on his way. If he wanted to stop at the hospital in Seaside before seeing patients, he had to hurry.

Still, he wanted to confide in her, for reasons he didn't wholly understand.

"This morning seemed to dredge up some things," he confided. "The last patient I performed CPR on didn't make it."

"Oh, Eli," she said. Her expression was drenched with compassion. "I'm sorry. That must be tough. But I can honestly say, seeing you in action today, I'm positive you did everything you could."

Had he? He wanted to think so but wasn't sure he would ever be convinced of that.

"You understand that not every battle we fight as health care professionals can or should be won," she went on softly.

"Yeah. I know. There have been plenty of times when I've had to accept I can't change the inevitable and that it is not in the patient's best interest to try." He paused. "It's harder when it's someone you know.

"The person you lost was someone you cared about."

He didn't know how she could possibly know that, yet she spoke the words as a quiet statement, not a question.

"Yes." He was appalled when emotions welled up in his throat, making it impossible for him to force any more words out around them.

"I'm sorry," she murmured again. She placed her hand on his arm in a small gesture of comfort.

"Thanks," he answered, more touched by her compassion than he could ever say. "I thought I had dealt with it, but apparently not."

"You didn't show your reaction when it mattered, in the heat of the moment, when you had work to do. I was right there beside you and had no idea what you were going through. You were professional, composed, in full command of the situation. I imagine that's something they teach you in the military. Do what has to be done when it matters, then react later."

"I guess."

"Was it another soldier you lost?"

He gripped Max's leash a little more tightly. "Justine was an aid worker. She was from a small town outside Paris, a doctor with Doctors Without Borders, in the last refugee camp where I was helping out. We... became friends."

More than friends, but he didn't want to tell Melissa that now.

"She died in a suicide bombing at a market square along with fifteen others." Including Miri. Sweet, smiling, innocent Miri. "I was a few hundred yards away when it happened, first on the scene."

"Oh, Eli. I'm so sorry. That must have been so difficult."

He acknowledged her sympathy with a nod. "It was. The situations aren't the same at all, except for the CPR part. For some reason, that brought everything back."

"Will you be okay?"

He forced his features into a smile, wishing he hadn't brought the subject up at all. "I'm fine. Thanks for worrying about me."

"In your professional opinion, Dr. Sanderson, is it appropriate for us to hug? I could sure use one, after everything that's happened this morning."

He didn't consider himself necessarily a physical person, but he really craved the comfort of Melissa's arms right about now. "I could use one, actually."

He wrapped his arms around her and she sagged against him with a little sigh, wrapping her arms around his waist.

It felt so damn good, warm and personal and kind. He had needed a hug for a long time.

He and Justine hadn't been in love. She was more concerned with saving humanity than starting up a relationship with him or anyone else. Still, their relationship had been a bright, happy spot in a miserable situation, and her death had filled him with a complex mix of guilt, grief and deep regret that her shining light to the world had been extinguished.

Melissa's arms tightened around him and she rested her head against his chest, soft and sweet and vulnerable.

After a few more moments, his sadness seemed to trickle away, replaced by something far more dangerous.

Maybe this hug between them wasn't such a good idea. His body was suddenly reminding him that he was still very much alive, and he could think of several excellent ways to reinforce that.

She made a soft, breathy sound and his groin tightened. He'd had a thing for Melissa for a long time. Having her in his arms now was better than anything he could have imagined.

And he shouldn't be here.

"I should, uh, probably go," he said.

She sighed and stepped away, and he instantly wanted to gather her close again. It was only a simple embrace. Why did it fill him with such peace?

"I'm proud of what you did. You saved a man's life,

and I was honored to be part of it." She smiled a little and, before he realized what she intended, she stood on tiptoe and kissed the corner of his mouth.

For a moment, he stood frozen, stunned into immobility. Her lips were soft and tasted like strawberries and cream, his very favorite dessert. He felt her breath on his skin, warm and delicious, and the heat of her where she stood close to him.

More.

That little taste wasn't enough. Not by a long shot. She eased her mouth away after that first little brush of her lips against his. He wasn't fully aware of moving his mouth to more fully meet hers, but he must have. One moment her lips were barely touching the edge of his mouth, the next he had turned his head so that he could capture her mouth in a true kiss.

She made a little sound in her throat, a gasp or a sigh, he wasn't sure which, and her breath seemed to catch, then she kissed him back. Her arms were still around his waist from their hug and now they tightened, pulling him closer.

She was the most delicious thing he'd ever tasted, and the sweetness of her kiss and the incredible *rightness* of her arms around him seemed to wash over Eli like cleansing, healing rain. He kissed her with an urgency bordering on desperation, afraid he would never have the chance again to stand with her between the ocean and a flower garden, afraid he would never again know a kiss like this, one that moved him to his soul.

He should *not* be doing this.

The thought whispered to him over and over, quietly at first, then with increasing intensity.

She worked for him. For his father, technically, but

right now for him. This was highly inappropriate, and he needed to stop this moment.

He started to pull away, but she made a soft, sexy little sound and pressed her body against him, as if she couldn't bear to let him go. It was like a match held to dry kindling, the only spark needed for him to ignite. He deepened the kiss, pulling her tightly against him.

He wanted her more than he remembered wanting anything in a long time.

All week as they had worked together, he had been trying not to admit that to himself. He had forced himself to view her strictly as a colleague, a nurse whose dedication and abilities he admired.

Now he could admit he had been lying to himself. Now, with her here in his arms, he could no longer deny it. He saw her as far more than that.

He had a thing for Melissa Fielding and had from the time he was eighteen. She had been the prettiest girl in town, with her big green eyes and her generous smile and the kindness that had always been part of her.

He couldn't have her then because she had eyes only for the jock and popular kid, Cody Fielding.

He couldn't have her now because of a hundred different reasons, mostly because he couldn't be the kind of man she needed.

All those reasons he needed to put a stop to this now, before things skyrocketed out of control, raced through his brain, and he tried to find the strength to heed the warnings. He couldn't do it. She felt too damn right in his arms, as perfect and lovely as a spring morning on Cannon Beach.

She was the one who finally pulled away, easing her

mouth slowly from his, her breathing ragged and her eyes dazed and aroused.

A mischievous wind seemed to slide around them, warm and rose scented, though that didn't make sense since it was too early for roses in the Brambleberry House gardens by about a month.

Eli lowered his arms from around her, the magnitude of what had just happened hitting him like a huge Japanese glass fishing ball dropped from the highest branches of the big pine tree on the edge of the garden.

He had just kissed Melissa Blake Fielding—and not a simple kiss, either, but a hot, passionate, openmouthed kiss that couldn't be mistaken for anything but what it was. A clear declaration that he wanted her.

"That was…not supposed to happen." Her voice sounded breathless, thready, sexy as hell.

"Agreed." He ran a hand through his hair, not sure how to respond.

"I'm not completely sure what *did* happen," she admitted. "I meant to just kiss you on the cheek and then somehow…things sort of exploded."

He had wanted them to explode. Something about the emotional turmoil of the morning had lowered all his defenses, allowing heat and aching hunger to filter through.

"We have both just been through something intense. Sometimes when that happens, when adrenaline spikes and then crashes, people can react in strange ways."

"That must be it." She didn't look particularly convinced and he couldn't blame her. He had been through plenty of intense things in the military and had never used that as an excuse to tangle tongues with anybody else.

"It was extremely inappropriate of me to kiss you," he said, his voice stiff.

"Was it?" She blinked, clearly at a loss to understand what he meant.

He sighed and took a step farther away, though he knew the opposite side of the beach wouldn't be far enough to make him want her less.

"Technically, I'm your boss. You work for me. In some corners, this might be considered workplace harassment."

She stiffened. "We are not in the workplace right now. And for the record, you did not harass me. I kissed you first."

"A kiss on the cheek. And then I turned it into something else."

"I wanted you to," she admitted. "I kissed you right back. Did you miss that part?"

He frowned. "It still shouldn't have happened."

"Maybe not, but nobody harassed anybody. And technically, I work for your father, not you. You're just the substitute doctor."

He gave a half laugh, not sure whether to be relieved or offended. "You're right. I'm leaving again as soon as my dad is on his feet."

Her features froze for a moment, then she gave a tight smile. "End of story, then. It happened, we can't change it, so let's just move on from here."

He sighed, not knowing what else to say. "Right. Well, I apologize for any inappropriateness on my part and promise it won't happen again."

Again, she offered that tight smile. "Great. Now I really do need to get going. You might not be justified in firing me because of the way I kiss, but you could if I'm an hour late to work."

"This morning's events more than excuse your tardiness."

"I'll let you try to get that one past Carmen and Tiffany," she said. "I'll see you at work."

He waited until she and her neighbor's dog moved out of sight before he gripped Max's leash and hurried toward his father's house, wishing he had time for a quick jump in the cold Pacific before he headed into the office.

Chapter Six

Though she wanted to find a nearby bench in the beautiful gardens at Brambleberry House and just collapse into a brainless, quivering heap, Melissa forced herself to keep walking toward the house, afraid Eli somehow might be watching.

The kiss they had just shared had shaken her to her core. The heat of it, the intensity behind it, the emotions stirring around inside her. Who would have guessed that Eli could kiss a woman until she couldn't think straight?

Her knees were trembling like she'd just run a marathon, and it was taking every ounce of concentration she had to stay on the path and not to wander blindly into the lilac bushes.

Oh. My. Word.

Dr. Sanderson Jr. packed one heck of a wallop in his kiss. She had been so very tempted to stay there in his arms for the rest of the day and simply savor the magic of it.

He was right, though. Their kiss was a mistake that never should have happened. At the first touch of his hard mouth on hers, she should have come to her senses and realized what a disaster this was.

She still wasn't sure why she hadn't done exactly that. Maybe it was the adrenaline crash from working on Jim, or maybe it was the highly inappropriate dreams she was still having about him, or maybe it had simply been the result of the long week of doing her best to fight her attraction to him.

Regardless, their kiss *had* happened. How on earth was she supposed to face him at work all day without remembering the taste of his mouth or the salty, musky scent of him, or the safety and security she found in his arms?

She had a serious crush on the man. This morning hadn't exactly helped her gain control of it, first watching him save a life and then sharing that amazing kiss.

As she headed with Fiona toward the house, Rosa walked out on the back porch to greet her. She could tell immediately that her friend had seen her and Eli together at the bottom of the garden. She must have been sitting here when they walked up, with a clear view down to the garden to the beach-access gate.

The only thing she could do was own it. "Yes. Okay. I just kissed my boss. We're both determined to forget about it. I would appreciate if you would try to do the same."

Rosa gave a laugh that she tried to disguise as a cough. "All right. Enough said. It's none of my business anyway."

Okay, she probably shouldn't have said anything. Now she'd only made things worse by bringing attention to the kiss, like in high school when girls used to walk into class and announce to everyone that they had a new pimple.

"Sorry," she mumbled.

"Nothing to apologize for. I only came for my dog so you did not have to walk her up the stairs."

"Thanks. You have no idea what kind of morning it's been. Eli and I happened upon a tourist who collapsed from a heart attack."

"Is that what the paramedics were doing? I heard the sirens and worried. How is he?"

"Better than he would have been if we hadn't been there. Eli gave him CPR, then shocked him with the AED and he came back. It was amazing to see."

"I can imagine. Good for Eli."

"The kiss you saw. That was kind of a crazy reaction to what happened. The adrenaline rush and everything. We shouldn't have… It won't happen again."

"We are not going to talk about that, though." Rosa smiled and Melissa felt a wave of gratitude for her.

"When do you leave for your hiking trip?" she asked.

"The plan was to take off tonight and be back tomorrow night, but my friend just texted me and had an emergency in the family, so now we're leaving tomorrow and will be back Sunday night. Fiona will be here until then, just in case you need her."

"I might. Thanks."

Fiona tugged at her leash, obviously wanting to be home, and Rosa gave the dog an exasperated look. "I'd better get her some water, then we've got to head into the office. Have a good day."

"Same to you."

As Rosa and Fiona headed up the stairs to her apartment, Melissa opened the door to her own.

Inside, she fought the urge to collapse on her bed for a few hours. Or maybe the rest of the day.

Rosa had wished her a good day. She had a feeling it

would be anything *but* good. How on earth was she supposed to make it through, especially having to face Eli again after that stunning kiss?

She could do it. She had tackled tough things before and she could do it again.

No matter how difficult.

By some miracle, she and Eli managed to get through the day's appointments at the clinic without too much awkwardness between them.

Melissa had decided on a strategy of avoidance. Though it was tough, she tried to pretend their kiss had never happened, that they hadn't spent a glorious five minutes with their mouths tangled together and his arms tightly around her.

It was one of the toughest things she'd ever had to do. Every time she passed him in the hall or shared an exam room with him while he spoke with a patient, she had to actively struggle to keep from staring at his mouth and remembering the heat and magic of their embrace.

The only saving grace was the clinic's caseload. They were both busy with patients all day and didn't have time for small talk. She almost made it through her shift without being alone with him, until she waved goodbye to Carmen and Tiffany and headed out to the parking lot at the end of the day, only to find Eli walking out just ahead of her. She almost turned around to go back inside but couldn't think on her feet quickly enough to come up with an excuse.

She found her urge to flee annoying and demeaning. So they'd shared a kiss. That didn't mean she had to be uncomfortable around him for the rest of his time here in Cannon Beach.

She put on a cheerful smile. She could do this. "Do you

have big plans for the weekend?" she asked, then instantly regretted the question. She did *not* want him thinking she was hinting that they should get together or something.

He shook his head. "Dad is hoping he'll be ready to come home soon, so I'll probably be busy making sure the house is ready for him. What about you?"

"Not really. Skye and I are running into Portland tonight to take Carol's things to her. The hotel has already packed them all up for her."

"That's very nice of you."

"It's the least I can do."

Jim had been airlifted to the hospital in Portland and Carol had flown with him, unwilling to leave his side even long enough to come back to Cannon Beach for their suitcases.

"What's the latest? Have you heard? When I talked to Carol earlier, she told me he was likely going to need a quadruple bypass."

"Then you know as much as I do. The surgery won't be until tomorrow, from what I understand. I feel good about his chances, but it's too early to say if he's out of the woods."

"At least he *has* a chance. He wouldn't have, if not for you."

"And you," Eli said.

It was a shared bond between them, one she never would have expected when she awoke that morning.

He smiled a little, more with his eyes than his mouth. Melissa fought a shiver. She also wouldn't have expected that kiss.

Why had he kissed her? And would it happen again?

She cleared her throat. "I'd better go. Skye will be waiting for me at the babysitter's."

"Right. Pizza night. Tell her I meant my invitation of the other day. The two of you are welcome to come to my dad's house so she can shoot some pool. Nobody else is using it. Who knows, maybe she can turn into a pool shark and start fleecing all the tourists over at A Slice of Heaven."

"You're a bad influence on my child," she said, shaking her head. And on *her*, she wanted to add, giving her all kinds of ideas she didn't need complicating her world right now.

She had a weekend away from him to regain her perspective, and the sooner she started the better chance she would have of putting that kiss out of her head.

She gave him a wave and had started to climb into her SUV when another vehicle pulled into the parking lot—a flashy red convertible carrying two people, a blond male and a darker-haired, more petite female.

She paused, ready to explain that the clinic was closed. The convertible pulled up next to her. When the driver pulled off his sunglasses and climbed out with athletic grace, Melissa let out an involuntary gasp.

"Cody! What…what are you doing here?"

Her ex-husband beamed his trademark smile that had appeared on surfing magazine covers for more than a decade. "I told you I was working on coming back to Oregon. And here I am."

"I didn't realize you meant you were coming back immediately."

"I wanted to surprise you, Missy."

"I'm surprised, all right." She couldn't have been more surprised if he'd come back to town with tattoos covering his face like a Maori warrior. "Are you…moving back to Cannon Beach?"

"No. We're just here hanging out with my buddy Ace. You remember him, don't you?"

"Oh, yes." Ace had been a jerk in high school and now had a string of used car lots along the coast. From what she heard, he was *still* a jerk.

"We're going to settle in Portland, near my folks. Since I lost my sponsorship, I need to find a more reliable paycheck. Got that baby on the way and all. My dad's been pushing me to join his office and this seemed as good a time as any."

Now he wanted to be financially stable? For the five years they had been married, he had been perfectly content to let her support them with her nursing career.

"You're going into real estate." She tried to process that shocking information, but it was too much for her brain, after the day she'd had.

"I guess I have to pass some kind of class and stuff before I can actually do any selling. But I'm going to start small and see where it goes."

Knowing her ex as she did, she had no doubt he would probably be brilliant at it. Cody had always been good at convincing people he had exactly what they needed.

After her dad died, Cody had been so sweet and attentive, making her feel like the most important person on earth. She had been grieving and lost, and he had helped remind her the world could still have laughter and ice cream and sweetness.

"You know how you've been bugging me to spend more time with Skye. This is my chance! We're moving into one of my dad's rentals in Portland and working out of his office there. We'll only be a few hours away."

"Great."

"Amalia can't wait to meet her. She's been asking every day."

"Amalia."

"My wife. That's one of the reasons I stopped by before we go out to dinner with Ace and his wife. I want you to meet her. Babe, get out here."

A young woman who looked to be in her early twenties rose from the passenger seat of the convertible with a grace that matched Cody's. She was dark and petite, tanned and fit and gorgeous. And very, very pregnant.

"Oh." The word escaped before Melissa could swallow it down.

Cody glowed like *he* was the pregnant one. He held out a hand to the woman, who moved to his side looking elegant and beautiful—so different from the way Melissa had looked when she was pregnant with Skye, when her ankles had disappeared and all the baby weight had somehow settled in her hips and butt.

"This is Amalia. I met her in Brazil. She doesn't speak much English."

"Hello, Amalia."

"'Ello." The woman's voice was low and throaty and exotic, though she looked nervous. Cody didn't speak a word of Portuguese, as far as she knew. If his new wife didn't speak much English, Melissa had to wonder how they communicated.

"Like I said, she's been dying to meet Skye. Where is she?"

"Not here," she said, pointing out the obvious. "This is my workplace. She's at the babysitter's."

"Oh. Right." He gave a little laugh. "I should have realized that. Where does the babysitter live? I can go see her there."

Skye would be thrilled to see her father. She adored him despite his chronic negligence.

"It would be better if I picked her up. Why don't you meet me at Brambleberry House in about an hour. Do you remember where that is?"

"I think so. Sounds good."

He started to lead his wife back to the car, then apparently noticed Eli, still waiting and watching the scene beside his father's Lexus SUV.

Cody's gaze narrowed. "You look familiar. Have we met?"

Eli coughed politely. "Yeah. Eli Sanderson. We went to school together. You and some buddies ambushed me in the parking lot once during a school dance."

Cody let out a rough laugh. "You're kidding me. Why would I do that?"

Eli shrugged. "You apparently weren't very happy with me for asking Melissa to dance."

"Kind of a dick move, dude, asking another guy's date to dance with you."

"Sometimes. In this case, I guess I figured you wouldn't care, since you had been ignoring her all night."

Cody laughed out loud at that. "I was an ass in high school. I hope there are no hard feelings."

He was *still* an ass, on many levels. She couldn't believe it had taken her so many years to figure it out.

"Why would there be?" Eli said coolly. "It was a long time ago."

She had completely forgotten about that school dance. As usual, Cody had abandoned her in the corner while he talked to his friends. She might as well have been invisible for all the attention her date paid her that night. That wasn't a unique situation. Even now, she wasn't quite sure why she had put up with it for so long.

"Anyway, we're staying the night at Ace's guesthouse, but I was hoping we could take Skye back to Portland with us tomorrow."

"Why?"

"We're buying some things for the new little munchkin, and I figured she might like to be involved in the whole baby thing."

As usual, he didn't think about anyone but himself. He didn't consider that she might have plans with her daughter. They were just supposed to drop everything for him.

According to the Gospel of Cody, the world revolved around him and always would. She hated thinking of the years she had wasted trying to make things different.

She glanced at the pregnant young woman beside him, who looked at Cody like he was the sun and the moon and the stars, all wrapped up in one perfect man.

She wanted to tell him to forget it, that she and Skye would be busy, but her daughter truly did adore her father and she would be sad to miss the chance to spend time with him.

"I'm sure she will be happy to see you."

The truth was, Cody wasn't necessarily a bad father. He did love their daughter, she just didn't come first, the way a child should.

"Perfect. We thought we would leave about eleven."

"I'll have her ready."

"Maybe we'll just wait until then to have Ami meet her. Save us time tonight, since we have to get ready for dinner. Does that work?"

"It should be fine."

"Thanks, Missy. This is gonna be great. You'll see."

With that use of the nickname she hated, he helped his pregnant young wife into the passenger seat of his impractical little red sports car, hopped into the driver's seat and pulled out of the parking lot, leaving Melissa feeling as if she had just been pounded by heavy surf against a seawall.

She closed her eyes for a moment, then opened them, wishing she could have dealt with that encounter alone, without any witnesses.

"Well, that seems like a pretty sucky way to start a weekend."

Eli's dry tone surprised a laugh out of her. "Congratulations, Dr. Sanderson. You officially get the understatement-of-the-week award."

"I was talking about me. It's tough being confronted with the guy who once tried to beat me up."

"Tried to?"

"I was tougher than I looked even when I was a tall, awkward geek."

He had *never* been awkward. She remembered that now, too late.

"I studied jujitsu from about age nine and had a few moves that still serve me well." He studied her. "I take it you're not exactly jumping for joy about your ex-husband's return. Is it the pregnant new wife?"

"No. Not exactly. Skye will be thrilled about having a new sibling to love and she'll be over the moon that she might see Cody more often. She loves her father."

"That's the important thing then, isn't it?"

His words struck with the ring of truth. "Yes. Thanks for the reminder."

He studied her for a moment, blue eyes glinting in the fading sunlight. "You've got your hands full tonight and don't need a trip to Portland. Why don't you let me take care of Jim and Carol's suitcases tonight?"

"I offered. It doesn't seem right to hand off the duty to you simply because it's become inconvenient."

"I don't mind. Max loves riding in the car, and it will give me the chance to check on my patient."

He was such a good man. Why couldn't she have seen past the skinny geekiness when she had been in high school instead of being drawn to the macho, sexy surfer type? She could have avoided so much heartache.

"That's very kind of you. They were staying at The Sea Urchin. The innkeeper has already packed up their suitcases for them. Thank you, Eli."

"It's no problem," he assured her. He gave her a smile that almost reached his eyes this time, and she surrendered even more of her heart to him.

He made it extremely difficult to resist him, and she was completely failing at the task.

"Didn't you say he was coming at eleven? That was forty minutes ago. Where is he? Do you think he forgot?"

Melissa could feel the muscles in her jaw ache and forced herself to unclench her teeth. "He'll be here," she assured her daughter, though she wasn't at all positive that was the truth.

As she looked at Skye watching anxiously out the window, Melissa was painfully reminded of all the nights she had waited for Cody to come home or call from the road when he said he would.

Cody was great at making promises and lousy at keeping them.

"He'll be here," she said again. "Let me text him again and see where he is."

She quickly shot off a text, only refraining from swearing at him by the same superhuman effort she was using to keep from grinding her molars.

It took him several long moments to reply.

Running late. Waves too good this AM at Indian Beach. On way now.

That was more of an explanation than she used to get from him but still not enough to placate a girl who adored him.

"Looks like he's on his way. Do you have everything you need to sleep over? Pajamas, a change of clothes, your emergency phone, some snacks, coloring paper and pens, your American Girl doll?"

"Yep. Got it all." Skye gave her gap-toothed grin, and Melissa's heart gave another sharp tug. She loved this kind, funny, creative little person with all her heart.

Her daughter was growing up. What would the future hold for this sweet, openhearted child?

"Why don't you practice your reading with me for a few more minutes while we wait?"

"Okay." Skye picked up the book she was reading about a feisty girl who resembled her greatly. They were both laughing at the girl's antics when the doorbell rang.

"That's him!" Skye exclaimed. She dropped the book and raced to the door eagerly.

It was, indeed, her father. Cody walked in with his exotically beautiful bride silently following along.

"Great place." Cody gave an admiring look around the big Victorian, with its high ceilings, transom windows and extensive woodwork. "I remember this from when that old biddy Abigail What's-Her-Name lived here. She never liked me."

"It's been a good apartment for us. The other tenants are wonderful and the landlords have been more than accommodating. It has worked out really well while I continue trying to save up enough for our own place."

"When you're serious about looking, make sure you let me help you. Who knows? I might even discount my commission."

She dug her nails into her palms and forced a smile, when what she really wanted to do was roll her eyes and remind him that if he were more dependable with child support, she could have bought a house when she first came back to town.

"Wow. Thanks. You might want to get your real estate license before you go around making that kind of generous offer."

"Working on it. Working on it. You ready, Skye-ster?"

"Yep." She threw her arms around Melissa's waist. "Bye, Mommy. Love you."

"Bye, sweetie."

"I'll bring her back tomorrow afternoon. Not sure what time. I was thinking we could maybe hit a baseball game in the afternoon."

No problem. She had nothing else to do but sit around and simply wait for him to drop off their child whenever he felt like it.

"Sounds like fun," she said, forcing another smile. "When you figure out your plans, I would appreciate a text or call so I know roughly when to expect you."

"You got it. Thanks, Missy."

He picked up Skye's suitcase and the booster seat she claimed she didn't need anymore but legally did because she was small for her age. At least Cody didn't argue about that as he led the way back to his flashy convertible. The booster seat barely fit in the minuscule back seat.

She stood on the sidewalk, watching as he helped Skye buckle in, opened the door for his new wife, then climbed in himself.

As Cody backed out of the driveway, Melissa whispered a prayer that her baby girl would be okay, then headed into her empty apartment.

Her remaining chores went quickly, especially without Skye to distract her with hugs and stories and eager attempts to help.

At loose ends, she couldn't seem to focus on her own book or on the television series she was working her way through on Netflix. If only her mother were in town, they could go for a long lunch somewhere, something they never seemed to have time to do.

She needed physical activity but couldn't summon the energy required for a run. After dithering for a few more moments, she finally decided to take a walk to deliver one of the loaves of banana nut bread she and Skye had made earlier that morning to her friends Will and Julia Garrett.

On impulse, she texted Rosa at work, asking if she was still around and, if so, could Melissa borrow Fiona for a walk.

Rosa immediately texted back a big YES with four exclamation points. Then she added, Both of us would thank you for that.

She smiled a little through her glum mood, grateful all over again that her wanderings had led her back here to this beautiful house and new friends.

She had a key to Rosa's apartment, and Fiona jumped

around excitedly when Melissa reached for her leash by the door.

"I'm taking a treat to the neighbors," she informed the dog. "You can only come along if you promise to behave yourself. They've got that handsome Labrador who is nothing but trouble."

Fiona shook her head as if she disagreed, which made Melissa truly smile for the first time since she had watched a red convertible drive down the road.

As she and Fiona walked down the stairs, she momentarily thought about inviting Sonia along, then remembered the second-floor tenant was out of town on one of the mysterious trips she took.

Every few months, an anonymous-looking car-service limousine would pick her up and Sonia would slip inside carrying a suitcase, then would return again by another limousine three or four days later.

Rosa had once asked her where she went, but Sonia, as usual, gave vague answers. She had offered some excuse about having to go away on a family matter, then had quickly changed the subject.

Considering she claimed she had no family, that excuse made no sense, but neither she nor Rosa had wanted to interrogate her about it.

The April afternoon was sunny and lovely, perfect for walking, with a sweet-smelling breeze dancing through the Brambleberry House gardens and the sound of waves in the distance.

She wanted to enjoy it and was annoyed with herself that she couldn't seem to shake this blue mood.

Unfortunately, when she and Fiona walked the three blocks to Julia and Will's beautifully restored home, nobody answered the door. She knocked several times but received no answer.

Too bad. She should have called first to make sure they were home. She could always freeze the banana bread, she supposed, though it was never quite as good as when it was fresh out of the oven.

She took a different way home, not realizing until she was almost to it that her route took her directly past Wendell Sanderson's house. She wouldn't have intentionally come this way, but apparently her subconscious had other ideas.

A sharp bark greeted them, and Fiona immediately started wagging her tail and straining at the leash when she spotted Max just inside the garden gate…in the company of Wendell's entirely too appealing son.

She really should have taken another way. Oh, she hoped he didn't think she was staking out the house in the hopes of seeing him.

She couldn't just walk on past, as much as she wanted to. Eli watched her approach, a screwdriver in his hand and an expression on his features she couldn't decipher.

"Hi," he said.

She gestured to the gate. He was installing some kind of locking mechanism, she realized. "This looks fun."

"Since my dad's surgery, Max has decided he's the canine version of Houdini. He's learned how to open the latch and take off."

The dog looked inordinately proud of himself.

"Oh, how sweet. I bet he's letting himself out so he can go look for your dad!"

"That is entirely possible. Or maybe he just doesn't enjoy my company."

That is not *possible*, she wanted to say, but didn't have the nerve.

"How is your dad? When is he coming home?"

"Not as early as he'd hoped. He's been doing so well, we thought he might be cleared to come home tomorrow, but I guess yesterday he had a little tumble during physical therapy."

"Oh, no!"

"He seems to be all right, but the doctor at the rehab center wants to keep him until at least Monday or Tuesday, to be safe."

"I'm sorry. That must be disheartening for both of you, especially if he thought he was going home sooner."

On impulse, she held out the loaf of banana bread. "Will you take this to him? Skye and I made it this morning for Julia Garrett and her family, but they're not home. Your dad particularly enjoys our banana nut bread."

Eli looked astonished. "Thanks. That's very kind of you, but are you sure you don't want to save it and give it to your friend later?"

"Banana bread is best when it's fresh. When Skye gets home from Portland, we'll make another batch."

"Portland. I forgot she was going with her dad. How are you holding up?"

"Super," she lied. "Except I couldn't stand how quiet my house was, so I borrowed my neighbor's dog and went for a walk so I wouldn't have to be alone there."

He smiled a little at that and patted Fiona, who gazed up at him with adoration.

She had been holding back her emotions all day, but the kindness in his eyes seemed to send them bubbling over. To her great and everlasting dismay she sniffled a little, a tear dripping down her cheek.

"Hey now. It's okay," Eli said, looking slightly panicky. "She won't be gone long."

"I know. She'll be back tomorrow."

Melissa felt so stupid! It was only an overnight visit. Fiona licked at her hand and it was the absolute last straw. She sniffled again and before she knew it, Eli had set the loaf of banana nut bread on top of the gate and reached for her, pulling her against his hard muscles.

"It's okay," he said again.

"She's never been away from me. Not one single night. She's seven years old and she's never slept somewhere she couldn't call out to me. Her father has taken her before but only for a few hours at a time. He doesn't know that she needs a night-light on and she has bad dreams if she eats too much sugar past eight, and when she wakes up, she does this sweet little stretchy thing."

"He'll figure all that out. The important parts anyway."

She let out a sigh, wishing she could stay here the rest of the evening so he could help keep her nerves away. "I know. You're right."

"Cody loves Skye, right? You said as much yesterday."

"He does. He doesn't always do things the same as I would, but that doesn't mean he doesn't love her."

"They will be fine. Skye strikes me as a clever girl. If there are any problems, she can always give you a call to come get her."

This was dangerous, being close to him like this. She couldn't help remembering their kiss the day before, and the way she had flung her arms around his neck and surrendered to her overpowering attraction toward him.

Holding him like this, being close to him and hearing his heartbeat against her cheek, was entirely too risky. It was making her think all kinds of wild thoughts. She was aware of a soft tenderness blooming to life inside her like the spring growth all around them. He was so kind, so concerned about her feelings. He made her feel like she mattered.

How was she supposed to resist that?

She had to. He was leaving again. He'd told her so himself. She couldn't afford to lose her heart to a man destined to break it into a thousand pieces.

Though it made her ache inside to do it, she forced herself to step away. "Thank you. I'm sorry you had to talk me down off the ledge."

"You're welcome. Anytime." He studied her. "You know what you need tonight? A distraction."

For one crazy second, her mind went into some completely inappropriate directions. She could come up with some pretty delicious ways to distract herself involving him, but she had a feeling that wasn't what he was talking about. "What did you have in mind?"

"Tiffany from work and her band are playing at The Haystacks tavern tonight. She gave me a flyer yesterday on her way out the door. I was thinking it would be nice to support her."

Melissa tried not to wince at the suggestion. She adored the young CNA for many reasons, but her musical ability wasn't among them.

"You haven't heard her sing, have you?"

"Is it that bad?"

"Taste can be such a subjective thing."

"In other words, you hate it."

"I don't hate it, exactly. Her band's style is what you might call an acquired taste."

"Well, hers isn't supposed to be the only band. According to the flyer, there are two other bands playing after hers. Who knows, we might get lucky and one might even be tolerable. What do you say?"

Why was he asking her? Because he felt sorry for her? Was he only being kind, or did he also dislike being alone on a Saturday night?

Did his reasons really matter? She didn't want to stay at home by herself watching television and feeling sorry for herself. He was offering a perfect distraction. If she didn't go, she would be alone all evening, without even Fiona for company, since Rosa was leaving town.

"I suppose it would mean a lot to Tiffany if we both came out to listen to her."

"There you go. A night on the town, plus supporting a coworker. You can't lose."

She wouldn't go that far. There was always the chance she would end up letting down her guard too much and inadvertently reveal the big crush she had on her boss.

She would simply have to be careful that didn't happen. The benefits of getting out of the house offset the small risk that she might make a fool of herself.

"What time?"

"Does eight work?"

"Yes. It's a d—" She caught herself before she said a word that rhymed with eight. This was *not* at date. They were simply two coworkers going out on the town to support someone else who worked with them.

"Deal. It's a deal," she improvised quickly. "Eight works for me."

"Perfect. I'll pick you up then."

"Great. Meantime, I hope your dad enjoys the banana nut bread. If you're lucky, he might even share some with you."

"I'll keep my fingers crossed."

She smiled, grabbed Fiona's leash and headed back toward Brambleberry House, feeling much better about the world than she had a few moments earlier.

Chapter Seven

As he drove up to the big, sprawling Victorian house where Melissa lived with her daughter, Eli was aware of a vague sense of danger.

He knew it was ridiculous. He had been in war zones, for heaven's sake, in countless hair-raising circumstances. He had operated on people with bullets flying, had jumped out of helicopters into uncertain territory, had tried to provide medical care in villages where he knew armed hostiles were hiding out.

Yeah, those things had been terrifying. Melissa Blake Fielding posed an entirely different sort of threat.

The woman got to him. She always had. He'd had a thing for her all those years ago when he was in high school, and apparently the intervening years had done nothing to work it out of his system.

This wasn't a date, despite the flowers on the seat next to him. They were friends and coworkers, he reminded himself. He had no intention of making things more complicated with her.

Sure, he liked her. The pretty cheerleader she had been in school had grown into a woman of strength and substance, someone who showed compassion and kindness to everyone.

She hadn't kissed him out of kindness. His abdominal muscles tightened at the memory of her sweet response the day before and the eagerness of her mouth against his. She had been as into the kiss as he was. He knew he hadn't misread the signs.

That didn't change the fact that he never should have let things go as far as they had.

Melissa had become an indispensable part of his father's practice. His father had told him how very much he relied on her. Eli had no business coming into town for a few weeks and messing with the status quo simply because he wanted something.

This wasn't a date, and he needed to remember that he wasn't the kind of man she needed. He couldn't be that man. She needed someone focused on home and family, not somebody who was simply marking time until he could go back and finish the job he had left undone overseas.

He found deep satisfaction working for the Army Medical Corps. He was helping other people and making a difference in the world, in whatever small way he could. Since Justine and Miri had died in that market square, however, his responsibilities had taken on vital urgency. Justine had been a dedicated physician, passionate about providing care to the desperate and helpless. He felt driven to continue her work.

Her life had held purpose and direction. Her death—

and Miri's—had been meaningless, the result of a cruel, fruitless act of violence. He was the trained military officer, and he should have picked up on the signs of unrest they had seen when they entered that village. He should never have let her go to the market that day. Instead, he had ignored his instincts and she had died as a result.

Because of him, she would no longer be able to help anyone, and he felt a sacred obligation to continue his own work in her memory. What else could he do?

He wasn't free to let himself fall for Melissa, no matter how attracted he was to her. It wouldn't be fair to either of them.

He wasn't in love with her. They'd only kissed once, for heaven's sake. She was his coworker and his friend.

He was half-tempted to throw the flowers his father had insisted he bring into the garbage can over there, but that would be wasteful. Friends could bring friends flowers. That didn't mean this was a date.

With that reminder firmly in his head, he walked up the porch steps of Brambleberry House and rang the doorbell just as another woman trotted down the steps carrying a backpack, with Fiona the Irish setter on her leash.

The woman was pretty, with warm brown eyes and wavy dark hair. She stopped and smiled at him, eyes widening a little when she spotted the flowers. He tried not to flush but had a feeling he wasn't very successful.

"Hello. You must be Dr. Sanderson's son. Eli, right? The army doctor."

What had she heard about him? And from whom? Had Melissa mentioned his name? He sighed, annoyed with himself. This wasn't junior high. It didn't matter if Melissa had mentioned him to her friend or not.

"That's right."

"Nice to meet you. I'm Rosa Galvez. I live upstairs, third floor."

"Any relation to Anna Galvez?" he asked as he petted the dog with his free hand.

Rosa nodded. "She's my aunt, sort of. I was adopted by her brother and his wife, anyway, when I was a teenager."

He sensed a definite story there, especially when the warmth in her eyes seemed to fade a little.

"Anna was always kind to me when I used to go into her gift shop. I understand you're running the place now."

"That's right. I love it," Rosa said. "How is your father doing?"

He couldn't go anywhere in town without people asking him that question, but Eli didn't mind. It was further proof of how beloved Wendell was around Cannon Beach.

"Okay. He had a little setback yesterday, but he should be home soon. The knees are better than ever, he says. Soon he'll be ready to chase all the ladies again."

She smiled. "Give him my best, will you? I like him very much. Your father, he is truly a good man and a good doctor."

"I'll tell him. Thank you."

"You are here to see my friend Melissa, no?"

"Yes. That's right." He found her trace of Spanish accent completely charming.

"Her doorbell is that one."

"Thanks."

She paused and appeared to be debating whether to add something. In the end, she gave a quick glance at Melissa's doorbell, then looked back at him. "I am glad you are here for Melissa tonight. She is having a struggle right now. It is hard to share a daughter."

"I imagine it would be."

"Thank you for being her friend. I am glad to know Dr. Sanderson's son is a good man like his father."

Was he? He was completely positive his father wouldn't have kissed one of his nurses until neither of them could think straight.

Fiona tugged on the leash before he could answer, and Rosa laughed a little. "I have to run. We are off on a little adventure and she is a little excited about it."

"Safe travels," he said.

"Thank you."

She hurried down the steps toward an SUV parked next to Melissa's vehicle, loaded her dog and backpack quickly and backed out.

At least the unexpected conversation had helped put the evening in perspective. Melissa needed a morale boost, and he was glad he had the chance to offer one.

He rang the doorbell, his hands tightening around the flowers in his hand.

When Melissa opened the door, his breath seemed to catch in his chest and, for a crazy moment, he forgot why he was there.

Friends, Eli reminded himself. They were only friends.

"Hi."

"Hi, yourself."

He couldn't think what to say for a long moment, then he remembered the flowers. "Here. These are for you. Peonies from my dad's garden. He was thrilled with the banana bread. It's one of his favorites. When I told him we were going to listen to Tiffany tonight, he insisted I cut some flowers to pay you back for the bread. They were my mom's favorite. The peonies, I mean."

Okay, he was babbling. He never babbled.

She looked touched by the gesture. "He showed me a

picture of your mother once. I wish I'd known her. She had the kindest eyes."

He felt the pang he always did when he remembered his mother, the ache that had become a part of him after all these years. "She did."

"How old were you when she died?"

"Twelve."

"I'm sorry. That must have been rough. I was fourteen when I lost my dad. The pain never quite goes away, does it?"

He shook his head, aware of yet another thread tugging him toward her. They both knew the void left behind from losing a parent at a young age.

He didn't know what to do with this soft tenderness unfurling inside him so he focused on the flowers, instead. "Anyway, the vase is from my dad. He made it in ceramics class at the rehab center. He wanted you to keep it."

Her features softened. "I'll cherish it even more, then. It's lovely. I have to tell you, I adore your father. If only he were thirty years younger!"

"Not the first time I've heard that phrase since I've been back in Cannon Beach," he said ruefully. His father was quite popular with women of all ages in town. Somehow Wendell managed to make every woman feel like she was the most important one in his world.

"Come in a moment while I find somewhere for these and grab my purse." She opened the door, and he followed her into the apartment.

He didn't know what the apartment had looked like before she moved in, but it was clear Melissa and her daughter had turned the space into a home. A large dollhouse stood in one corner, with a baseball bat propped against it and several stuffed animals on the roof, as if keeping watch. The room was cheery and open, with splashes of color from prints on the wall and bright pillows on the sofa and chairs.

"What a great view," he said, immediately drawn to the wall of windows facing the ocean.

"Killer, isn't it?" She moved to stand beside him and admired the rugged coastline outside the sunroom. "This is my favorite spot in the house. Sometimes I can't believe I really live here."

He glanced down at her features, pretty and open and genuine, and had to battle down a fierce urge to kiss her again. It would be so easy. He only had to close the small space between them and lean his head down just so. He could almost taste her, fresh and sweet as ripe strawberries.

His head dipped slightly, but he checked the movement just before he would have followed through on the powerful urge.

No. They were friends. That was all they could ever be. Melissa had enough complications in her life right now with her ex-husband moving back. She didn't need somebody with Eli's kind of baggage.

He was aware of her small swallow, of the way her gaze shifted from his eyes to his mouth and back again so quickly he wondered if he had imagined it.

It wasn't a good idea to be here alone with her in her warm, comfortable apartment. Not when she was everything he wanted and everything he couldn't have.

"We should go."

Was that disappointment he saw in her eyes? No. He was imagining that, too.

"We should. We wouldn't want to miss Tiffany in all her glory. Just give me a minute."

"Great."

He turned back to the window, hoping he had the strength to keep his hands off her all night.

She wasn't sure why, but Eli Sanderson seemed as uncomfortable as she felt as they walked into The Haystacks tavern.

Why? If she was the reason, what had she done to make him so edgy?

She had a feeling he was regretting whatever impulse had prompted him to invite her out tonight to hear Tiffany's band. She should have backed out when she had the chance. She could have made up some excuse, but she had been so grateful for the distraction she hadn't really thought through how awkward Eli might find it to spend time socially, after their heated kiss the day before.

It was too late now. He had invited her and she had accepted. The only thing she could do now was to make the best of it and try to relax and enjoy herself.

"Have you been here before?" she asked.

He looked around the tavern, with its brick walls and weathered plank bar. "Not recently. I may have stopped in with friends a time or two when I would come back to town during college, but I didn't have a lot of time for barhopping."

The Haystacks was one of those rare drinking establishments that didn't try to be trendy or hip. Its simple unpretentiousness made it popular with tourists and locals alike.

"It's not a bad place. They host some fun events, and on Saturday nights they feature all local musicians."

The place was already crowded and Tiffany's band was setting up on the small stage in the corner of the tavern. Eli managed to find them a table near the stage. He pulled a chair out for her and waited until she was settled before he sat across from her.

"I probably should warn you, I'm not much of a drinker," he admitted. "I've seen too many guys who spent every moment of their R & R hammered."

"You might change your mind and order a drink once the music starts."

He laughed roughly, a sound that seemed to ripple down her spine. "You've built it up so much, I can't wait."

"I shouldn't have said that. I'm sorry. Tiffany actually has an excellent voice. I'm just not sure Puddle of Love is the best venue for her talent."

"Her band is called Puddle of Love."

"I tried to warn you. It's not that bad. I'll be quiet and let you judge for yourself."

She ordered a mojito while Eli ordered one of the locally brewed ales.

She waved at a few people she knew from his father's practice and another couple who had gone to high school with her.

Their order came quickly. She sipped at her drink, then sat back in her chair. "Now that you've been here a week, what do you think?" she asked, making conversation. "Are you ready to stick around in Cannon Beach and go into practice with your dad?"

He shifted. "How did you know he was lobbying hard for that?"

She shrugged. "Lucky guess. I know how proud he is of you and how thrilled he is to have you back. It makes sense that he would want to make it permanent. He said your term of service is done but you're considering signing up for another few years."

He sipped at his beer, his gaze focused on the band setting up.

"Do you love the military that much?" She had to ask.

"It's not that I love it, necessarily. But I know I'm making a difference. I feel a certain…responsibility to continue doing what I'm doing."

"You could make a difference here, too."

"You make it sound so easy."

"Why isn't it?"

He was quiet, sipping at his beer again. "It's complicated."

"Doesn't seem like it to me."

"I'm good at what I do. I don't say that to be cocky, but there's something very fulfilling in knowing I'm helping people who have very few options available to them."

"I can see that."

"To be honest, I'm also not sure I'm ready to settle in one place. The idea of seeing the same patients day after day for the rest of my life seems so…final."

To her, that sounded like a dream come true. She yearned for roots. She had gone to nursing school before she and Cody were married and had barely earned her license before he decided it was time to move to Hawaii, where she had to retake her license requirements. They had lived in a half-dozen places during the five years they were married and she had to become relicensed three times.

She had loved staying in one place and having the chance to get to know their patients a little better.

She supposed everybody had different needs.

Before he could respond, Stew Peters, who ran the bar, went to the microphone. "Hey, everybody. Thanks for coming out. As you all know, it's locals' night tonight.

Performing for the first time here at The Haystacks, give it up for Puddle of Love."

She and Eli clapped with enthusiasm as Tiffany took to the stage, looking far different from the young woman Melissa had seen the day before, leaving the office in blue scrubs and a ponytail. Oddly, she also didn't resemble the leather-clad, big-haired rocker Melissa had seen fronting the band the last time she had seen them, at a little dive in Manzanita before Christmas.

This time she was dressed in a simple flowered dress, with her multicolored hair pulled back in a modest headband. Except for the multiple piercings and the vivid hair, she looked like a coed who had stopped into the bar between classes.

She took the microphone and the band behind her started up. As Melissa looked closer, she noticed several significant changes. The drummer was the same, but the guy on lead guitar and the girl playing bass were new to the band.

Tiffany's look and the band personnel weren't the only changes. She could tell after the first few bars. Puddle of Love had mellowed their sound significantly, cutting down on the screaming, angry lyrics and allowing Tiffany's strong contralto voice to come through.

By the time her friend finished the first song, Melissa was clapping along with the rest of the tavern crowd.

"I feel like I missed something here," he leaned in to say when there was a break in the music. "Were you deliberately trying to give me low expectations? They sound great to me."

"This isn't the same Puddle of Love I've heard before, trust me. This is Puddle of Love 2.0."

"I like it."

"So do I."

They both settled in to enjoy the music, mostly covers of rock ballads that somehow sounded evocative and unique with Tiffany's voice. When the set finished, the medical assistant walked through the crowd, greeting people she must have known, until she came to their table.

She looked impossibly young. "You guys came. Wow! I never thought you would."

"I'm glad I got to hear you before I leave town," Eli said. "That was terrific. You've got a gift."

The nurse's aide looked at Melissa.

"I enjoyed every minute of it," she said honestly.

"Thanks, you guys. Seriously, thanks. I like working for your dad—it's a good job—but I kind of feel like I need to take a break from everything and put all my energy into this, you know?"

Melissa remembered being young and passionate, ready to put all her faith into helping her husband follow his dreams.

What about her own dreams? What had she wanted?

"My parents think I'm crazy," Tiffany said with a little laugh. "Do you really think we're good enough to go for it anyway?"

She asked the question of Eli, who looked uncomfortable at being put on the spot. "I'm, uh, probably not the best person to ask. I'm not very musical."

"But you know what you like, right? I saw you getting into the groove."

He looked to Melissa for help, and she tried to tell herself they weren't really a team even when it felt like they were.

"You guys were terrific, Tiff. Seriously. If this is what

you really love, I say give it a try. You'll have another chance to get into nursing school, and you've already got your nursing assistant certification to help support you while you follow your dream."

As she spoke the words, she was fully aware of how hypocritical they were. She had given the same advice to Cody, to follow his dream and go for it, then had resented him for devoting all his time and energy to it.

It was too easy to fall into the trap of blaming all the problems in their marriage on his immaturity and lack of commitment. She held a fair share of the responsibility, had been completely unprepared when hard reality hadn't matched up to her rosy expectations.

Tiffany didn't need to hear that right now. Her friend glowed. "You're the best. Both of you! Are you guys staying for the next group? Glass Army is pretty good."

Melissa glanced over at Eli, who shrugged. "We've paid the cover. Might as well get our money's worth."

"Cool." Tiffany looked over her shoulder to where the drummer was gesturing to her. "Looks like J.P. needs me. Thanks again for coming. I'll see you guys Monday."

She gave Eli a radiant smile, hugged Melissa and returned to her bandmates.

Melissa sighed. "Did somebody just warp time in here? Because I feel about twenty years older than I did when we walked in."

He smiled. "I know what you mean. But for the record, you don't look a day older than Tiffany."

She told herself not to read anything into that. She picked up her drink again, determined to ignore the heat sizzling between them and focus on the music.

Chapter Eight

His date-who-wasn't-a-date was a little tipsy. She wasn't precisely drunk—she had only had two and a half mojitos over the past two hours—but he could tell she had let down some of her barriers and seemed more soft and relaxed than he'd seen her since he'd come back to town.

She yawned in the middle of a conversation about which band she preferred—Tiffany's, obviously—and he smiled a little. "We should probably get you home. It's late."

"I don't want to go home," she declared with a hint of defiance in her voice. "It's too quiet there."

The bar didn't close for another hour, but without the live music it had lost most of its appeal for him. Other than The Haystacks, the options for late-night entertainment in Cannon Beach weren't exactly what anyone could call extensive.

"I guess you're right, though," she said with a sigh. "We can't stay here all night."

She rose and started gathering her purse and the jacket she had brought along. She walked out to his dad's SUV with her usual elegant grace, but stumbled a bit when she reached to open the door.

"Here. Let me," he said.

She gave him a broad smile, another hint that she might not be completely sober. "You're just as sweet as your father. Don't tell him I said so."

"I won't," he promised. He made sure she had her seat belt on securely before walking around the vehicle, climbing in and starting it up.

"Oh, look at that dog," she exclaimed as they passed a late-night dog walker with a large yellow Lab on a leash. "I wish I had a dog. Too bad I can't borrow Fiona, but Rosa took her with her out of town. Everyone is gone."

She seemed genuinely sad, but that might have been the mojitos talking.

"Do you want to borrow Max for the night? I'm sure he would be happy to have a sleepover."

She leaned back in the leather seat. "Maybe." She closed her eyes. "He's so cute. He can sleep on the floor by my bed and warn me if any bad guys come around."

He had to smile a little at that and hope he didn't fall into that category. "He can be pretty fierce."

"That's what I need. A fierce dog like Max to protect me."

The idea of telling her he thought she needed a worn-out army doctor sounded ridiculous so he said nothing. "I'll stop at my dad's place and grab Max for you, and I can swing by in the morning to pick him up. Does that work?"

"You are the best boss ever. I mean it. The best!"

He couldn't help the laugh that escaped. For some reason, she gazed at him, an arrested expression on her features.

"I wish you would do that more often," she said.

"What?" The word seemed to hang between them, shimmering on the air.

"Laugh. I like it so much."

He caught his breath, aware of a strange tug, a softness lodged somewhere under his breastbone. This was dangerous territory, indeed. This woman threatened him in ways he wasn't at all prepared to handle.

"I'll keep that in mind," he murmured.

She smiled and closed her eyes, leaning against the leather seat back. A few moments later she was asleep, her hands tucked under her cheek like a child's.

At a stoplight, he looked over, captivated by her. In some ways, she resembled the sweet-faced cheerleader he'd had a thing for back in the day, but he could see now that was an illusion. She was so much more. She had grown into a woman of character and substance, her world changed and shaped by life.

At his father's house, he paused in the driveway for a moment, wondering if it was a stupid idea to loan her Max for the night. She would be fine without him and might find the dog more trouble than he was worth. But Eli had promised. If she would find some solace and comfort from having another creature in the house, Eli wasn't about to stand in the way.

As for Max, the dog would probably treat the whole thing as a fun adventure. He'd been at loose ends with Wendell in the rehab center and would probably enjoy being needed again.

Max trotted up to him as soon as Eli walked inside, making it an easy matter to scoop up the schnauzer, his food and water bowls, his leash and his favorite blanket. He carried all of it back to his dad's vehicle.

Melissa was still asleep, her breathing soft and measured. After another moment's hesitation, he set the dog and all his comfort supplies on the back seat, then reversed out of the driveway to head the short distance up the hill to Brambleberry House.

If anything, Melissa seemed to have fallen more deeply asleep, snuggling into the leather of the seat. He turned off the engine, reluctant to wake her. He could see Max was snoring away in the back seat, too. Apparently, Eli's company wasn't very scintillating to anyone.

He smiled ruefully and sat for a moment in the stillness of the vehicle. The rest of the world seemed far away right now, as if the two of them and Max were alone here in this quiet, cozy little haven.

Outside the windows, he could see the glitter of stars overhead and the lights of Arch Cape to the south, twinkling against the darkness. A strange, unexpected sense of peace seemed to settle over him like a light, warm mist.

The night was lovely, the sound of waves soothing and familiar. Little by little, he could feel the tension in his shoulders and spine begin to ease.

This...

This was the calm he had been yearning to find since he returned to town. How odd, that he would discover it here in his father's vehicle with a snoring dog in the back seat and a beautiful sleeping woman in the front.

He wasn't going to argue with it. He was just going to soak it in while he had the chance.

Eli closed his eyes, feeling more tension trickle away.

He hadn't even realized how tightly wound he had been, yet he found something unbelievably comforting about being here with her. He couldn't have explained it; he only knew she soothed something inside him that had been restless and angry for months and allowed him to set down the twin burdens of guilt and grief for a moment.

Like Max and Melissa, there was a chance he may have fallen asleep, too. He didn't intend to, but the day had been a long one and he felt so very relaxed here beside her.

He awoke sometime later, disoriented and stiff from the uncomfortable position.

Something was different. He opened his eyes and realized with some degree of wonder that she was in his arms.

How had that happened? He hadn't moved, was still behind the wheel, but now he held a woman against him. Her arms were around him, her head resting in the crook of his elbow, and he cradled her against him like a child.

He looked down at her lovely features, tucked against his chest, and was astonished at how absolutely right she felt in his arms.

No. This wasn't right at all. Hadn't he been telling himself all night how he couldn't be the kind of man she needed?

None of that seemed to matter, not here in the darkness. Here, he could admit the truth he had been running from since he'd returned to town.

He was falling for her.

More accurately, he supposed, he was finally allowing himself to acknowledge that he had fallen for her a long time ago and simply had been biding his time, waiting for life and circumstances to bring them together again.

He didn't want to admit it, even to himself. What good would it do? There was no happy-ever-after in the stars for them. He had obligations elsewhere.

His heart ached at knowing this was all they could ever have, these few stolen moments together in his father's SUV in the darkness while the waves pounded relentlessly against the sand.

He wasn't sure if his sudden tension communicated itself to her or if he made some sound or perhaps the dog did, but she began to stir in his arms. She opened her eyes, and for one startling moment there was a blazing joy in her expression, as if she were exactly where she wanted to be, then she seemed to blink a few times and the expression was replaced with confusion and uncertainty.

"Eli. Wh-what are you doing here?" She sat up a little and pulled back to the passenger side of the vehicle, hands in her hair. "What am *I* doing here?"

"We went to see Puddle of Love, remember? Then we stayed for the next group and the next, and there's a chance you may have had a little too much to drink. You fell asleep as I was driving you home. I waited in the driveway for you to wake up but I must have fallen asleep, as well."

She looked out the window, where a light, misty rain had started to fall.

"Okay. That's embarrassing."

"For you or for me? You at least had a moderate degree of alcohol consumption for an excuse. I had one beer all night."

She looked around. "Alcohol or not, I'm still not sure what we're doing *here* in your SUV in the middle of the night. And how did Max get here?"

Quite clearly, he was the one who should be embarrassed about the situation. "You, uh, didn't want to sleep alone tonight so I offered to bring Max up to stay with you."

She shook her head, massaging her forehead. "Well, that will go down in history as one of the most awkward episodes I've ever had with a coworker."

She glanced at the clock on the dashboard. "Is it really after one?"

"Yes. If it's any consolation, I think we only dozed off for an hour or so."

"I should probably go inside. Either that or go down to the beach and dig a giant hole in the sand to climb into."

"You have no reason to be embarrassed, Melissa. Seriously. It was kind of sweet, actually."

He shouldn't have said that. He knew it the moment the words were out. She gazed at him, her blond curls tousled and her eyes soft and her mouth parted slightly. It was all he could do not to yank her back into his arms.

"I'll walk you in," he said, a little more gruffly than he intended.

"Thanks."

"Would you still like Max to stay with you for the night? I can take him home if you'd rather not bother."

She looked at the dog in the back seat, who was beaming at her with that goofy look of his. "I'd like to say no, but I would actually appreciate his company. Having him here might help the house not feel as empty."

He opened the rear door for Max, and the dog trotted up the sidewalk as if he owned the place. Eli grabbed Max's blanket, leash and bowls.

As they walked toward the house, she pulled out her key. "I'm suddenly starving. Are you hungry? I've got stuff on hand to make an omelet, if you want."

He was torn between his conviction that it wasn't a very good idea to spend more time with her and his overwhelming desire to do exactly that.

As if to seal the deal, his stomach suddenly growled and he realized dinner had been hours ago, before he picked her up to go to The Haystacks. He had nibbled a bit on bar snacks, but apparently that wasn't enough.

"There you go," she said with a winsome smile. "Come in."

"I can grab a sandwich at home."

"I'm not super talented in the kitchen, but I do make a mean omelet. They're kind of a specialty of mine. Come on. It's the least I can do, after you were kind enough to let me sleep in your car."

It would be rude to refuse, he told himself. Plus, he wanted to make sure she would be okay on her own without her daughter.

"An omelet does sound good right now."

She smiled and unlocked the door. "It will hit the spot. Trust me."

He did. He trusted her more than any woman in a long time.

The question was, did he trust himself?

What had seemed like a brilliant idea while the two of them were standing outside on her porch suddenly lost a great deal of its shine once they walked inside her apartment.

Melissa was having a hard enough time resisting the man. Sharing late-night snacks alone in her kitchen when there was a chance she might still be slightly buzzed could very well be more temptation than she could resist.

She was still trying to deal with how perfect it had

seemed to wake up in his arms. She had felt safe and warm and cared for, though she knew that was ridiculous. How had she ended up there? She still wasn't quite sure. He had explained that she had fallen asleep in the vehicle on the way home from the tavern, but that didn't really explain how she had gone from sitting on her side of the vehicle to being cradled so tenderly in his arms.

Had she snored? Drooled? Done anything else completely mortifying? She had no idea. She also didn't understand how he had *let* her keep sleeping when he could have awakened her the moment he pulled up outside Brambleberry House. Why hadn't he just honked the horn or shouted in her ear? He could have just opened the door and pushed her out, for that matter.

Still, waking up in his arms had felt completely right, somehow.

She was falling for him and she had no idea what to do about it. She knew perfectly well it would only end up in heartbreak for her. He had made it clear he was leaving at the first opportunity. Under other circumstances, she might have followed after him and used her own skills to help those in need.

That was utterly impossible at this stage of her life. She had a daughter. They were settling into life here in Oregon. She didn't have the freedom to let herself fall for someone whose heart was somewhere else. Been there, done that.

She swallowed. She had invited him for an omelet, which was the least she could do after he had been so sweet about trying to distract her from being upset about Skye spending the night with her father.

So she had slept in his arms for a few moments and had awakened with a powerful urge to kiss the dark shadow of his jaw and pull his mouth to hers. She hadn't done that, which meant she had more self-control than she gave herself credit.

She only had to keep her hands off him for the ten minutes it would take her to fix him an omelet and the ten minutes it would take him to eat it. She could handle that.

She led the way into the kitchen, flipping on lights as she went, and quickly tied on an apron.

"This won't take long," she promised him.

"I can help."

"There's not much to do. I suppose you could cut the peppers while I do the onions."

"Sure."

She pulled a green pepper out of the refrigerator, pointed him to the cutting board and handed him a knife, then put on the food-grade gloves she used so onion juice didn't seep into her skin.

After sniffing around it, Max settled into the corner on the pillow Skye kept there for Fiona's visits, and a comfortable silence filled the kitchen, broken only by the sounds of chopping.

She was the first to break it.

"Who is Miri?"

His knife came down hard on the cutting board, and if she hadn't been watching him she might have missed the sudden bleak look that he quickly blinked away.

"How do you…know about Miri?"

"I'm not sure. I think you may have said her name in your sleep. I thought maybe I'd dreamed it, but obviously not."

He let out a breath and then another, and she could tell the question had upset him.

"I'm sorry. I shouldn't have said anything. I was only curious. You don't have to tell me."

He turned his attention to briskly cutting the peppers. Any smaller and they would disappear in the omelet. After a moment, she took them from him and added them along with her chopped onions to the sizzling oil in the omelet pan.

The smells made her mouth water even as her attention remained focused on him.

"I told you about Justine the other day."

"Your doctor friend who died in the suicide bombing. Or was she more than a friend?"

"I'm not sure what we were," he admitted, confirming her suspicion. "We had dated a few times, if you can call it dating when you're in a war zone, surrounded by people facing starvation and violence."

"You said she was there with Doctors without Borders. What was your role? Can you talk about it?"

He hesitated for a moment, and she wondered if she had overstepped, then he spoke. "For the last twelve months, I've been deployed to the Middle East, providing medical care in various refugee camps and setting up clinics in small struggling villages trying to recover from decades of unrest."

"Not an easy task."

"I've been deployed most of the last five years. After the first tour, I asked to go back. It had its challenges but there were many rewards. These are courageous people who have already lost so much, facing truly horrible circumstances."

Every time she heard about people living in rough conditions like Eli was talking about, Melissa regretted her propensity to feel sorry that her life hadn't turned out the way she'd planned. She had so many amazing things in her world. She had a job she loved, good friends, a great apartment next to one of the most beautiful beaches in the world. No, things weren't perfect, but on the whole, her life was extraordinary.

"We were trying to improve conditions," Eli said. "I like to think we were making progress. Justine was absolutely dedicated to the cause and was a real inspiration to everyone."

Features pensive, Eli pulled Max onto his lap and scratched the schnauzer beneath his chin. "As you can imagine, the camp had more than its share of orphaned children."

"How sad." She didn't like thinking about children who had no one to love them.

"There was one in particular who always wanted to help the aid workers. She used to ask to sweep the floor of the medical clinic."

"Miri."

"Yes. She was about seven or eight, the sweetest girl, with a huge smile."

He let out a soft, tortured sigh. "Everyone in the camp watched over her, but she and Justine had a special bond. Miri used to bring her little bouquets of flowery weeds or pretty rocks she'd found. Justine wanted to adopt her, take her back to France with her, and was trying to put the wheels in motion."

She wanted to say how wonderful that such sweetness could survive the horrors of war, but she sensed she didn't want to hear what was coming next. She could see by the tension in his shoulders and the way he gripped his hands tightly together that the rest of the story wasn't as tender.

"What happened?"

She flipped the omelet, wishing she hadn't asked any questions and started them down this grim road.

"One day, Justine asked me to go with her to a village about five or six kilometers away from the camp to help with a clinic for pregnant women and children. A routine trip, we both thought, something we'd done a dozen times in other villages. It was well within my mission as part of a PRT, Provincial Reconstruction Team, trying to help these war-torn areas rebuild." He paused. "She thought it would be fun to take Miri with us. The girl was very good at putting villagers at ease and convincing them to trust us."

He was silent, his eyes haunted by memories she couldn't begin to guess at.

"I didn't want to, but it made both of them happy so I relented. I liked to see them smile. Miri had started doing it more and more, especially when all three of us were together."

"What happened?"

"It was market day and the area was busy. We didn't stop working all morning and saw maybe twenty women, but then things began to slow down a little. I… Miri and Justine decided to walk to the market square to grab some lunch for us and look at some of the local goods on sale. I should have said no, that we should stick together. I'd been uneasy all day, feeling a weird energy."

"Would Justine have stayed behind simply because you asked her to?"

He made a face. "Probably not. She was fiercely independent. If I had told her I had a weird feeling, she would have laughed at me and called me *Monsieur Poule Mouillée*."

"Mr. Wet Hen," she said, smiling at his quite excellent French accent. Hers wasn't great, but she understood better than she could speak from studying it in school.

"I told myself I was imagining things. There was no potential threat. Why would there be? We were aid workers. I stayed behind at the clinic and didn't go with them because I was too busy showering all my knowledge on the village's young, inexperienced midwife. I had just about run out of things to yammer on about when we heard the blast."

"Oh, Eli."

His features were grim. "Apparently, there were still opposition forces in the area angry that the leadership of this village would accept foreign aid workers. They killed fifteen villagers at a peaceful market square for no reason, along with a sweet orphan girl who only wanted to help."

"Miri," she whispered, heart aching for the devastation she heard in his voice.

"She died instantly. Justine was conscious and in agony for only a moment after I arrived on scene. I tried to stabilize her, but she'd lost too much blood and the shock was too great. She went into cardiac arrest. I told you I did CPR while we tried to call for help but… It was too late. I couldn't save either of them."

She had no words, nothing that could comfort this sort of deep pain.

"Miri was only a girl, with a future that was much brighter than it had been a few months earlier, before Justine came into her life. I hate knowing that future was wiped out because of me."

"Why do you blame yourself?"

"I could have made other choices. I shouldn't have let

them go into the market alone. I should have been with them. We should have taken more protection with us."

"Could any of those things have stopped what happened?"

He looked helplessly at her and she knew the answer. No. He would have been a target, too.

She removed the omelet from the stove to a plate, choosing her words with care. "You can't blame yourself, Eli. You didn't plant the explosives and you couldn't have known someone else would. You were there to help people."

"I know that intellectually. Convincing my emotions isn't quite as easy."

The torment on his features broke her heart. She was a nurse, driven to ease suffering where she saw it, and she hated knowing she couldn't help him.

She couldn't resist going to him and wrapping her arms around his waist. She wanted to tell him not to blame himself, that she understood he had been there to help others and he couldn't hold himself responsible for the evil actions of a few, but she knew that would be cold comfort.

Still, something in her touch must have calmed him, as she hoped. After a few moments, she felt some of the tension in his muscles seep away. He returned her hug with a grateful embrace before he stepped away.

"I'm sorry. I keep thinking I've dealt with it. It was six months ago and most of the time I'm fine. Every once in a while, I let down my guard and the memories wash over me like a flash flood."

"I'm glad I was here to keep them from drowning you."

"So am I." He gestured to the table. "But I hate to waste a good omelet, especially when you've gone to all the trouble to make it. Should we eat?"

For all the sadness of his story, she found the meal surprisingly restful. They spoke of mutual acquaintances and some of the changes that had come over the town in the years since both of them had lived here. She didn't want their time together to end, but the long day finally caught up with her and she couldn't hold back a yawn.

He glanced at his watch, shook his head and rose. "I should go. It's nearly two. Thank you for the omelet and the evening. I enjoyed both."

"Thank *you*. I forgot all about missing Skye."

He shrugged into his jacket and headed for the door. She walked him there, with Max trotting at their heels.

"If you want to take Max home with you, I should be okay. I feel silly I was ever worried about being alone. This house just feels so big when I'm the only one here, especially when I know Sonia and Rosa aren't in town."

"Keep him until Skye gets home, if you want. He's good company. To be honest, you're better company to him than I will probably be. He's been lonely, I'm afraid. I think he misses my dad. And I'll be at the rehab center most of the day, so he would be alone otherwise."

He planned to spend his Sunday with his father, which filled her with a soft tenderness. "You're a very sweet man, Eli."

He raised an eyebrow. "Why? Because I have a good relationship with my dad?"

"You care. Too many people who have been through what you have would harden their soul against letting in any kind of softer feelings, but you haven't. You care about your father, you cared about Jim the other day on the beach, you care about our patients and about your refugee patients thousands of miles away."

She had to kiss him. Though she knew it was potentially dangerous, she couldn't resist rising on her tiptoes and pressing her mouth to his.

He remained frozen for one breathless moment, and then he lowered his mouth to hers and kissed her as she realized both of them had been craving all night.

It was raw and hot, his mouth searching hers, his body pressed against her. She realized as his arms tightened around her that she had been fooling herself. She hadn't kissed him out of tenderness or empathy but because she had been craving his kiss since those magical moments the day before, outside the beach gate.

She made a soft sound and wrapped her arms around his neck, her mouth angled to allow him better access. Her breasts ached where they were pressed against him. *Everything* ached.

His mouth was urgent and demanding on hers, and the hunger in it aroused her.

He wanted her.

She didn't need to feel the hard nudge of his arousal against her to sense it in his hands and his mouth and his body. They were alone in the house. She could take him by the hand and tug him into her bedroom, and they could spend the rest of this rainy, misty night wrapped together, pushing away the shadows.

The temptation consumed her. How easy it would be to take that step. It had been so very long since she had felt wanted and needed and cherished like this.

And then what? If she and Eli spent the night together, where would that leave them? He was still committed to leaving. He had just told her all his reasons for it. He was driven to continue the work he had been doing, providing medical care to people in need. She understood now that he was motivated by a complicated tangle of guilt and grief and obligation. She also understood that she would be a fool to think she would be enough to keep him here.

Her heart would be broken. Just like her marriage—which she had known even as she was saying *I do* was a mistake that never should have happened—it would be her own stupid fault.

One the best ways she had found to discipline Skye on the rare occasions her daughter misbehaved was to redirect, to encourage her to make a better choice. Those words, *make a better choice*, were often all she needed to say when Skye was throwing one of her rare tantrums or doing something Melissa had told her not to do.

She needed to listen to her own advice to her daughter. She had no hope of creating happiness in life if she made choices she knew from the outset would only lead to heartbreak and pain.

She couldn't make love with him, as much as she ached to feel his arms around her all night long, to learn all his secrets and explore that delicious body.

It would leave her too vulnerable. She was already half in love with the man. Spending what was left of the night together would push her headlong the rest of the way.

She had entrusted her heart and her life to one man who put something else ahead of her. Fixing her mistake had cost her dearly, and her child would pay the price for that the rest of her life, forever separated from one parent or the other through the tangled maze of custody and visitations.

She couldn't wander blindly into a similar situation. When he walked away to return to the military and the life that gave him such purpose and meaning, Melissa was very much afraid she would never put back together the pieces of her shattered heart.

She didn't want to end the kiss. She wanted to stay right here forever, with his warm, sexy mouth teasing out all her secrets. Just a few more moments...

He was finally the one who broke the embrace. He eased his mouth away and rested his forehead against hers.

She thought she smelled roses again, but this time the scent was wistful and almost sad.

"Didn't we say we weren't going to do this again?" he said, his forehead pressed to hers.

She wanted to make some smart response but couldn't think of anything. "Kisses don't count in the middle of the night."

"I think that's when they count the most."

After a moment, he stepped away, eyes haunted with regret. "I need to go, before I forget all the reasons why I can't stay."

Her chest ached and she wished with all her heart that things could be different, that she could be the woman for him.

"What about Max?" he asked.

Already the house seemed to echo with emptiness. For all that the ghosts of Brambleberry House seemed friendly enough, she wasn't sure she was strong enough to face them alone tonight. "He's here and he seems comfortable enough. If you don't mind, I'll keep him overnight."

"No problem."

He looked as if he had other things he wanted to say, but Eli finally headed for the door. When he opened it, Melissa saw the light rain of earlier had turned into a steady downpour. It matched her sudden mood—dank, dark, dismal.

"Good night," he said with one last, backward look that seemed filled with regret.

Was he regretting that he had to leave?

Or regretting that they both knew he couldn't stay?

After he walked out into the night, Melissa locked the door behind him, then went through her apartment turning off lights, grateful for Max's company as he followed along behind her.

Her heart ached as she thought of the story Eli had told and the sadness behind it. He must have cared about the woman very much to shoulder such a burden six months later. This Justine person must have been remarkable. Not the kind of woman who basically fell apart simply because her daughter was spending the night with her father.

She had learned to be tough after the divorce, and she needed to call on that strength. Something told her she would need all the courage she could find after Eli left Cannon Beach once more.

Chapter Nine

The next day, Sunday, she rose early despite her late night and took Max for a run along the beach. He didn't have Fiona's loping grade but toddled along beside her so cheerfully, it warmed her heart.

The day had turned cooler from the rain of the night before, with more precipitation predicted for later that evening. April could be fickle on the coast, with the rare warm, pleasant day often giving way to a spring snowstorm.

Things weren't supposed to be that drastic, but it was definitely cold enough first thing in the morning that she was grateful for her jacket.

They didn't bump into Eli, as she had half hoped and half feared. All in all, it was the most uneventful run she'd had on the beach in what felt like forever.

As if to remind her of previous fun times, her wrist ached more than it had in days as she and Max returned to the house. She ignored it and spent the rest of the morning trying not to watch the clock as she finished some of her coursework for her online nurse practitioner classes.

She had just hit Send on another assignment when Max suddenly scampered to the front door just moments before it opened.

"Mommy! Hi! Where are you, Mommy?"

She hurried out to the entryway to find Skye and Cody standing just inside the door. Skye must have used her key to come in.

"You're back! Hi, honey."

"Hi, Mommy." Skye hugged her but didn't stop frowning. "Hey, why do you have Dr. Sanderson's dog? Hi, Max!"

"He's babysitting me," she said. Skye giggled while Cody looked on, confused.

She didn't bother to explain to him. "How did things go?" she asked instead.

She didn't necessarily want Skye to rant about how miserable she'd been overnight. Melissa didn't want to think she was that small-minded.

Still, when her daughter beamed, Melissa had to smile through clenched teeth.

"So fun," Skye said. "We went to a baseball game last night and they had fireworks and everything. Then we had pizza and this morning we went to the store. We were going to go to another baseball game but decided not to. I got to see Grandma and Grandpa Fielding, too. Did you know they have a swimming pool at their new house?"

Her in-laws had only recently moved to Portland from Manzanita and she hadn't been to their house yet.

"I didn't know that. How fun."

Skye made a face. "Dad said it was too cold to go swimming, plus I didn't take my suit."

"Next time, though," Cody promised.

"Do we want to set up the next visit?" she asked her ex.

Cody looked a little distracted, as if he hadn't thought past this one. "I don't know what my schedule's going to look like next week. We might be heading down to Cali. What about two weeks from now?"

She forced a smile. "That could work. Just let me know."

"Thanks, Missy. Hey, Skye-ster. Thanks for hanging with me. I've got to run."

"Okay. Bye, Dad."

"Sorry to leave so fast. Amalia didn't do well on the drive here. She's a bit carsick so I'd better get her back to the city."

"No problem. Next time I could meet you halfway."

"That would be great. You're the best, Miss. Thanks!"

She waved him off, proud of herself for taking the high road this time. It made things go so much more smoothly when she tried to be the adult in their interactions.

After he hurried down the steps, she smiled at her daughter, who was busy petting Max.

"Why is he really here?"

"I wanted some company last night. The house was pretty empty since everyone but me was gone for the night."

"Even Fiona?"

"She went with Rosa on a hiking trip out of town. So, yes, it was just me."

"We should get our own dog."

It was not a new request. Skye had been pushing for their own dog since they had moved from Hawaii.

"Maybe when we get into our own house. I'm so glad you had a great time with your father and Amalia. Is she nice?"

"Really nice. She doesn't say much, but she's trying to learn English. She taught me a little Portuguese. That's what they speak in Brazil, not Brazilian, did you know that?"

"That I did know."

"I don't know why. It's weird, if you ask me. But she taught me how to say hello—*olá*, which kind of sounds like *hola*. And goodbye is *adeus*, which also sounds like *adios*. Thank you is *obrigada*. Dad would say *obrigado* but I'm not sure why. It was fun, except I missed you a ton. Maybe you could come next time."

Wouldn't that be delightful? She swallowed a groan and chose her words carefully. "That's sweet of you, honey, but it's important for you to enjoy your special time with your dad and new stepmom. And soon you'll have a new baby brother to love. You get plenty of time with me."

"I guess. I still missed you."

"I missed you, too. So much, I had to borrow Max here to keep me company."

"I wish we didn't have to give him back."

"I know, honey. But you like sleeping in your own bed and I'm sure Max does, too."

"I guess."

Melissa didn't want to fall into the trap of trying to compete with her ex for most fun parent, but she'd been without her daughter for an entire day and wanted to have a little fun with her while she could. "Why don't you go get your kite and we can take Max home, then fly your kite on that good stretch of beach by Dr. Sanderson's house."

Skye had been begging her to take the kite out for several weeks and she latched onto the idea with enthusiasm. "Yay! I'll go get it."

She skipped to her room, leaving Melissa to gather up the dog's things and try not to be nervous at the idea of seeing Eli again.

As he finished putting together the lift recliner he had purchased that morning, Eli wasn't sure whether his father would be happy about the gift or would accuse him of trying to turn Wendell into an old man before his time.

His father was recovering from a double knee replacement. Nobody would think less of him for using anything that might make his life a little more comfortable. And after all his father did for his patients around town, didn't he deserve a comfortable chair at the end of the day that he could get into and out of without pain?

It was a good argument, if Eli did say so himself. Whether his father would buy into it was another story entirely.

He pulled the chair into the corner where his father's beat-up old recliner held pride of place. He would never dare to get rid of the thing, but he could at least offer this one as an alternative. If nothing else, Max would probably like it.

He looked around automatically for the dog, then remembered. Max had spent the night with Melissa.

Lucky dog.

He pushed the dangerous thought away as he settled into the recliner to check it out. He couldn't think about her like that.

How had she made it through the night? It had taken all his strength that morning not to walk up to Brambleberry House to check on her.

That hadn't stopped him from thinking about her all

day. Their hot, intense kiss had haunted him, kept him awake most of the night.

What was he going to do about this attraction to her?

Absolutely nothing.

What could come of it? She deserved better than a long-distance relationship, and that was all he could offer her right now. He was leaving town as soon as his father was back on his legs. Eli had had an email just that morning from his commanding officer, asking when he would be back and whether he was ready to take off again to return to his job overseas.

For one crazy moment, Eli had been tempted to tell Dr. Flores that he was done, he wasn't going to re-up but would continue serving the National Guard, available when his country needed him.

He knew the woman would be disappointed but wouldn't think less of him. Many—in fact, most—army doctors didn't stay in as long as he had, at least not on active duty. His initial commitment had only been two years, but the work had been so fulfilling he hadn't been able to walk away then.

Could he walk away now? That was the million-dollar question. Before Justine and Miri died, he had been thinking about going into private practice while retaining his military benefits by serving in the Guard. That was the course most in the Army Medical Corps eventually took.

Since that horrible day in that dusty market town, he had felt driven to do more, try harder, dedicate himself more fully.

He owed both of them. Didn't he? He hadn't been able to save Justine, but he could help those she had cared about.

That left little place in his world for someone like Melissa, who had finally found her own place to belong here in Cannon Beach.

While he might accept that intellectually, it hadn't stopped him from thinking about her all day, remembering their kiss and feeling comforted all over again when he remembered the sweet way she had wrapped her arms around him in her kitchen, offering solace and concern.

He had it bad for Melissa Fielding. That was the plain truth. He was all tangled up over her and didn't know how to unravel the silken cords around his heart.

The doorbell startled him out of his thoughts, and it took him a minute to figure out how to work the control of the chair enough to put the footrest down so he could get out.

When he opened the door, he was greeted first by a familiar woof, and then by a grin and wave from a young curly-haired girl.

"Hi, the other Dr. Sanderson."

He was as charmed by Skye as he was by her mother, even though her bright smile reminded him so painfully of Miri. "Hi there, the other Ms. Fielding."

She grinned. "Mom said we had to take Max back to you today, even though I really, really, really wanted to keep him."

He glanced at Skye's mother and felt that peculiar tug in his gut that had also become familiar since he'd come back to town, the one he felt only around Melissa. He wanted to tell the girl she could keep the dog for another night, but he had a feeling Melissa would not appreciate his offer.

"Thank you. Both of you."

"Thanks for loaning him," Melissa said. "He was wonderful company, weren't you, Max?"

The dog yipped as if agreeing with her.

"Here's his stuff." Skye handed over the bowls and blanket he had taken to Brambleberry House the night before.

"Thanks." He took them and set them inside his father's house, then gestured to the colorful fabric kite in Melissa's hand. "I guess I can tell where you guys are going after this."

"Yep," Skye answered. "I've been begging and begging to fly our kite and today Mom said yes. We're going down to the beach by your house because the wind is always just right."

"Looks like a great kite."

It was shaped like a jellyfish, purple with rainbow-colored tentacles. "You should see how high it goes. Sometimes it goes up and up until I can barely even see it."

"Sounds amazing."

He and his mom used to fly kites on the beach often after school. It had been one of their favorite pastimes. After the cancer made her too weak, she used to sit at the window here and watch him down on the beach below their house. Some nights he would fly a kite past dusk, hesitant to come in when he knew she enjoyed the sight of it flying and dipping so much.

"You can come with us," Skye suggested. "We always have a hard time getting it up in the air. I can never run fast enough to have the wind take it. Maybe you could help us."

He darted a look at Melissa but couldn't tell by her veiled expression what she thought about her daughter's spontaneous invitation.

"It's been a long time since I've flown a kite. I'm not sure I remember how."

"We can show you," Skye said.

"I'm sure Dr. Sanderson has other things to do right now," Melissa said.

"Like what?" Skye asked.

"Skye. It's rude to expect him to drop everything and come with us."

He ought to let the girl down gently and tell her he had other plans. But suddenly he wanted to fly a kite more than he had wanted to do anything else in a long time… except, perhaps, to kiss her mother.

"Thank you for inviting me," he said instead. "I would very much enjoy helping you fly this beautiful kite."

It definitely wasn't a good idea to spend more time with Melissa or with her daughter, not when he was having a hard time resisting both of them, but he told himself he could handle it. He only had to keep things in perspective, remind himself he was leaving in a few weeks.

He couldn't tell how Melissa felt about the prospect of him coming along, but her daughter made her delight clear. She beamed at him, the gap in her front teeth more pronounced. "Yay! Can Max come with us?"

"Sure. I don't see why not."

"I'll hold his leash, if you want."

"Thanks," he said, trying to keep the dryness out of his tone. "That's very nice of you."

He picked up his sunglasses from the hall table where he'd left them and walked outside into a lovely Oregon afternoon. The rain of the evening before was nowhere in evidence, though he knew the forecast called for possible heavy waves and wind later in the week.

"Let me take that," he said to Melissa, reaching for the colorful kite she carried.

"It's a kite. It's not exactly heavy."

"If it were heavy, it wouldn't fly," Skye pointed out with irrefutable logic.

"It's big and bulky, though. I don't mind."

She held it out for him. "Here you go. Knock yourself out."

He reached for it and though he didn't plan to and, in fact, actively tried to avoid it, his hands brushed hers.

Heat seemed to race along his nerve endings and his stomach muscles clenched.

So much for keeping control around her. If he could have that kind of reaction from a little accidental slide of skin on skin, he was in big trouble.

As they took the closest beach access, a narrow trail between two houses, Skye hurried ahead of them with Max, leaving Eli to walk alone with Melissa.

"You really didn't have to come with us," she said after a moment. "Skye is right, we're not the greatest at getting the kite up in the air, but trying is half the fun."

Her cheeks were pink, but he couldn't tell if that was from embarrassment or from the breeze.

"I meant what I said. I'm looking forward to it. What better way to spend a windy April afternoon?"

When they reached the beach, she gave him a sidelong look.

"All morning, I've been thinking about how awkward it would be to face you again," she admitted, confirming his suspicion about the source of that rosy glow. "I'm kind of glad we got that out of the way now, instead of tomorrow morning in the office when you're seeing a patient."

Her words were a blunt reminder that she worked for his father. He had a strong suspicion that wasn't accidental, as if she needed both of them to remember their respective roles.

"You have nothing to feel awkward or embarrassed about," he assured her.

She snorted. "Sure. I only drank too much, which I never do, fell asleep in your car and then practically dragged you into my house and insisted on feeding you." She glanced at her daughter and then back at him. "And it's my fault we kissed again, when we both made it clear the first time that it shouldn't happen again."

Was she sorry it had happened? He couldn't tell from her response. He wasn't sure he regretted it. He should, he knew, but her kiss had been as warm and nurturing as the rest of her.

He wanted to kiss her again. Right now, right here. Instead, he gripped the kite more tightly and continued walking beside her while the April breeze that smelled of sand and sea danced around them. "It was a strange night. We're going to chalk it all up to that, right?"

She opened her mouth as if to argue, but her daughter interrupted before she could.

"What about here?" Skye asked. "Is this a good place to fly a kite?"

He managed to drag his gaze away from Melissa's mouth to focus on their surroundings, the beach a short distance from his father's house. "This looks like an excellent spot. No trees, no wires, no skyscrapers."

"I agree. It's a great place," Melissa said. She set her backpack on the sand and reached inside, pulling out a rolled sand mat. After spreading it out, she plopped down, then calmly pulled a book out of the backpack.

"I do believe this is a great spot for me to sit back and relax with a book while you guys run around and get all sweaty trying to get that big kite up in the air. I'll watch our stuff."

Eli snorted. "You're going to read a book while I help your daughter fly her kite. Why do I get the feeling I've just been played?"

She shrugged nonchalantly. "Nobody is playing any-body. If you remember correctly, I had no idea you would be here. We were only supposed to be dropping Max off at your place before coming down to fly the kite. I didn't plan things this way, but since you're here, I would be crazy to waste a chance to sit on the sand and enjoy this warm afternoon."

He laughed, completely delighted with her. Every time he was with her, he fell harder.

She stared at him, her features still and watchful, with an expression he couldn't read behind her sunglasses.

I wish you would do that more often. I like it so much.

He remembered her slightly tipsy words the night be-fore in his dad's SUV after he had laughed then, and his insides felt achy with need. That encounter seemed a hundred miles away right now on this sunny beach with the waves washing against the sand and the seagulls cry-ing out overhead.

After a moment, he turned to Skye. "Your mom wants to read her book and I can't argue it's a good plan. I guess it's up to us to fly this kite, then."

"We can do it," Skye said again. She jutted her chin into the air, looking like a mini pugilist version of her mother. "I know we can."

"You got it. Let's do this."

The afternoon turned into one of the most enjoyable he had spent in a long time.

He tried to steel his heart against Skye, using as a

shield an image of a little dark-eyed orphan with a shy smile, but he quickly realized it was pointless.

He couldn't resist her any more than he'd been able to resist her mother.

Skye was completely adorable. She chattered endlessly about everything under the sun. She told him about the haystacks, how they had been formed by wind and water eons ago. She waved energetically at the people on recumbent bicycles who rode past them with some frequency on the hard-packed sand close to the water, telling him about the time she and her mother had rented them once when they first moved back to town and it had been really fun. She talked about her father and his new wife and the baby on the way and how it was a boy and she couldn't wait to hold him.

She was smart and funny and as openhearted as her mother.

Max ran around in excitement as they worked to get the kite up. Once it was soaring and dipping above them on the currents, the dog seemed to lose interest and plopped down beside Melissa, who reached absently to pet him while turning the page of her book with her other hand.

Whenever he looked over at her, his chest seemed to ache all over again. The sunlight gleamed in her hair and she looked fresh and sweet and beautiful.

It was a perfect moment here, beside the water he loved. A girl laughing with glee, her mother soft and relaxed on the sand, the wind catching the colorful kite and tugging it ever higher.

The restlessness inside him seemed to settle for now, and he wanted the moment to go on and on.

He and Skye flew the kite for over an hour, taking turns holding it and letting it dip and dance on the currents.

He thought Melissa might have fallen asleep, but he couldn't tell for sure with her sunglasses.

Sometime later, she finally rose with her elegant grace and came over to where he and Skye were holding the kite. "You guys have done a great job."

"It's higher than we've ever got it!" Skye exclaimed. "Eli is the *best* at flying a kite. He said he used to do it with his mom when he was a kid and flying a kite always makes him think of her."

Melissa sent him a swift look, and Eli pointedly busied himself with the kite.

"We should probably go, kiddo. We still have to fix dinner and get you to bed."

"Oh. Do we have to?"

"I'm afraid so. You had a big weekend with your dad. You don't want to be too tired for school tomorrow, right? It's your big field trip."

"Oh, yeah!" To Eli, she said, "We're going to the lighthouse in Astoria and my teacher said we could maybe even fly paper airplanes off the top of it. We're going to write our names on them and see whose goes the farthest. I bet it will be mine."

He remembered flying paper airplanes off that lighthouse when he was in elementary school and still remembered the triumph of his particular design beating everyone else in his class. "Sounds like fun. You'll have to let me know if you're the winner."

"I will."

Together, they started the process of winding the string from the kite back onto the reel. The kite fought them on the currents until he was able to pull it back down to earth.

"What do you say to Eli?" her mother prompted once they had the colorful kite back on the sand.

"Thanks a ton for helping me, Eli."

Skye beamed at him. Before he realized what she intended, she threw her arms around his waist and gave him a tight hug.

Emotions came out of nowhere and clogged his throat, much to his embarrassment, his mind on another girl who would never have the chance to fly kites on a beautiful April afternoon.

"It was my pleasure. Truly."

"I hope we can do it again sometime."

He didn't know how to answer. He would be gone again soon. Even if his father wasn't yet up to full strength, Eli would have to go and let a substitute doctor take his place. "Maybe."

"And you said I could play pool at your dad's house. Can we do that tonight?"

"No," Melissa said firmly. "Maybe another time."

He regretted that he likely wouldn't have the chance to follow through on his offer to let her come over and practice before he left town. Maybe his father could take on billiards lessons while he was recovering from his knee surgery. He would suggest it to Wendell the next day when he went to his father's rehabilitation center.

"I'll walk you back," he said after Melissa had gathered up her things.

"You don't have to do that."

"Somebody needs to haul this guy back for you."

She didn't argue, but he could tell she didn't need or want his help.

He couldn't tell her he would find any excuse to spend more time with her, already dreading the moment he would have to say goodbye.

As she walked along beside him, with Skye again racing ahead of them holding tight to Max's leash, Melissa came to the grave realization that she didn't need to worry any more that she might do something stupid like fall in love with Eli.

She already had.

Watching him fly a kite with Skye, seeing his patience and his kindness and the sheer fun he seemed to have with her daughter, had made that truth abundantly clear.

How could any woman hope to resist him? He was sexy and sweet and wonderful.

What a complete disaster. He was going to leave again. What was she supposed to do then?

When they reached Brambleberry House, he opened the sea gate for her. She was relieved when she spotted Fiona, who immediately rushed across the lawn to greet Max, tail wagging.

"Looks like your neighbor is back."

She waved to Rosa, who was sitting on the swing looking out at the water.

Rosa waved back, and Melissa didn't need to see her expression to guess she was wearing a speculative look seeing her with Eli again.

Rosa could speculate all she wanted. They were only together temporarily. He would be leaving soon and she would be alone again.

"Thanks for letting me fly the kite with you," he said to Skye. "I had a great time."

"Thanks again for helping me. Me and my mom never would've been able to get it up that high."

"I don't know. You seem like a pro."

"Thanks." She beamed at him. "Now that you showed me what to do, I bet the next time I can get it as high as you did this time."

"I don't doubt it for a minute."

"You can come watch and tell me if I'm doing it right," she declared.

"Maybe."

He wouldn't be here. He would be off saving the world, leaving them here to figure out how to fly kites and play billiards without him. Melissa frowned but didn't want to ruin her daughter's happiness by pointing out that depressing truth.

"I guess I'll see you at the office tomorrow," she said instead.

"Right. I guess so."

With other friends, she might have hugged them or even given a kiss on the cheek before sending them on their way. With all these emotions churning through her, she didn't dare do anything but give Eli an awkward little wave.

He looked as if he wanted to say something else, but he finally nodded and waved, gripped Max's leash and headed back down the beach.

She did her best not to watch after him, though it took every ounce of self-control she had.

"I am so ready to have this baby, if only to be done with stirrups and paper gowns."

Melissa smiled at Julia Garrett, currently settled onto

the exam table in said paper gown. "It looks so lovely on you. Are you sure you don't want a few more children?"

Julia made a face. "No. This is it. Our house is bursting at the seams and Will says he can't build on again and I can't bear to move. So we have to be done."

"At least until Maddie and Simon go off to college next year. Then you'll have plenty of room for more babies."

She gave a rough laugh. "I hope you hear how ridiculous that sounds. We'll never be empty nesters at this rate."

This was Julia's fifth child. She and her husband, Will, had her teenage twin boy and girl from her previous marriage as well as an eight-year-old and a four-year-old. Melissa could only imagine the chaos at their house, but Julia always seemed calm and composed. Oh, how she envied her and wished some of that serenity would rub off on her.

Julia had once lived in Brambleberry House with her twins, when she was a single widow with twins, before she married Will. She had a soft spot for the house and the gardens and the stunning beauty of the place.

When Melissa came back to town, the two of them had bonded over that right after they met, a bond that had deepened and strengthened into real friendship in the months since.

"This is the last one, for sure."

She touched her abdomen protectively and Melissa felt a sharp little ache in her own womb.

She had wanted more children but hadn't been willing to bring more children into the uncertainty of a shaky marriage.

The little twinge of regret annoyed her. She had an

amazing daughter. She refused to waste the wonderful life she had, wishing she had made different choices.

"Dr. Sanderson should be here soon."

"When you say that, I keep picturing sweet Dr. Sanderson, then remember you're talking about someone else entirely. How is it, working for Wendell's son? He's quite gorgeous, isn't he?"

Oh, yes. Entirely *too* gorgeous. She had to brace herself against her instinctive reaction to him every time she came into the office. It had been three weeks since he came back to town, two since the day he had come with her and Skye to fly kites, and she was more tangled up than ever.

"Just like his father, Eli is an excellent doctor," she said. "I promise you'll be in great hands."

"Oh, I know. He was great when I came in for my checkup last week and the week before. Wendell has nothing but praise for him. Will remembers him, though Eli is a few years younger. Will said he was freaky smart in school."

Julia hadn't grown up in Cannon Beach but had spent summers here during her childhood. Will had been her first love, which Melissa found utterly charming.

"He was," she answered, wondering how they'd gotten on the subject of Eli. She had been doing her best *not* to think about him…which was particularly tough when they worked together each day. The only way she had survived the last few weeks was by staying busy with her classes and Skye and trying not to think about him leaving.

"How soon before his dad is back?"

"We're still not sure. His own doctors want him to take it easy, but you know Wendell. He is determined to come in next week for at least a few hours a day. Who knows, he might be back before you have the baby. When are you due again?"

"Three more weeks."

"Your chances are good, then."

She was aware with every passing day that Eli's time in Cannon Beach was drawing to a close. The prospect of him leaving filled her with a curious mix of dread and relief. She dreaded knowing he would be gone and she would be left to worry about him possibly being in harm's way. But she couldn't deny there would be a certain relief that she wouldn't have to pretend any more that she wasn't crazy in love with the man.

She had done her best to keep things polite and professional between them. She helped him in exams, she did triage assessment, she answered phone calls and forwarded prescriptions to him. And every time she was with him, she was aware of her feelings growing stronger by the moment.

He was an excellent doctor, compassionate and kind, as well as a devoted, loving son. She was head over heels and already aching at the idea that he wouldn't be in her life every day.

She pushed away the worry to focus on their patient. "Do you want Eli to wait a few minutes before doing your checkup, until Will can get here?"

"Better not. He wasn't sure if he would make it back to town in time. He's on a job up in Seaside, doing a bathroom remodel for a lady."

Her husband was a master carpenter who had done some amazing work at Brambleberry House and other places around town.

"I'll let Eli know you're ready, then."

When she opened the door, she found him pulling the chart out of the polished wood holder beside the door, which, she remembered now, Will Garrett had built right around the time she started working for Wendell Sanderson.

"Julia is ready when you are."

"Thanks." He gave her the same kind of careful smile they had both become experts at over the last few weeks. She had a feeling he felt as awkward and uncertain around her as she did around him.

He entered the exam room and she followed behind as he shook Julia's hand with a warm, comforting smile that made Melissa's ovaries tingle. Darn them.

"How are you feeling? Things are probably getting tight in there."

"Any tighter and I'm afraid I'm going to bust through the seams."

"Let's just take a look at things."

He listened to the baby's heartbeat first, then did a quick exam with brisk professionalism.

"Looks like you're only dilated to a one, so I think it's safe to say we still have a few weeks to go."

Melissa adjusted the sheet over her and then helped her sit up.

"The twins were a week early," Julia said, "but Tess was born the day before her due date and her brother was born the day after his."

Eli said. "You're the expert after five of these. I'm sure you can tell me a thousand ways every pregnancy is different, but it's good to know the pattern."

"No offense, Dr. Sanderson, but I was telling Melissa I would love it if your dad was back in action by the time I deliver. You've been great, but he delivered Will as well as my younger two kids and he's become kind of part of the family."

"None taken," Eli assured her. "I wish I had an answer for you. He's coming in for a few hours a day next week, though his surgeon and physical therapist want him to take it easy. Maybe he'll be back just in time to deliver your little girl."

"I hope so. He's home, right?"

"Yes. He came home a few weeks ago."

The day after they had flown kites and walked with Max along the beach, in fact, after rebounding quickly from the temporary setback of his tumble. Melissa had been by to see him twice on her lunch hour and once with Skye after school. All three times she had managed to miss Eli.

"How is he doing?" Julia asked.

"Bored out of his mind," Eli said with a smile. "My dad is the kind of guy who likes to be on the go. I knew the toughest part of his recovery would be the monotony of being sidelined. But his knees are already stronger than they've been in years, so the surgery was a good thing, for him and for his patients here in Cannon Beach."

He wrapped up the appointment a few moments later with another handshake and a warm smile.

After he left, Julia shook her head at Melissa. "I love Dr. Sanderson Sr., I'm not going to lie, but that son of his. Yum. Honestly, even though I'm extremely pregnant and extremely happily married, I don't know how you keep from constantly melting into a pile of hormones with that slow smile of his."

Melissa couldn't tell her friend she did exactly that. "He's my boss," she reminded Julia. "I have to keep my hormones—and everything else—to myself where he's concerned."

"Good luck with that," Julia said with a laugh.

Melissa forced a smile. She needed far more than luck where Eli was concerned.

Eli wasn't sure what had happened, but somehow over the last few weeks, since the Sunday afternoon when he had gone with her and Skye to fly the girl's kite, Melissa had withdrawn from him, treating him with a polite reserve that was far different from the friendship that had been growing between them.

She wasn't rude. In fact, she was respectful and professional, but as distant as if he were just some scrub who had stepped in to help out at his dad's practice in Wendell's absence.

He was glad, he told himself. He had crossed too many lines he shouldn't have with her.

Still, he missed her easy smiles and her funny sense of humor and the warmth that seemed to envelop him around her.

"You all know my dad wants to come in next week," he said to her, Carmen and Tiffany as the three women prepared to leave for the day on Friday.

"I hope he doesn't overdo," Carmen said with her characteristic frown. "My sister had knee replacement surgery and had to have the whole thing done all over again six months later."

"We'll all have to make sure he takes it easy. It's going to have to be a team effort. But the truth is, he's going crazy at home after three weeks away and thinks his patients need him. He won't be up for much patient care, but he should be fine handling consultations or refilling prescriptions, if he could do that from his desk. We'll all have to watch out for him."

"We can make sure he behaves," Tiffany said. "I'm glad he's coming in. I was hoping he'd be back before I leave."

The CNA had put in her notice the week before and had been talking nonstop about her plans to move to Los Angeles, where they already had a manager and a few gigs lined up.

"It will be good to have him back," Melissa said. "I've missed him."

"I'll add a few appointments into his schedule," Carmen said. "Nothing too drastic. Just consultations, like you said."

"He wants to jump back into things with both of his artificial knees, but I worry about him overdoing."

"Sounds good, especially since you're going to be leaving us soon," Carmen said.

Against his will, he glanced at Melissa. Had she stiffened at that?

"Yes. I'll be here until the end of next week, and then I have to report to duty again. I've already talked to the medical temp agency in Portland about sending a replacement until my dad is back up to speed."

"We'll miss you," Carmen said gruffly.

"Especially the female patients," Tiffany said with a teasing grin.

Eli could feel his face flush and he forced himself not to look at Melissa, who hadn't said a word.

"If that's everything, can I go?" Tiffany asked. "We're playing down in Manzanita tonight, at least until the power goes out from the big storm on the way."

"They're not canceling your gig?" Melissa finally asked.

Tiffany shook her head. "Not that I've heard. The storm's not supposed to be here until nine or so. We'll play until we can't play anymore."

"That's the spirit," Carmen said.

"Could be nobody else will show up, then we can all go home. So can I take off?"

"Yes. That's all," Eli said. "I just wanted to talk for a moment about the plan next week for my dad's return. Good luck with your show."

She flashed him a grin as she grabbed her backpack and hurried out the door, humming some of the lyrics he recognized from the night he and Melissa had gone to see her.

"I'm off, too," Carmen said. "I have to head to the grocery store. Every time the wind blows around here, the grocery stores run out of milk."

She hurried off after Tiffany. For the first time in longer than he could remember, he and Melissa were alone.

She jumped up from her desk and grabbed her sweater and her purse. "I need to go, too," Melissa said.

No, he wasn't imagining things. She was doing her utmost to avoid his company. He knew it was for the best so they didn't cross any more lines, but he missed her with a fierce ache.

"Big weekend plans?"

She made a face. "Cody's coming to pick Skye up again tonight. He wants to have her the whole weekend until Sunday this time, so I need to help her pack. He wants to get out of town before the storm hits. I tried to convince him it wasn't a good weekend for his visitation, but he insisted since he's going to be busy next weekend. Also, his sister is in town and she hasn't seen Skye in about a year."

"Go take care of what you need to at home. Don't worry about things here. I'll lock up."

"Thank you."

She gave him a stiff nod, gathered her purse from under her desk and hurried for the door.

That was the most personal conversation they had shared in days. He felt an ache, missing the warm, funny woman he had come to know since returning to Cannon Beach.

It was better this way, that she had put up these walls between them, but he felt an ache.

How had she reacted when he'd said he would only be there another week? He hadn't been able to read her. Had she been relieved? Or would she miss him as deeply as he knew he would miss her?

He rubbed at that ache in his chest. Somehow Melissa had worked her way inside his own careful walls. She was there, lodged against his heart, and he didn't know how he was going to push her out again.

Chapter Ten

The storm hit about four hours after Cody left for Portland with Skye in his impractical sports car.

Melissa sat in the window seat in the sunroom she loved, watching the waves grow higher as the sky darkened with rolling clouds.

Storms always made her blood hum. One good thing about formerly being married to a professional surfer—they had always lived next to an ocean. Whether it was Mexico or Hawaii or Australia, no matter what coastal area she and Cody and Skye had been living, she had always loved watching storms hit land, as long as she could observe the drama from somewhere safe.

She wasn't as crazy about being in the middle of them. She had been, a few times. Once she had been working at a hospital in Maui in the midst of a Category 3 hurricane and had worked for thirty-six hours straight when her coworkers couldn't make it to the hospital because of the storm.

Skye loved storms. She would have loved this one. Her daughter would have found it a great adventure to cuddle together and tell stories by candlelight. She missed her with a deep ache, which she knew was perfectly ridiculous. Somehow Melissa had to get used to these weekends without her child. She wanted her daughter to have a relationship with her father, and Skye and Cody couldn't truly have that through only occasional phone calls and video chats.

Melissa had lost her father when she was fourteen and still felt the emptiness of that. She didn't want Skye to grow up being resentful or angry that Cody wasn't in her life. Somehow she had to come to terms with being without her and fill the void with friends and hobbies.

The power went out two hours later, as she expected. Through the window, she could see only darkness, which told her Brambleberry House wasn't the only structure hit. It appeared power was out up and down the coast.

Fortunately, her e-reader was fully charged and would last for hours, and she had already gathered all the emergency supplies she might need during a storm.

She wasn't looking forward to a long night alone in the dark, but she tried to make her situation as comfortable as possible, lighting candles she had gathered earlier and carrying pillows and blankets to the window seat.

If the winds increased in intensity, she would probably feel safer away from the windows and the possibility of shattering glass from flying tree limbs or other debris, but for now she didn't feel in harm's way.

She was just settling in with her book when she heard a knock at the door.

"It's Rosa," she heard from outside. "And Fiona."

Melissa hurried to the door and found her friend standing in the entry holding two lit candles, her Irish setter at her side.

"This is some kind of storm, no?"

"It's crazy out there."

"Did I see our Skye go off with her father earlier tonight? Did they make it all right?"

She nodded, warmed by Rosa's use of the possessive pronoun when it came to her daughter. She loved having friends who cared. This was the reason she had come back to Cannon Beach, to forge this kind of powerful connection.

"He texted me that they were safely back in Portland and it wasn't even raining there."

"That's a relief." Rosa looked inside the apartment, where Melissa had lit a couple of emergency candles to push away the darkness. "I came down to check on you and make sure you had some kind of flashlight or candle, but it looks like you are all set."

This wasn't her first spring storm along the coast. Sometimes the big ones could wipe out power in the region for days.

"I should be fine. Thank you for worrying about me. Have you checked on Sonia?"

Rosa nodded, looking worried. "I know she doesn't like storms much."

Though it was nothing the other woman had told her, Melissa had the same impression during the most recent storm. Sonia became even more brusque than normal, her words clipped, and Melissa thought she glimpsed fear layering beneath it.

"I checked on her first. She assured me she is fine,

that she has plenty of LED candles. She had four or five going, with extra batteries if necessary, so they can go all night, if it comes to that."

"I hope it doesn't." Again, she wondered about Sonia and the mysterious past that left her afraid of the dark.

"Since Skye is not here, do you want me to leave Fiona with you for the company? I asked Sonia and she said she would be fine."

Poor Rosa, having to watch over everyone in Brambleberry House. It wasn't her job, but somehow they all had become her responsibility anyway.

She patted Fiona, wishing she could say yes. She never would have guessed she would find so much solace in canine companionship. She and Skye really needed to get serious about going to the shelter and picking out a rescue.

"That's so sweet of you, but I think I'm okay. Much better than last time Skye was with her dad."

Rosa gave her a sympathetic look. "I'm sorry. Being a mother is hard business, no? It never seems to become easier."

That seemed an odd statement, filled with more knowledge than she might have expected from a woman who didn't have any children, at least as far as Melissa knew. Maybe it was just Rosa's unique word choices, where English was her second language.

She couldn't deny the truth in what her friend said, though. "It's so hard," she agreed.

"If you want some chocolate and the sympathy, you know where to find me. I can maybe find a bottle of wine somewhere, also. We don't need light for that."

She managed a smile, tempted for a moment by the

picture Rosa painted. Wine and chocolate and sympathy might just be the perfect prescription during a storm.

On the other hand, she wouldn't be good company for anyone.

This time, she knew her dark mood was only partially about the pang she felt at being separated from her child. The rest was about Eli and this wild morass of emotions she didn't know what to do about.

He would be there another week, he had said that afternoon. She had nearly gasped aloud at his words as the shock of them had ripped through her like a sharp blade. She was still trying to process the idea that she only had one more week with him.

"Thanks," she managed, "but I think I'll watch the storm for little longer, then go to bed."

"No problem. If you change your mind, you know where to find me."

She smiled. "Thanks. Good night."

After Rosa left, she sat in the window seat for a while longer, feeling more alone than she had in a long, long time.

She awoke to absolute darkness and the strange, disorienting awareness that she didn't know where she was.

She blinked, aware of cold and wind and the faint hint of roses hanging on the air.

Was that what had awakened her? She blinked again as the sunroom of her apartment at Brambleberry House slowly came into focus. She was still curled up on the window seat, a blanket casually tossed over her. Her back ached from the odd position and her foot tingled, asleep.

She must have drifted off while watching the storm. She wasn't sure how she could have slept in the midst of the weather's intensity. Wind whined outside, fiercely hurling raindrops at the window.

Her phone suddenly rang and she had the feeling it wasn't the first time. It wasn't an alarm, but someone calling.

Skye!

Still trying to push away the tangled remnants of sleep, she scrambled for her phone and found it glowing under the throw blanket she must have tugged over her in the night.

"Hello?" She hardly recognized her own raspy voice.

"Melissa? Is that you?"

"I… Yes."

Not Skye, and not Cody. Some of her anxiety eased and she pulled the blanket tighter around her shoulders against the chill of the night and the storm.

"It's Julia Garrett. I'm so sorry to bother you, but I tried to call the clinic's emergency number and the phone lines must be down. I didn't have Eli's cell number and thought you might."

Her friend's words seemed to push away the last vestiges of sleep, and Melissa came fully awake. A hundred grim scenarios flashed through her head. It must be something serious for Julia to reach out at 1:00 a.m. in the middle of a storm.

"Are you all right? Is it one of the kids?"

"In a manner of speaking." Was that amusement she heard in Julia's voice? It hardly seemed appropriate, given the circumstances.

"I'm in labor."

Shock washed over her. "In labor. Now? Are you sure? Your cervix was only dilated to a one, eight hours ago when you left the office!"

"I've done this enough times, I'm pretty positive. I've had contractions all evening. I thought they were only Braxton Hicks, but in the past hour they've become much more regular."

"How far apart?"

"I'm down to about three minutes now."

Some of her wild panic subsided and she relaxed a little. "Okay. That's good. There's still time to make it to the hospital in Seaside."

"We thought so, too, but there's a problem. That's why I'm calling you. We were packing up the car and Will heard on the radio that the road is closed. The storm has knocked several big trees and power lines down between here and there."

Her voice cracked on the last word, and she started to breath heavily and regularly into the phone, obviously in the middle of a contraction. Melissa was already looking for her shoes by the door.

"That one was less than three minutes."

A new voice spoke into the phone. Julia must have handed the phone to her husband. Will was usually one of the most calm, measured people Melissa knew, but now he spoke briskly, his voice edged with the beginnings of panic. "I'm not sure what to do. Should I call for medevac?"

She wasn't at all prepared to make this sort of decision for the couple. "Let me call Eli and Wendell and see what they suggest. You told me you had a completely natural childbirth with your two youngest, with no complications. Eli may want to just have you meet us at the office."

"The only problem," Will said, "is that one of the downed power lines I heard about is apparently blocking the road between our place and Doc Sanderson's office.

The only way I could figure out to get there is to walk, which I don't feel good about in this wind and storm, or to head down the beach on the four-wheeler."

"We're not doing either of those things," she heard Julia declare.

"Stay put," she said, shoving on her raincoat and her boots. "I'm on my way. I'll be there in five minutes. I'll get in touch with Eli and see if we can come up with a plan. If I can't get through, I'll stop and bang on his windows until he wakes up. Meanwhile, breathe, both of you. And don't let her have that baby yet."

"I'll do my best, but you know Jules. She can be pretty stubborn," Will said.

"I heard that," Melissa heard Julia say in the background.

Despite her own efforts to grab a flashlight and rush out the door, Melissa had to fight a smile. Will and Julia were a darling couple, overflowing with love for each other and their children. She adored both of them.

"Hang tight. I'll be there in a few minutes."

"Be careful," Will said. "It's still pretty nasty out there. I don't like the idea of you going out in it, either."

"I won't let a little rain stop me," she assured him. "See you soon."

She hung up the phone as a particularly strong gust of wind rattled the windows of the old house.

She wasn't eager to go out into the teeth of the storm, but she also wasn't about to let her friend down. Not when Julia needed her.

He was having a delicious dream.

He and Melissa were walking through one of the dense ancient forests around Cannon Beach, her hand tucked in his. She carried a blanket in rich jewel tones and wore a sundress the same green as her eyes. Dappled light shot through the trees, catching in her hair.

She pulled her hand from his and raced ahead a little, turning around to look at him with that laughing, teasing smile that always stole his breath. He caught up with her and she wrapped her arms around his waist, pulling him close, where he was safe and warm and loved.

It was magic here, with a peace he hadn't known in months. He wanted to stay forever.

His phone jerked him awake and for an instant he was back in his residency, surviving on energy bars and rare, haphazard chunks of sleep.

He fumbled for it. "Hello?"

"Eli. It's Melissa."

The discord of hearing the woman who had just been holding him in his dreams jarred him. Unlike the relaxed, warm woman he'd been dreaming about, her voice was strained and she pitched her voice above howling wind.

That same storm howled outside his father's house. He had been sitting in his dad's old recliner awake most of the night but must have eventually drifted off. He had a feeling he hadn't been sleeping long.

Eli sat up, his surroundings coming sharply back into focus. Melissa was calling and she needed him.

"What is it? What's wrong? Are you hurt?"

"I'm not hurt. I'm fine. But Julia Garrett is in labor and apparently the storm has blocked the road between here and Seaside, as well as between her house and the clinic."

"She was barely dilated this afternoon!"

"Tell that to her baby. Apparently it's on its own schedule. Now she's having contractions that are less than three minutes apart. I'm heading to their place now."

"In this storm?" Fear for her washed over him like a twenty-foot-high swell. Anything could happen to her. She could get hit by flying debris, stumble into a downed power line, fall and injure herself in the deep, powerless darkness.

He couldn't lose her!

"I'm fine. She needs help. Can you meet me there?"

He was already throwing on his shoes. "I only need five minutes. Be careful!"

"I know. Same to you."

She hung up before he could argue with her and tell her to go back inside Brambleberry House, where she would be safe.

"What's happening?"

In the light of a lantern, Wendell stood in the doorway, holding on to the walker he detested but still needed for stability. His father's hair was messy, and in his flannel pajamas he looked his age.

"I'm sorry I woke you. Julia Garrett's in labor, and apparently power lines are down between here and the hospital in Seaside."

"You didn't wake me. I can never sleep through storms like this. I've been in here fretting, wondering how long it would be before someone called, needing help. I didn't expect it to be Julia. She's three weeks from her due date."

He wasn't surprised that his father knew exactly when Julia was due, despite the fact that Wendell had been dealing with his own health issues and subsequent recovery for weeks.

"It was actually Melissa. Julia called her first and she was letting me know what was going on. Melissa is on her way over there and I'm going to meet her."

"She shouldn't be out in the storm, but you and I both know we can't stop her, especially since Julia is a friend of hers."

"We just saw Julia in the office yesterday. She was barely dilated, but of course babies have their own opinions about when they're going to make an appearance."

"Oh, yes. They love showing up when it's least convenient for anyone. You can take my emergency kit if you need it. I already pulled it out earlier in the evening and set it by the door. It should have everything you need."

He had his own emergency kit he kept stocked with supplies in a backpack, but he was touched his father had survived enough storms around Cannon Beach to make sure Eli, as his designated representative, was ready for anything.

"Thanks. I'll keep you posted."

"Take care of Julia. I know you will. You're an amazing doctor."

He wasn't as convinced, but his father's vote of confidence warmed him through. "I'll try."

"And take care of Melissa, too. She shouldn't be out in this storm."

"Exactly what I told her," he said. He didn't have time to tell his father how very much he yearned to take care of Melissa forever, to walk through all the storms of life together.

He grabbed his father's case and his own backpack, and headed out into the wind and lashing rain.

Melissa somehow beat him to the Garretts' house, but he suspected she hadn't been there long. Her hair was drenched, despite the raincoat she was taking off, and she looked cold.

He wanted to kiss the raindrops off her cheeks and

hold her close to warm her up but knew both of them needed to focus on the crisis at hand.

"Thank you both for coming out in this crazy weather," Will Garrett said as he let Eli inside. "I'm sorry we had to call you in the middle of the night, but when we heard the roads were closed, we weren't sure what else to do."

"You did the right thing," Eli assured him.

"Trust Julia to make things more exciting," he said ruefully. "She's never content with the ordinary."

"You'll have a great story to tell this little one," Melissa said, her voice calm. She had so many strengths, but that was one he appreciated most: the calm that seemed to radiate from her.

"How do you have lights?" she asked.

"We have a whole-house generator. I put it in a few years ago. Believe me, I've never been so grateful for anything in my life," Will said gruffly.

When Eli pushed the door open, Melissa close behind him, they found Julia Garrett, dressed in a pale blue nightgown, sitting on the edge of the bed. A pretty teenage girl who had to be one of her twins sat next to her.

"Hey, Julia. Hi, Maddie." Melissa greeted both of them with more of that calm.

Julia managed a smile in response though her features were taut and strained. "This isn't quite the way I planned this."

"What is it with babies, deciding to make their appearances in the middle of the night in the worst possible weather?"

"Inconsiderate little stinks, aren't they?"

She smiled at them and then caught her breath, pressing both hands over her abdomen.

"That one was barely a minute since the last one," Maddie said, eyes huge and frightened in her pretty face.

"We're okay," Julia said, reaching out a hand to give her daughter's arm a reassuring squeeze. "The cavalry is here now. You and Will won't have to deliver your baby sister."

"Whew," the girl said, vast relief on her face.

Eli considered his options quickly. "How do you feel about a home birth? I don't think we have time to call the air ambulance and have them here in time for the delivery, and I'm not sure they can fly in this wind anyway. We can have them on standby in case there any complications."

"Women have been giving birth at home forever," Julia said. "As long as she's safe, I don't care how she gets here."

He had plenty of colleagues who would have disagreed and would have insisted a hospital was the only safe place for a woman to give birth, but Eli's experience in war zones and refugee camps had told him that women could be incredibly resourceful. Under the circumstances, this was the safest possible place for Julia to have her baby, not in a helicopter or an ambulance trying to make its way through the storm.

Even if they had called for a chopper, it turned out that Julia's labor progressed so quickly it was clear it wouldn't have arrived in time. He and Melissa barely had time to arrange her on the bed, put a nervous Will at ease and send Maddie for clean towels and to boil water to sterilize any tools he needed to use.

Ten minutes later, he watched a head emerge.

Sweat poured down Julia's face and she gripped her husband's hand tightly. "I have to push."

"That's good," Eli said. "I need you to do just that. Now is the perfect time to push. You've got this."

A moment later, he delivered a chunky, red-faced baby, who took a shuddering breath, then began to wail.

"Love that sound," Melissa said, wiping off the baby's face with an awestruck expression. "Welcome to the world, little Garrett girl."

"Miriam Renee," Will said, his voice raw with emotions. "We want to call her Miri."

Eli caught his breath. It was a coincidence, he knew, but hearing the name out of the blue like that still made him feel as if he'd been run over by a tank.

For a moment he was frozen, picturing a sweet girl, bloodied and torn, her smile cut down forever by hatred and violence. A strangled cry choked him and he couldn't breathe or think. He had to get out of here before the memories consumed him and he fell apart. In a panic, his muscles tensed and he was about to rise, to escape, when he felt the gentle pressure of fingers on his shoulder.

Melissa.

His gaze met hers, and he saw a knowledge and compassion there that made him swallow back the emotions. She knew. She knew and somehow she steadied him. He had no idea how she managed it. He only knew that the warm touch of her hand on him seemed to clear away the panic and the grief and shock until he felt much more in control.

He drew in a shuddering breath and cleared his throat. "Miri is a beautiful name for a beautiful little girl."

"She's gorgeous," Will said gruffly. "Like her mother."

He kissed Julia's sweat-dampened forehead, running a tender hand down her hair. After Eli helped Will cut the cord with the sterilized scissors he had in his kit,

Melissa took the baby and placed the naked, wriggling girl on Julia's chest. She instinctively rooted around, and Julia laughed a little before helping her latch on. Will stood next to them, his somewhat harsh features relaxed into an expression of love and amazement and a vast joy.

"Good job, Mama," Eli said.

His voice sounded ragged but he didn't care. He had delivered babies before, into the hundreds, but he couldn't remember when a birth had impacted him so deeply.

He was emotional about Miri but about so much more. He wanted this, what Will and Julia had created here. A family.

He had seen so much ugliness over the last five years of near-constant deployments. Pain and bloodshed and violence. Families torn apart, villages decimated, lives shattered.

All of it stemmed from hatred, from power struggles and greed and ideological differences.

He was so tired of it.

Maybe it was time he focused instead on love.

He had been doing important work overseas, helping people in terrible situations who had few options and little hope. He couldn't deny that what he had been doing *mattered*.

Justine had been doing important work, and some part of him would always feel a responsibility to try harder and be better because of her example and the tragic way she had died.

But this was important, too, these small but significant moments. Helping to bring new life into the world. Caring for neighbors and friends. Continuing his father's legacy in this community, where Wendell was so loved.

"Are you all right?" Melissa asked a short time later,

after the baby was bundled and the ambulance had been called. Both mom and baby were fine, but as soon as the road was cleared, Eli wanted them to be checked out at the hospital, where little Miri could have a full assessment and Julia could receive care while she recovered.

He wanted to tell her some of the many thoughts racing through his head, but now didn't seem the proper time.

"I'm fine. It's always amazing, seeing new life come into the world and remembering what a miracle it is, every time. I heard it said once that a baby is God's opinion that the world should go on. I think I needed that reminder."

Her features softened and she touched his arm again. The tenderness of the gesture made those emotions well up.

He was so deeply in love with her. How had he ever been crazy enough to think he could go on without her?

"I didn't know about the name. They were still trying to decide, the last I talked to Julia about it. If I had known, I would have warned you."

"It's a lovely name," he said. "I hope she's as sweet as the other little girl I once knew who carried it."

Before she could answer, Eli's phone rang. When he saw his father on the caller ID, he quickly answered it.

"Hey, son," Wendell said. "How are things going there? How's Julia?"

"Good. Both the mama and baby girl are doing fine."

"Oh, that's wonderful to hear. I knew you could do it."

His father's confidence in him warmed him. "Right now we're waiting for the road to open so we can get them to the hospital in Seaside. The crews are saying about another half hour."

"Great news. Listen, I just got a call from Elisa Darby. A branch came through her teenage boy's bedroom window about a half hour ago."

"Oh, no!"

"He's fine, just shaken up, but might need a couple of stitches. It's not a big deal, not big enough to try getting to the ER in Seaside in this storm, but she called to see if someone could come by, check things out and maybe stitch him up. You up for another house call?"

He assessed the situation with the Garretts. Will and Julia had things under control. Right now, their teenage daughter was holding the bundled baby and her siblings were waiting in line for their turn.

"I can do that. Text me the address. I'll wrap up with Julia and head there within the next fifteen or twenty minutes."

"If other people call, want me to start making a list? I can be your dispatcher."

"Sure."

He hung up from his father to find Julia watching carefully. "What's happened?"

"I've got a teenage boy with an injury from broken glass after a branch came through a window."

"I was worried about that very thing happening to me earlier. I fell asleep in the window seat while I was watching the storm and woke up thinking it probably wasn't a good idea."

"It wasn't. You should probably not do that again." He wanted to be here to hold her during the next storm. The two of them could keep each other warm and watch the clouds roll over the ocean together.

"Where did it happen?" she asked.

"The house of Elisa Darby. Do you know her?"

"Yes. She doesn't live far from here.

"Apparently, her son might need a few stitches."

"You'll need help."

To give someone stitches? Probably not. He'd been doing that since his first day of med school, but he couldn't deny the two of them made a good team. She seemed to know exactly what supplies he needed without being asked, and he definitely needed her amazing skill at calming any situation.

"I don't want to take you away if you think you're still needed here."

Will glanced over, obviously listening to the conversation. "We're fine. The ambulance should be here soon. You've done great work and I can't thank you enough for our little Miri here, but it sounds like somebody else needs you now."

"If you're sure."

Melissa seemed reluctant to leave, but she gathered up their supplies, gave Julia a kiss on the cheek and hugged Will. Then she kissed the baby's forehead before following Eli out into the pearly light of predawn.

The wind had finally slowed, though the rain continued. The sun was still an hour or so from coming up above the mountains to the east, but there was enough light for them to see some of the damage left behind by the storm.

On this street alone, nearly every house had at least one tree branch down, and he could see a metal shed collapsed at the Garretts' neighbors. This was only one small sample of what the storm could do. He had a feeling the rest of the region had been hit just as hard.

He met Melissa's gaze. "I have a feeling it's going to be a busy day."

Chapter Eleven

Eli's words turned out to be prophetic. By the time they finished at the Darbys' house, Wendell had called them to report three more people had phoned him looking for emergency medical care. They all had mild cuts and bruises, except for one man who sustained minor burns trying to start a malfunctioning generator. Eli patched him up as best he could but ordered him to the hospital as soon as he could make it there.

They made house calls at first, but as they started to receive reports that the roads were slowly being cleared throughout the morning, he and Melissa were finally able to retreat to the clinic, sending out word to the real dispatchers and the paramedics that they would stay open to take some of the more mild emergencies where a trip to the hospital wasn't necessarily warranted.

She loved seeing Eli in action during a crisis. Over

the last three weeks during routine office visits, she had observed that he was truly a wonderful doctor, one who spent as much time as each patient needed, dispensing advice and compassion.

Observing him during an emergency situation was something completely different. He was focused, concise, with an uncanny ability to take care of whatever situation walked through the door with skill and care.

No wonder he was so passionate about his military career. Eli was a man who truly thrived under pressure.

She couldn't expect someone with a gift like that to be content as a family physician in a small practice.

The realization depressed her, though she was not sure why. Maybe she had been holding out some slim hope that Eli might be able to find a place to belong here on the beautiful Oregon Coast where he had been raised, exactly as *she* had over the last seven months.

Around noon, she closed the outside doors after their last patient, a tearful eight-year-old girl who had stepped on a nail while helping her family clean up debris. When the family drove away, no cars were left in the parking lot. She locked the doors and turned the Open sign to Closed.

At last report, the dispatchers assured them all the roads were clear now along the coast and people in need could make it to the emergency room or the urgent-care clinics in Seaside or Astoria, if necessary.

"Good work," Eli said when she walked back. "You've been amazing today. An army medic trained in battlefield emergency care couldn't have done better."

His admiring words and expression left her flustered and not sure how to respond. "You were the one doing all the care. I've only been providing support."

"That's completely not true and you know it. Every time I needed something, you were right there with it before I had to ask, and you are amazing at calming down every panicked mother or crying child."

"We make a good team." For another week, anyway. The thought made her chest ache.

"Do you have any idea of how necessary you are to my father's practice? Why do you think I've tried so hard to..." He bit off his words, leaving her intensely curious about what he intended to say.

"Why you've tried so hard to what?" She had to ask.

His smile appeared forced. "Uh, make sure you know exactly how much you're appreciated."

She had a feeling that wasn't what he'd almost said at all, but he didn't appear inclined to add anything more.

"I was going to say the same to you," she said. "It's not every day you deliver a baby, sew thirty-six stitches in five different patients and give eight tetanus shots, all before noon."

He smiled. "All in all, a good morning. I'm glad we could help."

"If you hadn't been here, I'm not sure what people in Cannon Beach would have done."

"My dad is not the only doctor in town. Someone else would have stepped up."

Wendell might not be the only doctor, but he was one of the most beloved.

Eli was well on his way to matching his father's popularity. Everyone in town loved Eli, after he had been here only three weeks to fill in for his father.

Especially her.

She pushed the thought aside. Not now. She couldn't think about her impending heartache. He was leaving in a week, and somehow she was going to have to figure out how to go on without that slow, gorgeous smile in her life.

She had to say at least a little of what was on her mind. It seemed vitally important that she let him know what she had been thinking all morning as she watched him work.

"You're an amazing doctor, Eli. You make a great family physician in the proud tradition of your father, but today, working together in an emergency situation with you, showed me you're doing exactly what you need to be doing for the army. You obviously thrive in stressful situations. You care passionately about what you're doing and you're good at it—exactly the sort of person who can make a much-needed difference in the world."

He looked touched, his eyes warm, and he opened his mouth to answer, but his cell phone rang before he could say anything. He gave the phone a frustrated look that shifted to one of concern when he saw the caller ID.

"I need to get that. Looks like it's the Seaside hospital, probably the attending physician at the women's center, calling about Julia and Miri."

"While you talk to the Attending, I'll go straighten up the exam rooms we used today so they're ready for Monday."

She was just finishing up when Eli appeared in the doorway, again looking dark and lean and so gorgeous it made her catch her breath.

"Mom and baby are doing well," he reported. "I figured you'd want to know."

"Yes. I was going to call her later. I appreciate the update."

"Everyone is healthy. The attending physician suggests keeping them overnight, but it sounds like Julia is eager to be home with their other children. I'll go check things out, and if all appears okay she might be released by tonight."

"She'll be happy about that."

He leaned against the door frame and scratched his cheek. "Better yet, I'll pick up my dad and take him with me to do the honors. He'll want to see the baby and check on Julia himself."

Her heart melted at his thoughtfulness, both on his father's behalf and on Julia's, and she fell in love with him all over again.

"You are a good man, Eli Sanderson."

He made a face. "Why? Because I'm going to take my dad with me to the hospital to check on a patient?"

"Because you know how important it is for him to make sure she's all right and also how much it will set Julia's mind at ease to have him there."

"It's not a big deal."

"It is to me, just as it will be for Julia and your dad."

She smiled at him, and he gazed at her for a long moment, then growled something she couldn't hear and lowered his mouth to hers.

The fierce kiss came out of the blue and was the last thing she expected him to do, yet somehow was exactly what she needed.

His mouth was hard and intense on hers, searching and demanding at the same time. She answered him kiss for kiss, taste for taste. Heat raced through her and she wrapped her arms around him, but the hunger contained something else, something deeper.

This was goodbye.

He was leaving in a week, and this likely would be the last chance she would have to hold him like this before he left. She tightened her arms, trying to burn the taste and the feel and the smell of him into her mind. When he was gone, back doing the work he loved, and she was alone here in Cannon Beach, at least she would have these slices of memories to comfort her.

She tried to pour everything in her heart into the kiss. All her love and admiration and sadness, wrapped together and delivered on a breathless sigh. She had no idea how long they stayed locked together there in the doorway. She only knew the emotions in the kiss would leave her forever changed.

She would have stayed forever, but she was aware, always aware, that someone else needed him, too.

After long, heady moments, she finally pulled her mouth away and stepped back, her breathing ragged and her face flaming. Could he sense in her kiss all the love she couldn't say?

She looked away, hoping desperately that she hadn't revealed entirely too much by that kiss.

"Melissa."

His voice sounded raw, breathless. She could feel his searching gaze on her and forced herself to offer back a bland smile. "You should probably go check out Julia and Miri. The Garretts will be waiting for you."

"I… Yes."

She didn't want him to offer any explanations or apologies or, worse, ask any questions. Any conversation between them and she was afraid she would burst into tears she couldn't explain.

"I'll see you later. Drive carefully."

With that, she turned around and hurried out of the room, wishing with all her heart that things could be different between them.

* * *

Though she was tired down to her bones, Melissa spent the afternoon working with Sonia to clean up the battered gardens at Brambleberry House. Rosa was busy doing the same at the gift store in town, which had suffered some water damage from a roof leak.

The gardens looked sad, with broken limbs, crushed flowers, scattered leaves.

She felt a little like the landscaping around the house—damaged, scarred. She had to hope she could be like a few of the shrubs around the house, which had been bent by the storm but were already beginning to straighten again.

"I don't think we can save this one." Sonia sat before one of the brambleberry bushes, her lovely, perfect features creased with a grief that seemed out of proportion to a little storm damage.

"Are you sure we can't salvage some of the canes?"

"They won't be the same. I'm not sure they'll be able to produce much fruit at all."

She seemed devastated by the loss. Maybe she had an extreme fondness for that particular brambleberry bush, or maybe her grief was for something else entirely.

Melissa tried to choose her words carefully. "You know, my dad used to say that not everything that's broken is worthless. It might not ever be what it was, but that doesn't mean it can't be something else. Maybe something even better."

She wasn't sure if she had helped or made things worse. Sonia gave her a long look, nodded slowly, then went back to work.

"That's all we can do tonight," Sonia said sometime

later. "It's going to be dark soon. You look very tired. You need to rest."

Her exhaustion had deepened, and she thought she might fall asleep right here in the cool, storm-battered garden.

"I'll just stay with Fiona for a moment, then we'll come inside."

Sonia gave her a long look and she could see the concern on her friend's features. She didn't pry, though. One of the best things about Sonia was her ability to let other people keep their own secrets, too. After a moment, the other woman twisted her mouth into what other people might consider a smile and headed into the house.

Melissa sat for a few moments more, heart aching. She needed to go inside but couldn't seem to find the energy to do it.

She wanted her daughter here. A Skye hug always went a long way toward healing her soul from life's inevitable disappointments. Her daughter would be home the next day. They would have plenty of time for hugs then.

She was just about to head into the house when Fiona suddenly turned around and raced for the edge of the garden.

What on earth?

"Fiona," she called. "Come on, girl. Home."

The dog ignored her, headed with single-minded purpose in the other direction. There was probably some poor mole who had been foolish enough to set up shop in the gardens the Irish setter considered her own.

Fiona didn't stop when she reached the beach access gate. To Melissa's astonishment, she nudged open the latch and raced through, leaving her little choice but to chase after the dog.

She was too tired for this, but Fiona didn't seem to care about that.

Exasperated, Melissa followed the dog onto the beach. "Come on, Fi. Here girl," she called, then her voice faltered.

Fiona wasn't alone. She stood on the sand not far from the house, nose to nose with another dog. A little black schnauzer, whose leash was currently held by the one man she didn't feel strong enough to face again right now.

Her heart seemed to stutter, and she wanted to slip back through the gate and hurry into the house.

After that emotional kiss earlier when she had bared everything in her heart, she didn't want to face him right now...or ever again, if she could arrange it.

But he was here and she had no choice. She forced herself to move toward him. "Sorry. She got out somehow. Come on, Fiona. Inside."

The dog showed no sign of obeying her, and Melissa sighed, taking another step toward him and the two dogs.

"Julia and Will send their love and gratitude," he said when she was an arm's length away.

Despite her discomfort, she couldn't help a smile at that. "How is Julia? I wanted to go visit but thought I would give her a day or two to be settled at home."

"She's good. Glowing."

That made her smile again. "And baby Miri?"

"Beautiful. I held her for a good fifteen minutes while the infant unit nurses were giving me their report and she slept the whole time. She obviously likes me."

Why wouldn't she? The man was irresistible. Her heart ached when she pictured him in a hospital nursery, holding a tiny baby who shared the same name as someone dear to him, someone he had lost.

She was suddenly deeply grateful she would have the

chance to watch this Miri grow up. She would be here to see her learn to walk, to ride a bike, to go on dates. Melissa, at least, wasn't going anywhere.

"Maybe Julia can keep in touch with you after you're back on active duty and send you pictures of her."

He was quiet, his hands on Max's leash. "That would be great, except I'm not going back on active duty."

She stared at him in the gathering twilight. "You're... what?"

He returned her shocked look with an impassive one she couldn't read. "I called my commanding officer on my way back from the hospital and told her I wouldn't be signing up for another tour."

"But...but why? I thought you loved what you do in the military. You were doing important work. Necessary work."

"I am. I was. But today when we were delivering Miri, I realized something."

He gazed toward the ocean and the dramatic rock formations offshore, his features in shadow.

"There is more than one way to make a difference in the world," he said slowly. "Sometimes that involves focusing on helping out those in critical situations. That's a good and honorable thing to do, and I will always be grateful I had the experiences and learned the lessons I did."

He glanced back at her, blue eyes glittering in the fading light. "I'm glad I had the chance to serve. I'm a better doctor and a better person for it. But I have no obligation to do it forever. Even Justine was never planning to serve for the rest of her life. She was making plans for after she left Doctors Without Borders. She was going to adopt Miri and take her back to France with her."

"Yes. That's what you said."

"If she could make plans for a different future some-day, why can't I?"

"What kind of future?" Her heart now seemed to be racing in double time as she tried to absorb this shock-ing information.

"I want to be home. I want to help my neighbors and be around when my dad needs me and watch Miri and any other babies I deliver grow up and have babies of their own."

"You're leaving the army." She couldn't seem to pro-cess it even after his explanation.

He shrugged. "I'm leaving active duty. I'll stay in the reserves. If my country needs me, I may end up being called up in emergencies. I'm more than willing to do that on a temporary basis, but I want something else. I want to go into practice with my dad. Sanderson and Sander-son. Has a nice ring, don't you think?"

Oh, that would make Wendell happy beyond words. "Your dad will be thrilled."

"He will. With me here to share the burden, who knows? He might even slow down and little and start to enjoy life outside of medicine."

She wasn't sure that would happen, but she hoped so for his father's sake.

As she processed the news, the magnitude of what he was telling her began to soak through her shock. He was staying in Cannon Beach. Staying at the clinic where she worked. That would only mean one thing.

She would have no choice.

"That's great. I'm happy for you. You'll be gr-great."

Tears began to burn behind her eyes, and she had to hope he couldn't see them in the dusky light.

Unfortunately, she forgot how sharp-eyed the man could be. His gaze narrowed and he watched her with an intensity she couldn't escape.

"What's wrong? I was hoping for a…different reaction."

"I'm happy for you. I really am. This is exactly what your father would have wanted."

"So why do you look like I just started clear-cutting the Brambleberry House gardens?"

She wanted to come up with something clever that would explain the tears she was afraid he had seen, but she was too tired to tell him anything but the truth.

"I love working at your dad's practice," she said softly. "But if you're coming home for good, I'm afraid I'll have to quit."

His mouth sagged. "Quit? Why the hell would you do that?"

She had to tell him, especially now that she'd started. The words caught in her throat, but she forced them out.

"I can't work for you, Eli. I can't. Not when I…" She faltered, losing her nerve.

He looked thunderstruck, as if she'd just thrown a handful of sand in his eyes. "When you what?"

She closed her eyes, mortified to her soul that she'd said anything at all. She should have just let the dust settle for a week or so and then quietly tendered her resignation.

"Are you really going to make me say it? Fine. I'll say it, then. I can't work for you when I have…have feelings for you."

This was the most difficult conversation she'd ever had. She wanted to find a hole and let Fiona and Max bury her in it like a leftover soup bone.

"These last two weeks have been torture," she finally

admitted, "trying to keep things on a professional level when my heart wants so much more. I'm sorry. I can't do it. I'm not strong enough. I'll have to go somewhere else to work. I'm sure I can find another job somewhere else along the coast. I only hope your dad will be able to give me a good reference."

He didn't say anything for a full minute, his expression filled with shock and something else, something she couldn't identify.

"Say something," she finally couldn't help but say.

When he continued to stare at her, she grabbed Fiona's collar and turned to head to the house, wanting only to escape.

"Melissa. Stop. Please!"

Fiona plopped her hindquarters in the sand, refusing to move other step, while a warm, rose-scented breeze seemed to eddy around them.

She couldn't face him. Humiliated and miserable, she stood there outside the beach gate, not knowing what to do.

She thought she knew what love was. She had been married for five years, for heaven's sake. But everything she understood before seemed wholly insignificant compared to this vast ache of emotion coiling through her.

"Melissa."

He tugged her around to face him, and she finally slowly lifted her gaze to his. The emotions blazing there made her catch her breath. Her pulse in her ears seemed louder than the surf.

"I want to stay in Cannon Beach for dozens of reasons," he said, his voice low and intense. "And almost every single one of them is because of you."

She gazed at his strong, lean features, everything inside her tuned to this moment.

"I came back to town broken," he went on gruffly. "I didn't want to admit it to myself or anyone else, but something inside my head and heart shattered when Miri and Justine died. I wouldn't say it was post-traumatic stress disorder, but the whole world seemed empty, joyless. Wrong."

He smiled a little and reached for her hand. His skin was warm against hers, and she shivered at the contrast, wanting to lean into him but afraid to move.

"And then I came back to town and met up with the girl I had the biggest crush on when I was eighteen and she was just fifteen, and I started to heal."

"You did not have a crush on me."

He raised an eyebrow. "Do you remember that time we danced together at the prom? Your boyfriend tried to beat me up later, but I didn't care. I would have done it all over again. It was all worth it, for the few moments I got to hold you in my arms."

"Why didn't you say anything? Back then or now?"

"You were way out of my league back then. You still are. I know I'll never be good enough for you, but that doesn't seem to matter anymore. The only thing that matters is that I'm in love with you and want the chance to show you I can make you happy."

Joy exploded through her, fierce and bright and perfect. "You love me."

"I think I've loved you a little since we were in high school together. But when I came back to Cannon Beach and met you again—the strong, amazing, compassionate woman you've become—I fell in love all over again."

Warmth flowed over her, healing and blissful. He loved her. She would never get tired of those words.

She reached up on tiptoe and kissed him, and this time when his mouth met hers there were no reservations between them, no uneasiness or worry or doubts.

Only love.

He kissed her for a long time, until the sun had almost slipped into the ocean. She would never grow tired of his kisses, either.

"I love you, Elias Sanderson. I'm so in love with you, I've barely been able to function around you. I'm amazed I could do my job, I was so busy trying to hide my feelings about you."

"Whatever you did worked. I had no idea."

She wanted to laugh and dance barefoot in the sand and fly a hundred kites with hearts all over them. Joy soared through her, wild and fierce and perfect.

He wouldn't be returning to harm's way. He would be here in Cannon Beach with her where they could walk the dogs at sunset and teach Skye how to play billiards and listen to music at The Haystacks on Saturday nights.

They could work together, helping the neighbors and friends they cared about.

Storms would come. Tree limbs would fall and brambleberry bushes would be broken and torn. But they would get through it all together.

He kissed her, and that future seemed sweet and full of incalculable promise.

"I'm not that young, perky cheerleader anymore," she eventually felt compelled to remind him when his hands started to wander.

"I know," he murmured against her mouth. "You're so much more than that now. A loving mother, a com-

Epilogue

Humming one of her favorite Christmas songs, Rosa Galvez twisted another string of lights around one of the porch columns. She only had two more to go, then this part of her holiday decorating would be done.

She loved this time of year. Brambleberry House was at its most beautiful at Christmas. The old Victorian was made for the season. Wreaths hung on the front door and in every window and her neighbor Sonia had been busy for the past two weeks hanging lights around the garden. Well, busy supervising a crew of teenage neighbor boys, anyway, who were earning a little extra change while helping them decorate.

The house would be spectacular when they finished.

She twisted the last of the strand of lights around the column, grateful for her coat against the cool, damp afternoon.

Though it was barely December, a Christmas tree already gleamed in the window of the first-floor apartment and she could see Skye peeking out. The girl waved at Rosa and at Fiona, sprawled out on the porch watching her work, then disappeared from view, back inside where she was baking something with Melissa.

Rosa had to smile, though she felt a little pang in her heart. The house would seem so empty when Skye and her mother moved out, but at least she wouldn't have to worry about that for a few more months. Eli Sanderson and Melissa Fielding planned to marry here at Bramble-berry House in April, when the flowers were first beginning to bloom in the gardens. It would be a lovely place to marry. She wanted to think Abigail would have been happy at the romantic turn of events.

Melissa and Eli were already looking at houses and seemed to have found a lovely Craftsman home close to Wendell Sanderson's house.

She was happy for her friend but, oh, she would miss her and Skye. So would Fiona. Who was going to take the Irish setter on runs along the shore? Certainly not Rosa.

She was hanging the last of the lights when a big late-model pickup truck she didn't recognize pulled into the driveway and a tall, serious-looking man climbed out. He stood for a moment, looking up at the house, then walked toward her.

For reasons she couldn't have explained, Rosa tensed.

She hardly ever had the panic attacks and meltdowns that had afflicted her so much after the dark period of her youth, before she had been rescued by Sheriff Daniel Galvez and his wife, Lauren, who later adopted her. Those terrible months seemed a lifetime ago. She was a different person now, one who had worked hard to find happiness.

Every once in a while, she felt as if all the progress she had achieved over the last fifteen years was for nothing—that somewhere deep inside, she would always be a frightened girl, tangled in a situation out of her control.

"May I help you?" she asked as the man approached the porch.

"I hope so."

Up close, he seemed even more grim than he had appeared when he climbed out of his vehicle. No trace of a smile appeared on his features, only tight control.

"I'm looking for a woman. I'm pretty sure she lives here. Her name is Elizabeth Hamilton."

The name meant nothing to Rosa, who knew all the past tenants going back to the original owner. Still, she felt a stirring of unease.

"I know no one by this name," she said. She was nervous, which was probably the reason that her Spanish accent became more pronounced. "I believe you have the wrong house."

"It's not the wrong house," he said flatly. "I know she's here."

"And I know she is not," Rosa retorted. Like her accent, her unease was becoming more pronounced, as well. This man made her nervous, though she couldn't have said why.

She wondered, for one fleeting moment, whether she should pull her phone out and call 911. It was a crazy reaction, she knew. The man wasn't threatening anyone. He was only looking for a woman who did not live there. She could only imagine trying to explain why she had called the police for such a reason to the frustrating but gorgeous new police chief. Wyatt Townsend would look at her with even more suspicion than he usually did.

"Now, I must ask you to leave."

She saw frustration cross features that she would ordinarily call handsome. Right now, they only looked dangerous.

"Sorry, ma'am, but I've come too far to leave now."

There was a bit of a Western twang to his voice, one that seemed similar to those she heard throughout her teenage years living in Utah.

"The woman you are seeking, this Elizabeth Hamilton, she does not live here."

He let out a sigh and looked down at the piece of paper. "What about Sonia Davis. Is she here?"

Now her nervousness bloomed into full-on fear. What could he possibly want with their Sonia?

Her neighbor was home. Rosa had seen her come in earlier and make her painstaking way up to her second-floor apartment, looking more weary and sore than usual.

She wanted to tell him no. She wanted to tell him to go away and not come back. Some instinct warned Rosa that this man was a threat to her secretive, vulnerable neighbor, who had already been through so very much.

She opened her mouth to lie but closed it again. What if Sonia was expecting him? What if she wanted to see this handsome man in cowboy boots and a worn ranch jacket, who drove a pickup truck that had Idaho license plates and the words Hamilton Construction on the side.

"She lives upstairs." She couldn't see any point in lying. He obviously knew Sonia lived here. "If you would like, I can see if she is home. What name should I tell her? And is there a message you would you like me to give her?"

He glanced up, almost as if he could see through the porch ceiling to the floor above. Now the tight expression showed a crack of emotion, something stark and raw. She thought she saw longing, frustration, pain, before his features became closed again.

"Sure. My name is Luke Hamilton. And you can tell this Sonia—whose real name, by the way, is Elizabeth Sinclair Hamilton—that her husband has come to take her home."

* * * * *

*Watch for Luke and Elizabeth's story,
the next book in the Haven Point series,
available this September from HQN.*

*Rosa Galvez's story,
next in The Women of Brambleberry House series,
will be coming soon.*

THE DADDY MAKEOVER

Chapter One

On a scale of one to ten, Sage Benedetto would probably rate the concept of jogging before sunrise every day somewhere around a negative twenty.

While she highly doubted she would ever evolve enough that she could wholly enjoy these runs, after a month, she had at least grown to tolerate the activity. Her gut didn't automatically cramp at just the idea of throwing on her running shoes and her muscles no longer started to spasm after the first few steps.

She supposed that was a good thing.

This would probably never be her favorite thing to do, but she *had* promised, she reminded herself. And while she had many faults—all of which somehow seemed more glaringly obvious in the pale light of early morning—breaking her word was not among them.

Despite the random muscle aches and her inherent

dislike of just about any activity that involved sending her heart rate into heavy exertion mode, she had even come to discover an ethereal beauty in these quiet early-morning runs.

The towering sea stacks offshore glowed pink in the first, hesitant rays of the sun; this wide, gorgeous stretch of Oregon beach was empty, at least for a little while longer.

Soon the beach would be crowded with treasure hunters looking for shells or colored glass or any other gift the sea surrendered during the night. But for now it was hers.

Hers and Conan's, anyway.

A huge red beast emerged from behind a cluster of rocks and shuffled to her, scaring up a seagull.

She sighed. This was the reason she was here before sunrise, her thigh muscles burning and her breath sawing raggedly. This rangy, melancholy creature was her responsibility, her curse, her unexpected legacy.

"There you are. You can't keep slipping off your leash or we won't do this anymore."

Abigail's big mutt, rescued from the pound right around the time Abigail rescued Sage, cocked his head and gazed at Sage out of doleful eyes the murky dark green of the sea in a November storm.

Some days these jogs along the shore seemed to lift his spirits—the only reason she carried on with them when she would much rather be home in bed for another hour.

This apparently wouldn't be one of those days.

"I know," she murmured, rubbing his chin as she slipped the leash back on. "She loved these kind of mornings, didn't she? With the air clear and cool and sweet and the day just waiting to explode with possibilities. Anything-can-happen days, that's what she called them."

Conan whined a little and lowered himself to the sand, his head sagging to his forepaws as if he were entirely too exhausted to move.

"You've got to snap out of it, bud. We both do."

She tried to swallow down the lump of grief that had taken up permanent residence in her throat during the past month. Her eyes burned and she wondered when these raw moments of sorrow would stop taking her by surprise.

She blinked away the tears. "Come on, dude. I'll race you home."

He gave her a long, considering look, then heaved to his feet and shuffled off in the direction of Brambleberry House, still a mile down the beach. Even at his most ponderous pace, Conan could outrun her. A pretty sad state of affairs, she decided, and tried to pick up her speed.

Focusing on the sand in front of her, she had only made it a few hundred yards down the beach, when she heard a sharp bark. She turned in the direction of the sound; Conan was at the end of his long retractable leash, sitting with a small figure above the high-tide mark in the sand.

The figure was a young girl, one she wasn't even sure was old enough to be considered a tween. A young girl who was wearing only a pale green nightgown and what looked to be seashell-pink flip-flops on her feet.

To Sage's deep surprise, Conan's tail wagged and he nudged at the girl's hand in a blatant invitation to pet him. She hadn't seen Conan greet *anyone* with this kind of friendly enthusiasm for the better part of a month.

Sage scanned the beach looking in vain for the girl's companion. She checked her watch and saw it was barely 6:00 a.m. What on earth was a young girl doing out here alone on an empty stretch of beach at such an hour, and in nightclothes at that?

"Morning," she called out.

The girl waved. "Is this your dog?" she called to Sage with a big smile. "She's so pretty!"

Conan would just love being called pretty. When he wasn't grieving and morose, the beast had more prickly pride than a hedgehog with an attitude. "*She's* a *he*. And, yeah, I guess you could say he's mine."

Partly hers, anyway. Technically, she shared custody of the dog and ownership of Brambleberry House. But she wasn't about to let thoughts of Anna Galvez ruin one of Abigail's anything-can-happen days.

"His name is Conan," she said instead. "I'm Sage."

"Hi, Conan and Sage. My name's Chloe Elizabeth Spencer."

The girl had short, wavy dark hair, intense green eyes and delicate elfin features. If she'd been in a more whimsical mood, Sage might have thought her a water sprite delivered by the sea.

A cold, wet breeze blew off the Pacific and the girl shivered suddenly, drawing Sage's attention back to her thin nightgown and her nearly bare feet. "Chloe, what are you doing out here by yourself so early?"

She shrugged her narrow shoulders with a winsome smile. "Looking for sand dollars. I found four yesterday but they were all broken so I thought if I came out early enough, the tide might leave some good ones and I could get them before anybody else. I promised my friend Henry I'd bring one back to him and I can't break a promise. He lives in the apartment next door. He's only seven and won't be eight until December. I've been eight for two whole months."

"Where's your mom or dad? Do they know you left?"

"My mom's dead." She said the words in a matter-of-fact way that Sage was only too familiar with. "She died when I was six."

"What about your dad, then?"

"I'm not sure. He's probably still asleep. He got mad at me last night because I wanted to find more sand dollars so I decided to come by myself this morning."

Sage looked around at the few isolated cottages and guesthouses on this stretch of beach. "Are you staying close by? I thought I knew all the eight-year-olds in town."

"Every one?" With a lift of her dark eyebrow, the girl somehow managed to look skeptical and intrigued at the same time.

"I do," Sage assured her. "The ones who live here year-round, anyway. I'm sure I don't remember meeting you."

Cannon Beach's population was only a couple thousand year-round. In the summer, those numbers swelled as tourists flocked to the Oregon shore, but they were still a week or so away from the big crowds.

"We're only here for a few days. Maybe a week. But if it's longer, then my dad says he'll have to send me to stay with Mrs. Strictland so he can get some work done. She's my dad's assistant and she hates me. I don't like going to her house."

Though she knew it was unfair to make snap judgments about a man she had not even met, a clear image of the girl's father formed in Sage's mind—a man too busy to hunt for sand dollars with his motherless child and eager to foist her on his minions so he could return to conquering the world.

She fought down her instinctive urge to take Chloe

home with her and watch over her like a sandpiper guarding her nest.

"Do you remember where you're staying, sweetheart?"

Chloe pointed vaguely north. "I think it's that way." She frowned and squinted in the opposite direction. "Or maybe that way. I'm not sure."

"Are you in a hotel or a condo?"

The girl shook her head. "It's a house, right on the beach. My dad would have liked to stay at The Sea Urchin but Mr. Wu said they were all booked. He didn't look very happy when he said it. I think he doesn't like my dad very much."

No wonder she had always considered Stanley Wu an excellent judge of character. She hadn't even met Chloe's father and already she disliked him.

"But what I don't get," the girl went on, "is if he doesn't like my dad, why is he going to sell him his hotel?"

Sage blinked at that unexpected bit of information. She hadn't heard Stanley and Jade Wu were considering selling The Sea Urchin. They had been fixtures in Cannon Beach for decades, their elegant boutique hotel of twenty or so guest rooms consistently named among the best accommodations along the coast.

"Do you know if your rental is close to The Sea Urchin?"

Chloe screwed up her features. "Pretty close, but I think it's on the other side. I didn't walk past it this morning, I don't think."

Though she seemed remarkably unconcerned about standing on wet sand in only her nightgown and flip-flops, she shivered a little and pulled Conan closer.

Sage sighed, bidding a regretful goodbye to any hopes she might have entertained of enjoying a quiet moment for breakfast before heading to work. She couldn't leave this girl alone here, not when she apparently didn't have the first clue how to find her way home.

She shrugged out of her hooded sweatshirt and tucked it around Chloe's small shoulders, immediately shivering herself as the cool ocean breeze danced over her perspiration-dampened skin.

"Come on. I'll help you find where you're staying. Your dad will be worried."

Conan barked—whether in agreement with the plan or skepticism about the level of concern of Chloe's father, she wasn't sure. Whatever the reason, the dog led the way up the beach toward downtown with more enthusiasm than he'd shown for the ocean-side run. Chloe and Sage followed with the girl chatting the entire way.

In no time, Sage knew all about Chloe's best friend, Henry, her favorite TV show and her distant, work-obsessed father. She had also helped Chloe find a half-dozen pristine sand dollars the gulls hadn't picked at yet, as well as a couple of pieces of driftwood and a gorgeous piece of translucent orange agate.

"How do you know so much about shells and birds and stuff?" Chloe asked after Sage pointed out a surf scoter and a grebe.

She smiled at Chloe's obvious awe. "It's my job to know it. I'm a naturalist. Do you know what that is?"

"Somebody who studies nature?"

"Excellent! That's exactly what I do. I work for an organization that teaches people more about the world around them. When I'm not working on research, I get to show people the plants and animals that live here on the Oregon Coast. I even teach classes to kids. In fact, our first nature camp of the summer starts today. That's how I know so many of the local children, because most of them have been my campers at some time or another."

"Really? That's so cool!"

She smiled back, charmed by the funny little creature. "Yeah, I think so, too."

"Can I come to your camp?" The girl didn't wait for an answer. "My dad has another hotel in Carmel. That's in California, too, like San Francisco where we live. Once I went with him there and my nanny took me to see the tide pools. We saw starfish and anemones and everything. It was *super*cool."

Her nanny, again. Did the girl's father even acknowledge she existed?

"Did you at least tell your nanny where you were going this morning?" she asked.

Chloe stopped to pick up a chipped shell to add to the burgeoning collection in her nightgown pockets. "Don't have one. Señora Marcos quit two days ago. That's why my dad had to bring me here, too, to Cannon Beach, because he didn't know what else to do with me and it was too late for him to cancel his trip. But Señora Marcos wasn't the nanny that who took me to see the tide pools anyway. That was Jamie. She quit, too. And the one after that was Ms. Ludwig. She had bad breath and eyes like a mean pig. You know what? I was *glad* when she said she couldn't stand another minute of me. I didn't like her, either."

She said this with such nonchalance the words nearly broke Sage's heart. It sounded like a very lonely existence—a self-involved father and a string of humorless nannies unwilling to exert any effort to reach one energetic little girl.

The story had a bitterly familiar ring to it, one that left her with sick anger balled up in her stomach.

None of her business, she reminded herself. She was a stranger and didn't know the dynamics between Chloe and her father. Her own experience was apropos of nothing.

"Does any of this look familiar?" she asked. "Do you think your beach house is close by?"

The girl frowned. "I'm not sure. It's a brown house made out of wood. I remember that."

Sage sighed. *Brown* and *made of wood* might be helpful information if it didn't describe most of the houses in Cannon Beach. The town had strict zoning laws dictating the style and aesthetics of all construction, ensuring the beachside charm remained.

They walked a little farther, past weathered cedar houses and shops. Sage was beginning to wonder if perhaps she ought to call in Bill Rich, the local police chief, when Chloe suddenly squealed with excitement, which prompted Conan to answer with a bark.

"There it is! Right there." Chloe pointed to a house with an unobstructed view of the ocean and the sea stacks. Sage had always loved the place, with its quaint widow's walk and steep gables.

"Are you sure?" she asked.

Chloe nodded. "I remember the fish windchimes. I heard them when I was going to sleep and it sounded like angels singing. And I remember the house next door had those big balls that look like ginormous Christmas ornaments."

Sage shifted her gaze to take in the collection of Japanese glass fishing floats that adorned Blair and Kristine Saunders' landscape.

"Do you have a key?" she asked the girl.

Chloe held tight to Conan's collar. "No. My dad didn't

give me one. But I climbed out the window of my room.
I can just go back that way."

Sage was tempted to let her. A quick glance at her
watch told her it was now twenty minutes to seven and
she had exactly forty minutes to change and make it in to
work. Her life would certainly be easier if she let Chloe
sneak into her rental house, but it wouldn't be right, she
knew. She needed to make sure the girl's father knew
what Chloe had been up to.

"We'd better make sure your dad knows you're safe."

"I bet he didn't even know I was gone," Chloe muttered. "He's going to be mad when he finds out."

"You can't just sneak out on your own, Chloe. It's not
safe. Anything could have happened to you out on the
beach by yourself. I have to tell your dad. I'm sorry."

She rang the doorbell, then felt like the worst sort of
weasel when Chloe glared at her.

Before she could defend her action, the door opened
and she forgot everything she intended to say—as well
as her own name and how to put two words together.

Chloe neglected to mention the little fact that her father was gorgeous. Sage swallowed hard. The odd trembling in her thighs had nothing to do with her earlier run.

He had rugged, commanding features, with high
cheekbones, a square, firm jaw and green eyes a shade
darker than his daughter's. It was obvious he'd just
stepped out of the shower. His hair was wet, his chest
bare and he wore only a pair of gray trousers and an unbuttoned blue dress shirt.

Sage swallowed again. Why did she have to meet a
man like him *today* when she smelled like wet dog and
four miles of sweat? And she already disliked him, she
reminded herself.

"Can I help you?" he asked. She didn't mistake the shadow of irritation on those rugged features.

She blinked and tugged Chloe forward.

"Chloe?" he stared at his daughter, baffled concern replacing annoyance. "What's going on? I thought you were still sound asleep in your bed. What are you doing out here in your nightgown?"

She didn't answer for a moment then she shrugged. "Nothing. I just went for a walk to get some more sand dollars. I found a ton. Well, Sage helped me. Look." She thrust her armload at her father.

He didn't take them, gazing at his daughter's hard-won treasure with little visible reaction. Or so Sage thought, until she happened to catch the storm clouds scudding across his green eyes like a winter squall stirring up seafoam.

"What do you mean, you went for a walk? It's barely six-thirty in the morning!"

Chloe shrugged. "I woke up early but you were still sleeping and I didn't want to wake you up. I was just going to be gone for a minute, but…then I couldn't remember how to get back."

"You are in serious trouble, young lady."

His voice was suddenly as hard as a sea stack and Sage was automatically seven years old again, trying desperately to understand how her world could change with such sudden cruelty.

"I am?" Chloe's fingers seemed to tighten on Conan's collar but the dog didn't so much as whimper.

"You know you're not supposed to leave the house alone. You *know* that. *Any* house, whether our own or a temporary one."

"But Daddy—"

"You promised me, Chloe. Do you remember that? I knew bringing you along on this trip would be a huge mistake but you promised you would behave yourself, for once. Do you call running off down the beach by yourself behaving?"

He didn't raise his voice one single decibel but muscles inside Sage's stomach clenched and she hated it, hated it. The terrible thing was, she couldn't blame the man. Not really. She could imagine any parent would be upset to discover a child had wandered away in an unknown setting.

She knew it was a normal reaction, but still this particular situation had an entirely too-familiar ring to it.

"But I wasn't alone for very long," Chloe insisted. "I made two new friends, Daddy. This is Sage and her dog's name is Conan. She lives here and she knows all kinds of things about birds and shells and fish. She's a naturist."

"Naturalist," Sage corrected.

"Right. A naturalist. She teaches summer camp and tells kids about shells and birds and stuff like that."

For the first time since she rang the doorbell, the man shifted his gaze to her.

"I'm Sage Benedetto," she said, hoping her cool voice masked the nerves still jumping in her stomach. Though she wanted to yell and scream and ask him what the hell he thought he was doing trying to quash this sweet little girl's spirit, the words tangled in her throat.

"I live down the coast about a half mile in the big Victorian," she said instead.

He stared at her for a long second, an odd, arrested look in his eyes. She didn't know how long he might have stared at her if Conan hadn't barked. The man blinked a little then closed his fingers around hers.

She was quite certain she imagined the odd little sizzle when their fingers touched. She *didn't* imagine the slightly disconcerted expression that crossed his features.

"Eben Spencer. Thank you for taking the time to bring my daughter home."

"You're welcome," she said in that same cool voice. "You might want to keep a closer eye on her."

"Easier said than done, Ms. Benedetto. But thank you for the advice."

"No problem."

She forced a tight smile for him, then a more genuine one for his daughter. "Bye, Chloe. You need to rinse those sand dollars in fresh water until the water runs clear, then soak them in bleach and water for five or ten minutes. That way they'll be hard enough for you to take them home without breaking. Remember, Henry's counting on you."

The girl giggled as Sage called to Conan, who barked at her, nuzzled Chloe, then bounded off ahead as they headed back toward Brambleberry House.

He watched her jog down the beach, the strange woman with the wild mane of honey-colored hair and thinly veiled disdain in her haunting amber-flecked brown eyes.

She didn't like him. That much was obvious. He hadn't missed the coldness in her expression nor the way she clipped off the ends of her words when she spoke to him.

He wasn't sure why that bothered him so much. Plenty of people disliked him. Constantly striving to win approval from others simply for the sake of their approval wasn't in his nature and he had long ago learned some measure of unpopularity was one of the prices one paid for success.

He was damn good at what he did, had taken his family's faltering hotel business and through careful management, a shrewd business plan and attention to detail turned it into a formidable force in the luxury hotel business.

Over the years, he had bumped up against plenty of affronted egos and prickly psyches. But seeing the disdain in Sage Benedetto's unsettling eyes annoyed him. And the very fact that he was bothered by it only irked him more.

What did he care what some wind-tousled stranger with a massive, ungainly mutt for a dog thought of him?

She stopped at a huge, cheerful yellow Victorian with incongruent lavender trim some distance down the beach. He watched her go inside and couldn't stop thinking about that odd jolt when their hands had touched.

It was completely crazy but he could swear some kind of strange, shimmery connection had arced between them and he had almost felt as if something inside him recognized her.

Foolish. Completely unlike him. He wasn't the sort to let his imagination run wild—nor was he the kind of man to be attracted to a woman who so clearly did not share his interest.

"She's nice. I like her. And I *love* her dog. Conan is so cute," Chloe chirped from inside the room and Eben realized with considerable dismay that he still stood at the window looking after her in the early-morning light.

He jerked his attention away from thoughts of Sage Benedetto and focused on his daughter. Chloe had spread her treasures on the coffee table in their temporary living room, leaving who knew what kind of sand and grime on the polished mahogany.

He sighed, shut the door and advanced on her. "All right, young lady. Let's hear it."

He did his best to be firm, his tone the same one he would use with a recalcitrant employee.

These were the kind of moments that reminded him all too painfully that he didn't have the first idea how to correctly discipline a child. God knows, he had no childhood experience to draw from. He and his sister had virtually raised each other, caught in a hellish no-man's-land between two people who had had no business reproducing.

Between their mother's tantrums and violent moods and their father's shameless self-indulgence, it was a wonder either he or his sister could function as adults.

Cami had found happiness. As for him, he was doing the best he could not to repeat the mistakes of his parents.

"You know the rules about leaving the house by yourself. What do you have to say for yourself?"

Chloe shifted her gaze to the sand dollars in front of her and he hated himself when he saw the animation fade from her eyes. "I'm sorry, Daddy. I promise I won't do it again."

Eben sighed. "You say that every time, but then you find some other way to cause trouble."

"I don't mean to." Her voice was small, sad, and he found himself wishing fiercely that he were better at this.

"I try to be good but it's so *hard*."

He had to agree with her. Nothing was as hard as trying to do the right thing all the time. Even right now, some wild part of him wanted to call up Stanley and Jade Wu and tell them to go to hell, that he didn't want their stupid hotel if they were going to make him work this hard for it.

That same wild corner of his psyche wanted to toss Chloe onto his shoulders and run out into the surf with her in his bare feet, to feel the sand squishing between his toes and the cold water sluicing over his skin and her squeals of laughter ringing in his ears.

He tamped it down, containing it deep inside. "Try a little harder, okay?" he said sternly. "This deal is important to me, Chloe. I've told you that. You've got to be on your best behavior. I can't afford any distractions. It's only for a few more days, then I promise when we get back to San Francisco, we'll find a new nanny."

She nodded, her little mouth set in a tight line that told him clearly she was just as annoyed with him as Sage Benedetto had been.

"I'm supposed to have meetings with Mr. and Mrs. Wu most of the day so I've made arrangements for a caregiver through an agency here. All I'm asking is for you to behave. Can you try for a few hours?"

She looked up at him through her lashes. "When you're done with your meeting, can we buy a kite and fly it on the beach? Sage said Cannon Beach is the perfect place to fly kites because it's always windy and because there's lots of room so you don't run into people."

"If you promise to be on your best behavior, we can talk about it after my meetings."

She ran to him and threw her arms around his waist. "I'll be so good, Daddy, I promise, I promise, I *promise*."

He returned her embrace, his heart a heavy weight in his chest. He hated thinking of her going to boarding school at the end of the summer. But in the two years since Brooke died, Chloe had run through six nannies with her headstrong behavior. Some sort of record, he was certain. He couldn't do this by himself and he was running out of options.

"Maybe Sage and Conan can help us fly the kite," Chloe exclaimed. "Can they, Daddy?"

The very last thing he wanted to do was spend more time with Sage Benedetto of the judgmental eyes and the luscious mouth.

"We'll have to see," he said. He could only hope a day of trying to be on her best behavior would exhaust Chloe sufficiently that she would forget all about their temporary neighbor and her gargantuan canine.

Chapter Two

"Sorry, Conan. You've got to stay here."

Sage muscled her bike around Anna's minivan and wheeled it out of the small garage, trying to ignore the soulful eyes gazing back at her through the flowers on the other side of the low wrought-iron fence circling the house. "You'll be all right. I'll come back at lunchtime to throw a ball with you for awhile, okay?"

Conan didn't look convinced. He added a morose whine, his head cocked to one side and his chin tucked into his chest. She blew out a frustrated breath. They had been through this routine just about every day for the past month and the dog didn't seem to be adjusting.

She couldn't really blame the poor thing for not wanting to be alone. He was used to having Abigail's company all day.

The two of them had been inseparable from the moment Abigail had brought him home from the pound.

Conan would ride along with Abigail to the shops, his head hanging out the back seat window of her big Buick, tongue lolling. He would patiently wait for her on the porch of her friends' houses when she would make her regular round of visits, would sniff through the yard while Abigail tended her flowers, would curl up every evening beside her favorite chair in front of the huge bay windows overlooking the ocean.

Conan was lonely and Sage could certainly empathize with that. "I'm sorry, bud," she said again. "I'll be back before you know it."

The dog suddenly barked, his ears perking up like twin mountain peaks. He barreled to the front porch just as the door opened. From her place on the other side of the fence, Sage watched Anna Galvez—trim and proper in a navy blazer and gray slacks—set down her briefcase to greet the dog with a smile and a scratch under his chin.

Anna murmured something to the dog but Sage was too far away to hear. She wasn't too far to see Anna's warm smile for Conan trickle away when she straightened and saw Sage on the other side of the wrought-iron.

She brushed hair off her slacks and picked up her briefcase, then walked to the gate.

"Good morning. I thought I heard you come down the stairs some time ago. I figured you had already left."

Sage straddled her bike, not at all in the mood for conversation. Her fault for sticking around when she heard the door open. If she'd left then, she could have been halfway to town by now. But that would have been rude and she couldn't seem to shake the feeling Abigail wanted her to at least pretend politeness with Anna.

"I couldn't walk out in the middle of his guiltfest."

"He's good at that, isn't he?" Anna frowned at the dog.

"I expected him to be past this phase by now. It's been a month. Don't you think he should already be accustomed to the changes in his life?"

Sage shrugged. "I guess some of us need a little more time than others to grieve."

Anna's mouth tightened and Sage immediately regretted the low comment. So much for politeness. She wanted to apologize but couldn't seem to form the words.

"I wish I could take him with me to work," Anna said after an awkward moment.

Sage gave the other woman a disbelieving look. Anna couldn't possibly want a big, gangly dog wreaking havoc with the tchotchkes and whatnot in her book and gift shop in town. Conan would bankrupt her in less than an hour.

"I've been coming home for lunch to keep him company for awhile. Throw a ball, give him a treat. That kind of thing. For now, that's the best I can do."

For an instant, guilt flickered in Anna's brown eyes but she blinked it away. "I'm sorry. I should have realized you were doing so much. I'm a little preoccupied with some things at the store right now but it's only right that I do my share. Abigail left him to both of us, which means he's my responsibility as well. I'm sorry," she said again.

"Don't worry about it."

"I'm afraid I can't come back to the house today," she said with a frown. "But I'll try to arrange my schedule so I can take a few hours to be here with him tomorrow."

"I'm sure he would enjoy that," Sage said. As always, she regretted the awkwardness between her and Anna. She knew Abigail had wanted them to be friends but Sage doubted it was possible. They were simply too different.

Anna was brisk and efficient, her world centered on By-The-Wind, the shop she had purchased from Abigail two years earlier after having managed it for a year before that. Sage didn't believe Anna had even the tiniest morsel of a sense of humor—or if she did, it was buried so deeply beneath spreadsheets and deposit slips that Sage had never seen sign of it.

After two weeks of sharing the same house, though in different apartments, Anna was still a stranger to Sage. Tightly wound and tense, Anna never seemed to relax.

Sage figured they were as different as it was possible for two women to be, one quirky and independent-minded, the other staid and responsible. Yet Abigail had loved them both.

When she was being brutally honest with herself, she could admit *that* was at least part of the reason for her natural reserve with Anna Galvez—small-minded, petty jealousy.

A weird kind of sibling rivalry, even.

Abigail had loved Anna—enough to leave her half of Brambleberry House and all its contents. Sage knew she was being selfish but she couldn't help resenting it. Not the house—she couldn't care less about that—but Abigail's affection.

"I'd better get going," Sage said.

"Uh, would you like a ride since we're both going the same way?"

She shook her head. "I'm good. Thanks anyway. If you give me a ride, I won't be able to come home at lunch."

"Oh. Right. I'll see you later then."

Sage stuffed her bag in the wicker basket of her one-speed bike and headed off to town. A moment later, Anna pulled past in her white minivan, moving at a cautious speed on the curving road.

Sage knew the roomy van was a practical choice since

Anna probably had to transport things for the store, but she couldn't help thinking how the vehicle seemed to perfectly mirror Anna's personality: bland and business-like and boring.

Somebody had certainly climbed out of bed on the bitchy side, she chided herself, resolving that she would think only pleasant thoughts about Anna Galvez today, if she thought of her at all.

The same went for little sea sprites she had met on the beach and their entirely too-gorgeous fathers. She had too much to do today with all the chaos and confusion of her first day of camp to spend time thinking about Chloe and Eben Spencer.

The road roughly followed the shore here. Through the heavy pines, she could catch a glimpse of the sea stacks and hear the low murmur of the waves. Three houses down, she waved at a neighbor pulling out of his driveway in a large pickup truck with Garrett Carpentry on the side.

He was heading the other direction toward Manzanita but Will Garrett pulled up alongside her and rolled down his passenger-side window. "Morning, Sage."

She straddled her bike. "Hey, Will."

"Sorry I haven't made it over to look at the work you want done on the house. Been a busy week."

She stared. "Work? What work?"

"Anna called me last week. Said she wanted me to give her a bid for a possible remodel of the kitchen and bathroom on the second-floor apartment. She also wanted me to check the feasibility of knocking out a couple walls in Abigail's apartment to open up the floor plan a little."

"Oh, did she?"

Anger swept over her, hot and bright. Any warmth

she might have been trying to force herself into feeling toward Anna seeped out into the dirt.

How dare she?

They had agreed to discuss any matters pertaining to the house and come to a consensus on them, but Anna hadn't said a single word about any of this.

Abigail had left the house to both of them, which meant they *both* should make minor little decisions like knocking out walls and remodeling kitchens. Yet Anna hadn't bothered to bring this up, even when they were talking a few moments ago.

Was her opinion so insignificant?

She knew her anger was overblown—irrational, even—but she couldn't help it. It was too soon. She wasn't ready to go knocking down walls and remodeling kitchens, erasing any sign of the crumbling old house Abigail had loved so dearly.

"She didn't talk to you about it?"

"Not yet," she said grimly.

Something in her tone of voice—or maybe the smoke curling out of her ears—had tipped him off that she wasn't pleased. His expression turned wary. "Well, uh, if you talk to her, let her know I'm going to try to come by this evening to check things out, if that's still okay. Seven or so. One of you can give me a buzz if that's a problem."

He looked eager to escape. She sighed—she shouldn't vent her frustration on Will. It certainly wasn't his fault Anna Galvez was a bossy, managing, stiff-necked pencil-pusher who seemed to believe she knew what was best for the whole bloody world.

She forced a smile. "I'm sure it will be fine. See you tonight."

Though he didn't smile in return—Will rarely smiled

anymore—he nodded and put his truck in gear, then headed down the road.

She watched after him for only a moment, then continued pedaling her way toward town.

She still simmered with anger toward Anna's high-handedness, but it was tempered by her usual ache of sorrow for Will. So much pain in the world. Sometimes she couldn't bear it.

She tried her best to leave the world a better place than when she found it. But riding a bike to work and volunteering with Meals on Wheels seemed exercises in futility when she couldn't do a darn thing to ease the burden of those she cared about.

Will was another of Abigail's lost sheep—Sage's affectionate term for the little band of creatures her friend had watched over with her endless supply of love. Abigail seemed to collect people in need and gathered them toward her. The lonely, the forgotten, the grieving. Will had been right there with the rest of them.

No, that wasn't exactly true. Will had belonged to Abigail long before he had ever needed watching over. He had grown up in the same house where he now lived and he and his wife Robin had both known and loved Abigail all their lives.

Sage had lived at Brambleberry House long enough to remember him when he was a handsome charmer, with a teasing grin for everyone. He used to charge into Abigail's parlor and sweep her off her feet, twirling her around and around.

He always had a funny story to tell and he had invariably been the first one on the scene whenever anyone needed help—whether it was moving a piano or spreading a dump-truckload of gravel on a driveway or pumping out a flooded basement.

When Sage moved in upstairs at Brambleberry, Will had become like a big brother to her, offering her the same warm affection he poured out on everyone else in town. Robin had been just as bighearted—lovely and generous and open.

When Robin discovered Sage didn't having a dining room table yet, she had put her husband to work on one and Will had crafted a beautiful round piece of art as a housewarming present.

Sage had soaked it all in, had reveled in the miracle that she had finally found a place to belong among these wonderful people who had opened their lives to her.

If Abigail had been the heart of her circle of friends, Will had been the sturdy, reliable backbone and Robin the nerve center. Their little pigtailed toddler Cara had just been everyone's joy.

Then in the blink of an eye, everything changed.

So much pain.

She let out a breath as she gave a hand signal and turned onto the street toward work. Robin and Will had been crazy about each other. She had walked in on them once in a corner of Abigail's yard at a Fourth of July barbecue. They hadn't been kissing, had just been holding each other, but even from several yards away Sage could feel the love vibrating between them, a strong, tangible connection.

She couldn't imagine the depth of Will's pain at knowing that kind of love and losing it.

Oddly, the mental meanderings made her think of Eben Spencer, sweet little Chloe's abrupt, unfriendly father. The girl had said her mother was dead. Did Eben mourn her loss as deeply as Will did Robin and little Cara, killed two years ago by a drunk driver as they were walking across the street not far from here?

She pulled up to the center and looped her bike lock through the rack out front, determined to put Eben and Chloe Spencer out of her head.

She didn't want to think about either of them. She had learned early in her time at Cannon Beach not to pay much mind to the tourists. Like the fragile summer, they disappeared too soon.

Her resolve was tested even before lunchtime. Since the weather held through the morning, she and her dozen new campers gathered at a picnic table under the spreading boughs of a pine tree outside the center.

She was showing them intertidal zone specimens in aquarium display cases collected earlier that morning by center staffers when she heard a familiar voice call her name.

She turned to find her new friend from the morning barreling toward her, eyes wide, her gamine face animated.

Moving at a slower pace came Eben Spencer, his silk, undoubtedly expensive tie off-center and his hair slightly messed. He did *not* look as if he were having a great day.

Of course, when Sage was having a lousy day, she ended up with circles under her eyes, stress lines cutting through her face and a pounding headache she could swear was visible for miles around.

Eben Spencer just looked slightly rumpled in an entirely too-sexy way.

Heedless of the other children in the class, Chloe rushed to her and threw her arms around Sage's waist.

"It's not my fault this time, I promise."

Under other circumstances, she might have been annoyed at the interruption to her class but she couldn't ignore Chloe's distress—or the frustration stamped on Eben's features.

"Lindsey, can you take over for a minute?" she asked her assistant camp director.

"Of course." The college student who had worked for the nature center every summer since high school stepped forward and Sage led Eben and Chloe away from the interested campers.

"What's not your fault? What's going on?"

"I didn't do *anything*, I swear. It's not my fault at *all* that she was so mean."

Sage looked to Eben for elucidation.

"The caregiver the agency in Portland sent over was… unacceptable." Eben raked a hand through his wavy hair, messing it even more.

"She was mean to me," Chloe said. "She wouldn't let me walk out to the beach, even when I told her my dad said it was okay. She didn't believe me so I called my dad and she got mad at me and pulled my hair and said I was a bad word."

From that explanation, she gathered the caregiver hadn't appreciated an eight-year-old going over her head.

"Oh, dear. A bad word, huh?"

Chloe nodded. "She called me a spoiled little poop, only she didn't say poop."

"I'm sorry," Sage said, trying to figure out exactly what part she played in this unfolding drama.

"I didn't care about the name but I didn't like that she pulled my hair. She didn't have to be so mean. I think she was a *big* poop."

"Chloe," her father said sternly.

"Well, I do. So I called my dad again and told him what she did and he came right over from The Sea Urchin and told her to leave right now. He said a bad word, too, but I think she deserved it."

She gave a quick glance at her father, then mouthed H-E-L-L.

Sage had to fight a smile. "I see," she said. She found it admirably unexpected that Eben would rush to his daughter's defense.

"And now the place that sent her doesn't have anybody else to take care of me."

Sage raised her eyebrows and glanced at Eben. "I suppose the temp pool is probably pretty shallow right now since the tourist season is heading into full gear."

"I'm figuring that out," he answered. "The agency says it will be at least tomorrow or the next day before they can find someone else. In the meantime, I've got conference calls scheduled all day."

Sage waited to hear what all of this had to do with her, though she was beginning to guess. Her speculation was confirmed by his next words.

"I can't expect Chloe to entertain herself in a strange place while I'm occupied. I remembered you mentioning a summer camp and hoped that you might have room for one more."

"Oh, I'm sorry. We're completely full."

The center had always maintained a strict limit of twelve campers per session to ensure an adequate adult-to-student ratio. Beyond that, she had her hands full this year. Three of the children had learning disabilities and she had already figured out after the first few hours that two more might be on their way to becoming behavior problems if she couldn't figure out how to channel their energy.

Even as she thought of the trouble to her staff if she added another camper, her mind raced trying to figure out how to accommodate Eben and his daughter.

"I was afraid you would say that." He smiled stiffly. "Thank you for your time anyway. We'll try to figure something else out."

He looked resigned but accepting. His daughter, on the other hand, appeared close to tears. Her shoulders slumped and her chin quivered.

"But I really wanted to come to camp with Sage," she wailed. "It sounded super, super fun! I don't want to stay in a boring house all day long while you talk on the phone!"

"Chloe, that's enough. If the camp doesn't have room for you, that's the way it is."

"You think I'm a little poop, too, don't you?" Chloe's chin was definitely quivering now. "That's why you don't want me in your camp. You don't like me, either."

"Oh, honey, that's not true. We just have rules about how many children we can have in our camp."

"I would be really good. You wouldn't even know I'm here. Oh, please, Sage!"

She studied them both—Chloe so dejected and her father resigned. She had to wonder how much pride he had forced himself to swallow for his daughter's sake to bring her here and ask Sage for a favor.

How could she disappoint them?

"We're at capacity," she finally said, "but I think we can probably find room to squeeze in one more."

"You mean it? Really?" The girl looked afraid to hope. Sage nodded and Chloe squealed with delight and hugged her again. "Yes! Thank you, thank you, thank you!"

Sage hugged her in return. "You're welcome. You're going to have to work hard and listen to me and the other grown-ups, though."

"I will. I'll be super super good."

Sage glanced up to meet Eben's gaze and found him watching her with that same odd, slightly thunderstruck expression she had seen him wear earlier that morning. She didn't fathom it—nor did she quite understand why it made her insides tremble.

"I'm busy with the class out here," she spoke briskly to hide her reaction, "but if you go inside the center, Amy can provide you with the registration information. Tell her I said we could make an exception this once and add one more camper beyond our usual limit."

"Thank you, Ms. Benedetto." One corner of his mouth lifted into a relieved smile and the trembling in her stomach seemed to go into hyperdrive, much like the Harder twins after a little sugar.

Somehow that slight smile made him look even more attractive and her reaction to it alarmed her.

"Amy will give you a list of supplies you will need to provide for Chloe." Annoyance at herself sharpened her voice. "She's going to need waterproof boots and a warmer jacket this afternoon when we go out to Haystack, though we can probably scrounge something for her today."

"Thank you."

"May I go with the other children?" Chloe asked, her green eyes gleaming with eagerness.

"Sure," Sage said. She and Eben watched Chloe race

to the picnic table and squeeze into a spot between two girls of similar ages, who slid over to make room for her.

She turned back to Eben. "Our class ends at four, whether your conference calls are done or not."

He sent her a swift look. "I'll be sure to hang up on my attorneys if they run long. I wouldn't want to keep you waiting."

"It's not me you would be letting down. It's Chloe."

His mouth tightened with clear irritation but she watched in fascination as he carefully pushed it away and resumed a polite expression. "Thank you again for accommodating Chloe. I know you're stretching the rules for her and I do appreciate it."

Without waiting for an answer, he turned around and walked toward the center. She watched him go, that fast, take-no-prisoners stride eating up the beach.

What a disagreeable man. He ought to have a British accent for all the stuffy reserve in his voice.

She sighed. Too bad he had to be gorgeous. Someone with his uptight personality ought to have the looks to match, tight, thin lips, a honker of a nose, and squinty pale eyes set too close together.

Instead, Eben Spencer had been blessed with stunning green eyes, wavy dark hair and lean, chiseled features.

Didn't matter, she told herself. In her book, personality mattered far more than looks and by all indications Eben Spencer scored a big fat zero in that department.

"Ms. B., Ms. B.! What's this one? Lindsey doesn't know."

She turned back to the picnic table. She had work to do, she reminded herself sternly. She needed to keep her attention tightly focused on her day camp and the thirteen children in it—not on particularly gorgeous hotel magnates with all the charm of a spiny urchin.

Chapter Three

"Your daughter will just *love* the day camp." The bubbly receptionist inside the office delivered a thousand-watt smile out of white teeth in perfect alignment as she handed him the papers.

"It's one of our most popular summer activities," she went on. "People come from all over to bring their children to learn about the rocky shore and the kids just eat it up. And our camp director is just wonderful. The children all adore her. Sometimes I think she's just a big kid herself."

He raised an eyebrow, his mind on Sage Benedetto, and her honey-blond curls, lush curves and all that blatant sensuality.

"Is that right?" he murmured.

The receptionist either didn't catch his dry tone or chose to ignore him. He voted for the former.

"You should see her when they're tide-pooling, in her

big old boots and a grin as big as the Haystack. Sage knows everything about the coastal ecosystem. She can identify every creature in a tide pool in an instant and can tell you what they eat, how they reproduce and who their biggest predator might be. She's just amazing."

He didn't want to hear the receptionist gush about Sage Benedetto. He really preferred to know as little about her as possible. He had already spent the morning trying to shake thoughts of her out of his head so he could focus on business.

He smiled politely. "That's good to hear. I'm relieved Chloe will be in competent hands."

"Oh, you won't find better hands anywhere on the coast, I promise," she assured him.

For a brief second, he had a wickedly inappropriate reaction to that bit of information, but with determined effort, he managed to channel his attention back to the registration papers in front of them.

He quickly read over and signed every document required—just a little more paperwork than he usually faced when purchasing a new hotel.

He didn't mind the somewhat exorbitant fee or the tacked-on late-registration penalty. If not for Sage and her summer camp, his options would have been severely limited.

He didn't have high hopes that the agency in Portland would find someone quickly, which would probably mean he would have to cancel the entire trip and abandon the conference calls scheduled for the week or fly in his assistant to keep an eye on Chloe, something neither Chloe nor Betsy would appreciate.

No, Sage Benedetto had quite likely saved a deal that was fiercely important to Spencer Hotels.

He would have liked to surrender Chloe to someone a little more…restrained…but he wasn't going to quibble.

"All right. She's all set, registered for the entire week. Now, you know you're going to need to provide your daughter with a pair of muck boots and rain-gear, right?"

"Ms. Benedetto already informed me of that. I'll be sure Chloe is equipped with everything she needs tomorrow."

"Here's the rest of the list of what you need."

"Thank you."

He took it from her with a quick glance at his watch. He was supposed to be talking to his advertising team in New York in twenty minutes and he wasn't sure he was going to make it.

Outside, steely clouds had begun to gather with the capriciousness of seaside weather. Even with them, the view was stunning, with dramatic sea stacks offshore and a wide sandy beach that seemed to stretch for miles.

He shifted his gaze to the group of children still gathered around the picnic table. Chloe looked as if she had settled right in. As she chattered to one of the other girls, her eyes were bright and happy in a way he hadn't seen in a long time.

He was vastly relieved, grateful to see her natural energy directed toward something educational and fun instead of toward getting into as much trouble as humanly possible for an eight-year-old girl.

This next few days promised to be difficult with all the new conditions Stanley Wu was imposing on the sale of his hotel. Having a good place for Chloe to go during the day would ease his path considerably.

His attention twisted to the woman standing at the head of the table. In khaki slacks and a navy-blue knit shirt, Sage Benedetto should have looked stern and official. But she was laughing at something one of the children said, her blond curls escaping a loose braid.

With her olive-toned skin and blonde hair, she looked exotic and sensual. Raw desire tightened his gut but he forced himself to ignore it as he walked the short distance to the cluster of children.

Chloe barely looked up when he approached. "I'm leaving," he told her. "I'll be back this afternoon to pick you up."

"Okay. Bye, Daddy," she chirped, then immediately turned her attention back to the other girls and their activity as if she had already forgotten his presence.

He stood by the table for a moment, feeling awkward and wishing he were better at this whole parenting thing. His love for his daughter was as vast and tumultuous as the ocean and most of the time it scared the hell out of him.

He looked up and found Sage watching him, a warmth in her eyes that hadn't been there earlier. Sunlight slanted beneath the clouds, turning the hair escaping her braid to a riotous halo of curls around her face.

She looked like something from an old master painting, lush and earthy, and when her features lightened into a smile, lust tightened inside him again.

"Don't worry, Mr. Spencer. We'll take good care of Chloe."

He nodded, angry again at this instinctive reaction to her. The only thing for it was to leave the situation, he decided, to avoid contact with her as much as possible.

"I have no doubts you will. Excuse me. I've got to return to work."

At his abrupt tone, the warmth slid away from her features. "Right. Your empire-building awaits."

He almost preferred her light mockery to that momentary flicker of warmth. It certainly made it easier for him to keep his inappropriate responses under control.

"I'll be back for Chloe at four."

He started to walk away, then paused, feeling churlish and ungrateful. She was doing him a huge favor and he couldn't return that favor with curt rudeness.

"Uh, thank you again for finding space for her. I appreciate it."

Her smile was much cooler this time. "I have no doubts you do," she murmured.

He studied her for a moment, then matched the temperature of his own smile to hers and walked to the nature center's parking lot where his rented Jaguar waited.

His mind was still on Sage Benedetto as he drove through town, stopping at a crosswalk for a trio of gray-haired shoppers to make their slow way across the road, then two mothers pushing strollers.

He forced himself to curb his impatience as he waited. Even though it was early June, the tourist season on the Oregon Coast seemed to be in full swing, something that boded favorably for someone in the hotel business.

He had learned that the season never really ended here, unlike some other resort areas. There was certainly a high season and a low season but people came to the coast year-round.

In the summer, families came to play in the sand and enjoy the natural beauty; winter brought storm watchers and beachcombers to the wide public beaches.

Though his ultimate destination was his temporary quarters, he automatically slowed as he approached The Sea Urchin. He could see it set back among Sitka spruce and pine: the graceful, elegant architecture, the weathered gray-stone facade, the extravagant flower gardens already blooming with vibrant color.

He wanted it, as he hadn't coveted anything in a long, long time. In the four months since he had first seen the hotel on a trip down the coast to scout possible property locations, he had become obsessed with owning it.

His original plan had been to build a new hotel somewhere along the coast, possibly farther south in the Newport area.

But the moment he caught sight of The Sea Urchin—and Cannon Beach—the place called to him in a way he couldn't begin to explain.

He had no idea why it affected him so strongly. He wasn't one for capricious business moves, heaven knows. In the dozen years since he'd taken over his family company at the ripe age of twenty-four, he had tried to make each decision with a cool head and a sharp eye for the bottom line.

Building a new property made better business sense—everything was custom designed and there were more modern amenities. That would have been a far more lucrative choice for Spencer Hotels and was the option his people had been pushing.

But when he saw The Sea Urchin, with its clean lines and incredible views of the coast, his much-vaunted business acumen seemed to drift away with the tide.

It had been rainy and dismal that February day, a cold, dank wind whistling off the Pacific. He had been calling himself all kinds of fool for coming here in the first place, for packing his schedule so tightly when he was supposed to be leaving for the United Kingdom in only a few days.

But on the recommendation of a local woman, he had

driven past The Sea Urchin and seen it silhouetted against the sea, warm, welcoming lights in all the windows, and he had wanted it.

He had never known this sense of *rightness* before, but somehow he couldn't shake the odd sense that he could make this small hotel with its twenty guest rooms the glimmering crown jewel of Spencer Hotels.

He sighed and forced himself to drive past the hotel. *He* might be certain his destiny and The Sea Urchin's were somehow intertwined, but Stanley and Jade Wu were proving a little harder to convince.

Renewed frustration simmered through him. A week ago, this sale was supposed to be a done deal. All the parties involved had finally agreed on an asking price— a quarter million dollars more than Eben had planned to pay when he and the Wus first discussed the sale in February.

He thought all the legalities had been worked out with his advance team before he flew to Portland. The only thing left was for Stanley and Jade to sign the papers, but they had been putting him off for two days.

He could feel the property slipping through his fingers and for the first time in his business life, he didn't know how the hell to grab hold of something he wanted.

He understood their ambivalence. They had run The Sea Urchin for thirty-five years, had built it through skill and hard work and shrewd business sense into a stylishly beautiful hotel. Surrendering the family business to a stranger—seeing it folded into the *empire* Sage Benedetto had mocked with such disdain—could only be difficult for them.

He understood all that, Eben thought again as he

pulled into the driveway and climbed out of the car, but his patience was trickling away rapidly.

He fiercely wanted The Sea Urchin and he wasn't sure how he would cope with his disappointment if the deal fell through. And in the meantime, he still had a company of a hundred hotels to run.

Oh, she was tired.

Right now the idea of sliding into a hot bath with a good book sounded like a slice of heaven. In the gathering twilight, Sage pedaled home with a steady drizzle soaking her to the skin.

So much for the weather forecasters' prediction of sunshine for the next three days. Having lived in Oregon for five years now, she ought to know better. The weather was fickle and erratic. She had learned to live with it and even enjoyed it for the most part.

She tried to always be prepared for any eventuality. Of course, this was the day she had forgotten to pack her rain slicker in her bike basket.

She blamed her negligence on her distraction that morning with Eben and Chloe Spencer, though maybe that was only because she was approaching their beach house.

She wiped rain out of her eyes as she passed it. A sleek silver Jaguar was sprawled arrogantly in the driveway.

Of course. What else would she expect?

Against her will, her eyes were drawn to the wide bay window in front. The blinds were open and she thought she saw a dark shadow move around inside before she quickly jerked her attention back to the road.

Wouldn't it be just like her to have a wipeout right in front of his house, with him watching out the window?

She stubbornly worked to put them both out of her head as she rode the half mile to Brambleberry House. The house came into view as she rounded the last corner and some of her exhaustion faded away in the sweet, welcome comfort of coming home.

She loved this old place with its turrets and gables and graceful old personality, though some of the usual joy she felt returning to it had been missing since Abigail's death.

As she pedaled into the driveway, Conan barked a halfhearted greeting from the front porch.

Stubborn thing. He should be waiting inside where it was warm and dry. Instead, he insisted on waiting on the front porch—for her or for Anna or for Abigail, she didn't know. She got the sense Conan kept expecting Abigail to drive her big Buick home any moment now.

Conan loped out into the rain to greet her by the fence and she ached at the sadness in his big eyes. "Let me put my bike away, okay? Then you can tell me about your day while I change into dry clothes."

She opened the garage door and as she parked her bike, she heard Conan bark again and the sound of a vehicle outside. She glanced out the wide garage door to see Will Garrett's pickup truck pulling into the driveway.

Rats. She'd forgotten all about their conversation that morning. So much for her dreams of a long soak.

He climbed out into the rain—though he was at least smart enough to wear a Gore-Tex jacket.

"Hi, Will. Anna's not here yet."

"I'm sure she'll be here soon. I'm a little early."

"I never told her you were coming. I'm sorry, Will. I knew there was something I forgot to do today. I honestly don't have any idea when she'll be home."

The man she had met five years ago when she first

moved here would have grinned and teased her about her bubbleheaded moment. But the solemn stranger he had become since the death of his wife and baby girl only nodded. "I can come back later. Not a problem."

Guilt was a miserable companion on a rainy night. "No. Come in. You're here, you might as well get started, at least in the empty apartment. Without Anna here, I don't feel right about taking you into Abigail's apartment to see what to do there, since it's her territory now. But I have a key to the second floor. I just need to run up and get it."

"Better change into something dry while you're up there. Wouldn't do for you to catch pneumonia."

His solemn concern absurdly made her want to cry. She hadn't had anybody to fuss over her since Abigail's death.

"I'll hurry," she assured him, and dripped her way up the stairs, leaving him behind with Conan.

She returned five minutes later in dry jeans, a sweatshirt and toweled-dry hair. She hurried down the stairs to the second-floor landing, where Will must have climbed with Conan. The two of them sat on the top step and the dog had his chin on Will's knee.

"Sorry to leave you waiting." She pulled out a key and fitted it in the keyhole.

Will rose. "Not a problem. Conan's been telling me about his day."

"He's quite the uncanny conversationalist, isn't he?"

He managed half a smile and followed her into the apartment.

The rooms here, their furnishings blanketed in dust covers, had a vaguely forlorn feeling to them. Unlike the rest of the house, the air was stale and close. Whenever she came in here, Sage thought the apartment seemed to be waiting for something, silly as that seemed.

Abigail had rented the second floor only twice in the five years Sage had lived at Brambleberry House. Each time had been on a temporary basis, the apartment becoming a transitional home for Abigail's strays for just a few months at a time.

The place should be lived in. It was comfortable and roomy, with three bedrooms, a huge living room and a fairly good-sized kitchen.

The plumbing was in terrible shape and the vinyl tiles in the kitchen and bathroom were peeling and outdated, in definite need of replacement. The appliances and cabinets in the kitchen were ancient, too, and the whole place could use new paint and some repairs to the crumbling lathe and plaster walls.

Despite the battle scars, the apartment had big windows all around that let light throughout the rooms and the living room enjoyed a particularly breathtaking view of the sea. Not as nice as the one from her third-floor apartment, but lovely still.

She wandered to the window now and realized she had a perfect view of Eben and Chloe Spencer's place, the lights still beating back the darkness.

"Hey Sage, can you come hold the end of the tape measure?"

She jerked out of her reverie and followed his voice to the bathroom. For the next few minutes she assisted while Will studied, measured, measured again and finally jotted figures on his clipboard.

They were in the kitchen when through the open doorway she saw Conan suddenly lift his head from his morose study of the peeling wallpaper. A moment later, she heard the squeak of the front door and reminded herself to add WD-40 to her shopping list.

Conan scrambled up, nosed open the door and galloped for the stairs. A moment later he was back, with Anna not far behind him.

"Hey, Will. I saw your van out front. I didn't realize you were coming tonight."

Sage fought down her guilt. She wasn't the one in the wrong here. Anna had no business arranging all this without talking to her.

"I meant to call you but the day slipped away from me," she said. "I bumped into Will this morning on the way to work and he told me he was coming out tonight to give us a bid on the work we apparently want him to do."

Anna didn't miss her tight tone. Sage thought she saw color creep over her dusky cheekbones. "I figured there was no harm having him come out to take a look. Information is always a good thing. We need to know what our initial capital outlay might be to renovate the apartment so we can accurately determine whether it's cost-effective to rent it out."

Sage really hated that prim, businessy tone. Did any personality at all lurk under Anna's stiff facade? It had to. She knew it must. Abigail had cared about her, had respected her enough to sell her the gift shop and to leave her half of Brambleberry House.

Sage had seen little sign of it, though. She figured Anna probably fell asleep at night dreaming of her portfolio allocation.

She didn't want to battle this out tonight. She was too darn tired after wrestling thirteen energetic kids all day.

Instead, she reached into her pocket for the dog treat

she had grabbed upstairs when she had changed her clothes. She palmed it and held it casually at thigh level.

Conan was a sucker for the bacon treats. Just as she intended, the dog instantly left Anna's side and sidled over to her. Anna tried to hide her quick flicker of hurt but she wasn't quite quick enough.

"Dirty trick," Will murmured from behind her.

Having a witness to her sneakiness made her feel petty and small. She wasn't fit company for anyone tonight. She let out a breath and resolved to try harder to be kind.

"I think we're done up here," Will said. "Should I take a look at the first floor now?"

Anna nodded and led the way down the stairs. Sage thought about escaping to her apartment and indulging in that warm bath that had been calling her name all evening, but she knew it would be cowardly, especially after Will had witnessed her subversive bribery of Conan.

She followed them down the stairs to Abigail's apartment. With some trepidation, Sage stood in the doorway. She hadn't been here since Anna moved her things in two weeks ago. She couldn't help expecting to see Abigail bustle out of the kitchen with her tea tray and a plateful of Pepperidge Farm Raspberry Milanos.

All three of them—four, counting Conan—paused inside the living room. Shared grief for the woman they had all loved twisted around them like thorny vines.

Anna was the first to break the charged moment as she briskly moved into the room. "Sorry about the mess. If I'd had warning, I might have had time to straighten up a little."

Sage couldn't see much mess, just a newspaper spread out on the coffee table and a blanket jumbled in a heap on the couch, but she figured those few items slightly out of place probably affected Anna as much as if a hurricane had blown through.

"What I would like to do is knock down the wall between the kitchen and the dining room to make the kitchen bigger. And then I was wondering about the feasibility of taking out the wall between the two smaller bedrooms to make that a big master."

Abigail's presence was so strong here. While Will and Anna were busy in the kitchen, Sage stood in the middle of the living room and closed her eyes, her throat tight. She could still smell her here, that soft scent of freesia.

Abigail wouldn't have wanted her to wallow in this wrenching grief, she knew, but she couldn't seem to fight it back.

For one odd second, the scent of freesia seemed stronger and she could swear she felt a soft, papery hand on her cheek.

To distract herself from the weird sensation, she glanced around the rooms and through the open doorway to one of the bedrooms and suddenly caught sight of Abigail's vast doll collection.

Collecting dolls had always seemed too ordinary a hobby for Abigail, given her friend's other eccentricities, but Abigail had loved each piece in the room.

She moved to the doorway and flipped on the light switch, enjoying as always that first burst of amazement at the floor-to-ceiling display cases crammed full of thousands of dolls. There was her favorite, a mischievous-looking senior citizen wearing a tie-dyed shirt and a peace medallion. Golden Flower Child. She was certain the artist had handcrafted it specifically for Abigail.

"You should take some of them up to your apartment."

Sage quickly dropped her hand from the doll's familiar smile to find Anna watching her.

"They're part of the contents of the house, which she left jointly to both of us," Anna went on. "Half of them are yours."

She glanced at the aging hippie doll with longing, then shook her head. "They belong together. I'm not sure we should split up the collection."

After a long pause, Anna's expression turned serious. "Why don't you take them all upstairs with you, then?"

She had a feeling the offer had not been an easy one for Anna to make. It touched her somewhere deep inside. The lump in her throat swelled and she felt even more guilty for the dog-treat trick.

"We don't have to decide anything like that today. For now, we can leave them where they are, as long as you don't mind."

Before Anna could voice the arguments Sage could see brewing in her dark eyes, Will joined them. "You want the good news or the bad?"

"Good news," Anna said instantly. Sage would have saved the best for last. Good news after bad always made the worst seem a little more palatable.

"None of the walls you want to take out are weight-bearing, so we should be okay that way."

"What's the bad?" Anna asked.

"We're going to have to reroute some plumbing. It's going to cost you."

He gave a figure that staggered Sage, though Anna didn't seem at all surprised.

"Well, there's no rush on this floor. What about the work upstairs?"

Those figures were no less stunning. "That's more

than reasonable," Anna said. "Are you positive that will cover your entire overhead? I don't want you skimping your profit."

"It's fair."

Anna gave him a careful look, then smiled. "It *will* be fair when we tack back on the twenty percent you cut off the labor costs."

"I give my friends a deal."

"Not these friends. We'll pay your going rate or we'll find somebody else to do the work."

Anna's insistence surprised Sage as much as the numbers. She would have expected the other woman to pinch pennies wherever she could and she had to admit she was impressed that she refused to take advantage of Will's generosity.

"You'll take a discount and that's final," he said firmly. "You'll never find another contractor who will treat Brambleberry House with the same loving care."

"You guys can hash this out better without me," Sage announced. She wasn't sure she could spend any more time in Abigail's apartment without breaking into tears. "I'm tired and I'm hungry. Right now all I want to do is fix some dinner and take a long, hot soak in the tub with a glass of wine. You can give me the details tomorrow."

"I'll walk Conan tonight. It's my turn," Anna said.

She nodded her agreement and headed up the stairs to her veggie burger and silence.

Chapter Four

This was the reason he wanted The Sea Urchin so desperately.

Eben leaned his elbows on the deck railing off the back of their beach house watching dawn spread out across the Pacific the next morning, fingers of pink and lavender and orange slicing through the wisps of fog left from the rains of the night before.

The air smelled of the sea, salty and sharp; gulls wheeled and dived looking for breakfast.

He was the only human in sight—a rare occurrence for him. He wasn't used to solitude and quiet, not with chattering Chloe around all the time. He wasn't completely sure he liked it—but he knew that if he could package this kind of morning for all his properties, Spencer Hotels would never have a vacancy again.

Normal people—people very much unlike uptight Californian businessmen—would eat this whole relaxation thing up. The Sea Urchin would be busy year-round, with people booking their suites months, even years, in advance.

He sipped his coffee and tried to force the tension from his shoulders. Another few days of this and he would be a certifiable beach bum, ready to chuck the stress of life in San Francisco for a quiet stretch of shoreline and a good cup of coffee.

Or maybe not.

He had never been one to sit still for long, not with so much to do. He'd been up since four taking a conference call with Tokyo in preparation for a series of meetings there next week and in two hours he would have to drive the ninety minutes to Portland to meet with his attorneys.

Despite the calm and beauty of the morning, his mind raced with his lengthy to-do list.

In the distance he saw a jogger running up the beach toward town and envy poked him. He would give his coffee and a whole lot more to be the one running along the hard-packed sand close to the surf, working off these restless edges.

Others found calm and peace in the soothing sound of the sea. For Eben, a good, hard run usually did the trick. But with Chloe asleep inside, that was impossible. He couldn't leave her alone in a strange place, even if he left a note and took his cell phone so she could reach him.

The jogger drew closer and recognition clicked in at exactly the same moment he heard a bark of greeting. A moment later, Sage Benedetto's big gangly red dog loped into view.

The dog barked again, changed directions and headed straight toward him. After an odd hesitation, the big dog's owner waved briefly and followed her animal.

Though he knew it was foolish, anticipation curled through him like those tendrils of fog on the water.

She was still some distance away when the dog nuzzled his head under Eben's hand, looking for attention. He had never had a pet and wasn't very used to animals, but he scratched the dog's chin and was rewarded by the dog nudging his hand for more.

When Sage approached, he saw she was wearing bike shorts and a hooded sweatshirt with an emblem that read Portland Saturday Market across the front.

She looked soft and sensual in the early morning light, like some kind of lush fertility goddess. Her exotic features were flushed and her hair was in a wild ponytail.

She looked as if she had just climbed out of bed after making love all night long.

His insides burned with sudden hunger but he hid his reaction behind a casual smile. "Great morning for a run."

She raised an eyebrow. "You think?"

"I was just now pondering how much I'd love to be out there doing the same thing if only Chloe weren't asleep inside."

She gave a sudden delighted smile that made him feel as if the sun had just climbed directly above his beach house. Before he could catch his breath, she grabbed the coffee mug straight out of his hand and sipped it, pressing her mouth exactly where his own lips had been.

"Problem solved. I'll stay here in case Chloe wakes up and you can take Conan."

She made a shooing gesture with the hand not holding his coffee. "You two boys go on and run to your little hearts' content and I'll go back to sleep for a few moments."

She slid into one of the wide, plump rockers on the deck and closed her eyes, his mug still cradled in her hands.

She was completely serious, Eben realized, not quite sure whether to be amused or annoyed. But with a sudden anticipation zinging through him, he couldn't help but smile. "At least come inside where it's warm while I throw on some jogging shoes."

She opened her eyes and her gaze flashed down to his bare toes then back at him with an inscrutable expression on her features. "I'm fine out here, but if you would feel better having me inside in case Chloe wakes up, I have no problem with that, either."

She followed him inside to the living room with its floor-to-ceiling windows overlooking the shore.

"Nice," she murmured.

He was intensely aware of her, more than he had been of any woman in a long, long time.

He was also cognizant of the fact that they were virtually alone, with only his daughter sleeping on the other side of the house, something he *didn't* want to think about.

"Give me five minutes to grab my shoes."

She was already nestling into the comfortable leather couch that faced the windows, her eyes already closing, her muscles going slack. "No problem. Take your time. This is perfect. Absolutely perfect."

He threw on his shoes quickly and hurried back to the family room. She gave all appearances of being asleep. He watched her for only a moment, entranced by the wisp of honey-colored hair curling over her cheekbone.

When he realized he was gazing at her like some kind of Peeping Tom, he hurried out the door to the deck and whistled to Conan, who was busy marking every support of the deck.

The dog stopped mid-pee, barked with an eagerness that matched Eben's and the two of them set off down the beach.

With a sense of freedom he hadn't known in a long time, he ran on the hard-packed sand, dodging waves and the occasional long, ragged clump of kelp. The dog raced right along with him, easily matching his stride to Eben's and in no time they had a comfortable rhythm.

By the time they reached the headlands on the north end of the beach, he felt loose and liberated, as if the jog had chased all the cobwebs from his mind.

He paused for a moment to enjoy the full splendor of the sunrise slanting out across the water while the dog chased a couple of seagulls pecking at something in the sand.

After some time, Eben checked his watch with some regret. "We'd better hustle back. Some of us need to go to work," he told the dog, who tilted his head with a quizzical look then barked as if he understood exactly what Eben had said. The dog turned and charged back down the beach the way they'd come.

The beach had been largely empty on their way north but on the run back, they passed several other joggers and beachcombers, all of whom greeted him with friendly smiles—or at least offered smiles to Conan.

Several called the dog by name and gave them curious looks that Eben deflected with a wave. All the locals were probably wondering who was running with Sage Benedetto's dog but he didn't have the breath to enlighten any of them, even if he'd wanted to.

"Wait out here," he ordered the sandy dog when they reached the beach house, his breath still coming fast and hard. Conan flopped onto the deck and curled his head in his paws, apparently content to rest.

He let himself into the house and found Sage exactly where he'd left her, sound asleep on his couch.

A quick peek into Chloe's room showed him she was still asleep as well, the blankets jumbled around her feet.

He closed her door with gentle care and returned to the family room. Okay, so he hadn't worked all the restlessness out of his system, apparently. Some of it still simmered through him, especially as he watched Sage sleep on his couch. She looked rumpled and sexy, her lashes fluttering against the olive skin of her high cheekbones and the slightest of smiles playing over those lush lips.

What was she dreaming about? he wondered, hunger tightening his insides.

Maybe it was a reaction to the blood still pumping through him from the good, hard run—or, he admitted honestly, probably just the delectable woman in front of him—but Eben wanted her more than he could remember ever wanting a woman.

He cleared his throat, again fighting back his heretofore unknown voyeuristic tendencies. "Uh, Ms. Benedetto. Time to go. The run's over."

Her mouth twitched a little in sleep but her eyes remained stubbornly closed. She made a little sleepy sound and rolled over, presenting her back to him, looking for all the world as if she were settling in to nap the morning away.

Now what was he supposed to do?

"Sage?" he said again.

When she still didn't respond, he sighed and reached a hand out to her shoulder. "Sage, wake up. You have to go to work, remember? We both do."

After a moment, she heaved a long sigh and turned over again. She blinked her eyes open and gazed at him in confusion for a moment before he saw consciousness slowly return like the tide coming in.

She sat up, gave a yawn and stretched her arms above her head. Eben swallowed and did his best to remember how to breathe.

"I have to say, that had to be just about the best jog I've had in a month," she murmured with a sleepy, sexy smile.

She rose, stretching again with graceful limbs, and Eben stared at her a long moment—at the becoming flush on her features, at the wild tangle of her hair, at her slightly parted lips.

He sensed exactly the instant his control slipped out the window—when she smiled at him again, her head canted to one side. With a groan, he surrendered the battle and reached for her.

She was soft and warm and smelled of the leather sofa where she had been sleeping and an exotic spicy-sweet flowery scent that had to be purely Sage.

He told himself he would stop with just a tiny taste. He had taken her dog out running, after all. Didn't she owe him something for that? Stealing a little morning kiss seemed like small recompense.

He didn't expect her mouth to taste of coffee and mint and he certainly didn't expect, after one shocked second, for her to make a low, aroused sound in her throat then wrap her arms around his neck as if she couldn't bear the idea of letting him go.

From that point on, he lost all sense of time and space and reason. His foolish idea of giving into the heat for only an instant with one little taste went out the window along with the rest of his control.

The only thing he could focus on was the woman in his arms—her intoxicating scent and taste, the texture of her sweatshirt under his hands, the soft curves pressing against him.

He needed to stop, for a million reasons. He barely knew the woman. She barely knew him. Chloe could wake and come out of her room any moment. He had just jogged three miles down the beach and back and probably smelled like a locker room.

All these thoughts flickered through his mind but he couldn't quite catch hold of any of them. The blood singing through him and the wild hunger burning up his insides were the only things that seemed to matter.

He deepened the kiss and she sighed against his mouth. He was intensely aware of her soft fingers in his hair, of the other hand curving around his neck. Even with the heat scorching him, the wonder of feeling her hands on him absurdly drew a lump to his throat.

How long had it been since he'd known a woman's touch? Brooke's shockingly sudden death from an aneurysm had been two years ago and he hadn't been with anyone since then. Even for months before her death, things had been rocky between them. He knew he had failed her in many, many ways.

The specter of his disastrous marriage finally helped him regain some small measure of control.

He stilled, then opened his eyes as the sensation of being watched prickled down his spine.

Not Chloe, he hoped, and swept the room with a glance. No, he realized. Sage's big red dog watched them through the wide windows leading to the deck. And if Conan had been human, Eben would have sworn he was grinning at them.

Though he ached at the effort, Eben forced himself to break the kiss and step back, his breathing uneven and his thoughts a tangled mess.

"Well. That was…unexpected," she murmured.

Her color was high but she didn't look upset by their heated embrace, only surprised.

He, on the other hand, was stunned to his core.

What the hell was he thinking? This kind of thing was not at all like him. He was known in all circles—social, business and otherwise—for his cool head and detached calm.

He had spent his life working hard to keep himself in check. Oh, he knew himself well enough to understand it was a survival mechanism from his childhood—if he couldn't control his parents' tumultuous natures, their wild outbursts, their screaming fights, and substance abuse, at least he could contain his own behavior.

Those habits had carried into adulthood and into his marriage. In the heat of anger, Brooke used to call him a machine, accusing him of having no heart, no feeling. She *had* to have an affair, she told him, if only to know what it was like to be with a man who had blood instead of antifreeze running through his veins.

This new, urgent heat for an exotic, wild-haired nature girl sent him way, *way* out of his comfort zone.

"My apologies," he said, his voice stiff. "I'm not quite sure what happened there."

"Aren't you?"

He sent her a swift look and saw the corner of her mouth lift. He didn't like the feeling she was laughing at him.

"You can be certain it won't happen again."

A strange light flickered in the depths of her dark eyes. "Okay. Good to know."

She studied him for a moment, then smiled. He wanted to think the expression looked a little strained but he thought that was possibly his imagination.

"Thank you for taking Conan jogging for me. I admit, I'm not crazy about the whole morning exercise thing. I'm trying to warm up to it but it's been slow going so far. I thought after a month I would enjoy it more, but what are you going to do? It seems to cheer him up a little, though, so I guess I'll stick with it."

He couldn't seem to make his brain work but he managed to catch hold of a few of the pieces of what she said.

"You're telling me your dog is depressed?" he asked, feeling supremely stupid for even posing the question.

"You could say that." She glanced out the window where Conan still watched them and lowered her voice as if the dog could hear them through the glass. "He misses his human companion. She died a month ago."

The dog's *human companion* had died a month ago and Sage had been jogging with Conan for a month. Even in his current disordered state, he figured the two events had to be connected.

"She left you her dog?"

"That and a whole lot of other problems. It's a long story." One she obviously had no intention of sharing with him, he realized as she headed for the door.

"I'd better go. I've got thirteen eager young campers who'll be ready to explore the coastline with me in just an hour. I'm sure you've got things to do, people to see, worlds to conquer and all that."

His mouth tightened at the faint echo of derision in her voice, but before he could defend himself from her obviously harsh view of his life, she opened the door and walked out into the cool morning air, to be greeted with enthusiasm by the dog, who jumped around as if he hadn't seen her in months.

Just now the animal looked far from the bereft, grieving animal she had described. She patted his sides, which had the dog's eyes rolling back in his head. Eben couldn't say he blamed him.

"Thanks again for exercising Conan," she called back.

"No problem. I enjoyed it."

Stepping outside, he decided he wasn't going to think about anything else he might have enjoyed about the morning.

"The run was good for me," he said instead. "Helps keep my brain sharp while I'm swindling retirees and gullible widows out of their life savings."

Her mouth quirked a little at that but she only shook her wild mane of hair and took off down the stairs of his deck and across the beach, the dog close on her heels.

Chapter Five

She tried to tell herself that heated kiss was just a one-shot deal, some weird anomaly of fate and circumstance that would never, ever, *ever* be repeated.

She and Eben were two vastly different people with different values, different tax brackets. Their lives should never have intersected in the first place—and their mouths certainly shouldn't have either.

But as she showered and dressed for work, Sage couldn't shake the odd, jittery feeling that something momentous had just happened to her, something life-changing and substantial.

It was silly, she knew, but she couldn't shake the feeling that her life had just turned a corner down a route she was not at all sure she was prepared to follow.

Just a kiss, she repeated in a stern mantra as she gave Conan one last morning scratch, pulled her bike out of the garage and cycled through the strands of morning fog that hadn't yet burned off. Two people reacting to their unlikely attraction to each other in the usual fashion. One never-to-be-repeated kiss certainly was not about to alter the rest of her life, for heaven's sake.

She was still working hard to convince herself of that when she arrived at the nature center and let herself into her office. She was answering e-mail from a school group interested in arranging a field trip between her camp sessions when Lindsey poked her head into her office.

"So the weirdest thing happened this morning," Lindsey said without preamble.

Sage raised an eyebrow. "Good morning to you, too."

Her assistant director grinned. "Yeah, yeah. Hello, how are you, great to see you and all that. I've been up at the bakery since four already helping my dad so it feels more like lunchtime to me by this time. But back to my weird morning."

She pushed away the lingering memory of Eben and that stunning kiss and tried to focus on Lindsey's story. "Don't tell me you had another creepy dream about old Mr. Delarosa walking down Hemlock Street in a Speedo again."

Lindsey screwed up her face. "No! Ew. Thanks for putting that visual in my head again. I just spent the last three months in intensive therapy trying to purge it."

Sage fought a smile. "Sorry. What happened this morning?"

"I was making the usual morning deliveries of muffins to The Sea Urchin and suddenly this huge dog comes running at me out of nowhere. Scared the bejabbers out of me."

"Yeah?"

"It was Conan, of course."

"Of course. He is the only dog in Cannon Beach, after all."

"Well, maybe not, but you have to admit he's pretty distinctive-looking. There's no mistaking him for anyone else. So when I couldn't see you or Anna anywhere, I thought maybe Conan broke out of your place and was running loose. I was trying to grab hold of his collar so I could take him back to Brambleberry House when suddenly, who should show up but this extremely sexy guy who looked familiar in an odd sort of way?"

Sage didn't even want to think about just how extremely sexy *she* found Eben Spencer.

"He whistled to Conan and the two of them just kept running down the beach."

"That *is* strange," Sage murmured.

"I couldn't help but wonder what on earth our newest little camper's father was doing running with your dog at six in the morning. That *was* Chloe Spencer's hottie of a dad, wasn't it?"

Sage could feel warmth soak her cheeks. She could only be grateful the coloring she inherited from the Italian side of her family hid her blushing.

"It was. Conan and I bumped into Eben this morning on our daily jog and he, uh, graciously offered to exercise Conan for me."

Lindsey raised an eyebrow—the one with the diamond stud in it. "You sure that's all there is to the story? I'm sensing more. Come on, give me all the juice."

She would *not* allow anything resembling a guilty expression to cross her features, she vowed. They'd shared one kiss, that's all, and she was absolutely not going to share that information with anyone else—especially not

Lindsey, who had a vivid imagination and would be spinning this whole thing way out of control.

"What juice?" she said. "You think I spent the night ripping up the sheets with Eben Spencer while his daughter slept in the next room, then I kicked him out of bed so he could go take my dog for a run?"

Lindsey laughed. "Okay. Stupid hypothesis. I have a feeling if a woman had a man like that in bed, she wouldn't kick him out if the house was on fire, forget about making him walk her dog."

"He's here to buy The Sea Urchin and will only be in town for a few days. Not even long enough for a summer fling, if I were into that kind of thing. Which I most assuredly am not. It happened just as I told you. I was jogging past his house and he was outside and offered to take Conan for his jog. Since you know I'm not excessively fond of that particular activity myself, I decided I would be stupid to refuse."

"Too bad." Lindsey grinned. "I like my version better. For a man like that, I might reconsider my strict hands-off policy toward tourists."

"He's too old for you."

"Mr. Delarosa in his Speedo is too old. Eben Spencer? Not even close."

To her relief, Sage was spared having to continue the conversation by the arrival of the first campers.

She was showing the children how to identify the different tracks of birds in the sand—and doing her level best *not* to pay more than her usual attention to the front door—when it opened suddenly and a little dark-haired sprite rushed through and headed straight for her.

"Hi Sage! My dad says he went running with Conan this morning while I was still sleeping."

Her skin suddenly itchy and tight, she drew in a breath and lifted her gaze to find Eben standing a short distance away watching her out those glittering green eyes.

She couldn't read anything at all in his expression—regret, renewed heat, even mild interest.

Fine. She could pretend nothing happened, too. "True enough," she answered Chloe.

"Why didn't anybody wake me up?" she pouted. "I would have gone jogging, too!"

"Conan has pretty long legs, honey. It's hard for me to keep up with him sometimes."

"I'm a slow runner," Chloe said glumly, then her face lit up. "I could ride a bike, though. I do that sometimes back home. I ride my bike and my dad has to run to catch up with me."

Sage couldn't help giving Eben a quick look, endeared despite herself at the image of Eben jogging while his daughter rode her bike alongside.

It seemed incongruous with everything else she had discerned about the man—but she supposed one brief kiss didn't automatically make her an expert.

"If I can find a bike, can I go with you next time?"

"I don't know if there will *be* a next time," she pointed out. "You're leaving in a few days."

That apparently was the wrong thing to say. Chloe's bottom lip jutted out and her green eyes looked as wounded as if Sage had just kicked her in the shins.

"I don't want to go. I like it here. I like you and I like your dog and I like finding sand dollars."

Sage gave her a little hug. "It's fun going on vacation and meeting new people, isn't it? When you came in, did you notice that Lindsey has some sea glass in a jar? Whoever guesses how many pieces are inside gets a prize."

Distracted for the moment, Chloe's truculence faded. "Really? What kind of prize?"

"A toy stuffed sea otter. It's really cool."

"I bet I can win it! I'm really good at guessing stuff." Chloe rushed away, leaving Eben and Sage alone.

She was intensely aware of him, the smell of expensive cologne that clung to his skin, his tailored blue shirt, the crisp folds in his silk power tie.

His business attire ought to be a major turn-off for her. It should have reminded her just how very far apart they were.

She had always thought she preferred someone like Will, who wasn't afraid to get his hands dirty. But she couldn't seem to control the wild impulse to loosen that tie a little, to spread her hands over the strong muscles beneath the expensive tailoring.

She cleared her throat and forced herself to meet his still-veiled gaze. "Chloe should have a great day today. We have lots of fun things planned for the children."

"Great. I know she's excited—more excited than she's been about anything in a long time."

"That's what we like to hear."

"Okay, then. I guess I'll see you later."

He turned away and headed out the door. Sage watched him for only a moment—but even that was too long and too revealing, apparently. When she turned back to her campers she found her assistant director watching her with a knowing look.

"You know, it's really too bad you're not the kind of woman who would consider a summer fling," Lindsey murmured as Eben closed the door behind him.

Wasn't it? Sage thought, but she quickly turned her attention to the children.

* * *

He was dead meat.

Roast him, fry him, stick him on a spit. Sage Benedetto was going to kill him.

With one eye on the digital clock on the dashboard, Eben accelerated to pass a slow-moving minivan towing a pop-up trailer. He was supposed to have been at the nature center to pick up Chloe twenty minutes ago and he was still an hour away from Cannon Beach.

Sage might have disliked him before—their disturbing, heated morning kiss notwithstanding—but her mild antipathy was going to move into the territory of loathing if he didn't reach her soon to explain.

He was beyond tardy, approaching catastrophically, negligently late.

He steered the Jag off the highway and dialed the center's number again, as he had done a half-dozen times since the moment he had emerged late from meeting with his team of Portland attorneys.

He'd gotten a busy signal for the last half-hour, but this time to his relief the phone rang four times before someone picked up. He recognized Sage's low, sexy voice the moment she said hello.

"Hello. Eben Spencer here," he said, feeling far more awkward and uncomfortable than he was accustomed to.

Somehow she seemed to bring out the worst in him and he didn't like it at all.

"I've, uh, got a slight problem."

"Oh?"

"I'm afraid I'm just leaving Portland. I had a meeting that ran long and, to be perfectly honest, I wasn't paying attention to the time. I'm hurrying as fast as I can, but I won't be there for another hour, even if the traffic cooperates. I'm very sorry."

He heard a slight pause on the line and could almost hear her thinking what a terrible father he was. Right now, he couldn't say he disagreed.

"No problem," she finally said. "I'll just take her to Brambleberry House with me. Conan will be over the moon to see her again."

"I can't ask you to do that."

"You didn't ask. I offered. And anyway, I certainly can't leave her here by herself. I could take her to your beach house but I wouldn't feel right about leaving her alone there either. I don't mind taking her home with me. Like I said, Conan will love the company."

"In that case, thank you." He had to struggle not to grovel with gratitude.

Until this week when he'd been forced by circumstance to bring Chloe along, he wasn't sure he had fully comprehended how much he relied on nannies to take care of details like making sure Chloe was picked up on time. It was all a hell of a lot harder on his own.

He always considered himself a pretty good employer but he was definitely going to make sure he paid the next nanny more.

"You live in the big yellow Victorian down the beach, right?"

"Right. It's got a wrought-iron fence and a sign above the porch that says Brambleberry House."

"I'll be there as soon as I can." He paused. "Thank you again. I owe you."

"No problem. You can pay me back by taking Conan for another run in the morning."

Her words conjured up that kiss again, Sage all sleepy

and warm and desirable in his arms, and his stomach muscles tightened.

"That's not much of a punishment. I enjoyed it more than he did," he said, his voice suddenly rough. He had to hope his sudden hunger didn't carry through the phone line. "I'll be glad for the chance to do it again."

"Don't speak too quickly. The weather forecast calls for a big storm the rest of tonight and in the morning. You'll be soaked before you even make it out the front door. I, on the other hand, will be warm and dry and cozy in my bed."

He didn't even want to go there. "I still think I'll be getting the better end of the stick, but you've got a deal."

"We'll see you in a while, then. And Eben, you really don't have to rush. Chloe will be fine."

He severed the connection and sat for a moment in the car, surrounded by lush green foliage in every direction.

He shouldn't be filled with anticipation at seeing her again. He couldn't afford the distraction—and even if he could, he shouldn't want so much to be distracted by *her*.

What was the point, really? He wasn't interested in anything short-term. How could he even think about it, with his eight-year-old daughter around? And he certainly wasn't looking for any kind of longer commitment or if he were, it would never be with a wild, free-spirited woman like Sage.

With a sigh, he put the Jag into gear again and pulled back onto the highway. Best to just work as hard as he could to finalize the deal with the Wus so he could take Chloe back to San Francisco, back to his comfort zone where everything was safe and orderly and predictable.

The storm Sage had mentioned hit just as he reached the outskirts of town. The lights of Brambleberry House gleamed in the pale, watery twilight, a beacon of warm welcome against the vast, dark ocean just beyond it.

The house was a bit more than she described, a rambling Queen Anne Victorian with a wide front porch, elaborate gingerbread trim and a voluptuous tangle of gardens out front. Painted a cheery yellow with multi-colored pastel accents, it looked bright and homey, the kind of place that for some reason always made him picture bread baking and the sweet, embracing scents of home.

He blinked the random image away and hurried through the rain to ring the doorbell, grateful for the wide porch that kept him mostly dry.

Despite the sign above the porch, he thought for a moment he might have come to the wrong house when a stranger answered the door. She had dark hair, solemn eyes, and an air about her of efficient competence.

Her mouth lifted in an impersonal, slightly wary smile. "Yes?"

"Hello. I was certain I was in the right place but now I'm beginning to doubt myself. This is Brambleberry House, isn't it?"

"Yes." She still kept the door only slightly ajar— probably a smart self-defense move so she could slam it quickly shut if he should try anything threatening.

"I'm Eben Spencer. I believe Sage Benedetto is expecting me."

She seemed to relax a little and the door opened wider, letting out a bigger slice of light and warmth to fight back the rainy evening. "You must be Chloe's father."

He held out a hand and she took it. Again, he gathered the vague impression of competence, though he wasn't sure what about her spoke so solidly of it.

"I'm Anna Galvez. I live on this floor and Sage is upstairs, all the way at the top."

"Which means you probably get roped into answering the door for her more often than you'd like."

Her smile warmed. "I don't mind, usually, unless I'm in the middle of something. Sage has a separate doorbell to her apartment but it hasn't been working for awhile. We're working on it. Sage's apartment is all the way to the top of the staircase."

The wide, sweeping staircase was the center core of the magnificent house, he saw, rising straight up from the entry through two other floors. A shame the house had been split into apartments, he thought. It would have made a stunning bed and breakfast, though he supposed it could be converted back if someone had the money, time and energy.

"Thank you," he said to Anna. "Sorry to bother you."

"Not a problem."

He followed the curve of stairs, his hand on the mahogany rail that had been worn smooth over generations.

Outside the door at the top, he heard laughter, then a dog's loud barking. He picked up Chloe's voice, then Sage's. The sound of it, rich and full and sexy, strummed down his spine.

He knocked and the dog's barking increased. He heard Sage order the dog to be stay and be quiet. It seemed to work—when she opened the door, Conan was sitting perfectly still beside the door, though he was practically vibrating with impatience.

Sage had changed yet again—the third outfit he'd seen her in that day. Instead of her jogging clothes or the conservative navy knit shirt and khaki slacks she wore to work, she wore a flowery tunic-style blouse in some kind of sheer material over a pale pink tank top, dangly earrings and a pair of faded jeans.

She looked heart-stoppingly gorgeous, lush and appealing, and he couldn't seem to focus on anything but their kiss that morning.

He knew he didn't mistake the memory of it flaring in her dark eyes. Her mouth parted slightly and beneath the memory was a faint sheen of trepidation.

Did she think he was going to grab her right here in front of her dog and his daughter for a repeat performance?

"You made good time from Portland." In seconds, she shunted away the brief flicker of remembered heat from her gaze and became as coolly polite as her downstairs neighbor.

"I was afraid you'd be ready to string me up if I didn't hurry."

"I told you not to worry about it. Chloe's a joy."

He raised an eyebrow at that, not used to hearing such praise of his daughter. Before he could respond, Chloe rushed to him.

"Hi Daddy! I had a *super* day today. We learned about the different habitats in the ocean at camp and then when we came here, we went outside on the beach and played catch with Conan and then we made lasagna with zucchini and carrots! It's almost ready. Sage says I can stay and have some. Can I, Daddy?"

He glanced at Sage and saw her mouth tighten slightly. He was quite certain the invitation would never have been extended if she had expected him to be here before the meal was ready.

But how could he disappoint Chloe by telling her they

needed to go, that they had already imposed on Sage enough for the day?

Sage must have sensed his indecision. She smiled brightly, though it didn't quite reach her eyes. "You're certainly both welcome to stay. There's plenty for everyone and Chloe did work hard to help me fix it. It's only fair she get to enjoy the fruits of her labor."

"Did we put fruit in there too?" Chloe asked, a baffled expression on her face. "I thought it was just vegetables."

"Well, remember, technically tomatoes are a fruit. So I guess that counts. Seriously, you're both welcome to stay."

Though he knew it was a mistake to spend more time with Sage, he couldn't figure out any way out without hurting Chloe.

"All right. Thank you."

He was quite certain *he* was the one with trepidation in his eyes now as he stepped into her apartment. Only after he crossed the threshold did Conan hurry to him for attention and Eben could swear the dog looked pleased.

Chapter Six

Sage had always considered her apartment to be a perfect size, roomy without being huge. The rooms were all comfortably laid out and she loved having an extra bedroom in case any friends from college came to stay. It had always seemed just right for her.

How was it that Eben Spencer seemed to fill up every available inch?

His presence was overwhelming. He wore the same pale blue dress shirt he'd had on that morning, though his tie was off and his sleeves were rolled up. Afternoon stubble shadowed his jawline, giving him a slightly disreputable look she guessed he would probably find appalling if he were aware of it.

He looked so damn gorgeous, it was infuriating.

She shouldn't even be noticing how he looked, not after she had spent all day sternly reminding herself they had nothing in common, no possible reason for this un-wanted attraction that simmered between them.

He represented wealth and privilege and all the things she had turned her back on after a lifetime of struggling—and failing—to find her place there. He was no doubt just like her father, obsessed with making and keeping his money.

Good grief, the cost of his tailored shirt alone could probably feed a family of four for a month.

She didn't like him, she told herself. While her brain might be certain of that, the rest of her was having a tougher time listening to reason when she just wanted to curl against his strength and heat like Conan finding a sunbeam shooting through the window.

She sighed and pulled her lasagna out, attributing her flushed and tight skin to the heat pouring from the oven.

"Can I help with anything?" he asked, standing in the doorway.

Yeah. Go away.

She forced herself to stuff the thought back into the recesses of her mind. She was a strong, independent woman. Surely she was tough enough to endure an hour or so with the man.

"Everything's just about ready. Chloe and I were finishing things up in here when you arrived. Would the two of you mind setting the table?"

She regretted the question as soon as she asked it. Eben Spencer probably had a legion of servants to do that sort of grunt work at his house. To her surprise, he didn't hesitate.

"No problem. Come on, Chloe."

Through the doorway beyond him, Sage saw Chloe get up from the floor where she had been playing with

Conan. She and the dog both tromped into the kitchen, making Sage even more claustrophobic.

"You'll have to point me in the right direction for plates and silverware," Eben said.

"I'll grab them for you."

She pulled out her favorite square chargers—she'd bought them from a ceramics studio in Manzanita, attracted by their wild, abstract designs—and the contrasting plates she always used with them, then held them out for Eben to take.

Their hands connected when he reached for them and a spark jumped between them.

Sage flushed. "Sorry. It's the, uh, hardwood floors. Makes electricity jump in the air, especially when there are a lot of negative ions flying around from the storm."

She was babbling, she realized, and forced herself to clamp her lips shut. She didn't miss the long, considering look Eben gave her.

"Oh, is that what it's from?" he murmured.

Before she could formulate what would no doubt be a sharp retort, he grabbed the plates and carried them out of the kitchen. Only after he left did she release the breath she suddenly realized she was holding.

"Silverware is in the top drawer to the left of the dishwasher," she told Chloe. "Glasses are in the overhead cupboard."

She didn't have the luxury of a dining room in her apartment, but she had commandeered a corner of the good-sized living room for the table Will Garrett had made her.

The chairs were a mismatched jumble picked up here and there at thrift stores and yard sales, but she coordinated them with cushions in vivid colors to match the placemats and chargers.

She always thought the effect was charming but she imagined to someone of Eben Spencer's sophisticated tastes, her house probably reeked of a lousy attempt at garage-sale chic.

She didn't care, she told herself.

It was a waste of time even worrying about what he might think of her and her apartment. In a week, Eben and Chloe Spencer would just be a memory, simply two more in a long line of transitory visitors to her corner of the world.

The thought left her vaguely depressed so she pushed it away and pulled the salad she and Chloe had tossed earlier out of the refrigerator. After a few more moments of them working together, the meal was laid out on the table.

"Everything looks delicious," Eben said, taking the seat across from her.

"Sage is a vegetarian, Daddy," Chloe announced with fascinated eagerness.

"Is that right?"

"Not militant, I promise," she answered. "Steak lovers are usually still welcome at my table."

A corner of his mouth lifted. "Good thing. I do enjoy a good porterhouse, I'm sorry to say."

"You can enjoy it all you want somewhere else, but I'm afraid you won't find any steaks here tonight."

"I can be surprisingly adaptable." Again that half smile lifted his features, made him seem much less formidable. Her insides trembled but she stubbornly ignored them, serving the lasagna instead.

They were all quiet for a few moments as they dished breadsticks and salad.

Sage braced herself for a negative reaction to her favorite lasagna dish. She wasn't the greatest of cooks but after choosing a vegetarian lifestyle in college, she had worked hard to find dishes she found good, nutritious and filling.

But her tastes were likely far different than Eben's. He probably had at least one Cordon Bleu-trained personal chef to go along with the legion of servants she'd imagined for him.

To her relief and gratification, he closed his eyes in appreciation after the first taste. "Delicious. My compliments to the chefs."

Chloe giggled. "There weren't any chefs, Daddy. Just Sage and me."

"You two have outdone yourselves."

"It's super good, Sage," Chloe agreed. "I wasn't sure I'd like it but I can't even taste the carrots and stuff."

Sage smiled, charmed all over again by this little girl with the inquisitive mind and boundless energy.

"Thank you both. I'm glad you're enjoying it."

"Maybe you could give me the recipe and I could make it sometime at home, if the new nanny helps me," Chloe suggested. "I like to cook stuff sometimes, when I have a chance."

"I'll do that. Remind me before you leave and I'll make a copy of the recipe for you."

"Thank you very much," Chloe said, with a solemn formality that made Sage smile again. She shifted her gaze from the girl to her father and immediately wished she hadn't.

Eben watched her, an odd expression in those brilliant green eyes. It left her breathless and off balance.

He quickly veiled it in that stiff, controlled way of his she was coming to despise.

"This is a beautiful house," he said into the sudden silence. "Have you lived here long?"

"Five years or so—I moved in a few weeks after I came to Cannon Beach."

"You're not from here? I wondered. You have a slight northeast accent every once in a while, barely noticeable."

Her mouth tightened as if she could clamp down all trace of the past she didn't like remembering. "Boston," she finally said.

"That's what I would have guessed. So what brought you to Oregon?"

"When I graduated from Berkeley, I took an internship at the nature center. I spent the first few weeks in town renting a terrible studio apartment a few blocks from here. It was all I could afford on an intern's salary, which was nothing."

"You worked for free?" Chloe asked and Sage had to smile a little at the shock in her voice.

"I was fresh out of college and ready to see the world, try anything. But I did hate living in that terrible apartment."

"How did you end up here?" Eben asked. He sounded genuinely interested, she realized, feeling ashamed of herself for being so surprised by it.

"One day at the grocery store I helped a local woman with her bags and she invited me home for dinner." Her heart spasmed a little and she suddenly missed Abigail desperately.

She managed a smile, though she suspected it didn't look very genuine. "I've been here ever since."

Eben was silent for a long moment. By the time he spoke, Sage had regained her composure.

"How many apartments are in this place?"

"Three. One on each floor, but the middle floor is empty right now."

"Your neighbor on the first floor let me in."

"Right. Anna."

Conan barked a little from under the table when she said Anna's name and Sage covered her annoyance by taking a sip of the wine she had set out for her and Eben.

Eben and Anna Galvez would be perfect for each other. The hotel tycoon and the sharp, focused businesswoman. They were both type A personalities, both probably had lifetime subscriptions to *The Wall Street Journal*, both probably knew exactly the difference between the Dow Jones and the NASDAQ—and how much of their respective portfolios were tied up in each, down to the penny.

Sage could barely manage to balance her checkbook most months and still carried a balance on her credit card from paying a down-on-his-luck friend's rent a few months earlier.

Yeah, Eben and Anna would make a good pair. So why did the idea of the two of them together leave her feeling vaguely unsettled?

"You said the second floor is empty?"

"Yes. We're still trying to figure out what we want to do, whether we want to fix it up and rent it out or leave things as is. Too many decisions to make all at once."

"I didn't understand that you owned the place. I thought you were renting."

She made a face. "I own it as of a month ago. Well, sort of."

"How do you sort of own something?"

"Anna and I co-inherited the place and everything in it, including Conan."

He looked intrigued and she didn't like feeling her life was one interesting puzzle for him to solve. "So the dog came with the house?" he asked.

"Something like that."

"So are you and Anna related in some way?"

"Nope." She sipped at her wine. "It's a long story."

She didn't want to talk about Abigail so she deliberately changed the subject.

"I understand from Chloe you're in town to buy The Sea Urchin from Stanley and Jade Wu."

Frustration flickered in his green eyes. "That's the plan, anyway."

"When do you expect to close the sale?"

"Good question. There have been a few…complications."

"Oh?"

"Everything was supposed to be done by now but I'm afraid the Wus are having second thoughts. I'm still working hard to convince them."

"My daddy has a lot of other hotels," Chloe piped up, "but he really, really wants The Sea Urchin."

Of course. No doubt it was all about the game to him, the acquisition of more and more. Just like her own father, who had virtually abandoned his child to the care of others, simply to please his narcissistic, self-absorbed socialite of a second wife.

"And I imagine whatever you want, you get, isn't that right?"

She meant to keep her voice cool and uninterested, but she was fairly sure some of her bitterness dripped into her words.

He studied her for a long moment, long enough that she felt herself flush at her rudeness. He didn't deserve to bear the brunt of an old, tired hurt that had nothing to do with him.

"Not always," he murmured.

"Can I have another breadstick?" Chloe asked into the sudden awkward silence.

Her father turned his attention to her. "How many have you had? Four, isn't it?"

"They're so good, though!"

Sage had enough experience with both eight-year-olds and dogs to know exactly where the extra breadsticks were going—under the table, where Conan lurked, waiting patiently for anything tossed his way.

She handed Chloe another breadstick with a conspiratorial smile. "This is the last one, so you'd better make it last."

"I'm going to have to roll you down the stairs, I'm afraid."

Chloe snickered at her father. "Conan could help you carry me down. He's way strong."

"Stronger than me, probably, especially with all those breadsticks in his system."

Chloe jerked her hand above the table surface with a guilty look, but her father didn't reprimand her, he only smiled.

Sage gazed at his light expression with frustration. Drat the man. Just when she thought she had him pegged, he had to act in a way that didn't match her perception.

It was becoming terribly difficult to hang on to her dislike of him. Though her first impression of him had been of a self-absorbed businessman with little time for his child, she was finding it more difficult to reconcile that with a man who could tease his daughter into the giggles.

She had always made a practice of looking for the good in people. Even during the worst of her childhood she had tried to find her stepmother's redeeming qualities. So why was she so determined to only see negatives when she looked at Eben Spencer?

Maybe she was afraid to notice his good points. If she could still be so attracted to him when she was only focusing on the things she disliked, how much more vulnerable would she be if she allowed herself to see the good in him?

The thought didn't sit well at all.

What was her story? Eben wondered as Sage dished out a simple but delicious dessert of vanilla ice cream and fresh strawberries. She was warm and approachable one moment, stiff and cool the next. She kissed like a dream then turned distant and polite.

Her house was like her—eclectic, colorful, with a bit of an eccentric bent. One whole display case in the corner was filled with gnarled pieces of driftwood interspersed with various shells and canning jars filled with polished glass. Nothing in the house looked extravagant or costly, but it all seemed to work together to make a charming, cozy nest.

He was intensely curious about how she came to own the house after five years of renting it, but she obviously hadn't want to talk about it so he had let her turn the conversation in other directions. He wondered if that had something to do with the pain that sometimes flickered in her gaze.

"I *love* strawberries," Chloe announced. "They're my very favorite thing to have on ice cream."

"You need to try some of the Oregon berries sometime," Sage said with a smile.

She maintained none of her stiff reserve with Chloe. She was genuinely warm all the time and he found it entrancing.

"And before you leave, remind me to give you some of the wild raspberry jam I made last summer," she went on.

"You made jam all by yourself?"

"It's not hard. The toughest thing is not eating the berries the minute you pick them so you've got enough left to use for the jam."

Before Chloe could ask the million questions Eben could see forming in her eyes, Sage's dog slithered out from under the table and began to bark insistently.

"Uh-oh. That's his ignore-me-at-your-peril bark," Sage said quickly, setting her unfinished dessert down on the table. "I had better let him out."

"I'll do it!" Chloe exclaimed. Her features—so much like her mother's—were animated and excited.

She had been remarkably well-behaved through dinner—no tantrums, no power struggles. It was a refreshing change, he thought. Sage Benedetto had a remarkably positive effect on her. He wasn't sure what she did differently, but Chloe responded to her in a way his daughter hadn't to anyone else in a long time.

"Thanks, Chloe," Sage said. "Just make sure the gate is closed around the yard so he can't take off. He's usually pretty good about staying on his own territory, but all bets are off if he catches sight of a cat."

Chloe paused at the door. "Can I ask Miss Galvez if I can look at the dolls while I'm downstairs?"

Sage shifted her gaze to meet Eben's. "You'll have to ask your father that."

"Someone will have to clue me in. What dolls?"

"The woman who left the house to me and to Anna Galvez had a huge doll collection. It takes up an entire room in Anna's apartment now. I promised Chloe we could take a look at them before dinner, but time slipped away from us and then you arrived."

"Can I see it, Daddy?"

"If Miss Galvez doesn't mind showing you, I can't see any reason why not."

"Yay!" Chloe raced out the door, though Conan shot ahead of her and Eben could hear his paws click furiously down the stairs.

The moment they left, Eben realized he was alone with Sage—not a comfortable situation given the tension still simmering between them. She was obviously suddenly cognizant of that fact as well. She jerked to her feet and started clearing away their dinner dishes.

He finished the last of his dessert and rose to help her. "Thank you again for dinner. I can't remember a meal I've enjoyed more."

It was true, he realized with surprise. Chloe was usually in bed when he returned home from work, but on the rare occasions he dined with her, he typically found himself bracing for her frequent emotional outbursts.

It had been wonderful to enjoy his daughter's company under Sage's moderating influence.

Sage didn't look convinced by his words. "It was only vegetarian lasagna. Probably nothing at all like you're used to. You don't have to patronize me."

Her words surprised a laugh from him. "I don't think I could patronize you, even if I tried. I doubt anyone can. I mean it. I enjoyed the meal—and the company—immensely."

She studied him for a moment then nodded. "So did I."

"You sound surprised. It's not very flattering, I must admit."

"I am surprised, I suppose. I don't entertain a great deal. When I do, it's usually friends in my own circle."

"I appreciate you making an exception in our case."

He was intensely aware of her, of the way her dangly earrings caught the lamplight, the smell of her, feminine and enticing, her mobile expressions. He wanted to kiss her again, with a fierce ache, though he knew it was impossible, not to mention extremely unwise.

He didn't want to destroy this fragile peace—especially when his intentions could never be anything other than a quick fling, something he guessed wasn't typical for her, either.

In an effort to cool his growing awareness, he searched his mind for a change of topic as he followed her into the small kitchen with his hands full of dishes.

"Tell me the truth, now that Chloe is gone for a moment. How was she today?"

Surprise widened her eyes at the question. "Fine. She's a little energetic, but no worse than any of the other eight-year-olds at the camp. Better than some. She's very sweet."

She studied him and he was certain some of his relief must have shown on his features.

"You look like you expected a different answer."

He sighed and put the dishes down on the countertop next to the sink. "I love my daughter, but I have to admit that *sweet* is not an adjective many people use to describe her these days."

"That surprises me. She seems to me a typical kid, just like the others in the class."

"I think you have an extraordinary rapport with her.'"

"I'm not sure why that would be."

"I'm not, either. Chloe is…challenging. She's bright and creative and funny most of the time, but she has these mood swings. Her mother's death two years ago affected her strongly. She and Brooke were very close. Her mother doted on her—maybe too much."

"I don't think you can ever love a child too much."

There was that stiffness in her voice again. "I don't, either. Please don't misunderstand. I only meant that losing her mother was a fierce and painful blow to Chloe. As a parent, I'm afraid I'm a poor substitute for my wife."

Her gaze flashed to his and he regretted exposing so much truth about himself.

"I tried to give her some leeway for her grief for several months but I'm afraid I let her get away with too many things and now that's her expectation all the time. In the last year and a half she's been through four schools and a half-dozen nannies. She's moody and unpredictable. Defiant one moment, deceptively docile the next."

Without really thinking about it, he started to load the dishes in the dishwasher. "The other morning was a perfect example," he continued. "She could have been seriously hurt sneaking out so early. I wouldn't do as she demanded the night before and stay out late hunting up seashells with her, so she countermanded me by sneaking out on her own."

She opened her mouth slightly then closed it again.

"What were you going to say?" he pressed.

"Nothing. Never mind." She turned away to run water in the sink for the soiled dishes.

Eben leaned against the counter next to her, enjoying her graceful movements.

"You probably would have been right out there with her in the middle of the night with a flashlight and a bucket looking for sand dollars, wouldn't you?"

She gave him a sidelong look, then smiled. "Probably."

"I let her get away with too much right after Brooke died and I need to set some boundaries now. Children needs rules and structure."

"Is that the kind of childhood you had? Regimented, toe-the-line. Military school, right?"

He laughed, though he heard the harsh note in it and wondered if she did as well. "Not quite. I would have given my entire baseball card collection for a little structure and discipline. My parents were of the if-it-feels-good-just-do-it school of thought. It destroyed them both and they nearly took me and my sister along with them. I can't do that to Chloe."

Her hands paused in the sink and her eyes widened with sympathy. He shifted, uncomfortable. Where the hell had that come from? He didn't share these pieces of his life with anyone. He wasn't sure he'd ever even articulated that to Brooke. If he had, maybe she wouldn't have expected so many things from him he wasn't at all sure he had been capable of offering.

He certainly had no business sharing them with Sage. She was quiet for a long moment, watching him out of intense brown eyes. The only sound was the rain clicking against the window and the soft sound of their mingled breathing.

"I'm sorry," she finally murmured.

He shrugged. "It was a long time ago. I just don't want to make the same mistakes with Chloe."

"But you can go too far in the other direction, can't you?"

"I'm doing my best. That's all I can do."

He didn't want to talk about this anymore. With her so close, he was having a tough time hanging on to any coherent thought anyway. All he could think about was kissing her again.

But he couldn't.

The thought had no sooner entered his head than he could swear he felt a soft hand in the small of his back from out of nowhere pushing him toward her.

She gave him a quick startled look then her gaze seemed to fasten on his mouth.

What other choice did he have but to kiss her?

Chapter Seven

She sighed as if she'd been waiting for his kiss and she tasted heady and sweet from the wine and the strawberries.

Having her in his arms felt *right*, in a way he couldn't explain. On an intellectual level, it made absolutely no sense and every voice in his head was clamoring to tell him why kissing her again was a colossal mistake.

He shut them all out and focused only on the silky smoothness of her hair, her soft curves against him.

Her hands were warm, wet from the dishwater. He could feel the palm prints she left against his shirt, a temporary brand.

He had been thinking of their earlier kiss all day. As he drove to Portland and back, as he listened to his attorneys ramble on and on. Like the low murmur of the sea outside, she had been a constant presence in his mind. Their kiss that morning had been heated and intense, more so because it had been so unexpected.

This, though, was different. Eben closed his eyes at the astonishing gentleness of it, the quiet peace that seemed to swirl around them, wrapping them together with silken threads.

He still wanted her fiercely and the hunger thrumming inside him urged him to deepen the kiss but he kept it slow and easy, reluctant to destroy the fragile beauty of the moment.

"All day long, I've been telling myself a thousand reasons why I shouldn't do that again," he murmured after a long, drugging moment.

He could see a pulse flutter in her throat, feel her chest rise and fall with her accelerated breathing. She dropped her hands from his shirt, but not before he was certain he felt their slight tremble.

"I can probably give you a couple thousand more why I shouldn't have let you."

"Yet here we are."

She sighed and he heard turmoil and regret in the sound. "Right. Here we are."

She stepped away from him and immersed her hands in the dishwater, a slight brush of color on her cheeks as she started scrubbing a pan with fierce concentration.

He sighed, compelled to honesty. "I'm not looking for anything. You need to know that. This just sort of… happened."

The temperature in the room suddenly seemed to dip a dozen degrees and he could swear the rain lashed the windows with much more force than before.

When she spoke, her voice was as cool as the rain. "That makes two of us, then."

"Right."

He was digging himself in deeper but he had to attempt an explanation. "We just have this…thing between us. I have to tell you, I don't quite understand it."

"Don't you?" Her voice was positively icy now and he realized how his words could be construed.

He sighed again, hating this awkward discomfort. "You're a beautiful woman, Sage. You have to know that. Any man would be crazy not to find you attractive. But I swear, until this morning I have never in my life kissed a woman I haven't at least taken on two or three dates. I've never known anything like this. You just do something to me. I can't explain it. To be honest, I'm not sure I like it."

The ice in her eyes had thawed a little, he saw, though he wasn't sure he was thrilled with the shadow of amusement that replaced it.

"I'm sure you don't."

"I haven't dated in a decade," he confessed. "My wife and I were married for seven years and Brooke has been gone for two years now. I'm afraid I'm out of practice at this whole man–woman thing."

She sent him a sidelong look he couldn't read. "I wouldn't exactly say that."

Oddly, he could swear he heard a ripple of low laughter coming from the other room. He shifted his gaze to the doorway into her living room and saw Sage do the same, almost as if she could hear it, too.

No one was there, he could tell in an instant, but his attention was suddenly caught by a picture he hadn't noticed before hanging on the wall of the kitchen.

He stared at the image of two women on what looked like a sea cliff, their cheeks pressed together as they embraced, deep affection in their eyes.

One was Sage, a lighthearted joy in her expression he hadn't seen before. But his shock of recognition was for the other person, the one with the wrinkled features and mischievous eyes…. He moved closer for a better look.

"I know this woman!"

Sage blinked a little at his abrupt change of topic. "Abigail? You know Abigail?"

"Yes! Abigail, that's her name!"

"Abigail Dandridge. She's the one who left me this house. She was my best friend in the world."

"I never knew her last name. She's dead, then." An obvious statement, but he couldn't for the world think of what else to say.

She nodded, her eyes suddenly dark with emotion. "It's been almost five weeks now. Her heart just stopped in her sleep one night. No warning signs at all. I know she would have wanted to go that way, but… I didn't have a chance to say goodbye—you know?—and everything feels so *unfinished*. I still feel her here, in the house. At random moments I think I smell her favorite scent or feel the touch of her hand in my hair. It's a cliché, but I still keep thinking I'll hear her voice any minute now, calling me down the stairs to share some gossip over tea."

He suddenly understood the sorrow he glimpsed every once in a while in Sage's eyes. He wanted to comfort her but couldn't find the words, not through his own shock and sadness.

She looked at him with puzzlement in her eyes. "I'm sorry. How did you say you knew her?"

"I suppose I can't really say I knew her. I met her only briefly but the encounter was…unforgettable."

She smiled, a little tremulously. "Abigail often had that effect on people."

"I should have figured it out. You know, I thought

Conan looked familiar but I didn't put the pieces together until right this moment. I can't believe she's gone."

"You met her then? She didn't say anything about it."

"It probably wasn't as significant a meeting for her as it was for me. I came to town scouting locations for a new property. I was jogging early one morning and I saw her and I guess it was Conan. I don't know why I stopped to talk to her—maybe I stopped to tie my shoe or something—but we struck up a conversation. It was the oddest thing. After we talked for awhile, she insisted on taking me to breakfast at The Sea Urchin—and I went, which isn't at all like me."

What also hadn't been like him was the way the woman's warm, kind eyes had led him to telling her far more about himself than he did with most people.

By the time they'd finished their divine breakfast of old-fashioned French toast with mountains of fresh whipped cream and bacon so crisp it melted in his mouth, Abigail knew about Chloe, about Brooke's death, even about those last years of their troubled marriage.

"Abigail was always doing things like that, grabbing a stranger to take out for a meal," Sage said into his sudden silence. "She loved to meet new people. She used to say she knew everything there was to know about the locals and she got damn sick and tired of hearing the same boring old stories a hundred times."

"She was wonderful. Sharp. Funny. Kind. After breakfast at The Sea Urchin, she suggested I talk to Stanley and Jade Wu about buying it. You know, the whole thing was her idea. She told me they were thinking about retiring, but I have to say, until I approached them with an offer, I don't think it had even occurred to them to sell the place."

"I told you Abigail knew everything about the locals, sometimes things they didn't even know themselves."

Abigail had certainly been able to see deep into Sage's own mind. From the moment Sage arrived in Cannon Beach, Abigail had seemed to know instinctively how much Sage longed for a family and home of her own.

The remarkable thing had been her way of finding the best in everyone she met and helping them see it as well.

Why on earth would Abigail have picked Eben Spencer to be one of her pet projects? Sage couldn't for the life of her figure it out. And she had steered him toward buying The Sea Urchin? It didn't make sense. Abigail would never have suggested he buy the place if she didn't trust him to take care of it.

Maybe Sage needed to reconsider her perceptions of the man. If Abigail had approved of him to that extent, perhaps she saw deeper into him than Sage could.

"That morning at breakfast with Abigail felt like an omen. I have to admit, from the moment we stepped into the place, I set my heart on purchasing The Sea Urchin and I'm afraid I haven't been able to even entertain the idea of any other property for Spencer Hotels' next project. I'm only sorry I didn't have the chance to meet up with her again."

What weird twist of fate had led her to Chloe on the beach that morning, to someone peripherally connected to Abigail? Or *had* it been a coincidence? She shivered a little, remembering how Conan had greeted Chloe like an old friend, as if he had been expecting her.

"Everything okay?" Eben asked.

He would probably mock any woo-woo speculation on her part. She had a feeling Eben was a prosaic man not given to superstition.

"Fine. Just thinking how odd it was that you're here now, in Abigail's house."

"*Your* house, now."

"In my mind, it will always belong to her. She loved every inch of this place."

Before he could answer, they heard footsteps bounding up the stairs. A moment later, Chloe and Conan burst into the apartment, with Anna Galvez in tow.

"Daddy, Daddy, guess what?"

"What, sweetheart?"

"There's a whole room of dolls downstairs. It's huge. I've never *seen* so many dolls. Miss Galvez says if it's okay with you, I can pick one out and keep it. May I, Daddy? Oh please, may I?"

"Chloe—" He shifted, obviously uncomfortable with the idea.

Sage sent a swift look to Anna, surprised she would make such an offer. She wouldn't have expected such a generous gesture from Anna, especially after their conversation the day before about keeping the collection intact.

But somehow it seemed exactly the right thing to do, precisely what Abigail would have wanted, for them to give this sweet daughter of the man Abigail had known one of her beloved dolls.

"Several of the dolls have resin faces and aren't breakable. They're completely safe for her," Anna said somewhat stiffly.

Eben looked at Sage with a question in his eyes. She nodded. "Abigail would have wanted her things to be loved," she said. "She adored showing them off to children."

She got the impression it wasn't an easy thing for

Eben to accept anything from anyone. He was a hard, self-contained man, though it appeared he had a soft spot for his daughter, something she wouldn't have expected just a few days before.

"All right," he finally said. "If you're certain you don't mind."

Chloe squealed with excitement. "You have to help me choose one. Both of you."

She grabbed Sage with one hand then Eben with the other and started tugging them both toward the stairs. Conan barked once and Sage could swear he was grinning again.

She didn't know which she found more disturbing, her dog's pleased expression or Anna's speculative one.

For the next ten minutes, she, Anna and Eben helped Chloe peruse Abigail's vast collection, doing their best to point her toward the sturdier, more age-appropriate dolls.

Sage had never been one to play with girlie things, but even she had to admit how much she enjoyed walking into the doll room. She couldn't help feeling close to Abigail here, amid the collection that had been such a part of her friend.

Abigail never married and had no children of her own. She had a great-nephew somewhere, but he hadn't even bothered coming to his great-aunt's funeral. In many ways, the dolls were Abigail's family, the inanimate counterpoints to the living, breathing strays she collected.

Sage loved seeing them, remembering the joy Abigail had found every time she added a new doll to her collection.

She especially loved the dolls Abigail had made herself over the decades, with painted faces and elaborate hand-sewn clothes. Victorian dolls with flounced dresses and parasols, teenyboppers with ponytails and poodle skirts, dolls with bobbed hair and flapper dresses.

There was no real rhyme or reason to the collection—no common theme that Sage had ever been able to discern—but each was charming in its own way.

"I can't decide. There are too many."

A spasm of irritation crossed Eben's features at Chloe's whiny tone. Sage could tell the girl was tired after their big day on the shore then coming back to Brambleberry House afterward. She hoped Eben was perceptive enough to pick up on that as well.

To her relief, after only a moment his frustration slid away, replaced by patience. He pulled his daughter close and kissed her on the top of her dark curls and Sage could swear she felt her heart tumble in her chest.

"Pick out your favorite three and maybe we can help you make your final choice," he suggested, a new gentleness in his voice.

That seemed a less daunting task to his daughter. With renewed enthusiasm she studied the shelves of dolls, pulling one out here and there, returning another, choosing with care until she had three lined up in the middle of the floor.

They were an oddly disparate trio: a little girl with pigtails holding a teddy bear, a curvy woman in a grass Hawaiian skirt and lei, then an elegant woman with blond hair and a white dress.

Chloe studied them for a moment, then reached for the one in white. "You don't have to help me pick. This is the one I want. She looks just like an angel."

The doll was simple but lovely. "Good choice," Sage said, admiring the doll when Chloe held her out.

"Her name is Brooke."

"Of course it is," Eben murmured.

Sage glanced at him and was surprised to see a pained look in his eyes as he studied the doll. Only then did she remember his wife's name had been Brooke.

For the first time, Sage picked up the resemblance in the doll's features to Chloe's. Only their hair color was different.

Chloe must have picked the doll because it looked like her mother. Oh, poor little pumpkin. Sage wanted to gather her up and hold her tight until she didn't hurt anymore.

So much pain in the world.

"I'm going to put her on my bureau at home," Chloe announced. "That way I can see her every morning."

"Good plan," Anna said. Her eyes met Sage's and Sage could see her own supposition mirrored there.

"Okay, kiddo," Eben interjected, the shadows still in his gaze, "you need to say thanks to Sage and Ms. Galvez for the doll, then we should head home. You've had a big day and need to get some rest so you'll be a good little camper in the morning."

"Thank you very much for the doll. I will love her forever," the girl said solemnly to them, then turned back to her father. "I'm not tired at all, though. I would like to stay longer."

Eben smiled, Sage could see the lines around the corners of his mouth that only served to make him look more ruggedly handsome.

"*You* might not be tired, but I certainly am and I imagine Sage and Ms. Galvez are as well. Come on, let's take your new friend home."

Chloe paused, then ran to Anna and threw her arms

around her waist. "I mean it. Thank you for the doll. I'll take super good care of her, I promise."

Anna looked discomfited by the girl's hug, but there was a softness in her eyes Sage hadn't seen before. "I'm glad to hear that. Bring her back anytime to see the rest of her friends."

Chloe giggled, then turned to Sage and embraced her as well. That tumble in her heart before was nothing compared to the hard, swift fall she felt as she fell head over heels for this sweet, motherless little girl.

"Thank you for letting me help you make vegetable lasagna and play with Conan and see where you live. I think Brambleberry House is the most beautiful house in the world."

Sage hugged her back. "You're very welcome. I'll see you in the morning, okay? Don't forget your raincoat. We're in for some nice Oregon sunshine. That means rain, by the way."

Chloe giggled, then slipped her hand in her father's.

Though Anna and Conan stayed in her apartment, Sage followed them outside. The rain had nearly stopped and only a light drizzle fell.

On the porch, she stopped, feeling as awkward as if they'd been on a date. That stunning, gentle kiss in her apartment seemed to shimmer through her mind and she couldn't seem to think of anything but his warm mouth and his strong, hard arms around her.

Though Chloe ran ahead and climbed into the back seat of the Jag, Eben paused and met her gaze, the recessed porch lights reflecting in his eyes. He grabbed her hand, his fingers enfolded around hers. "Thank you again for taking Chloe later than you planned, and for dinner and everything."

"You're very welcome. She was no trouble."

"Only because you're amazing with her."

Sage shook her head, slipping her hand from his, needing the safety of physical distance from him even as her emotions seemed to tug her ever nearer. "I find her a joy. I told you that."

"I'll be ready in the morning to run with Conan."

"I promise, I won't hold you to that. I was joking."

"I'm looking forward to it. This morning was wonderful and I'd love a repeat. The, uh, run I meant."

She was certain if the light had been brighter she would have seen faint color on his features. Somehow his discomfort over their unexpected kiss charmed her beyond measure.

She didn't need to spend more time with him or with Chloe. Both of them were already sneaking their way into her heart. More time would only make their departure that much more difficult. She already dreaded thinking about when they left Cannon Beach.

"Don't count on it," she answered. "If I'm lucky, my furry alarm clock will sleep in tomorrow."

"I'll be waiting if he doesn't."

Without another word, he turned and hurried down the steps into the drizzle.

Chapter Eight

Long after the car drove away, headlights reflecting on the wet streets, Sage stood on the porch of Brambleberry House, hugging her arms to her against the evening chill and worrying.

She had to find it in her heart to push them both away. That was the only solution. Her emotions were too battered right now, raw and aching from Abigail's death.

She wasn't strong enough to sustain another devastating loss. That's what it would be, she feared, if she let them inside any farther. She was afraid she would find it entirely too easy to fall for both of them. Already she was halfway to being in love with Chloe, with her sweet eyes and her quirky sense of humor and her desperate eagerness to please.

She sighed as an owl called somewhere in the distance, then Sage opened the door into the house.

She expected Anna to be cloistered in Abigail's apart-

ment by the time she returned. Instead, she found her waiting in the foyer, one hand absently rubbing Conan's head.
She looked softer, somehow, more approachable—perhaps
because she'd changed out of her work clothes while Sage,
Eben and Chloe had been upstairs having dinner.

She should have invited Anna to join them, she
thought, ashamed of herself for not thinking of it.

"Thank you for the whole doll thing," she said. "It
seemed to be a big hit with Chloe."

"I probably should have talked to you first about giving her one before I suggested it to her. I know what you
said the other day about the collection staying together.
Technically, they belong to both of us and they're not really mine to give away."

Would she ever escape the complexities of that blasted
will? "Despite what you might think, I honestly don't
want to hoard all of Abigail's things forever, to freeze
everything in the house just as it is and never alter so
much as a nail hole."

"I know you don't," Anna said stiffly. "I'm sorry if I
gave you the impression I thought otherwise."

Sage sighed. "I'm sorry to be short with you. This is
all so awkward, isn't it?"

Anna was quiet for a moment. "I know you loved Abigail deeply and she felt the same way about you. There
was an unbreakable bond between the two of you. Everyone could see it. I understand how painful her death
is for you. Believe me, I understand. Maybe you loved
her longer but… I loved her, too. I miss her."

Guilt lodged in her throat at her weeks of coldness toward Anna, at her ridiculous resentment—as if it were
Anna's fault they found themselves in this tangled ar-
rangement.

She had never felt so small and petty.

Abigail would have been furious with her, would have given her a stern look out of those blue eyes and told her to put on her big girl panties and just deal.

"Would you...like to come in?" Anna asked at Sage's continued silence. "I was about to have some tea and you're welcome to share it. You don't have to, of course."

She was exhausted suddenly, emotionally and physically. Her day had been tumultuous from that first kiss in Eben's beach house and she wanted nothing more than to climb into her bed and yank the quilt over her head and shut out the world.

But how could she rebuff such a clearcut overture of friendship?

"Sure. Okay."

Anna looked surprised, then thrilled, which only added to Sage's guilt level. The other woman led the way into her apartment, toward the little kitchen that still looked as it had the day Abigail died. Her gaze landed on the calendar still turned back to April and Abigail's handwritten little notes in the date squares.

Conan, shots, 10:30.
Lunch with the girls.
Will's birthday.

It was a snapshot of her life, busy and fulfilling. Why hadn't Anna taken it down? Sage would have thought that to be one of the first things an efficient, orderly woman like Anna would make an effort to do when she moved her own things in.

Did she find some kind of comfort from this small

reminder of Abigail and her life? Sage resolved to try harder to forge a connection with Anna.

"What kind of tea would you like? I think there's every kind imaginable here."

Chai was her favorite but she wasn't sure she could drink it here in this kitchen out of Abigail's favorite teacups, not with her emotions so close to the surface.

"It's late. I don't need more caffeine with my head already buzzing. I'd better go for chamomile."

Anna smiled and found teabags in the cupboard, then pulled a burbling kettle off the stove and poured it over the bags.

Sage watched for a moment, awkward at the silence. "Thank you again for the doll thing," she said. "It was a great idea. Chloe was thrilled."

"She picked an angel doll and named her Brooke. Am I crazy or was there some deeper significance to that?"

"It was her mother's name."

Anna pursed her lips in distress. "That's what I thought. Poor little thing."

Anna studied her for a moment as if she wasn't sure whether to ask the questions Sage could see forming in her eyes. "You do know that's Eben Spencer, the CEO of Spencer Hotels, right?" she finally said.

"I hope so. If not, he's doing a fairly credible job of masquerading as the man."

"And do you realize he's brilliant? I read about him in *Fortune* a few months ago. The man has single-handedly rescued a small, floundering hotel company and turned it into a major player in the hospitality industry with small luxury properties around the globe."

"Yippee for him."

And she had fed him vegetarian lasagna and breadsticks at her dining table with the mismatched chairs. She wanted a do-over on the whole evening.

No, she corrected herself. She wouldn't allow him to make her feel ashamed of her life or what she had worked hard to build for herself. After severing the last fragile ties with her father, she had started with nothing and had built a rich, fulfilling life here.

"While we were looking at the dolls, Chloe told me he's looking to buy The Sea Urchin."

"That's what I understand."

"It's a perfect property for Spencer Hotels. It will be interesting to see what he can do with the place."

"I like The Sea Urchin exactly the way it is," she muttered.

"So do I," Anna assured her. "But Spencer Hotels has a reputation for taking great properties and making them even better. It will be interesting to watch."

"If Stanley and Jade ultimately decide to sell. I don't believe Eben has convinced them yet."

"If what I've heard about him is halfway true, he will." She paused and gave Sage a careful look as she handed her the cup of tea. "Was I crazy or did I pick up some kind of vibe between you two?"

Sage could feel herself flush and was grateful again for her Italian heritage. She could taste his mouth again on hers, feel the silky softness of his hair beneath her fingertips. "You have a much more vivid imagination than I ever gave you credit for."

She immediately wished she could call the words back, but to her surprise, Anna only laughed. "Sorry. Not much imagination here, but I do pride myself on my keen powers of observation. Comes from reading too many mysteries, I think."

"What did you see?" Sage asked warily.

"Wet handprints. They were all over his shirt. Unless the man has some kind of weird, acrobatic agility, I don't believe he could put handprints on his own back. And since you were the only one in the apartment with him, I guess that leaves you. Not that it's any of my business."

Sage could feel herself flush and for the life of her, she couldn't think how to respond.

"I hope this doesn't offend you," Anna went on, "but I have to tell you, he doesn't seem like your usual type."

"I wasn't aware I had a *type*."

"Of course you do. Everyone does."

She told herself she was grateful the conversation had turned from handprints—or anything else she might have put on Eben. "Okay, I'll bite. What's my type?"

Anna added at least three teaspoons of sugar to her own cup as she gave Sage a sidelong look. "I don't know. Maybe some shaggy-haired, folk-singer guy who smells like patchouli and drives a hybrid with a Peace-Out bumper sticker on the back bumper."

She was too tired to be offended, she decided. Besides, she had to admit it was a pretty accurate description of the guys she usually dated. She sipped at her tea and grinned a little, astonished to find a sense of humor in Anna Galvez—and more astonished to find herself enjoying their interaction.

"All right, Ms. Know-it-All. What's your type, then?"

She was certain Anna's smile slipped a bit. "Well, probably not shaggy-haired folk singers."

Her evasion only made Sage more curious. She had never given much thought to Anna's social life, though she thought she remembered something about a broken engagement in the last few years.

"Seriously, are you dating anybody? Since we're living in the same house, it would be good to be prepared if I encounter some strange man on the stairway in the middle of the night."

Anna sighed. "No. I'm currently on sabbatical from men."

For some reason—probably because of her exhaustion—Sage found that hilarious. "Is there a stipend that goes with that?"

The other woman laughed and shook her head. "No, it's all purely gratis. But the benefits to my mental health are enormous."

No wonder Abigail had loved Anna. It was a surprising revelation in a day full of them, but by the time Sage finished her tea fifteen minutes later, all her misconceptions about Anna Galvez had flown out the window. The other woman wasn't at all the stuffy, serious businesswoman she presented herself as most of the time, at least the way she had always presented herself to Sage.

Why the facade? Sage wondered. Why had she always acted so cool and polite to her? Was it only a protective response to some latent, unconscious hostility Sage might have been projecting? She didn't want to think so, especially tonight when she was too tired for such deep introspection, but she had a feeling she may have been largely to blame for the awkwardness between them.

At least they had made this shaky beginning to building a friendship. They had a house and a dog and a life in common now. They should at least get a friendship out of the deal, too.

As the thought flickered through her mind, the scent of freesia seemed to drift through the room.

"Can you smell that?"

An odd look sparked in Anna's dark eyes and she set

down her teacup. "I smell it all the time. It's like she's right here with me sometimes. But of course that's crazy."

"Is it?"

"I don't believe in ghosts. I'm sorry. I'm sure I'm a little more prosaic than you. I can't buy that Abigail still lingers at Brambleberry House."

"So what explanation do you have for it?"

Anna shrugged and spoke so quickly Sage was certain she must have given the matter some thought. "Abigail loved the smell of freesias. I think over her eighty years of living here and wearing the scent, some of it must have just absorbed into the walls and the carpet. Every once in a while, it's released by a shifting of molecules or something."

Sage wasn't convinced but she wasn't about to risk this tentative friendship by arguing. "Maybe," she answered. "I like it, whatever the explanation."

Anna smiled a little tremulously. "So do I."

"I should go. It's getting late." When Sage set down her teacup and rose, Conan didn't move from his spot curled up on his side by Anna's feet like a huge red foot-warmer. Apparently he was settled for the night. She felt a little twinge of jealousy but pushed it away. For some reason, she sensed Anna needed his company more than she did right now.

"I guess he's yours for the night."

"I guess."

"Good night. I, uh, enjoyed the tea."

Anna smiled. "So did I."

"Next time it's my treat."

"I'll count on it."

She said good-night to Conan, who slapped his tail against the floor a few times before going back to sleep, then she headed up the stairs to her apartment.

No freesia lingered in the air here, only the spicy scent of lasagna—and perhaps a hint of Eben's expensive cologne.

What was she going to do about the man?

Nothing, she answered her own question. What could she do? He would be leaving in a few days when his business here was done and she would go back to her happy, fulfilling life.

What other choice did she have? They were worlds apart in a hundred different ways. He was the CEO of a multinational corporation and she was a vegetarian nature-girl with a spooky, omniscient dog and a rambling old house full of ghosts and problems.

Yeah, the two of them seemed to generate this unlikely heat between them, but even if she were stupid enough to indulge herself by playing with it for awhile, dry tinder could only burn so long. Without the steady fuel of shared interests and emotional compatibility, the heat between them would probably flare and burn out quickly.

That thought depressed her more than it ought to.

She had a great life here in Cannon Beach, she reminded herself. Everything she could ever need. She knew that eventually this ache in her heart over losing Abigail would ease. She hurt a little less again than she had yesterday, a little less then than the day before that.

She would never stop missing her friend, but she knew eventually she would find her way back to homeostasis and begin to find happiness and joy in her life again.

Eben and Chloe Spencer would leave Cannon Beach in a few days and be just another memory. A pleasant one, yes, like all her many birdwatching hikes with Abigail and their hundreds of shared cups of tea, but a memory nonetheless.

* * *

"It's a good thing you're cute or I could definitely grow to loathe you for these morning tortures."

The object of her ire simply sat waiting by the door with an impatient scowl for Sage to lace up her running shoes. Despite spending the night in Anna's apartment, Conan must have squeezed out of his doggie door so he could come up the stairs and bark outside her door at the usual time to go running.

She yawned and tied her other shoe, dearly wishing she were back in her bed, that she had the nerve to send the mongrel down the beach to Eben's rental unit to drag him out of bed.

Since that conjured up too many enticing images of wavy dark hair against a pillow, of whisker-roughened skin and sleepy smiles, she jerked her mind back to Conan, who was quivering with impatience. He barked again and she sighed.

"All right, all right. I'm ready. Let's do this."

Conan bounded down the stairs of Brambleberry House, dancing around in the foyer in his eagerness to be gone as she followed more slowly, yanking her hair back into a ponytail as she went.

The morning air was cool and the rain had stopped sometime in the night, leaving wisps of fog to wrap through the garden and around the coastal pines beyond.

She stood on the porch stretching her hamstrings and listening to the distant sound of the sea and the call of that screech owl she'd heard the night before.

Maybe she didn't hate these runs with Conan after all, she decided. If not for them, she would miss all this morning splendor, simply for the sake of an extra hour of sleep.

The dog seemed wildly eager to go, whining impa-

tiently and racing back and forth in the yard. Apparently
he'd never heard of pulled muscles or torn ligaments, she
thought sourly, then gave up stretching and followed him
to the backyard, to the latched gate there that led directly
to the beach.

The dog rushed out but Sage had to pause for a moment to prop the gate open so they could return that way
instead of having to take a more circuitous route to the
front of the house.

She straightened from the task and nearly collided
with a solid wall of muscle.

"Oh," she exclaimed. She would have fallen if strong
arms hadn't reached to keep her upright.

"Sorry," Eben murmured, heat flaring in his green
eyes. "I thought you saw me."

"No. I wasn't paying attention."

After a moment's hesitation, he released her arm and
she managed to find her footing as she caught sight of
Conan a few yards away, racing around a giggling Chloe.

"Chloe! You're up early."

"Don't I know it." Eben looked at his daughter with
disgruntled affection. "She woke me an hour ago, begging me to take her jogging with Conan this morning. We
couldn't quite figure out the logistics, though. We didn't
want to bang on your door at 6:00 a.m. just to pick up
your dog, but then we saw your lights go on and headed
over, hoping to catch you."

"Conan didn't give me a lot of choice this morning. He
seemed particularly insistent on running today. Sometimes I think he's psychic. Maybe he knew you and Chloe
were going to be here and wanted to make sure we didn't
miss you."

"We came to take him running, so you can go back to bed," Chloe said with her guileless smile.

Tempting offer, Sage thought. That would certainly be the prudent course, to climb back into her bed, yank the covers over her head and pretend this was all a weird dream.

She couldn't do it, though. The morning was too lovely and she discovered she wasn't willing to relinquish the chance to be with them again, even though she knew it couldn't possibly be healthy for her.

"I've got a better idea," she said suddenly. "Come on inside to the garage for a moment."

Eben looked puzzled but he followed her and Chloe and Conan did the same. Sage quickly programmed the code to open the garage door. Inside she found one of Abigail's favorite toys propped against one wall and wheeled it out to where they waited for her.

Chloe's eyes widened when she saw Sage pushing the tandem bike out of the garage.

"Cool!" she exclaimed. "Is that yours?"

"It belonged to a friend of mine. We used to love to take bike rides together."

What a wealth of information that revealed about Abigail, she thought, that an independent woman in her eighties who lived with only an upstairs tenant for family would invest in a tandem bike. With her skill of gathering people around her, she never had a dearth of people to take rides with, from Will Garrett to Mr. Delarosa to the high school kids who delivered the newspaper.

"Can we ride it? You and me?" Chloe asked.

"I think that's a great idea. Your dad and that beastly dog can run if they want and get all sweaty and gross. We girls will enjoy a leisurely morning ride."

Chloe's glee nearly matched Conan's excitement. Sage glanced over at Eben and found him watching her with a murky look in his eyes that made her suddenly as breathless as if she'd just biked up the hill to Indian Beach.

It took Chloe a few moments to get the hang of the tandem bicycle, but by the time they made it a block, she was riding like a pro, giggling for the sheer joy of it.

Sage knew just how she felt. She wanted to laugh, as well. How could she ever have thought staying back in her apartment in bed would be preferable to this?

They stuck to pavement since she knew the soft sand of the beach would prove a challenge for Chloe. On impulse, she guided them south, away from town, with a specific destination in mind.

They encountered little traffic here this early in the morning. Conan and Eben ran ahead of them, Conan resigned to the leash. She had to admit, she enjoyed watching the play of Eben's muscles as he ran. Not a bad way to start the day, she decided.

She lifted her face to the pale streaks of sunlight shining toward the ocean. A strange emotion fluttered through her and it took her a while to recognize it.

She was happy, she realized.

For the first time since Abigail's death, she remembered what it was to savor life.

It was a gift, she decided, one she wasn't about to waste.

Chapter Nine

On a purely intellectual level, Eben knew he shouldn't be enjoying himself so much.

It was only a run, after all, just a brief interlude before he jumped right back into his normal routine of business calls and strategy sessions.

But the air was cool and sweet, his muscles had that pleasant burn of a good workout and the scenery was beyond spectacular, with the broad expanse of beach below them and the needles and sea stacks jutting into the sky offshore.

He wasn't sure where he was going, but Sage obviously had a destination in mind. Every once in a while she called out a direction—turn here, over that hill. They continued to head south until they finally turned into a parking area with no cars in sight.

She parked the bike on the pavement, then led them down a short trail to a gorgeous, isolated beach, complete with an intriguing sea cave and gnarled, funky rocks.

He let Conan off the leash when they were away from the road and the dog and Chloe both jumped around in the sand with delight.

Sage watched them, the seabreeze playing in her hair.

"This is one of my favorite spots along the northern coast."

"I can see why."

"I like it not only for its beauty, but for its interesting history. It gives a rare glimpse into an earlier time."

"How?"

She led him to a rocky outcropping that looked as if it had been blasted through at one point. "See that? That was once a road carved into the headland there."

"A road?" Chloe asked. "For what?"

"Well, the highway we came here on wasn't built until the 1930s. Before then, this was the only way carriages and early cars could move up and down the coast, right on the beach."

For the next fifteen minutes, she gave them a guided tour of the place she called Hug Point. She pointed out many features Eben knew he wouldn't have paid any attention to had he been on his own and many more he wouldn't have understood even if he'd noticed them.

He was particularly fascinated by the stoplight still embedded high on the rocky headland, more evidence of the beach highway.

"You have to be careful here, though," Sage said with a serious look. "The tide comes in faster than you expect. I have a friend who was trapped in the cavern for several hours by the tide and had to be rescued by the Coast Guard."

"I love it here." Chloe twirled her arms around, whirling across the sand with Conan barking alongside her.

Sage smiled at her with a soft affection that did weird things to Eben's insides. "I do, too. I think it's my favorite place on earth."

"Can we come back here tomorrow, Daddy?"

Eben wasn't quite sure how to answer. On the one hand, he hoped he could conclude his business with Stanley and Jade today and be back on his way to San Francisco by morning.

On the other hand, he hated the thought of leaving behind this smart, fascinating woman who made him feel things he never thought he would again.

"We'll have to see," he said, giving the classic parental cop-out. Chloe didn't seem to mind, especially when Sage picked up a piece of driftwood and tossed it far down the beach. An exuberant Conan bounded through the sand after it, then delivered it back, not to Sage but to Chloe. His daughter giggled and threw it again—not quite as far as Sage had, but far enough to make Conan work for it.

He and Sage stood some ways off and he was astonished again at the peace he felt with her.

He wasn't used to these moments of quiet. Usually his life was busy with troubleshooting and meetings and conference calls. Taking a few moments to pause the craziness, to focus only on breathing in sea air and savoring the morning, seemed healing in a way he wouldn't have expected.

He caught a glimmer of something in the sand and reached to pick it up—a baby-pink agate.

"Wow! That's really rare. Finding one is supposed to be lucky. Go ahead, make a wish."

He glanced at Chloe, too far down the beach with Conan to overhear them, then spoke with heartfelt—

though no doubt unwise—honesty. "Okay. I wish I could kiss you again right now."

She froze and sent him a quick, startled look. Heat flashed there for a moment but she quickly veiled it. "Probably not a good idea."

"On several levels," he agreed. "I'll give it to Chloe and let her make the wish."

They were quiet for several moments as they watched the delighted dog and equally delighted child romp across the sand.

"Did you say you expect to be done with The Sea Urchin purchase in a few days?"

It was an obvious play to change the subject but he didn't argue. They were both probably better off pretending to ignore this heat they seemed to generate.

"I have to be," he answered. "I'm due in Tokyo by Tuesday of next week."

She gave him a piercing look as she pushed a strand of wind-tossed hair out of her face, tucking it behind her ear. "Are you planning to take Chloe along?"

He couldn't contain a little shudder at the idea of letting Chloe loose in a foreign country. The havoc she could wreak boggled his mind.

"While we're here enjoying the beaches of Oregon, my assistant has been busy interviewing new nanny applicants. She e-mailed me with the names of a couple of possibilities. I'll try to choose one when we return home this weekend."

He wasn't completely surprised to see storm clouds scud across her dark-eyed gaze. She stopped stock-still on the sand and stared at him.

"Let me get this straight. You're going to dump your

daughter on a stranger picked by your *assistant* while you go out of the country?"

Despite her deceptive calm, she certainly knew just how to raise his hackles and put him on the defensive.

"I said I was choosing the nanny. My assistant is merely offering me a list of possibilities."

"Are you planning on actually meeting any of these worthy applicants before you fly out of the country and leave your daughter with them?"

"Yes. I'm not completely irresponsible, contrary to what you apparently think."

"But you won't stick around to see how she gets along with Chloe?"

"My plans can't be changed at this late date."

"So why don't you just take her and the new nanny with you?"

"Haul Chloe halfway across the world to Tokyo so she can sit in a hotel room with a stranger for a week?"

"Why not? At least then she wouldn't feel completely abandoned. You're the one stable thing in her life right now. You're all she has, Eben. Can't you see that?"

"Of course I see that!" He was astonished how quickly his own much-vaunted calm seemed to be slipping away with the tide. "I live with the responsibility of it every moment of my life. I love my daughter, Sage, despite what you might think."

"I know you do. I can see it. But I'm just not sure Chloe is quite as convinced."

"What do you mean? I've never given her any reason to doubt it." At least he didn't think so.

"Children are resilient and bend with the wind like that seagrass over there, but they're not unbreakable, Eben."

"I have to go to Tokyo next week. Taking her along

sounds perfectly reasonable in theory. But have you ever tried to keep an eight-year-old happy on a ten-hour flight?"

"I'm sure it's not easy. But isn't your daughter's sense of emotional security worth a little inconvenience?"

"It's more than inconvenience! It's impossible."

"Nothing is impossible for a man like you. You have the money and the power and the resources at your disposal to make anything happen. You just have to want to make it work."

He started to lash back at her—what the hell did this do-gooder know about his life?—then he took a good look at her. She was angry with him, unquestionably, but there was something else in her eyes, something deeper. An old hurt he couldn't begin to guess at.

He opened his mouth to ask why this seemed so important to her. Before he could formulate the words, Conan raced to them, with the driftwood in his mouth, and dropped it at their feet.

He was followed immediately by Chloe, wind-whipped color on her cheeks and her hand outstretched.

"Look at this cool thing I found. What is it?"

He was fascinated to watch Sage inhale and exhale a long breath and then pick up the item in Chloe's hand. "Cool!" she exclaimed, with no trace of hurt or anger in her voice. "That's a little piece of petrified wood. You and your dad are great at beachcombing. He found a baby-pink agate. Maybe he'll let you make a wish on it."

"Oh, may I, Daddy?"

Grateful he hadn't tossed it back in the sand, he dug it from the pocket of his Windbreaker and handed it to her. She screwed her eyes shut for a moment, her mouth moving with words he couldn't understand, then she opened her mouth and handed it back to him.

"What did you wish?"

"Not telling. Then it won't come true."

"Fair enough. We should probably be heading back."

Chloe shook her head. "I want to keep looking for cool stuff on the beach."

"It's getting late," he insisted after a quick look at his watch. "Nearly a quarter to seven."

"No!" she said hotly. "I'm going to find more shells!"

He should have picked up on the signs. Chloe had been up for several hours already and was overstimulated by the excitement of the bike ride and playing hard with Conan. But she'd been on such good behavior in Sage's presence that her recalcitrance took him completely by surprise.

"Maybe we can make time later to look for shells, but we already have to hurry so you and Sage aren't late at the center."

"Not later! Now!"

"Chloe, get back here, young lady!"

Instead of obeying, she ran farther down the shore, coming dangerously close to the cold Pacific waters.

He headed after her, but the closer he got to her, the faster she ran, sending backward glances over her shoulder.

He saw truculence and defiance in her gaze, all the things he had become accustomed to seeing there the last two years. Though he tried to hang on to his temper, it was fraying already from his argument with Sage and he could feel it slipping through his fingers.

"Chloe Elizabeth Spencer, get your behind back here right now," he ordered. "You're in serious trouble."

"I don't care! I want to find more petrified wood."

And Sage thought he should subject the good citizens of Tokyo to Chloe?

He wouldn't put it past her to cause some kind of international incident and get them both thrown out of Japan.

He was within a few yards of grabbing her and tossing her, shrieking like a banshee, over his shoulder when Sage suddenly rode up on the tandem bike. He had no idea how she'd retrieved it from the parking lot so quickly or how she maneuvered it with such ease across the soft sand. He only knew he'd never been so grateful to see anyone in his life as he was to see Sage placidly pedaling toward them.

"Come on, Chloe. I need help getting back across the sand," she said calmly.

His daughter paused, still poised for flight but with a confused look on her features, as if she didn't quite how to react. "I want to find more petrified wood."

"I'm sure you do. But I'm afraid if we don't leave now, you and I will both be late for nature camp. Today I promised we were going to Ecola and Indian Beach, remember? I'm sure you'll find all kinds of shells there. You wouldn't want to miss it, would you?"

After a moment's reflection, Chloe shook her head and climbed onto the bicycle seat behind Sage.

"We'll have to use all our muscles to get across the sand. It's hard work. Are you ready?"

"Ready!" Chloe exclaimed, all signs of defiance miraculously gone.

Frustration simmered through him as Eben watched them work to pedal back toward the trail to the parking lot.

Even strangers were better at dealing with his daughter than he was. He was far too reactionary, far too quick to let her push his buttons. She knew just how to make him lose his temper and she didn't hesitate to push her advantage.

Perhaps sending her to boarding school to learn control would give him at least a semblance of the upper hand in their relationship.

"Are you coming?" Sage asked at the parking lot. With a sigh of defeat, he nodded and jogged toward them.

The trip back toward town wasn't nearly as pleasant as the trip away from it. Conan seemed to be the only one enjoying himself, even with the leash he obviously despised firmly attached to his collar.

Sage seemed pensive and Chloe sulked while pedaling along on the back half of the bike.

Eben was almost glad they were all working harder to go back uphill. He didn't have the breath left to make conversation, even if he'd been able to find the inclination.

He wouldn't have expected it earlier in the morning, but he was relieved when they finally reached Brambleberry House.

"Why don't you take the bike the rest of the way back to your beach house?" Sage asked. "You'll get home faster on it. Perhaps you can find time to use it tonight or tomorrow to see some sights around town if you're still here. You can just drop it back here on your way out of town."

He didn't like thinking about saying goodbye, despite their earlier conflict and the inevitability of their parting. "Thank you," he answered. "And thank you also for the inside tour of Hug Point. It was nice to have our own private naturalist."

"You're very welcome."

She mustered a smile that didn't quite reach her eyes. In the widening sunlight, she looked lovely—fresh and untamed, her honey-gold hair slipping from its ponytail and curling riotously around her face, her cheeks flushed from the wind and the exercise.

"Bye Sage," Chloe chirped. "I'll see you in a while."

Sage waved to them as they took off down the road. Eben, busy with figuring out a tandem bike for the first time, could spare only one quick look behind him. She was watching after them, one hand on her dog, the other in her pocket.

Was that sadness he saw in her eyes? he wondered. He didn't have time to look closer, since he had to turn his attention to the road in order to keep both him and Chloe upright.

A curious ache caught in her throat as Sage watched them ride away on Abigail's bike. She told herself it was just because the fragile loveliness of the morning was ending. She had found unexpected pleasure in sharing the morning with Eben and Chloe, even the rough patch at the end.

She shouldn't have been so critical of his parenting. It had been presumptuous and rude and she winced now, remembering it. No wonder he had reacted so strongly.

Eben was not Tommy Benedetto, she reminded herself sharply. She was finding it far too easy to forget that, to project her own childhood and her father's emotional abandonment onto the dynamics between Eben and Chloe.

She had all but accused him of neglect. She supposed she needed to find a way to apologize to the man.

Conan barked what sounded suspiciously like agreement and settled at her feet, for all appearances completely worn out from the morning run.

She sighed. She was becoming entirely too wrapped up in the lives of two strangers she likely would never see after a few more days. Still, she couldn't help wishing she could find a way to help Eben see how very much his daughter needed him.

The strength of her desire took her by surprise. Gathering strays had been Abigail's specialty, not Sage's.

She had many friends in town but she had no misconceptions about herself. Most of her friendships were casual, superficial. She didn't allow people into her life easily. She wasn't standoffish or rude—at least she didn't think she was—but she was uncomfortable letting people see too deeply into her psyche.

Those protective instincts had been learned early at the prestigious boarding school she'd been sent to when she was around Chloe's age, around the time her father's new wife decided she didn't like competition for Thomas's attention.

At school, Sage had been immediately ostracized, marginalized. The stench of new money had clung to her—an insurmountable obstacle, especially since it was new money obtained only through her father marrying it.

She didn't want to think those years had shaped the rest of her life, but she couldn't deny that she was as cautious as a hermit crab about letting people too close to her.

What was different about Eben Spencer and his gamine little daughter? Already she cared about them and she couldn't quite figure out how it had happened so quickly. They were transitory in her life, she knew that, yet in only a few days they had both become dear to her—so dear she wanted to do all she could to smooth their path.

Maybe she had inherited that from Abigail, along with a rambling old house and a mongrel of a dog.

"Everything okay out here?"

She glanced up at the front porch to find Anna just leaving the house, dressed in a black pinstriped suit with a leather briefcase slung over her shoulder.

Neat and orderly, with her dark hair pulled back into a sleek chignon, she made Sage feel frumpy and sweaty. Big surprise there. She *was* frumpy and sweaty.

Anna also looked worlds different from the soft, approachable woman who had shared tea with her the night before.

"It's fine," she finally answered. "Just woolgathering for a moment but I suppose I'd better get moving if I want to have any chance of making it to work on time."

"Since Conan was gone when I woke up, I figured he was with you. Looks like you've been out early this morning."

"He doesn't give me a whole lot of choice some days. It's hard to roll over and go back to sleep with him barking outside my apartment. I'm not sure which is worse, his insistent call outside the door or his big wet nose nudging me out of bed."

Anna grimaced. "I'm sorry. I've been letting you carry most of the burden for taking care of him and it's not fair to you. I'll take my turn tomorrow on the morning run."

"I complain about it but I don't really mind," she said quickly, and realized it was true. Somehow over the last month she had come to enjoy their solitary mornings.

"Well, I'll take a turn sometime, I promise. And don't worry about him this afternoon, either. I've got meetings this morning for my new store in Lincoln City and I should be home early."

She stared. "You never told me you were opening a store in Lincoln City. I had no idea."

Beneath her trim exterior, Anna brimmed with suppressed excitement. "The grand opening is in two weeks. We were trying to have it ready before the summer tourists started showing up, but we didn't quite make it."

"If it's opening by mid-June, you'll hit most of the high season, anyway."

"That's the plan."

Anna was quiet for a moment then she sighed. "I'm scared to death," she admitted.

Sage had a feeling that kind of raw truth was something the brisk, in-control Anna didn't share with many people and it warmed her to know Anna trusted her with it.

"Are you crazy? By-The-Wind rocks here in Cannon Beach. You're always busy. The new store will be great."

"I know, but we're entering a whole new demographic in Lincoln City. I've done the market studies and it looks like it will be feasible, but you never know what's going to click with people. Entering a new market is always a risk."

"If anyone can handle it, you can."

Anna look surprised, then pleased. "Thanks. That means a lot." She paused. "Everything has been so overwhelming the past month, with Abigail's death and the house and everything. If I could postpone the opening of the new store for a few weeks until I find my feet again, I would, but this has been planned for months. I don't have any choice."

No wonder Anna seemed so stressed and stiff all the

time. Sage regretted again her rudeness, the deliberate distance she had imposed between them.

Eben and Chloe weren't the only ones she was letting deeper into her life, she realized. She was coming to consider Anna a friend as well.

Somehow she suspected that was exactly what Abigail had intended.

Chapter Ten

"Did everybody have fun at Ecola?" Sage asked the thirteen tired, sweaty children gathered around her at the end of the day.

"Yeeeessss!" came the resounding cheer from the campers.

"I did, too. Remember, if the weather cooperates, tomorrow is our beach day. We're going to spend the whole day on Cannon Beach, so make sure you have your hats and your sunscreen and a warm jacket. We'll be tide-pooling near Haystack Rock, flying kites and having a sand-castle competition."

She smiled as the campers cheered with excitement. "Now your parents will be here in a few moments. It's time to gather up your backpacks and the projects we did today so you're all ready to hit the road."

The campers jumped up and dispersed to the classroom where they stowed their gear. As she helped find missing jackets and refereed arguments over whose watercolor of aggregating anemone was better, she was aware of the anticipation curling through her.

Your parents will be here in a few moments, she had told the children, but it was the thought of only one parent's arrival that churned her pulse and sent wild-edged nerves zinging through her.

Ridiculous, she reminded herself.

Eben Spencer was just another parent and that's exactly the way she had to treat him. She certainly should not have spent what seemed like the entire day remembering their morning together—his powerful muscles as he ran beside her toward Hug Point, his slow smile as he enjoyed the sunshine, his low words when he said he wished he could kiss her again.

Even though they had argued, she couldn't seem to stop thinking about him.

She needed a good dousing in the Pacific.

Perhaps if she had seen him when he dropped off Chloe in the morning she wouldn't feel this glittery anticipation, but she had been busy on the phone arranging a field trip for the next session of camp. By the time she emerged from her office, Chloe had been working with Lindsey and several of the other children in a gathering activity to identify different sea creatures and their typical habitat and Eben had been nowhere in sight.

"Sage! There you are! I've been trying to catch you all week."

She groaned at the perky voice ringing through the center. Damn Eben Spencer anyway! If she hadn't been so distracted by thoughts of him, she might have been able to employ her usual tactics to avoid Tracy Harder. Now she had nowhere safe to go.

"Hi, Tracy. How are you?"

The other woman beamed at her. "Just great. I got the listings for two new properties today, right next to each other in Manzanita. They're half a block from the ocean and ought to move fast. So how were my two little terrors?"

She forced a smile. Tracy had been bringing her twins to camp for three years, ever since they turned old enough to attend, and right around the time their parents divorced.

The boys *were* terrors but she liked to chalk it up to high energy, not maliciousness.

"We had a great day today. I tried to keep them too busy to get into trouble."

"You are amazing with them, Sage. Thanks for putting up with them every year. I just wish you had camp year-round. I'd pull them out of school in a heartbeat and sign them up to every session."

Sage managed to contain a slight shudder. Fortunately, Tracy didn't require an answer before she went on. "So, let's talk," she said abruptly. "Brambleberry House."

Though she mentally groaned, she managed to keep a polite expression. "We've had this discussion already, Tracy. Several times. And nothing has changed at all since the last time we discussed it. I'm sorry, but Anna and I aren't selling."

"You two are crazy! Do you realize how much I can ask for a fifteen-room mansion on the beach? The place is a gold mine! With a little creative investment, you and Anna could be set for life."

"We can't do that, Tracy. I'm sorry, but Abigail would have hated to see us sell it."

"Abigail is not the one who will have to deal with all the repairs and the property taxes and the gigantic utility bills. Do you want to be tied to that house for the rest of your life?"

She had a brief, stark image of living forever in her turret apartment, growing old like Abigail, alone except for a big furry red dog who had been rescued from the pound.

A week ago, she would have found that image comforting. She wanted nothing more than to emulate Abigail, to be as feisty and independent as her friend for the rest of her days.

She wasn't sure what she wanted anymore. Her old childhood dreams of having a family of her own, born out of empty loneliness, had somehow re-emerged.

"You need to think long and hard about this," Tracy pressed. "I know you're still grieving for Abigail—we all are—but you're a young, beautiful woman. Trust me, someday you're going to want options."

She opened her mouth to answer but Tracy cut her off. "I've got a couple of Portland clients looking for a property for a bed and breakfast in town. Brambleberry House would be perfect. They have money to spare and I'm sure we could push the asking price well into seven figures. Talk to Anna about it. You have to!"

Sage shook her head. "No, Tracy. We're not selling."

The other woman's attention suddenly caught at something in the doorway, at the same time a tiny shiver skittered down Sage's spine.

Tracy's eyes widened and she let out a long breath. "Oh. My. Word. Who's the yummy guy? No, don't turn around."

She didn't need to turn around to know who it must be. Since this session of camp contained mostly local children, Tracy had to know all their parents—except one.

"How can I know who it is if you won't let me turn around to look?" she asked.

Tracy's eyes widened. "He's coming this way! Unless my eyes deceive me—and I don't think they do, trust me, I've got radar for these things—I can't see a ring. How's my hair?"

Sage studied her polished friend. Her makeup was perfect and not a strand of her highlighted blonde hair dared escape its trendy style.

In contrast, Sage didn't need a mirror to tell her what she must look like. Her dratted hair was probably falling out of the ponytail again, her skin felt tight and itchy, probably from a slight sunburn, and she didn't doubt she smelled as if she'd been chasing thirteen active elementary school students all day.

She sighed. "You look beautiful, as always."

"Liar!" Tracy purred, then her white teeth widened and she thrust out a hand, complete with the French manicure Sage knew she drove to Astoria to get and no trace of a callus or wrinkle.

"Hi there. I don't believe we've met. I'm Tracy Harder with Harder Realty. Welcome to Cannon Beach! Are you a summer visitor or are you moving in? Before you answer, let me just say how much I sincerely hope it's the latter. We just love new faces around here, don't we, Sage?"

"Uh, sure."

Eben blinked a few times at her gushing warmth, but finally held out his hand. "Hello. Eben Spencer. I'm afraid my daughter and I are only here until the weekend."

Tracy's face fell and she didn't look like she wanted to let go of his hand, as if she could change his mind just with her force of will. Eben finally managed to slip it away.

"Too bad for us. But if you ever think about moving back permanently, give me a call. Let me give you my card. Now you hang on to that, promise? I have listings up and down the northern/central coast, from Astoria to Newport. From luxury beachside houses to small two-room cottages, I can hook you up with anything you want. Anything."

Sage certainly didn't mistake the intent in that single, flirtatious word and Eben obviously didn't either.

"Uh, thank you."

"Oh, you're welcome. For instance, I just picked up two new listings today in Manzanita. The master suite in one of them is huge with one full wall of windows over-looking the ocean. Truly stunning and it's listed at several thousand dollars below appraisal. At that price, it's not going to last long. And the other one has four bedrooms, including one that would be perfect for an in-law suite."

Before Tracy could get revved up into a full-scale sales pitch, Sage took pity on Eben's glazed expression and stepped in. "Mr. Spencer, I imagine you're probably looking for the hiking trail guides we talked about this morning, aren't you?"

He looked baffled for only half a second, then seized on the excuse. "Yes. Exactly. I'm very anxious to see the area."

"I'm sorry, I meant to have them ready for you when you arrived to pick up Chloe, but it's been a rather busy day. It won't take me a second to dig them out of my files, though. They're back in my office, if you want to come with me. Tracy, will you excuse us?"

Tracy opened her mouth to object, but Sage didn't give her a chance, she just led Eben through the center to her office.

"Trail guides?" he murmured when they were safely out of earshot.

"I couldn't think of anything else. Sorry. Tracy's a

sweetheart but she can be a bit of a piranha if she smells fresh meat."

He raised an eyebrow and Sage could feel herself flush. "Completely in the real estate sense of the word, I mean. Potential customers."

"Right."

He looked tired, she thought. His shirtsleeves were rolled up, his tie loose and that hint of disreputable stubble was back on his jawline. No wonder Tracy went into hungry mode.

"Uh, long day?"

He shrugged. "We're having some labor issues with a couple of our European properties. It took some serious negotiations, but I think we've finally got a handle on it."

He studied her for a long moment, a light in his eyes that left her suddenly breathless. "How about you?"

"It's been a good day. The kids seemed to enjoy Ecola. What's not to love? The place looks prehistoric, like dinosaurs will come stalking through the plants any minute now."

"How was Chloe today?"

"Tired, I think."

"I suppose that's what happens when she wakes us both up before five o'clock."

"Probably. She was a little bit cranky, but we didn't have any real problems. She fell asleep for a few moments in the van on the way back."

"She'll probably zonk out right after dinner, which will be good since I'm suddenly slammed with paperwork my assistant sent by courier."

She had a sudden fierce longing to run a finger down the tired lines at the corner of his mouth, as if she could soothe them. The impulse appalled her. "And are you the proud owner of a certain Cannon Beach landmark yet?"

"Not yet. They're stalling with every possible tactic they can come up with."

"Yet you're not giving up?"

He sighed. "I don't know. At this point, I'm not sure what else I can do. I can't force Stanley and Jade to sell, nor would I want to."

"Someone unscrupulous probably could figure out a way to do just that."

To her surprise, hurt flickered in his gaze. "Is that what you think of me?"

She considered the idea then rejected it. "Not at all. I think you're very determined but I don't believe you're ruthless."

"We need The Sea Urchin. I'm afraid nothing else will do."

"You need it or you want it? Big difference, Eben."

"Both. The more time I spend in Cannon Beach, the more I know this is the ideal location for another Spencer Hotel. It's perfect."

Before she could answer, Chloe skipped in and threw her arms around Eben's waist. "Hi Daddy. What are you doing in here?"

"Just talking to Sage."

She seemed to accept that with equanimity. "I'm hungry. Can we have dinner at Brambleberry House again tonight?"

Eben looked taken aback at Chloe's question and sent a swift look toward Sage. Her first inclination was to go ahead and extend the invitation Chloe was angling for in her not-so-subtle manner, but she quickly checked the impulse. Eben said he had paperwork to finish.

Beyond that, she needed a little space and distance from the two of them to see if she could rebuild the protective barriers around her heart.

She forced a smile to Chloe. "I'm sorry, honey, but I've got other plans tonight."

It wasn't a lie. She was supposed to have her monthly book club meeting at By-The-Wind tonight, though all day she had been planning to do her best to wiggle out of it.

"What about tomorrow?" Chloe asked.

"We'll have to see," Eben stepped in. "Come on, Chloe. We'd better get out of Sage's hair and it looks like you need to get cleaned up before dinner. What do you say to pizza tonight?"

"I say *yum*," Chloe chirped.

Sage walked them to the door of the center. "Bye, Chloe. Don't forget your hat tomorrow. Remember, it's beach day."

"I can't wait! Can we ride bikes again tomorrow morning while Daddy and Conan run and go to Hug Point?"

She'd had a tough enough time getting the image of Eben's muscles out of her head all day today. She didn't need a repeat performance in the morning. "Guess what? I get to sleep in tomorrow since Anna wants to take a turn running with Conan in the morning."

To her surprise, disappointment sparked in Eben's gaze but he said nothing about it. "Come on, kid."

"Bye Sage," Chloe said reluctantly. She hugged Sage then grabbed her father's hand and walked outside.

This was becoming a habit Eben had a feeling would be tough to break when they returned to San Francisco. Early the next morning, Eben stood at the deck railing watching the ocean change color with the sunrise, from black to murky blue to a deep, rich green. He was coming to depend entirely too much on these moments of solitude, when he had the vast beach to himself, sharing it only with the occasional shore bird.

He had intended to sleep in at least until six, but he woke an hour before his travel alarm had been set to go off. Restless and edgy, he had opted to come out here and enjoy the morning.

The beauty of the Oregon coast had somehow seeped into him. Despite the frustration over The Sea Urchin, he felt calmer here than he had in a long time. Maybe since those rough last few months of his marriage.

He shifted. He didn't like dwelling on Brooke and all the ways he had failed her. The worst of it was that now he wasn't even sure when he had stopped loving his wife.

She had been a friend of his sister Cami's and he had known her since she was a girl. He had been her escort at her debutante ball, had dated her through college. Theirs had never been a grand passion, but in the early days at least it had been comfortable.

And then after Chloe was born, she had wanted so much more from him. She had become clingy, demanding. She had hated his work schedule, had resented the hours he spent rebuilding the company, then had started accusing him of a long string of affairs.

Her emotional outbursts had all seemed so much like his parents' marriage—with the exception that his father *had* been having affairs, buckets of them, and no one could ever have called Hastings Spencer a workaholic. Alcoholic? Yes. Workaholic? Not a chance.

The last few years of their marriage had been miserably unhappy and he had worked even more to avoid the tumult he hated so much at home. He imagined if Brooke hadn't died, they would have been well on their way to divorce by now.

And most of it had been his fault. He acknowledged that now. He had been consumed with proving he was *not* his father, that he had inherited nothing from his unstable mother. As a result, he had refused to fight with Brooke, had refused to show much emotion at all.

He had lived with that guilt for two years now. The past couldn't be changed. Perhaps it was time to let it go.

He watched a black oystercatcher hop down the shore and his muscles hummed with a fierce desire to be out there on the hard-packed sand running for all he was worth.

He couldn't leave Chloe sleeping alone inside their beach house, so he had to be content with watching the daybreak from the sidelines.

He sipped his coffee, remembering the morning only a few days ago when Sage had taken it out of his hand and sent him off running with her dog. Had it only been a few days ago? It seemed like forever since he had returned to find her asleep on the couch, warm and tousled and sexy, and had stolen a kiss.

He jerked his mind away from the memory and focused instead on the day ahead. He was meeting with Stanley and Jade that afternoon, for possibly the last time. If they still balked at the sale, he knew he would have to return to San Francisco and all the work waiting for him there. He couldn't linger here indefinitely, hoping he could change their minds.

He sighed, depressed at the realization that this would likely be his last Oregon sunrise for some time.

It was a glorious one, he had to admit. The sun coming over the Coast Range to the east tinted the sky above the ocean a pearly pink, with shades of lavender and pale orange.

Sage would love this.

He sighed. Couldn't he go five seconds without thinking about her? He was obsessed. He definitely needed to return to San Francisco soon so he could start shaking her from his mind.

As if in response to the direction of thoughts, he suddenly spied two shapes running down the beach, one of which was unmistakably a familiar shaggy red dog.

Anticipation curled through him and he knew with grim realization this was the reason he stood here at the railing—not to watch the sunrise, but on the off chance she might run past with Conan.

As they drew closer, he saw immediately his subconscious hope of seeing her would be dashed. Conan's companion didn't have unruly honey-gold curls. Instead, she had dark hair scraped back into a sleek ponytail.

Anna Galvez was taking her turn with the dog's morning run, just as Sage had told them the day before she planned to do.

The depth of his disappointment shocked the hell out of him.

How had a wild-haired nature girl become so important to him in a few short days? His fingers curled around the coffee mug. He should have done a much better job of keeping her out. What was the point of coming to care about her? He was leaving soon, tomorrow at the latest.

With sudden, hard dread lodged in his gut, he hated the idea of saying goodbye to her.

Conan barked an exuberant greeting and rushed over to his deck. Eben unlatched the gate and headed down the wooden stairs.

"Hey bud. No Chloe this morning. She's still sleeping." He scratched the dog's chin and was rewarded by furious tail-wagging.

Anna arrived several moments after the dog, panting hard. "My gosh, he's fast. I had no idea. Morning."

He smiled. "Good morning."

"How does Sage do this every morning? It's torture!" She straightened and he thought again that she was a remarkably lovely woman, with her glossy dark hair and delicate features.

He could appreciate her loveliness on a purely detached basis but he realized she did nothing for him. The realization was unsettling. He wasn't at all attracted to Anna Galvez—because all he could think about was Sage and her winsome smile and her untamed beauty.

"I guess you're the reason he insisted on dragging me in this direction," Anna said.

"Sorry."

She smiled. "I'm not. At least he's giving me a breather for a minute. Anyway, the ocean view is spectacular in any direction. I never tire of it."

"You're lucky to see it every day."

"I think so, too." She paused. "I never intended to stay here forever but I came a few years ago for a... vacation and I never left. I think seawater seeped into my blood or something. Now here I am a homeowner, a business owner. Settled. Life takes some strange twists sometimes."

He sensed there was more to her story, but didn't feel he knew her well enough to pry.

"I understand you may be joining the ranks of Cannon Beach property owners."

"Your mouth to God's ear."

She smiled again. "Will you be sticking around if you buy The Sea Urchin?"

Three days ago he would have given an unequivocal no to that question. The fact that he couldn't honestly offer her the answer he knew he should stunned him.

"Sorry. Not my business," she said, her voice somewhat stiff and he abruptly realized he must have been staring at her without speaking for several seconds.

"No, it's not that. I just don't quite know how to answer. Our hotel corporate office is in San Francisco, so I would have to say probably not. But I have a couple of great people in mind to run the place after we finish a few upgrades."

Conan barked and for some reason, Eben was quite certain that look in his eyes was disapproval. Did he need to consult a dog now on his business decisions?

"Well, Cannon Beach is a great place to raise a family if you should decide differently."

"I'll keep that in mind," he answered.

"Good luck with the Wus," she said. "I've read a little about Spencer Hotels and I think your company would treat The Sea Urchin exactly as it deserves."

"Thank you. Now if you wouldn't mind stopping at the hotel on your run and telling Stanley and Jade just what you told me," he joked, "maybe I could wrap things up here before Independence Day."

She laughed. "I'm not sure they'd listen to me. I've only been here three years so I'm still very much a newcomer."

Conan suddenly wriggled away from Eben and started heading up the beach. Anna gave a rueful smile. "I guess that's the boss's way of telling me it's time to head off. Thanks for giving me a chance to catch my breath."

"No problem."

She waved and headed off after the dog.

* * *

Six hours later, Eben wished for a little of Anna Galvez's encouragement as he sat in the elegantly appointed conference room of The Sea Urchin, frustration burning his insides.

He had been running his family's hotel company since he graduated from The Wharton School in his early 20s. The company's assets and reputation had increased exponentially under his command.

With a far-ranging strategic plan, he had worked as hard as he knew how, had sacrificed and planned and maneuvered Spencer Hotels to emerge from near-bankruptcy to its current healthy market share.

Through all the years of toil and negotiations, he had never felt as completely inept as he did right this moment, gazing at Stanley Wu's smooth, inscrutable features.

The man was harder to read than the framed Chinese calligraphy hanging on the wall above his head.

"Mr. Wu, I'm sorry, but I don't know what else you and Mrs. Wu want from me. I have tried to convince you Spencer Hotels doesn't plan any radical changes to The Sea Urchin. You've seen our business plan and the blueprints for the minor renovations we would like to see. You have physically toured each of our two other hotels in Oregon as well as two in Washington and I've showed you multimedia tours of several others. I've given you my personal promise that I will treat this establishment with the same care and attention you and Mrs. Wu have showered on it for thirty-five years. I want this hotel, I've made no secret of that fact, but my time here is running out. What else can I do to convince you?"

Stanley studied him for a full minute without saying anything—an eternity, Eben thought. Finally Stanley's mouth lifted slightly in what Eben supposed passed for a smile.

"Come to dinner tonight. Seven o'clock. Bring your daughter."

Eben gave a mental groan. Of all the things he might have expected, that was way down at the bottom of his list. It was also the one thing he did *not* want to do. The way things were going, Chloe would pitch a fit and destroy any chance he had of making this deal.

This was one more hoop the Wus were making him jump through. Perhaps one too many.

"I don't know if that's a good idea. Chloe's only eight. Her manners are not exactly what you might call impeccable."

"Bring her," Stanley said sternly. "My father used to say, if you want to know the health of the tree, study the fruit."

Eben had to fight to keep from banging his head on the conference table a few times as he felt his chances for buying The Sea Urchin slipping through his fingers like sand.

This was a certifiable nightmare. His entire plans—all the months of study and work—hinged on the table manners of a moody, unpredictable eight-year-old girl.

He should just tell the man to go to hell. Eben had worked harder on this deal than anything in the dozen years since he took over at the helm of Spencer Hotels. If it wasn't enough for Stanley Wu, so be it.

Even as he opened his mouth to tell the man to forget the whole thing, something stopped him.

"Of course," he found himself murmuring instead, at the same moment a germ of an idea sprouted.

He thought of Chloe a few nights before at dinner, how polite and patient she had been while they ate vegetarian lasagna at Brambleberry House. If he could somehow replicate that behavior, there was a tiny—miniscule—chance he might pull this off.

Sage's presence had made all the difference. She had some uncanny moderating effect on Chloe's misbehavior. If she could distract his daughter long enough, convince her to behave for one simple evening, perhaps all hope was not completely lost.

"Do you mind if I bring along a guest?" he asked before he gave himself time to think it through.

Stanley studied him across the conference table. "What guest is this?"

How exactly did he explain? "My daughter and I have befriended a Cannon Beach resident, Sage Benedetto. I would like to bring her along, if it would be acceptable to you and Mrs. Wu."

This time the cool look in the other man's eyes was replaced with the first genuine smile Eben had seen there. "Ah. Sage. Yes. A beautiful woman always improves the digestion."

"More wisdom from your father?"

Stanley laughed. "I don't need my father to tell me this truth. I have eyes, don't I?"

"Uh, right."

"So you will come for dinner and bring your daughter and our friend Abigail's beautiful wild rose, yes?"

"Yes," he answered.

Now he just had to convince Sage.

Chapter Eleven

"Now remember, what's the most important tide-pool rule?"

"Look but don't touch!" the six campers in her group recited as one and Sage beamed.

"Exactly right. The rocky shore ecosystem is very fragile and you never know what harm you could do even by picking up a piece of kelp. It's much better just to take pictures and look. All right, everybody grab your disposable cameras and let's start recording our observations."

The kids broke off into their pre-assigned teams of two and, chattering with excitement, headed on their field assignments to record as many tide-pool creatures as they could find.

Sage watched their eager faces and had to smile. This was close to her idea of a perfect day. The sun, making a brief appearance between storms, was bright and warm on her face, the water a spectacularly beautiful shade of deep olive. She had a bright group of children soaking in knowledge like little sea sponges.

For the next half hour, she wandered through the three teams, answering questions, making observations, pointing them toward species they may have missed: tiny porcelain crabs and Hopkin's roses.

She loved it out here. She didn't need anything else, certainly not any sharp-eyed executives who smelled like heaven and kissed like a dream.

She pushed thoughts of Eben away—again—and focused on the tide-poolers until her stopwatch beeped, then she gathered them around to compare notes.

"Excellent job, all of you. You're now official junior naturalists for Cannon Beach."

"Ms. B., when can we have the crab race? You promised you'd let me whip your butt this year."

She laughed at Ben Harder, one of Tracy's twins. "Excuse me, but I believe I promised I would let you *try* to whip my butt. Big difference there, kiddo."

"When? Can we do it now?"

She checked her watch. They had split the campers into two groups so they didn't stress the tide-pool residents with too much attention at once. Lindsey had the other group down the beach flying kites and they weren't due to switch places for another twenty minutes.

"Okay. Crab races it is. We need start and finish lines."

Two of the boys found a piece of driftwood and charted a race course of about thirty feet—far too long in Sage's book, but the children insisted they could go that far.

Her idea was for one-on-one races, but eventually everybody wanted to compete against her and it turned into a free-for-all.

It was a fight to the finish but she came in a respectable third—behind Ben Harder and Leilani Stein. At the finish line, panting and aching, she collapsed into the sand. How did she seem to forget every year until the first camp of the summer how blasted hard it was to walk backward on her hands and feet? It took her abs all summer long to relearn how to crab race.

"Good race," she said, gasping. "But I think you got a head start."

"No way," Ben exclaimed. "It was totally fair!"

"Need a hand up?"

At the low, masculine voice, Sage opened her eyes and found Eben standing over her, his hand outstretched.

Her heart gave a sharp kick in her chest at his features silhouetted in the sunshine. He looked gorgeous in a pair of khaki slacks and a casual cotton shirt.

Of course he would. She was hot and sweaty and probably smelled like a tide-pool again. She wanted to burrow into the sand like a geoduck clam. Instead, she released a tiny sigh, reached for his hand and let him help her to her feet.

"I have to say, the kid's right. It looked fair to me. If anybody jumped the gun, I think it was you."

She brushed sand off her butt. "Whose side are you on?"

He grinned and she forgot to breathe. She had no idea he could look so lighthearted. It was a disturbing revelation.

"Did you need Chloe?" she asked to cover her reaction. "Her group is down the beach. See the kites down there?"

"No. I saw them first and already stopped to talk to

her," he answered. "Your assistant—Lindsey, I think is her name—told me I could find you out here."

Note to self, she thought, *remind Lindsey not to send gorgeous men out searching for me when I'm crab-walking in the sand.*

She pushed wind-tossed hair out of her face. "Is there some problem with Chloe?"

"In a way."

His temporary lightheartedness seemed to slide away again and he shifted a little, looking suddenly uncomfortable.

She had no idea what he wanted and he didn't seem in any big hurry to enlighten her. "Do you need me to keep her after camp ends again?" she said, hazarding a guess. "It's really no problem."

"It's not that." He let out a long breath. "The truth is, I need to ask a huge favor and I'm not sure quite how to go about it."

The kids in her group seemed happy enough with continuing their crab races so she led him down the sand a little. "Just ask, Eben."

"You make it sound easy." He paused. "All right. Will you come to dinner at The Sea Urchin tonight?"

She gave a surprised laugh. "This is your huge favor? Inviting me to dine at the finest restaurant on the northern coast? By the tone of your voice, I was expecting you to ask me to donate a kidney or something."

"That might be less painful in the long run. The truth is, I need help with Chloe. Stanley has invited me to dinner tonight." He paused. "No, that's not right. There was no invitation involved. He *ordered* me to come to dinner tonight and to bring Chloe along. Apparently, before the man will make a final decision to trust me with his hotel, he wants to see how I interact with my daughter."

Sage flushed, embarrassed that she had initially allowed herself to feel flattered, to imagine he might have been asking her on a date. "And how do I fit into the picture?"

"You're so good with Chloe. With you, she's a different girl. She's polite and well-mannered. Happy. I need her to be on her best behavior and you seem to bring the best out in her where I seem to usually have the opposite effect."

It was ridiculous to feel this hurt that spread out from her stomach like the paralyzing venom of a jellyfish sting.

"So you're inviting me as your daughter's handler in order to help you clinch the deal?"

He winced. "Put like that, it sounds pretty damn nervy, doesn't it?"

"Yes," she clipped off the word.

"I'm asking you to help me for one night. This is important to me. You have the magic touch with Chloe. Everything seems to go more smoothly when you're around. Please, Sage. It's one night."

All her instincts cried out for her to tell him to go to hell. She thought of that kick in her heart when she first saw him. How ridiculous. She was allowing herself to have feelings for a man who only viewed her as a convenient caregiver for his daughter.

With every ounce of her, she wanted to tell him no. She even started to form the word, but her mouth seemed to freeze.

She couldn't do it.

He wanted The Sea Urchin desperately—he had made no secret of that—and she cared about him and about

Chloe enough that some part of her wanted to help him reach his goal.

Four days ago she might have scoffed and told him to go back to his business meetings and his conference calls. But that was before she had come to know him.

The truth was, she had become convinced Spencer Hotels would be good for Cannon Beach and The Sea Urchin. Abigail must have thought so or she never would have suggested the idea. It seemed a betrayal of her friend to refuse to help Eben simply because some foolish part of her hoped he wanted more from her than etiquette lessons for his daughter.

"Please," he repeated.

She was going to bleed from a thousand gashes in her heart when he and Chloe left. Helping him tonight would only accelerate that inevitable heartbreak. She knew it perfectly well, could already feel the ache, but from somewhere deep she still managed to dredge up a smile.

"What time?"

The pure delight on his face almost broke her heart right there. "Seven. Will that work for you?"

Her mind raced with the million things she would have to do between the time she finished work and seven o'clock. Foremost was the purely feminine lament that she had nothing to wear and no time to run to her favorite vintage boutique in Portland to find something.

"If Anna's home to stay with Conan, it should be fine."

He reached for her hands and she was certain if they weren't standing on a public beach in broad daylight with a hundred other people, he would have kissed her right then.

"My debt to you seems to grow larger by the minute. Somehow I'll find a way to pay you back, I swear it."

"Don't worry about it. I'll see you at seven."

* * *

"No, no, *no!*" Sage wailed, her breath coming in short gasps as she pedaled hard up the hill toward Brambleberry House. With one hand on the handlebars, she used the other to hold her umbrella over the dress that had just cost her an entire week's paycheck.

It was wrapped in plastic but she bemoaned every single raindrop that made it around the umbrella to splatter against her precious cargo. The whole dress was going to be ruined, she just knew it. Worse, her hair was drenched and would take hours to dry.

She had exactly forty-five minutes to ride the half-mile home and to shower and primp for her dinner with Eben and Chloe and the damn pouring rain wasn't making this any easier.

She could barely see and didn't have a spare hand to wipe the rain out of her eyes and she lived in mortal dread her tires were going to slip in the mud at the shoulder of the road and dump her *and* the dress.

A vehicle drove slowly past and she shifted the umbrella over the dress until it was almost vertical like a warrior's shield, just in case the driver hit a puddle and splattered it everywhere.

Instead, the vehicle slowed even further, then she saw brakelights through the rain. She could barely make out that the truck belonged to Will Garrett until the driver's door opened and he climbed out.

"Get in," he called. "I'll throw your bike in the back of the truck and drive you the rest of the way home."

"I'm almost there."

"Get in, Sage. It's not safe for you to be riding your bike in these conditions. It's slick and visibility is terrible, though I have to say, the bright pink umbrella does tend to draw the eye."

She winced at the ridiculous picture she must make. "I bought a fancy new dress. I didn't want it to get wet."

Will's eyes widened, but to her relief, he said nothing as he took the bicycle from her and effortlessly lifted it into the back while she rushed to open the passenger door. Inside the cab, she laid her dress carefully on the bench seat then climbed in behind it, closing her vivid umbrella.

Will's heater blared full force and she relished the warmth seeping into her chilled muscles for the few moments before he joined her and pulled back onto the road toward Brambleberry House.

"Do I dare ask what's up with the dress? It's not your usual kind of thing, is it?"

She could feel her face flame. "I'm having dinner at the Sea Urchin tonight and it occurred to me I don't have a lot of grown-up clothes to wear. I splurged a bit."

She glanced at it, a sleek midnight blue dream of a dress shot through with the barest trace of iridescent rainbow thread. *Splurge* was a bit of an understatement. She had spent more on this one dress than she usually spent on clothes all year long. Her Visa balance would probably never recover.

It had been purely an impulse buy, too. She hadn't really intended a whole new dress. Since she couldn't make it to her favorite shop in Portland, she thought she would only take a quick look at some of the local stores on the off chance she might find a blouse on clearance she could wear with her usual black dress skirt.

She had just about given up on finding anything when

she wandered into a new shop and saw this dress hanging in a corner.

The moment she saw it, she had fallen in love, despite the hefty price tag.

"So what do you think?" she asked Will.

He smiled ruefully. "I'm the wrong guy to ask. Afraid I'm not the best judge of that kind of thing. Robin used to throw a fit because I usually didn't even notice when she bought something new."

He didn't often refer to his late wife or their life together and she could tell it still bothered him to do so because he quickly changed the subject.

"The Sea Urchin, huh? Hot date?"

If only. She burned with embarrassment again, remember her first conclusion when Eben asked her. "Not quite. I'm taking an eight-year-old. One of my day campers. Her dad is negotiating with Stanley and Jade to buy the hotel and he and his daughter have been invited to dinner. Eben, in turn, invited me. They're coming in exactly—" she glanced at her watch as they pulled into the Brambleberry House driveway "—forty minutes now."

"You'd better hurry then. Run in and put on your fancy dress. I'll put your bike away in the garage for you."

On impulse, she leaned across her dress and kissed his cheek, smelling sawdust and sweat, a surprisingly pleasant combination.

"Thanks, Will. I owe you. Come for dinner next week, okay?"

"As long as there's no tofu on the menu."

"I'll see what I can do."

She opened her umbrella, clutched her dress to her as if it were spun gold—a fair description, really, penny for penny—and dashed out into the rain.

She reached the porch just as Anna opened the door to let Conan out. The dog barked a greeting, but to her vast relief he didn't jump all over her in his usual away, almost as of the uncanny beast knew she didn't have time to play.

"That looks like something fabulous," Anna exclaimed, gazing at the dress. "Let's see."

Sage held it up, gratified by Anna's moan of appreciation.

"Gorgeous!" she exclaimed. "What's the occasion?"

"I'm having dinner at The Sea Urchin tonight with Eben and Chloe."

Anna gave her a careful look, then smiled. "Do you have any jewelry to match?"

Ha. After buying the dress, her budget barely stretched to a new pair of pantyhose. "I'll find something."

"Don't forget we have Abigail's whole glittery collection to choose from. Go get dressed and I'll bring her jewelry box up and see what we can dig out."

Sage raced up the stairs two at a time. This excitement pumping through her was only adrenaline, she told herself, just a normal reaction to her urgency and the ever-ticking clock.

She hadn't been on a date in a long time. Did this qualify, since Chloe would be along? Probably not. But she still couldn't shake the bubbling anticipation and she took the fastest shower on record.

She raced through her makeup—something she rarely bothered with—then took a page out of Anna's fashion book and pulled her still-damp hair into as smooth an updo as she could manage with her unruly frizz.

She had just slipped into the dress and was working the zipper when Anna knocked on the door.

"It's open. Come in," she called.

Anna's arms overflowed with Abigail's huge jewelry box, but all Sage focused on was the astonished admiration in her eyes.

"Wow. That's all I can say. Wow. That dress is perfect for you. The coloring, the style, everything."

"That's why I spent far more than I could afford on it. Stupid, isn't it, for a dress I'll probably only wear once."

"Every girl needs something completely, outrageously impractical hanging in her closet."

"I guess I'm covered, then."

"Not yet. Let's see what Abigail has in her magic box." She held out the jewelry box that contained what had been another of Abigail's passions—vintage costume jewelry, which she wore loads of at every opportunity.

Even when she worked in the garden, Abigail would wear some kind of gorgeous jeweled earbobs and a matching necklace.

"I need to glitter," she used to say with that mischievous gleam in her blue eyes. "It takes the attention away from my wrinkles."

To Sage's shock, Anna turned the box with its jumbled contents and upended the whole thing onto her bed.

The two of them stared at the huge sparkly pile for a long moment. Sage hadn't given much thought to the collection, but now she couldn't seem to look away.

"Do you suppose any of it's real?" Sage whispered.

"I don't know." Anna spoke in the same hushed tone. "I'm not sure I *want* to know."

She started pawing through the collection, pulling out a gleaming strand of pearls here, a chunky citrine and topaz necklace there.

Finally she stopped and pulled out an Art Deco choker

in stones the exact midnight shade of the dress. "This is it. It's perfect."

The stones felt as smooth and cool as polished sea glass. After another moment of treasure hunting, Anna pulled out a pair of matching dangly earrings that seemed to capture the light and reflect it back in a hundred different shades of blue.

"I guess we really should have this collection appraised," Anna said while Sage put them in.

"You don't sound any more enthusiastic than I am."

"They're Abigail's. I hate the idea of parting with *any* of her things. But let's face it, the upkeep on the house is going to be more than either of us can afford. The heating bill alone is almost as much as I was paying for rent on my condo."

"We'll figure it out."

"You're right. No depressing talk," Anna said firmly. "Let's just get you ready. We can worry about heating bills and extravagant jewelry collections another day."

Already Sage could feel her hair slipping out of the style. Before the whole thing could fall apart, Anna fiddled with a few strands, smoothed a few more, then stepped back to admire her handiwork.

"All done. What do you think?"

Sage stared at her full-length mirror at the stranger gazing back at her. Not a stranger, she corrected. She only had a single picture of the slim, lovely mother she barely remembered, a picture rescued and hidden away when her father started to purge that part of his life after his second marriage.

She hadn't looked at it in a long time, but somehow she knew if someone snapped a picture of her right now and compared it with that precious photograph, the two women would be nearly a match.

Tears burned behind her eyelids, but she choked them back. "Oh, Anna. Thank you. The necklace and earrings are exactly right."

Anna stepped back and studied her. "It's almost spooky the way they match, as if Abigail bought them just to go with that dress."

Maybe because she had been thinking of her mother, but Sage could swear she felt invisible fingers gently brush her cheek.

She shivered a little and was grateful when the door-bell rang.

"There's Eben," she said, then felt ridiculous for the inanity. Who else would it be?

"Have a wonderful time," Anna said. "Give my love to Stanley and Jade."

"I will."

Anna looked bright and animated, Sage thought, so very different from the stiff businessman she had always considered her. She really was becoming a dear friend, something Sage never would have expected.

She reached out and gave Anna a quick, impulsive hug. "Thank you again."

Anna looked stunned but pleased. "You're very wel-come. I'll go let him in. Wait up here a moment so you can make a grand entrance down the stairs."

"Oh, for heaven's sake. I'm not in high school."

"Trust me. Stay here."

Anna flew down the stairs and a moment later, Sage heard Eben's deep voice greeting her. She tried to count to twenty but only made it to fifteen before she started down the stairs, certain she was going to trip in the un-accustomed high heels and break her neck.

Eben stood at the bottom of the stairs waiting for her in a dark suit and tie. He looked sinfully gorgeous and she had to admit his thunderstruck expression more than made up for the sheer extravagance of the dress.

By the time she reached the bottom step, Anna was ushering Conan into her apartment and closing the door behind them both with one last delighted smile at Sage and Eben in the entryway.

Eben grabbed her hand and brought it to his mouth in a gesture that should have felt foolish but seemed exactly right.

"You look stunning," he murmured.

"I feel like I'm on the way to the prom."

He gave a surprised laugh. "I sincerely hope I've moved beyond the arrogant jackass I was at seventeen."

"Well, I have to admit my prom date didn't bring along his eight-year-old daughter."

"Left her home with a sitter, did he?"

She laughed at the sheer unexpectedness of his teasing. "Something like that."

"I should probably tell you, Chloe's over the moon about spending the evening with grown-ups. We had to rush out and buy her a new dress and everything."

Thank heavens they hadn't bumped into each other in the few Cannon Beach clothing stores. "The Wus have a dozen grandchildren. Trust me, they're going to adore her."

He drew in a deep breath, his eyes filled with doubt. "I guess we'll find out in a few moments, right?" He held out his arm. "Shall we?"

She slipped her arm through his. The rain forced them

to stand close together and share his umbrella and she could smell the deliciously spicy scent of his aftershave.

This was a make-believe night, she reminded herself as he helped her into his luxurious rental car. She needed to remember that by morning this would all be a memory.

A wonderful, glorious, heartbreaking memory.

Chapter Twelve

"Mrs. Wu, this fortune cookie is delicious. I like it very much. Would you mind if I had a second one?"

Eben observed his daughter's careful politeness with amazement. What kind of well-mannered gremlin had snuck in when he wasn't paying attention and replaced his headstrong daughter with this sweet, polite little person?

He glanced over at Sage and caught her suppressing a smile.

Jade Wu only beamed at Chloe, her lovely, ageless features glowing with delight. "You have as much as you want, child. Fortune cookies are not really from China, did you know that?"

"I didn't know that. Really?" Chloe looked enthralled.

"They were invented right in your town of San Francisco by a smart baker at a Japanese restaurant. But our guests expect them, so we have perfected our own recipe."

"You make them here?"

Jade smiled at her. "They are not hard. I can show you how, if you would like."

Chloe's eyes widened with delight. "Oh, could you? That would be so cool! Can you show me now?"

Sage made tiny sound in her throat, enough that Chloe gave her a careful look, then moderated her glee to a respectful smile toward Jade Wu. "Only if it wouldn't put you to too much trouble, of course."

Jade looked as amused as Eben had ever seen her in their brief acquaintance. "Not at all. Not at all. I am certain we could find a good apron to put over your lovely dress."

"Thank you very much," Chloe said calmly but Eben could see her nearly vibrating with excitement.

He couldn't help breathing a huge sigh of relief. Chloe had been perfectly behaved all evening. She had been respectful of both of the Wus, had waited her turn to interject a comment or question and had used impeccable table manners.

He knew exactly who deserved the credit for the remarkable transformation—the stunning woman sitting beside him. Sage caught his gaze again and smiled in a conspiratorial way and his heart seemed to stutter in his chest.

Emotions tangled in his throat as he looked at her— tenderness and admiration and something else, something deeper he wasn't sure he could afford to examine closely.

"You should ask your father first, of course."

Chloe grabbed his hand and pressed it between both of hers in her dramatic way, as if she were pleading to save a life instead of only asking permission to bake a cookie. "Oh, please, may I, Daddy?"

"Of course, as long as Mrs. Wu doesn't mind showing you and you do exactly what she says."

She kissed his cheek and Sage smiled at him again. For some silly reason, Eben felt as if he had just hand-delivered the moon to both of them.

"Sage, would you care to come with us?" Jade asked her. "I will find an apron for you as well."

"I'd love to see how it's done," she answered. "But I believe I'll just watch, apron or not."

Eben rose when the three lovely females did and watched them head for the kitchen, Jade in the lead, leaving him alone with Stanley.

The other man didn't seem in any hurry to resume his seat even after the door closed behind the women, so Eben stayed on his feet as well. "Thank you for dinner. It was exceptional, as usual. Tonight, I especially enjoyed the duckling."

Stanley continued to study him out of impassive eyes. Just before the pause between them would have turned awkward, Stanley turned and headed away from the table. "Come with me, Eben Spencer."

Baffled and more than a little edgy, he followed Stanley to the suite of rooms that contained the hotel's administrative offices.

Stanley sat behind his elegantly simple desk and with a solemn look in his eyes he gestured for Eben to take a seat.

"My wife and I have loved this hotel," he said after a long moment. "It has been our home and our lives for many, many years. We have raised two strong sons here and had hoped one of them would choose to carry on for us, but our sons have chosen other paths to follow."

Eben wasn't quite sure where Stanley was steering

the conversation so he opted to remain silent and let the man lead.

"My wife and I are old and we are tired. We spend so much time caring for those who stay here that we have no time to enjoy our older years. The moment has come for us to make a decision about the future of this place we love."

Eben held his breath, doing his best to contain the nerves shooting through him.

"I know you have been impatient with us for the delays. But I hope you understand how difficult it is for us to let go and surrender our dream to another. We needed to be certain. Completely certain. Tonight, seeing you with your beautiful daughter, we are sure of our decision. A man who could raise such a delightful child will take good care of this hotel, the child of our hearts."

The other man pulled out the file Eben knew contained the paperwork for the sale of The Sea Urchin to Spencer Hotels. He signed it in his small, neat script, then handed the papers over to Eben.

He had negotiated hundreds of deals in his dozen years at Spencer Hotels, but Eben couldn't remember any victory tasting as sweet as this one. He wanted to laugh out loud, to throw his fists in the air.

To find Sage and kiss her senseless.

She deserved every bit of credit for this. If not for her and her miraculous effect on Chloe, he wouldn't be sitting here watching Stanley Wu hand him exactly what he wanted, ownership of this graceful old hotel.

Instead of leaping up to go in search of Sage, he settled for holding his hand out across the desk to shake the other man's hand.

"Thank you, Mr. Wu. I give you my solemn vow that you will not regret this."

They would have to go through this again in the morning with attorneys present, but Eben knew Stanley would not change his mind now, not after he had given his word.

They spent several moments discussing a few of the myriad details involved in the sale. He tried his best to focus, but inside he couldn't wait to find Sage and tell her.

Stanley must have finally sensed his impatience.

"All this can wait until tomorrow with the lawyers. Tonight is for being with those we love," Stanley said, then paused. "Our Sage, I have never seen her looking so lovely."

An odd segue, he thought, rather discomfited. "Uh, right."

"And she is just as lovely on the inside. A man would be a fool to let such a rare and precious flower slip through his fingers."

Eben couldn't have said why this particular conversational detour left him slightly panicked. Would Stanley rip up the papers if Eben told him things weren't serious between him and Sage?

He searched the other man's features but could see nothing behind Stanley's serenity.

"Shall we join our women in the kitchen? I am always looking for good fortune."

Still feeling a bit off center, Eben followed Stanley into the kitchen. They stood in the doorway, admiring the lovely picture of women across three generations working together.

The delicious-smelling kitchen was busy and crowded as the head chef and his workers served the other dinner guests. Jade had taken over a workspace in the corner and was overseeing as Chloe and Sage—aprons tucked carefully over their dresses—folded thin circles of soft-cooked cookies into half-moons around little slips of paper, then curved and tucked them into the traditional fortune-cookie shape.

Chloe was laughing with delight as she worked, he saw, and so was Sage, her lovely features bright and animated.

He could barely look away.

Something shivered in his chest, a sense of rightness, of belonging, that had been missing for a long time.

She glanced up and for a tiny sliver of time, their gazes locked together. Her smile slid away, her eyes suddenly as deep and fathomless as the Pacific.

He would be leaving her tomorrow. The grim knowledge churned through him and he suddenly hated the very thought of it. But what other choice did he have?

Chloe caught sight of him. "Daddy, come and see my fortune cookies! I made one just for you. I even wrote the fortune and put it inside and everything."

He jerked his gaze away from Sage, from that stunning, tensile connection between them, and smiled at the cookie in her outstretched hand. "Thanks, kiddo. It's too pretty to eat, though."

"But if you don't eat it, you won't get to see the message."

Four sets of eyes watched him as he broke open the cookie and pulled out the folded slip of paper inside. He unfolded it, only to find Chloe's girlish handwriting, much tinier than usual, was almost indecipherable.

With effort, he was finally able to read the message aloud. To the best Daddy ever. I love you better than all the fortune cookies in the world.

To his complete astonishment—and no small amount of dismay—tears welled up in his eyes. Eben blinked them back rapidly, shoving them down as far as he could into his psyche.

"It's great," he said brusquely when he trusted his voice again. "Thank you very much."

Chloe was obviously looking for more from him. Her features fell. "You don't like it."

"I do." He tried a little more enthusiasm. "I love it. The cookie tastes great and the fortune is...well, it's not true."

Now she looked close to tears. "It is *too*. I do love you more than all the fortune cookies in the world."

He would have preferred this conversation anywhere else than in the busy, noisy kitchen of the hotel he had just agreed to buy—and anywhere else but in front of Stanley and Jade Wu and Sage Benedetto. "I know you do, sweetheart. I just meant the first part isn't true. I'm far from the best daddy in the world, but I'm trying."

She smiled her relief and threw her flour-covered hands around his waist. "Well, I think you're the best."

He hugged her back. "That's the important thing, then, isn't it?"

He had won. The Sea Urchin was his.

Neither Eben nor Stanley mentioned the matter for the rest of the evening. Even after the three of them took their leave of the Wus, Eben didn't say anything, but Sage somehow knew.

She didn't need to possess any kind of psychic ability to correctly read the suppressed excitement in his features.

So this was it. They would be leaving soon. His mind was probably already spinning as he made plans. For all she knew, he may even have made arrangements for a flight out tonight.

She sat beside him battling down a deep ache as he drove down the long driveway of The Sea Urchin, then turned in the direction toward Brambleberry House.

She wasn't ready for another loss so soon. She was still reeling from Abigail's death and now she would lose Eben and Chloe as well. How could she ever be happy in her quiet life without them?

She should never have let them so far into her world. It had been a huge mistake and she was very much afraid she would be paying the price for that particular error in judgment for a long time.

He would probably return to Cannon Beach at some point. She could at least console herself with that. His company had dozens of other hotels around the world, but The Sea Urchin was important to him, he had made no secret of it.

Now that she knew how much he cared about the hotel, she couldn't imagine him just buying the place for acquisition's sake alone. While Sage doubted he would have direct involvement in the future management of the hotel, she expected he would at least have some participation in decision-making.

Even if he left tonight, she knew it was unlikely she would never see him again.

In many ways, she almost thought she would prefer that alternative—that he leave Cannon Beach now that the papers were signed and never look back. How much harder would those occasional visits be, knowing she would have to steel herself to say goodbye to him again?

The rain had eased to a light, filmy drizzle. They were

almost to Brambleberry House when she knew she had to say something.

"It's done, then?" she asked.

His brilliant, boyish smile cut through the darkness inside the Jaguar and, absurdly, made her want to weep. "It's done. The papers are signed. We'll need to have our attorneys go over everything in the morning but as far as I'm concerned, it's official."

"Congratulations."

She thought she had done a fairly credible job of cloaking her ambivalence behind enthusiasm, but some of it must have filtered through.

Eben sent her a swift look across the vehicle. "I know The Sea Urchin is a local landmark and has great meaning for the people of Cannon Beach. I've told you this before, but I think it bears repeating. I promise, I don't plan any major changes. A few coats of paint, maybe, a few modernizations here and there, but that's it."

"I believe you." She smiled, a little less feigned this time. "I'm thrilled for you, Eben. Really, I am. You got exactly what you wanted."

He opened his mouth to say something, then closed it again and she couldn't read his expression in the dim light. "Yes. Exactly what I wanted," he murmured.

"You said you had papers to sign tomorrow. I guess that means you're not leaving tonight, then?"

She saw his gaze shift to the rearview mirror, where Chloe was admiring her substantial pile of fortune cookies and not paying them any attention.

"No. We'll wait until the morning. The Wus and I will have to go through everything with the attorneys at The Sea Urchin first thing and then I'll have my pilot meet Chloe and me at the airport in Seaside when we're done."

She thought of the field trip they had planned all week for their last day of camp, to visit the Cape Meares Lighthouse and Wildlife Refuge. Chloe would be so disappointed to miss it but she knew Eben no doubt had many things to do back in the Bay Area and wouldn't delay for a little thing like a camp field trip.

As they reached Brambleberry House, some of Eben's excitement seemed to have dimmed—or perhaps he was merely containing it better.

Sage, on the other hand, felt ridiculously close to tears. She wasn't sure why, she only knew she couldn't bear the thought of saying goodbye to them in the car.

Besides that, Conan would never forgive her if she let them leave without giving him one last chance to see his beloved Chloe.

She injected an enthusiasm she was far from feeling into her voice. "Do you both want to come in for a few minutes? I've got a frozen cheesecake Abigail made me a…a few weeks before she died. I've been looking for a good occasion to enjoy it with some friends."

"I *love* cheesecake," Chloe offered from the back seat.

"You love anything with sugar in it, monkey."

She giggled at her father. "It's true. I do."

"It's settled, then." Sage smiled.

"Are you sure?" Eben asked.

"Absolutely. We need to celebrate. I'll have to take it out of the freezer but it should only take a few moments to thaw."

He seemed as reluctant as she for the evening to end. "Thank you, then," he said.

He reached behind the seat for the umbrella and came around to her door to open it for her. As he reached to help her from the vehicle, her nerves tingled at the touch of his hand.

"You and Chloe take the umbrella," he said. "You're the ones with the fancy dresses."

Sage found it particular bittersweet to hold Chloe's little hand tightly in hers as the two of them raced through the drizzle to the porch.

Oh, she would miss this darling child. Again she had to swallow down the ache in her throat.

Water droplets glistened in Eben's hair as he joined them on the porch while she unlocked the door.

"Is Conan upstairs or with Ms. Galvez?" Chloe asked when they were inside the entryway.

"He would have been lonely upstairs in my apartment by himself. I think he and Anna were watching a movie when I left."

"Can I take him upstairs with us for cheesecake?"

"Well, we can get him but I should warn you that Conan doesn't like cheesecake. His favorite dessert is definitely apple pie."

Chloe giggled, as Sage had intended. She kept her hand firmly in Sage's as they knocked on Anna's door. For just an instant, Sage caught Eben watching her and she shivered at the glittery expression there.

Conan rushed through the door the moment Anna opened it. "Hey," Anna exclaimed. "How was dinner?"

"You know The Sea Urchin. It couldn't be anything other than exquisite," Sage answered. "Sorry to bother you but we're having an impromptu little party. I'm going to take out the frozen cheesecake Abigail made."

"What's the occasion?"

"We're celebrating," she said, forcing a smile. "Stanley and Jade agreed to sell to Spencer Hotels."

"Oh, that's wonderful! Congratulations."

Eben smiled, though in the better lighting of the entry-way, Sage was certain he didn't look quite as thrilled as he had earlier.

"You and Conan have to join us while we celebrate," she said.

"May I look at the dolls first?" Chloe asked.

Anna sent a quick look at Sage and Eben. Her dark eyes danced with mischief for a moment in an expression that suddenly looked remarkably like one of Abigail's.

"Sure," she finally answered. "You two go ahead. Conan, Chloe and I will be up in a moment. Well, probably closer to ten or fifteen."

She ushered the girl into her apartment and closed the door firmly before Conan could bound up the stairs, leaving Eben and Sage alone in the entryway.

Feeling awkward—and more than a little mortified by Anna's not-so-subtle maneuvering to give her and Eben some private time—Sage led the way up the stairs and into her apartment.

Eben closed the door behind him. She wasn't quite sure how he moved so quickly, but an instant later she was in his arms.

His kiss was firm, demanding, stealing the breath from her lungs. She wrapped her arms around him, exulting in his strength beneath her fingers, in the taste and scent of him.

For long, drugging moments, nothing else mattered but his mouth and his hands and the wild feelings inside her, fluttering to take flight.

"I've been dying to do that all night." His low voice sent shivers rippling down her spine.

She shivered and pulled his mouth back to hers, wondering if he could taste the edge of desperation in the kiss. She forgot about Chloe and Anna and Conan downstairs, she forgot about The Sea Urchin, she forgot everything but the wonder of being in his arms one more time.

One *last* time.

"I don't want to leave tomorrow."

At the ragged intensity of his voice, she blinked her eyes open. The reminder of her inevitable heartbreak seemed to jar her back into her senses.

What was the point in putting herself through this? The more she touched him, experienced the wild joy of being in his arms, the harder she knew it would be to wrench her heart away from him and return to her quiet, safe life before he and Chloe had stumbled into it.

She swallowed. "But you have to."

"I have to," he agreed, reluctance sliding through his voice. "I can't miss these Tokyo meetings."

He pressed his forehead to hers. "But I could try to rearrange my schedule to come back in a few weeks. A month on the outside."

She allowed herself a brief moment to imagine how it might be. Despite the heat they generated and these fragile emotions taking root in her heart, she knew she would merely be a convenience for him, never anything more than that.

She drew in a shuddering breath and slid out of his arms, desperate for space to regain her equilibrium. "I should, uh, get the cheesecake out of the freezer."

He raised an eyebrow at her deliberate evasion but said nothing, only followed her into the kitchen. She opened the small freezer and quickly found Abigail's foil-wrapped package.

Her hands shook a little as she pulled it out—from the

embrace with Eben, but also from emotion. This was one more tie to Abigail that would be severed after tonight.

She looked at Abigail's handwriting on the foil with the date a few weeks before her death and one simple word: Celebrate.

Eben looked at the cheesecake from over her shoulder. He seemed to instinctively know how difficult it was for her to lose one more connection to Abigail. "Are you certain you don't want to save this a little longer, for some other occasion?"

She shook her head with determination. "I have the oddest feeling Abigail would approve. She was the one who introduced you to the Wus, after all. She never would have done that if she didn't want you to buy The Sea Urchin. I think she would be happy her cheesecake is being put to good use. In fact, if I know Abigail, she's probably somewhere lifting a glass of champagne to you right now."

He tilted his head and studied her for a long moment, then smiled softly. "I have you to thank as much as Abigail."

"I didn't do anything."

"Not true. You know it's not. I honestly think Stanley and Jade were ready to pull out until dinner tonight, until you and Chloe both charmed them."

He grabbed her fingers. "You reach Chloe in ways I don't think anyone has since her mother died."

She shifted and slid her hand away, uncomfortable with his praise. How could she tell him she understood Chloe's pain so intimately and connected with her only because her life had so closely mirrored the little girl's?

"What can I do to reach her that way?" Eben asked.

By all appearances, he looked completely sincere. "You need to give me lessons."

"Just trust your instincts. That's the only lesson I can give."

"Following my instincts hasn't turned out well so far. Maybe if I had better success at this father business, I wouldn't have to send her to boarding school in the fall."

At first, she thought—hoped—she misheard him. He couldn't possibly be serious.

"Boarding school? You're sending her to *boarding school?*"

He shrugged, looking as if he wished he hadn't said anything. "Thinking about it. I haven't made a final decision."

"You have. Admit it."

She was suddenly trembling with fury. She was again eight years old, lost and alone, with no friends and a father who wanted little to do with her. "You've probably already signed her up and paid the first year's tuition, haven't you?"

Guilt flitted across his features. "A deposit, only to hold her spot. It's a very good school outside Newport, Rhode Island. My sister went there."

"Half a world away from you!"

"What do you want me to do, Sage? I've been at my wit's end. You've seen a different child this week than the one I've lived with for two years. Here, Chloe has been sweet and easygoing. Things are different at home. She's moody and angry and deceitful and nothing I do gets through to her. I told you she's been through half a dozen nannies and four different schools since her mother died. Every one of them says she has severe behavior problems and needs more structure and order. How am I supposed to give her that with my travel schedule?"

"You're the brilliant businessman. You don't need me to help you figure it out. Stop traveling so much or, if you have to go, take her with you. That's your answer, not dumping her off at some boarding school and then forgetting about her. She's a child, Eben. She needs her father."

"Don't you get it? I'm not the solution, I'm the damn problem."

As quickly as it swelled inside her, her anger trickled away at the despair in his voice. She longed, more than anything, to touch him again.

"Oh, Eben. You're not. She's a little girl who's lost her mother and she's desperate for her father's attention. Of course she's going to misbehave if that's the only time she can get a reaction from you. But she doesn't need a boarding school, she needs you."

"How do you know it won't help her?"

"Because I lived it! You want to know how I'm able to reach Chloe so well? Because I'm her with a few more years under my belt. I was exactly like Chloe, shunted away by my father to boarding school when I was eight simply because I no longer fit his lifestyle."

Chapter Thirteen

Eben stared at her. Of all the arguments he might have expected her to make, that particular one wouldn't have even made his list.

"Sage—"

She let out a long breath. Still in her party clothes, she looked fragile and heartbreakingly beautiful.

"My mother died when I was five," she went on. "I was seven when my father married his second wife, a lovely, extremely wealthy socialite who didn't appreciate being reminded of his previous wife and the life they had together. I was an inconvenience to both of them."

An inconvenience? How could anyone consider a child an inconvenience? For all his frustration with Chloe, none of it hinged on a word as cold as that one.

"I was dumped into boarding school when I was eight. The same age as Chloe. For the next decade, I saw my father about three weeks out of every year—one week during the Christmas holidays and two weeks in the summer."

He remembered her disdain for him early in their acquaintance, the contempt he saw in her eyes that first morning on the beach, the old pain he had seen in her eyes when they argued about whether he should take Chloe with him on his trip to Tokyo.

No wonder.

She thought of him as someone like her father, someone too busy for his own child. He ached to touch her but couldn't ignore the *hands-off* signals she was broadcasting around herself like a radio frequency.

"I'm so sorry, Sage."

Her chin lifted. "I survived. Listen to me complain like it was the worst thing that could ever happen to a child. It wasn't. I was always fed, clean, warm. I know many children endure much worse than an exclusive private boarding school in Europe. But I have to tell you, part of me has never recovered from that early sense of abandonment."

He pictured a younger version of Sage, lost and lonely, desperate for attention. He ached to imagine it.

But she was right, wasn't she? If he sent Chloe to boarding school, she would probably suffer some of those same emotions—perhaps for the rest of her life.

What the hell was he supposed to do?

"Boarding school doesn't have to be as you experienced it," he said. "My sister and I both went away for school when we were about Chloe's age. We did very well."

For him and, he suspected, for his sister, school had offered security and peace from the tumult and chaos of their home life. He had relished the structure and order he found there, the safety net of rules. He had thrived there in a way he never could have at home with his parents. In his heart, he supposed he was hoping Chloe would do the same.

"You don't have any scars at all?"

"A few." The inevitable hazings and peer cruelty had certainly left their mark until he'd found his feet. "But I don't know anyone who survives childhood without a scar or two."

"She's already lost her mother, Eben. No matter how lofty you tell yourselves your motives might be, I can promise that if you send Chloe away, she'll feel as if she's losing you, too."

"She won't be losing me. I'm not your father, Sage. I don't plan to send her away and ignore her for months at a time."

All his excitement at closing The Sea Urchin deal was gone now, washed away under this overwhelming tide of guilt and uncertainty.

"Besides, I told you I haven't made a final decision yet. This week has been different. *Chloe* has been different and I probably have been, too. If I can recapture that when we're back in our regular lives, there's no reason I have to follow through and send her to boarding school."

A small gasp sounded from the doorway. In the heat of the discussion with Sage—wrapped up in his dismay over inadvertently putting those shadows in her eyes— he had missed the sound of the door opening. Now, with a sinking heart, he turned to find Chloe standing there, her little features pale and her eyes huge and wounded.

"Chloe—"

"You're sending me to *boarding school?*" she practically shrieked. "You can't, Daddy. You *can't!*"

She was hitching her breath in and out rapidly, on the brink of what he feared would be a full-blown tantrum.

Helpless and frustrated, he went to her and tried to hug her, tangentially aware as he did so of Anna Galvez and Conan standing behind her in the hallway outside Sage's apartment.

"I didn't say I was sending you to boarding school."

She was prickly and resistant and immediately slid away from him. "You said you might not have to but that means you're thinking about it, doesn't it?"

He couldn't lie to her. Not about something as important as her future. "We don't have to talk about this right now. We're all tired and overexcited. Come on, let's have some of Sage's cheesecake."

"I don't want cheesecake! I don't want *anything.*"

"Chloe—"

"I won't go! Do you hear me? I'll run away. I'll come here and live with Sage."

She burst into hard, heaving sobs and buried her face in Conan's fur. The dog licked her cheek then turned and glared at Eben.

Join the club, he thought. Everybody else in the room was furious with him.

He didn't know what to do, certain that if he tried to comfort his daughter he would only make this worse. To his vast relief, Sage stepped in and sat on the floor right there in the doorway in her elegant dress and pulled Chloe onto her lap.

She murmured soft, soothing words and after a few tense moments, Chloe's tears began to ease.

"I don't want to go to boarding school," she mumbled again.

"I know, baby."

Sage ran a hand over her hair but he noted she didn't give Chloe any false reassurances. "Do you think you're going to be up for cheesecake tonight? If you're not, you could always take some home with you."

"I'm not hungry now," Chloe whispered. "If it's okay with you, I'll take it home. Thank you."

By the time Sage cut into her friend's ironically labeled cheesecake—he had never felt *less* like celebrating—and packaged up two slices for them, Chloe had reverted to an icy, controlled calm that seemed oddly familiar. It took him a moment to realize she was emulating the way he tried to stuff down his emotions and keep control in tense situations.

Somebody ought to just stick a knife through his heart, Eben thought. It would be far less painful in the long run than this whole parenting thing.

Anna had disappeared back to her apartment earlier during the worst of Chloe's outburst and Sage and Conan walked them down the stairs and to his car.

The rain had stopped, he saw. The night was cool and sweet with the scent of Abigail's flowers.

Chloe gave Sage an extra-long hug. If he wasn't mistaken, he saw Sage wipe her eyes after Chloe slid into the back seat, but when she lifted her gaze to his, it was filled with a Zen-like calm.

"This isn't the way I wanted the evening to end," he murmured. *Or the week, really.*

Their time with her had been magical and he hated to see it end.

He gazed at her features in the moonlight, lovely and exotic, and his chest ached again at the idea of leaving her.

"Will you come running with Chloe and me in the morning? Just one more time?"

She drew in a sharp breath. "I don't know if that's a good idea. It's late and Chloe probably will need sleep after tonight. Perhaps we should just say our goodbyes here."

"Please, Sage."

She closed her eyes. When she opened them, they brimmed with tears again and his heart shattered into a million pieces.

"I can't," she whispered. "Goodbye, Eben. Be well."

She turned and hurried up the sidewalk and slipped inside the house before he could even react.

After a long moment of staring after her, he climbed into the car, fighting the urge to press a hand to his chest to squeeze away the tight ache there.

Despite his halfhearted efforts to engage her in conversation, Chloe maintained an icy silence to him through the short distance to their rented beach house.

He couldn't blame her, he supposed. It had been a fairly brutal way to find out that he was considering sending her to boarding school. He had planned to broach the idea when he returned from Tokyo and slowly build to it over the summer, give her time to become adjusted to it.

"You know you're going to have to talk to me again sometime," he finally said when they walked to the door of their rented beach house. In answer, she pointedly turned her back, crossed her arms across her chest and clamped her lips shut.

He sighed as he unlocked the door and disengaged the

security system. The moment they were inside, Chloe raced to her bedroom and slammed the door.

Eben stood for a moment in the foyer, his emotions a thick, heavy burden. He didn't know what the hell to do with them.

He needed a drink, he decided, and crossed to the small, well-stocked bar. A few moments later, snifter in hand, he sat in the small office calling his assistant to set up the meeting with his attorneys at The Sea Urchin in the morning and to arrange for the company Learjet to meet them at the airport in Seaside.

After he hung up, he sat for a moment wondering how a night that had started out holding such promise could have so quickly turned into an ugly disaster.

Now Sage was angry and disappointed in him, his daughter wasn't speaking to him, he was even getting the cold shoulder from a blasted dog, for heaven's sake.

The way his evening was going, he would probably be getting a phone call from the Wus telling him they had changed their minds *again*.

By the time he finished the tiny splash of brandy, he knew he had to face Chloe, if only to address her fears.

He knocked on her bedroom door. "Chloe? Let's talk about this. Come on."

Only silence met his knock. Surely she couldn't have fallen asleep already, could she? He knocked harder and tried the door, only to find it locked.

He didn't need this tonight. Frustration whipped through him and he banged even harder. "Chloe, open this door, young lady. Right now."

Still no answer. For the first time, unease began to filter through his frustration. He should never have let her come here and stew. It had been only a cowardly attempt to delay the inevitable. He should have just confronted the problem head-on the minute they walked into the house.

The lock on the bedroom door was flimsy. He quickly grabbed a butter knife from the kitchen, twisted the mechanism, then swung the door open.

A quick sweep of the darkened room showed the bed was still made, with no sign of his daughter.

"Chloe? Where are you hiding? This isn't funny."

He flipped on the light. The dress she had adored so much was discarded in a pile of taffeta on the floor and the shelves of the bureau were open, their contents spilling out, as if she had rummaged through looking for something in a hurry.

He barely saw any of that. His attention was suddenly focused on the curtains fluttering in the breeze and instantly Eben's unease turned to cold-edged fear.

The window was open to the sea-soaked night air and there was no sign of his daughter.

"Yeah, I know. I don't need a second piece of cheesecake. Or the first one, for that matter. You're one to talk. You pig out on *dog food*, for crying out loud."

Conan snickered and dipped his head back to his forepaws as he watched her lame attempts to drown her misery in a decadent swirl of sugar and cream cheese.

"It's not working, anyway," she muttered, setting the plate down on the coffee table in front of her.

She should be in bed, she knew. The day had been long, the evening painfully full and her muscles ached with exhaustion, but she knew she wouldn't be able to sleep.

Her emotions were too raw, too heavy. She had a sinking suspicion that when the sun rose, she would probably still be sitting right here on her couch in her bathrobe, red-eyed and wrung-out and three pounds heavier from the cheesecake.

Damn Eben Spencer anyway.

He had no business sweeping into her life, shaking up her status quo so dramatically, then riding off into the blasted sunset—especially not when her grief for Abigail still had such a stranglehold around her life.

Conan made a sad sound suddenly, as if he sensed she was thinking about his human companion.

He had seemed much less depressed these last few days with Eben and Chloe. How would their leaving affect him, poor dog? She had a feeling her quad muscles were in for some good workouts the next few mornings.

He had been acting strangely ever since Eben and Chloe had left for the evening. Now he stood again. Instead of going to the door to signal he needed to go out, he went to the windows overlooking the ocean and stared out into the night for a long moment then whined plaintively.

That was the third time he had repeated the same odd behavior in the last half-hour. It was starting to freak her out.

"What's the matter, bud?" she asked him.

Before the words were even out of her mouth, she heard a sharp knocking at the door downstairs.

Who on earth would be coming to call at—she checked her clock—eleven o'clock at night?

She went to the opposite windows but couldn't see a car in the driveway. The caller knocked again and Sage moved warily down the stairs, one hand on Conan's collar.

The best Conan would do was probably sniff an intruder to death but he was big and could look menacing if the light wasn't great and the intruder had bad eyes.

She left the chain in the door and peered through, but her self-protective instincts flew out into the night when she saw Eben standing on the porch, a frantic expression in his eyes.

"Eben! What is it? What's happened?"

He studied her for a moment, then raked a hand through his hair. "She's not here, is she?"

She blinked, trying to make sense of his appearance on her doorstep so late. "Chloe? No. I haven't seen her since the two of you left. She's not at home?"

"I thought she was just sulking in her bedroom. I gave her maybe twenty minutes to get it out of her system while I made a few calls. But when I went into her room to talk to her, she was gone and her window was open. I was certain she must have come here to find you. That's what she said, right? That she would run away and find you."

Conan whined and ran past them sniffing around the perimeter of the wrought-iron fence.

"You checked the beach?" Sage asked.

"That's the way I came. I ran the whole way, sure I would bump into her any minute, but I couldn't see any sign of her. I called and called but she didn't answer."

His eyes looked haunted. "I have to find her. Anything could happen to her alone in the middle of the night!"

His desperation terrified her as nothing else could. "Let me throw on some clothes and get a jacket and shoes. Perhaps we can split up, cover more ground."

Anna's door suddenly opened and she poked her head out, her hair as messy as Sage had ever seen it and her dark eyes bleary with sleep. "What's wrong?"

"Sorry we woke you." Sage spoke quickly. "Chloe's missing. She was angry with her father about what happened earlier and it looks as if she snuck out her window."

She couldn't help but be impressed at the rapid way Anna pushed aside the cobwebs and became her normal brisk, businesslike self. "What can I do? Do you want me to call the police?"

Eben drew in a sharp breath. "I don't know. I just keep thinking she didn't have enough time to go far. Where could she have gone? There aren't that many places she's familiar with around here."

"I don't know. We've explored the area around here quite a bit this week in camp." Her voice trailed off and she gazed at Eben and saw the exact same realization hit him.

"Hug Point," Sage said. The beach they had visited when they took the tandem bicycle.

"Would she have time to get there?"

"She's fast. She could make it."

"That's a hell of a long way for an eight-year-old in the dark," Eben said, and she ached at the fledgling hope in his eyes.

"She has a flashlight. It's part of the survival kit we did the first day of camp."

"That must have been what she was rummaging through her room to find. That's something, isn't it?"

"Maybe." She paused, loathe to tell him more bad news but she knew she had no choice. "Eben, the tide is coming in fast. High tide will be in about ninety minutes."

She saw stark fear in his eyes and knew it mirrored her own.

"We should split up," he said. "One of us search down the beach in case she hasn't made it that far yet and is still on her way and the other one start at Hug Point and head back this direction."

"Good idea. I'll drive to Hug Point and start back-tracking this way. You take Conan with you."

She thought of the way the dog had immediately gone to Chloe that first day, as if he'd been looking just for her. "If she's out there, he'll help us find her."

"Okay."

She grabbed his hand, heartsore for him. "Eben, we'll find her."

He looked slightly buoyed by her faith and squeezed her fingers, then took off through the backyard to the beach access gate.

"Maybe I ought to call the police chief and give him a heads-up, just in case your hunch is wrong," Anna said.

"Do it," Sage said on her way up the stairs two at a time.

For all her reassurances to Eben, she knew exactly what dangers awaited a little girl on the beach in the dark at high tide and she couldn't bear to think of any of them.

Though it only took a few moments to reach Hug Point by car, it felt like a lifetime. The whole way, Sage gripped the steering wheel of her aging Toyota and tried to battle back her terror and her guilt.

She was as much to blame for this as Eben. If she hadn't overreacted so strongly at his mention of board-ing school for Chloe, they wouldn't have been arguing about it and Chloe wouldn't have overheard.

It was none of her business what school Eben sent his daughter to. She had been presumptuous to think otherwise. In her usual misguided attempt to save the world, she had ended up hurting the situation far more than she helped.

She pulled into the parking lot as a light drizzle started again. Heedless of the rain or the wind that whipped the hood of her Gore-Tex jacket, she cupped her hands and called Chloe's name.

She strained hard to hear anything over the wind and the murmur of the sea. In the distance, somewhere beyond the headland, she thought she heard a small cry.

Though she knew well how deceiving sounds could be out here—for all she knew, it could have been a nocturnal shorebird—she decided she had to head in the direction of the sound.

In the dark, the shore was far different than it was in the daylight, though it had a harsh beauty here as well, like some wild moonscape, twisted and shaped by the elements.

She rounded the cluster of rocks, straining to see anything in the darkness.

She heard the same cry again and aimed her flashlight along the beach but it was a pitiful weapon to fight back the vast, unrelenting dark.

Suddenly on the wind, she could swear she heard Chloe's voice. "Help. Please!"

She turned the flashlight toward the water and her heart stopped when she saw several yards away a small figure in a pink jacket on one of the rocks they had played on the other day. She was surrounded by water now and the tide was rising quickly.

Far down the beach from the direction of Brambleberry House, she saw a tiny spark of light on the beach and knew it was Eben. There wasn't time to wait for him but she whistled hard, hoping Conan would hear and come running. Perhaps Eben would pick up on the dog's urgency.

"I'm coming, baby," she called as she hurried down the sand. "Stay there. Just hang on."

When she was parallel on the shore with Chloe on her watery perch, she headed through the surf. She was prepared for the cold but it still clutched at her with icy fingers and she couldn't contain a gasp. No matter how cold she knew the ocean could be along the Pacific Northwest coast, even in June, it still took her by surprise.

She knew hypothermia could hit out here in a matter of minutes.

Chloe's rock was probably only twenty yards from shore but that seemed far enough as she waded through the icy water, now up to her knees. She was laboring for breath by the time she reached her. "Hi, sweetie."

The sobbing girl threw her arms around Sage. She was wet and shivering and Sage knew she had to get her out of the water immediately.

"You came for me!" she sobbed. "I was so scared. I want my daddy."

Sage held her close and buried her face in the girl's hair, her heart full. She could barely breathe around the emotions racing through her.

"I know you want your daddy, honey. I know. He and Conan are coming down the beach from my house looking for you, but they'll be here in a minute. He'll be so happy to see you."

"Am I in big trouble?"

"What do you think?" she asked, trying to sound stern through her vast relief.

"I snuck out again, even though I promised I wouldn't. I went on the beach at night, even though you told me

I shouldn't. I broke a lot of rules. I bet my dad's really mad."

Sage kept one eye on the rising tide. A wave hit her, soaking her to her waist and she knew they had to move. "Let's worry about that when we get out of here, okay? How about a piggyback ride?"

"Okay. My hands are really cold, though. I don't know if I can hang on."

"You can. Just pretend you're a crab and I'm your dinner and you don't want to let me go."

Chloe giggled and gripped her arms around Sage's neck. Sage could feel her shiver even through her jacket.

It was tough going on the way back. She couldn't see where she was going and she felt as if she were walking through quicksand. For the first time, she was grateful for the last month of morning runs that had built up her muscles. If not for those runs, she wasn't sure she would have had the endurance to get to shore.

A journey that had only been twenty yards on the way out now seemed like miles. They were almost to the sand when a sneaker wave came out of nowhere and slammed into the backs of her legs.

Tired and off balance with Chloe on her back, Sage swayed from the force of it and stumbled to her knees. She managed to keep her hold on Chloe but then another one washed over them and drove her face into the surf.

Spluttering and coughing, she wrenched her face free of the icy water. She had to get to her feet now, she knew, but she felt as if she were fighting the whole ocean.

At last, with a great surge of adrenaline, she staggered to her feet. Chloe was crying in earnest now.

"We're okay. We're okay. Only a little farther," she managed, then she heard the most welcome sounds she had ever heard—a dearly familiar bark and Eben's strong voice.

"Chloe! Sage!" he called. "Hang on. I'm coming."

She sobbed out a breath of relief and made it only another few feet before he reached them and guided them all back to safety.

Chapter Fourteen

By the time he reached them, both Sage and Chloe were soaked and shivering violently. He grabbed Chloe in one arm while he drew Sage against his body with the other. Together, the three of them made their way to the shore. Only when they were above the high tide line did Eben pause to take a breath.

His heart still pounded with rapid force from that terrible moment when he saw them both go down in the water and struggle so hard against the waves to come up.

"Are you both okay?" he asked.

In his arms, Chloe nodded and sniffled. "I'm sorry, Daddy. I'm sorry. I'm sorry. I shouldn't have run away. No wonder you want to send me away to boarding school."

He closed his eyes, pained that they had come back to this. "We need to get you both warmed up. Come on. Let's get you home."

"There's a trail back to the road from here. That's

probably the easiest way to get to the parking lot and my car."

After the longest fifteen minutes of his life, they made it to Sage's car.

"There's a b-blanket in the b-back for Chloe," she mumbled. "It's probably covered in dog hair but it's the b-best I can do."

He found it quickly and also a fleece jacket of Sage's, which he handed to her.

"I'll drive," he insisted. "You work on getting warm."

After Chloe was settled in the back wrapped in the blanket and cuddled next to Conan's heat, Eben climbed into the driver's seat and turned her heater on high.

His emotions were thick, jumbled, and his heart still pounded with remembered fear as he drove toward Brambleberry House.

"I should call Anna, tell her to call off the police," Sage said after a moment. Her trembling had mostly stopped, he saw with vast relief.

"The police were looking for me?" Chloe asked in a small voice from the back seat. "I'm in big trouble, aren't I?"

"Everybody was worried about you," Eben said.

Sage called Anna on her cell phone and for the next few moments their one-sided conversation was the only sound in the small vehicle.

"She's fine. We're all fine. Cold and wet but everybody's okay. Yeah, I'll be home in a minute. I'll tell her. Thanks, Anna."

She closed her phone and turned to the back seat. "Anna says to tell you she's so glad you're okay."

"Me, too," Chloe said sleepily. "I was so scared. The

water wasn't high when I went out to the rock but then it started coming in fast and I didn't know what to do."

"You did the right thing to stay where you were," Sage said.

"I remembered what we talked about in camp. I tried to do just what you said."

He couldn't bear to think about what might have happened if Chloe hadn't had a little survival training through Sage's camp or if they hadn't found her in time.

With the resilience of the young, Chloe was nearly asleep by the time they reached Brambleberry House, her arms wrapped around Conan and her cheek resting against the top of his furry head.

He feared it would be as tough to wean her from the dog as it would be to leave this place.

"Just drop me off," Sage said. "I can pick up my car at your place tomorrow on my way to the center."

In the driveway, he put the car in park and finally reached for her hand. "Sage, I don't know how I can ever thank you."

She shook her head. "Don't. You know you don't need to thank me. I'm just so grateful everything turned out okay."

He was quiet for a moment, hot emotion choking his throat. He wanted to shunt it all away as he usually did, to lock it down deep inside him, but this wild tangle was too huge, to overwhelming.

He knew he couldn't leave things between them like this, tainted by this stilted awkwardness, not after everything that had happened.

"I know it's late but… I need to talk to you. After I get Chloe settled into bed, I would like to call Stanley and

Jade, see if they could send someone over to stay with her for a little while."

She drew in a breath that ended in a little shiver, though he wasn't sure if it resulted from the cold or something else. "We don't really have anything left to say, do we?"

He squeezed her fingers. "I think we do. Please, Sage."

After an agonizingly long moment, she shrugged. "I'll try to watch for you so you don't have to ring the doorbell and wake Anna again."

He nodded. He had no idea what he wanted to say to her, he only knew he couldn't return home in the morning without seeing her again.

She opened the rear door for Conan and gave Chloe another hug, then hurried into her house.

Chloe said little as they drove back to their cottage. She was nearly asleep by the time he pulled into the driveway behind his rental, her head lolling back against the upholstery.

"Just a few more minutes, baby," he said as he helped her inside. "A hot shower will help warm you up the rest of the way and wash away the saltwater."

She sighed. "I'd rather just go to bed. I'm so tired."

"I know, but you'll feel better, I promise. You're not going to fall asleep in there, are you?"

"No," she said, her voice subdued. "I'll be okay."

While he listened to the sounds of the shower, he changed out of wet khakis and shoes. He'd had it easy compared to Chloe and Sage and had only gotten wet up to mid-calf, but just that slight dousing left him cold.

He called The Sea Urchin front desk and, to his surprise, Jade answered. He left out a few details but explained he needed someone to come and sit with Chloe. Despite his best efforts to dissuade her, she insisted on coming herself and said she would be there in a few moments.

He was waiting in the living room when Chloe came out of the shower in her warmest flannel nightgown.

She hurried to him at once and wrapped her arms around his waist. She smelled sweet, like lavender soap and baby shampoo, and he held on tightly as more emotions caught in his throat.

"I really am super sorry I ran away, Daddy. I was just so mad at you but I wasn't thinking right."

He kissed the top of her head. "Trying to escape our problems doesn't work and usually only creates more trouble. Either they come right along with us or they're waiting where we left them when we get back."

She nodded, her damp hair leaving a mark against his shirt.

"I love you, baby," he said after a moment. "Please don't forget that. No matter what, I love you."

"I want to stay with you, Daddy. Please don't send me away. I'll try harder, I promise."

Sage had been right. He couldn't do it. Imperfect though he was—inadequate as he felt as a father—his daughter needed him.

"Same here, okay? I'll try harder, too. We both have to figure out how to make this work. I'll try to cut down my travel schedule so I'm home to spend more time with you."

"Oh, would you?"

More guilt sliced him at the stunned disbelief in her voice. "Yes. But you have to promise me that you'll settle down and work harder in school and that you'll take it easy on the new nanny when we get one."

Though she was about to fall over with exhaustion,

she still managed to get a crafty look in her eyes. "Can I help pick her?"

"Well, I can't promise I'll let you make the final decision but you can have input. Deal?"

"Deal." She beamed at him. "I know just what I want. Somebody like Sage. She's pretty and she smells good and she's super nice."

That just about summed it up, Eben thought. "We'll have to see what we can do. I think Sage is one of a kind."

"You like her, too, don't you, Daddy?"

"Sure, baby." He wasn't quite ready to examine his emotions too closely—nor did he want to explain them to his eight-year-old daughter. Instead, he scooped her into his arms, earning a sleepy giggle.

"Come on, let's get you into bed, okay? Jade Wu is coming over to stay with you so I can take Sage's car back to Brambleberry House after you're asleep."

"Okay. Give Sage and Conan a big kiss for me, okay?"

He grimaced. He wasn't sure either of those creatures in question were very happy with him right now. "I'll see what I can do," he murmured as he tucked her into her bed, then kissed her forehead and slipped from the room to wait for Jade.

What the hell was he doing here?

Twenty minutes later, Eben drove Sage's car into the driveway of Brambleberry House, turned off the engine and sat for a moment in the dark silence.

He should just leave her car here, tuck the keys under the doormat and walk back down the beach. The smartest thing to do would be to leave things as they were and continue with his plans to leave in the morning.

But just the thought of it made him ache inside. He sighed, still not certain what he wanted to say to her.

He was still trying to puzzle it out when the porch light flipped on. A moment later, she opened the door and stood in the doorway, a slim, graceful silhouette, and his heart bumped in his chest.

Her hair was damp and she had a blanket wrapped around her shoulders and one hand on the dog. He let out a long breath and slid from the car. The night air was cool and moist from the rains earlier, sweet with Abigail's flowers and the salty undertone of the ocean.

Neither of them spoke until he reached the porch.

"I wasn't sure you were coming." Her voice was low and strummed down his spine as if she'd caressed his skin.

"I probably shouldn't have."

"Why are you here, then? You're not a man who does things he shouldn't."

He gave a rough laugh. "Aren't I?" Unable to resist, he stepped forward and framed her face in his hands. She was so achingly beautiful and the air eddying around them was sweetly magical and he had no choice but to kiss her.

She was perfect in his arms and as her mouth moved softly under his, he felt something tight and hard around his heart shudder and give way.

This was why he came. He knew it with sudden certainty. Because somehow when he was here, with this woman in his arms, all the tumult inside him seemed to go still.

He found a peace with Sage Benedetto he had never even realized had been missing in his life.

She wanted to cherish every second of this.

Sage twisted her arms around his neck, trying to burn

each memory into her mind. She couldn't quite believe she had the chance to touch him and to taste him again when only a few short hours ago she thought he would be leaving her world forever.

"You're shivering," he murmured.

She knew it was in reaction to the wild chaos of emotions storming through her, but she couldn't tell him that. "I'm fine. My hair's just a little damp. That's all."

"You shouldn't be out here in the cool night air."

She was silent for a moment, gazing at the masculine features that had become so dear to her. "You're probably right," she finally murmured. "Come inside."

She knew exactly what she was offering—just as she knew she was signing herself up for even more heartache.

But she loved him. The truth of it had hit her the moment she saw him coming walking up the path. She was in love with Eben Spencer, billionaire hotelier and the last man on the planet a wild, flyaway nature girl from Oregon would ever have a forever-chance with.

This was all she would have with him and she couldn't make herself turn away now.

She walked up to her apartment without looking back. Over the pounding of her heart, she heard his footsteps behind her but he didn't say anything as they climbed the two flights of stairs.

Once inside, she frowned. She could swear she had left several lights on when she walked downstairs to let him in, but now only a single lamp was burning.

She had been reading while she waited and watched for him, listening to a Nanci Griffith CD but she must have bumped her stereo on her way out the door because now soft jazz played.

The whole room looked as if she had set the scene for

romance, which she absolutely had *not*. Despite her conviction that she wanted this, wanted him, she felt her face flame and hit the overhead light switch.

Nothing happened. The bulb must have burned out, she thought, mortified all over again.

Eben came into the room alone and she looked behind him. "Where's Conan?"

"I think he went through his door into Anna's apartment."

"Ah."

They stood looking at each other for a long moment and Sage could swear she could hear the churn of her blood pulsing through her body. She didn't think she had ever wanted anything in her life as much as she wanted him right now.

She opened her mouth to ask if he would like a drink or something—not that she had much, just some wine left over from the other night—but before any words could escape, he stepped forward and kissed her again.

Who needed alcohol when Eben Spencer was around? It was the last thought she had for a long time as she lost herself in the wonder of his strength, his touch.

After several long, glorious moments, he lifted his mouth away and pressed his forehead to hers. "I don't want to lose you, Sage."

She raised an eyebrow. "You can't lose what you don't have. An astute businessman like you should already know that."

He laughed, a low, amused sound that rippled over her nerve endings. "You're very good at putting me in my place, aren't you?"

She smiled, liking the place he was in very, very much.

"I mean it," he said. "I have to leave in the morning but I don't want this to be the end for us."

She didn't want to think about his leaving or about the emptiness he would leave behind. "Eben—"

He stepped away from her, raw emotion on his face. He was usually a master at concealing his thoughts. To see him in such an unveiled moment shocked her.

He gripped her hands in his and brought them to his chest, where she could feel the wild pulse of his heartbeat. Had she done that to him? She wondered with surprise.

"I was terrified tonight," he said, his voice low. "I've never known anything like that."

"You were worried for your daughter," she said. "That was completely normal."

"My fear wasn't only for Chloe." His gaze locked with hers and she couldn't look away from the stunning tenderness in the glittery green depths of his eyes. "My world stopped when I saw that wave hit. All I could think was that I couldn't bear the thought of anything happening to either of you."

Sharp joy exploded inside her and she couldn't breathe around it.

"I care about you, Sage. You've become desperately important to me and to my daughter this week."

Close on the heels of the joy was an even bigger terror. This couldn't be real. Hadn't she just spent a week convincing herself of all the reasons there could never be anything between them?

"You'll go back to California and forget all about me."

"I don't think so." He brought their clasped hands to his mouth, his gaze still locked with hers. "I'm in love with you, Sage."

She swallowed, feeling lightheaded with shock. "You're not," she exclaimed.

"I've been fighting it with everything I have. Falling in love is not what I planned in my life right now—or ever."

He let go of her hands and stepped away from her. "My marriage was a mess, Sage. It taught me that love is complicated and confusing and…messy. I didn't want that again. I've done everything I can to talk myself out of it this week, but I can't deny it anymore. I'm in love with you, Sage. I don't want to be, but there it is. I think I have been since you showed up on my doorstep with Chloe that first morning."

I don't want to be in love with you.

She heard his words as if from a long distance, but they still managed to pierce the haze of disbelief around her.

He didn't want to love her. He had done all he could to talk himself out of it, had been fighting it with everything he had. He didn't want to be in love, didn't want the complications or the mess.

Panic fluttered through her and she was suddenly desperate for space to breathe, to think.

She couldn't do this. She *couldn't*. She had spent her childhood trying desperately to gain the attention of a man who didn't want to love her, who had shut his emotions off abruptly when he married her stepmother, leaving Sage with nothing.

She couldn't put herself through this again.

It was a simple matter of self-preservation. She loved him. The surety of it washed over her like the most powerful of sneaker waves.

She loved him and she knew all about how messy and

painful love could be. She was terrified that she would give everything to Eben and he would destroy her.

She drew in a shaky breath and pressed a hand to her stomach, to the fear that roiled and churned there. He was watching her out of those vivid green eyes and she knew she had to say something.

Something cold and hard.

Final.

She was weak, desperate, and very much feared she had no willpower at all when it came to Eben Spencer.

"You're not in love with me, Eben. You're attracted to me, just as I am to you, but it's not love. How could it be? We barely know each other. We're far too different. We...we want different things out of life. You want to conquer the world and I want to clean it up and leave it a better place."

"A little simplistic, don't you think?"

She grabbed the blanket that had fallen during the heat of their embrace and wrapped it around her shoulders again, hoping he wouldn't notice her trembling.

"Maybe it is simplistic. But look at us! You're the CEO of a billion-dollar hotel dynasty and I'm perfectly happy here in my little world, showing kids how to tell the difference between a clingfish and a sculpin. When you think about it, you have to see we have nothing in common."

"We can get past the few differences between us."

"I don't *want* to get past them."

For once in her life, she desperately wished she were a better liar. She could only pray he wouldn't look closely enough to see right through her. "I'm physically attracted to you, Eben, I can't deny that. I'm attracted to you and I adore Chloe. But I'm... I'm not in love with you. You're not the kind of man I want."

She was trembling in earnest now, sick with the lie and had to pull the blanket tighter around her shoulders to hide it from him.

He gazed at her for a long moment and she forced herself to lift her chin and return his gaze, praying she could keep all trace of emotion from her features.

"Fair enough," he finally said, his voice quiet. "I guess that's all that really matters, isn't it?"

A few more moments, she told herself. *Keep it together just a few more moments and he'll be gone.*

"I'm sorry," she murmured.

His laugh was rough, humorless. "You don't have to apologize for not sharing my feelings, Sage. I told you love was messy. There's nothing messier than one person feeling things that aren't returned."

She could say nothing, could only clutch the blanket around her with nerveless fingers.

"I guess this is goodbye, then," he said, reaching for the doorknob. "I have to come back to Cannon Beach. There's no avoiding that—I just bought a hotel here. But on the rare occasions I come back to oversee the transition of The Sea Urchin to Spencer Hotels ownership, I'll do my best to stay out of your way."

She thought her heart would crack apart again. How many times was she going to have to say goodbye to him? She couldn't bear this. "You don't have to do that."

One corner of his mouth lifted in a grim ghost of a smile. "Yeah. Yeah, I do."

He opened the door but turned back before he passed through it for the last time. "Goodbye, Sage. Thank you again for tonight, for Chloe. You gave me back my daughter and I don't just mean by rescuing her from the tide. I'm not sending her to school, if that makes you feel any better. The two of us will tough it out and try to figure things out together."

"That's good. I'm happy for you both."

Oh, please go! She couldn't bear this.

He gave that ghost of a smile again then walked out, closing the door behind him.

She managed to keep it together, her hands gripping the blanket tightly while she listened to his footsteps down the stairs and then the creak of the outside door opening and closing.

She waited a few more moments, until she could be certain he was on his way back to his beach house, then a wild sob escaped her, then another and another.

By the time Conan climbed the stairs a few moments later, she had collapsed on the couch and was sobbing in earnest.

Her dog raced into the room, sniffed around the entire apartment, then barked. She opened her gritty eyes to find him giving her what she could only describe as an accusing stare.

She was *not* in the mood to deal with another contrary male.

"Don't look at me like that," she tried to snap, though it came out more like a wail. "You're supposed to be on my side, aren't you?"

Conan barked and she could swear he shook his head.

"It's better this way. You're smart enough to know that," she muttered. "It never would have worked out. We're just too different. Eventually he would figure out I'm not what he needs or wants. I can't go through that. You understand, don't you? I *can't*."

She knew the tears she was wiping away probably negated some of the resoluteness of her voice but she couldn't seem to make them stop.

After another moment of glaring at her, Conan made a snorting, disgusted kind of sound. She thought he would amble back down to Anna's apartment. Instead, he came to her and licked at the tears on her cheeks, then settled beside her.

Sage wrapped her arms around his solid mass and wept.

Chapter Fifteen

She finally fell into a fitful sleep sometime in the early hours of the morning, only to be awakened a short time later by a cold nose snuffling the side of her neck.

"Oh, for the love of Pete," she grunted. "Why don't you go harass Anna for once?"

Now the cold nose was joined by a paw on her shoulder. Conan threw in a whine for good measure.

She glanced at her alarm clock. Six o'clock. He'd at least given her an extra half-hour of sleep. She supposed she ought to be grateful for that much. She scrubbed at her face with one hand and sat up. Every single muscle in her body ached.

Her penance, she supposed, for a night of only a few moments' sleep. Conan whined impatiently at the emerging signs of life from her.

She frowned at him. "I guess a broken heart doesn't win me any amnesty when it comes to your daily run, does it?"

He moved his head from side to side in that uncanny way he had. Obstinate male. He barked and cocked his head toward the door. *Come on. Let's go, lazybones.*

For a nonverbal creature, he was remarkably communicative. She sighed, surrendering to the inevitable. She had to be up soon for work anyway. Perhaps a few moments of fresh sea air would help clear this wool from her head.

Ten minutes later, still aching and exhausted but now in her workout clothes, her hair yanked back into a ponytail, she followed Conan down the stairs at a much slower pace than his eager gallop.

Outside, the sun was just beginning its rise above the Coast Range. The sweetness of Abigail's flowers mingled with the sharp, citrusy scent of the Sitka spruce and pines. It was a beautiful morning. She only wished she had room in her heart past this pain to enjoy it.

Still, the cool air did help her wake up and by the time she propped open the beach access gate and took off across the sand, she was moving a little less gingerly.

As usual, the moment they hit the beach, he tugged the leash for her to head downtown—exactly the direction she did not want to go. She couldn't take the chance that Eben might be outside his beach house again. She just couldn't face him this morning.

Or ever.

"No, bud. This way."

Conan barked and kept going to the very limit of his retractable leash. She managed to find the strength to give him the resistance to keep him from dragging her up the beach with him.

Sage pointed stubbornly in the other direction, as far

away from Eben's beach house as she could get. "This way," she repeated.

Conan whined but had no choice but to comply. When she started a halfhearted jog down the beach, he came along with a huffy reluctance that might have made her smile under other circumstances.

"It's no fun when somebody makes you go somewhere you don't want to, is it?" she muttered, wondering if his keen communication skills stretched to understanding irony.

After a few moments of running, she had to admit she felt slightly better. The slanted light of day breaking across the wild, rugged shoreline didn't calm her soul, but at least the endorphins helped take the edge off the worst of her despair.

She had the grim feeling it would take many more of these morning runs before she could find the peace her heart needed.

Why did Eben and Chloe have to come into her life now—and leave it again—when she was still reeling from losing Abigail? It hardly seemed fair.

If she had met them both before Abigail died, would she have even let them into her life? She didn't know. Perhaps she wouldn't have been as vulnerable to falling for both of them if her emotions hadn't been so raw and unprotected.

No, that was a cop-out. She had a feeling she would have fallen hard for them no matter what the circumstances. Chloe was completely irresistible and Eben... well, Eben reached her heart in ways no man ever had.

Or ever would again, she was very much afraid.

She sobbed out a little breath. Just from exertion, she

told herself. It was good for her. Maybe if she ran hard enough, she could outpace the pain.

The tide rose and fell on Oregon's coast approximately every twelve hours. It was almost low tide now, the perfect time for beachcombing. She passed a few early-morning adventurers as she ran, most of them tourists who waved at her and smiled at Conan's friendly bark.

After a mile and a half, she stopped, her breath heaving in her lungs. That first rush of endorphins could only take her so far. She wasn't up for their full five-mile round trip, she decided. Three would have to do for today. She started to turn around, when suddenly Conan barked sharply and tugged his leash so hard he nearly toppled her into the sand.

"What's the matter with you?" She pulled after him to follow her but he gave another powerful lunge away from her and the leash slipped out of her perspiration-slicked hands.

In seconds, he was gone, tearing down the beach in the direction of Hug Point.

"Conan, get back here!" she yelled, but he completely ignored her, racing toward a couple of beachcombers several hundred yards away.

He was going to scare the life out of them if he raced up to them at full-speed, a big hairy red beast rocketing out of nowhere. She had to hope it wasn't a couple of senior citizens with an aversion to dogs and a team of attorneys on retainer.

She groaned and hurried after him.

"Conan! Get back here."

From here, she saw him jump all over one of them and she groaned.

And then she saw a small figure hugging Conan, heard

a high, girlish giggle drift toward her on the breeze, and her heart seemed to stop. She shifted her gaze to see the other person on the beach who stood watching her approach, his dark hair gleaming in the dawn.

Eben and Chloe.

She wanted to turn and run hard in the other direction. She couldn't handle this. Not now. She needed time to restore the emotional reserves that had been depleted by her crying jag the night before.

Were her eyes as puffy and red as they felt? Oh, she hoped not.

It was far too late to turn and run back to the safety of Brambleberry House. Conan was already wriggling around them both with enthusiasm and Chloe was waving for all she was worth.

"Sage! Hi Sage!"

Somehow from deep inside her, she dug around until she found the courage to meet Eben's gaze. His features were impassive and revealed nothing as he watched her approach.

I'm in love with you.

For an instant, she could hear nothing but those words, not even the low murmur of the ocean.

He had offered her a priceless gift and she had rejected it with cruel finality.

I don't love you. You're not the kind of man I want.

She wanted to sob all over again at the lie. How could she face him in the cold light of day?

She looked away quickly and turned her attention back to Chloe. "Hey. Good morning. I didn't expect to see you today."

Or you can bet I would have been back at my house with the covers over my head right now.

"My dad woke me up. He said we had to try to find a few more sand dollars to take home today so we can always remember our trip together. Look at how many we have. He's the best at finding them."

"You're lucky to get them before the gulls do. That's terrific."

"I'm going to make something cool with them. I don't know what yet but I'll figure something out."

"Great."

Oh, she did not want to be here. She wanted to grab her dog and run as far and as fast as they could until both of them collapsed in the sand.

"Look! My dad doesn't have his shoes on, either. Don't you think that's funny? He said he wanted to wriggle his toes in the sand one more time before we leave."

Against her will, Sage shifted her attention to Eben and saw that, indeed, his bare feet were covered in sand. She couldn't seem to look away from the sight.

"This isn't going to last long." His voice sounded tight, slightly strangled, and her gaze flew to his. A glimmer of emotion slipped through his steely reserve and she could swear he looked as if this was as awkward for him as it was for her. "To be honest, it's not what I expected. The sand is much colder than I thought it would be and I'm a little nervous about being pinched by a hermit crab."

"But you tried it, just like you said you wanted to, didn't you, Daddy?" Chloe chirped, oblivious to the currents zinging between them.

He smiled, more than a little self-consciousness in his expression, his eyes shimmering with love for his daughter.

As she gazed at him, something inside her seemed to shatter apart.

The stiff, controlled businessman she had mistaken him for early in their relationship was nowhere in sight. She was stunned by the transformation. His jeans were rolled up, his toes were bare and he had his hands full of sand dollars.

She thought of him that first day when she had taken Chloe home to their beach house. He had been angry and humorless and she never would have imagined in a million years that one day she would find him digging his toes in the sand, laughing with his daughter, hunting for the treasures delivered by the sea.

Or that she would come to love him so dearly.

"Did *you* get pinched by a crab?" Chloe asked her. "You look funny."

Everything inside her began a slow, achy tremble and she suddenly felt as if her heart was like one of the gulls overhead, wheeling and diving across the sky.

"I'm… I'm fine."

Her voice sounded scratchy, and drew Eben's gaze. She saw echoes of longing in his eyes and a pain that matched her own.

She let out a breath, trying so hard to hang on to some shred of sanity. Nothing had changed. Not really. She was still terrified she would be left bruised and bloody.

No. She gazed at his bare feet and at the sight of them, it seemed as if her fear ebbed out to sea with the tide.

She loved him. More than that, she trusted him. He might not be comfortable digging his feet into the sand, but he had done it for his daughter's sake. And for his own. Because he wanted to know what it was like, even if it wasn't the most comfortable feeling in the world.

He was a good man. A wonderful man. If she didn't reach for the priceless gift he had offered her, she suddenly knew she would spend every moment of the rest of her life regretting it.

She wanted desperately to tell him but knew she could say nothing in front of Chloe. As if reading her mind, Conan, bless him, suddenly barked and took off after a gull down the beach.

"Hey! Get back here," Chloe giggled, running after him.

"I'm sorry," Eben finally said when the two of them were alone. He sat on a rock and started slipping his shoes back on. "I assumed with the late night and…everything… that you and Conan probably wouldn't be running this morning. I didn't mean to make you uncomfortable by forcing you to have to see us again."

She shook her head. "I'm not uncomfortable."

"No?" He rose from the rock. "Well, that makes one of us."

How difficult must it be for him to meet up with the woman who had coldly rejected him the night before?

"Don't be uncomfortable. Please."

"Sorry. I haven't had a lot of experience with this. I'm not exactly sure the correct protocol here. How does a man act smooth and urbane around the woman in front of whom he's made a complete ass of himself?"

She closed her eyes, hating the echo of hurt in his voice. She couldn't do this. She had to tell him the truth, no matter how painful.

"I lied, okay?" she finally blurted out. "I lied."

A dead silence met her pronouncement, with no sound at all but the waves and the gulls overhead.

"You…lied about what?"

She went to him and reached for his hand, wishing she wasn't disheveled and sweaty for this. He seemed to always see her at her worst.

Yet he loved her anyway.

"I lied when I told you you weren't the kind of man I want, that I didn't love you. I've never told such a shocking untruth."

He suddenly looked as astonished as if she had just knocked him into the cold waves.

"You don't have to do this."

"Yes, I do." She squeezed his fingers. "I love you, Eben. I have from the beginning."

"Sage—"

She didn't give him time to say anything, just blurted out the rest. "I'm such a coward. I never realized that about myself until last night. I always thought I had everything figured out, that I was so in control of my world. I thought I had worked through all the stuff of my past and become a capable, well-adjusted adult."

"You are."

She shook her head, fighting tears. "No. Inside I'm eight years old again, watching my father walk away without a backward look. I was so afraid to admit my feelings, a-afraid to give you that same kind of power to hurt me. Instead, I decided I would be the one doing the walking."

He said nothing, just continued to watch her, as if he didn't quite know what to believe.

She drew in a breath and reached for his other hand. "I love you, Eben. I'm sorry if I…hurt you by lying and saying I didn't."

He gazed at her for one stunned moment and then he gave a little, disbelieving laugh and tugged her into his arms. As his hard mouth covered hers, Sage wrapped her arms around his waist and held on for dear life. The tight ache inside her eased and she could finally breathe again, for the first time in hours.

This was right. This was exactly where she belonged, right here in his arms.

"It was ripping my heart out to leave you," he murmured against her mouth. "I came down to the beach with Chloe one more time because I wanted one last connection to you. I felt closer to you here by the ocean than anywhere."

She kissed him again and the tenderness in his touch brought tears to her eyes.

"Don't cry," Eben murmured, kissing her cheeks where a few tears trickled down.

She laughed, wondering if her heart could burst from happiness. "These are happy tears. Not like the ones I cried all night. Conan had to drag me out of bed to run. All I wanted to do was pull the covers over my head and hibernate there for a few weeks."

"What if I'd missed you this morning?" he asked. "If I hadn't decided to bring Chloe here one last time? If you and Conan had decided to go in the other direction?"

She hugged him. "We're both here. That's the important thing."

"I think you're the reason I came back for The Sea Urchin, why it seemed so vital to me that I buy it. The hotel was only part of it. Call it fate or destiny or dharma or whatever, but I think everything that's happened was leading me right here, to this moment and to you."

It was the perfect thing to say and she could swear she tumbled even deeper in love with him. This was her prosaic, austere businessman, talking of fate and destiny? Dharma? Had she ever been so wrong about a person in her life?

"I think it was Abigail."

He blinked. "Abigail?"

"I think she met you and fell for those gorgeous green eyes of yours."

She could swear a touch of color dusted his cheekbones. "She did not."

"You didn't know her as well as I did. She always was a sucker for a gorgeous man. Since she couldn't have you for herself, I think she handpicked you for me and she's been doing everything she can since she met you to throw the two of us together."

Eben didn't look convinced, but since he reached for her and kissed her again, she decided the point wasn't worth arguing.

She received confirmation of it a moment later, though, when a sudden bark managed to pierce the lovely fog of desire swirling around her. She wrenched her mouth from Eben's to gaze at her dog.

Conan watched them from a few feet away with that uncanny intelligence in his eyes. He barked again, a delighted sound. It seemed ridiculous, but she could swear he looked pleased.

Chloe was close on the dog's heels and she studied them with startled concern in her green eyes. "Daddy, why are you holding on to Sage? Did she fall?"

His expression filled with sudden panic, as if he hadn't quite thought far enough ahead about explaining this to his daughter. Sage took pity on him and stepped in.

"You're exactly right. I fell, really hard. Harder than I ever thought I could. But you know what? Your dad was right there to pick me back up and help me find my feet. Isn't that lucky?"

Chloe's brow furrowed as she tried to sift through

the layers of the explanation. Sage could tell she wasn't quite buying it. "So why is he still holding on to you?"

She laughed and slanted Eben a look out of the corner of her eyes. "I'll let you answer that one," she murmured.

He gave her a mock glare then turned to his daughter, "Well, after I helped her up, I discovered I didn't want to let her go."

Chloe seemed to accept that with surprising equanimity. She studied them for a moment longer, then shrugged. "You guys are weird," she finally said, then chased Conan across the sand again.

"I meant it. I *don't* want to let you go," Eben repeated fiercely after they were gone.

She wrapped her arms around his neck and held on tight. "I'm not going anywhere."

As he kissed her again, she could swear she heard Abigail's wicked laughter on the wind.

* * * * *

We hope you enjoyed reading
A Soldier's Return

&

The Daddy Makeover

by *New York Times* bestselling author

RAEANNE THAYNE

SPECIAL EDITION

Life, Love and Family

From passionate, suspenseful and dramatic
love stories to inspirational or historical,
Harlequin offers different lines to
satisfy every romance reader.

New books available every month.

HARLEQUIN®

"Do you know of any celebrities staying in the area?" Bea asked their aunt. "We saw this gorgeous guy outside the grocery store tonight in a big SUV limo. He looked familiar but I couldn't quite place him. He had eyes only for Daisy."

"Do tell!" Stella's own eyes widened.

Daisy felt herself flush. "He thought he knew me. I told him he was mistaken."

"You didn't tell me you talked to him!" Bea exclaimed.

"Apparently I missed the family rule where I had to tell you everything going on in my life in a twenty-four-hour period."

"Not everything, just the juicy parts about gorgeous strangers who show up in Cape Sanctuary and act like they know you."

"Well, that rule is stupid since that has only happened the one time."

"You're stupid if you think I wouldn't want to know you talked to him!" Bea said.

Stella laughed. "We all do. Tell us everything."

"Nothing to tell. I bumped into him in the toothpaste aisle. Like I said, he thought he knew me. I said he didn't. We went our separate ways. End of story."

Bea, she knew, wouldn't have let that be the end of the story. Bea would have flirted with the man, would have tucked one of those long, luxurious curls behind her ear as she turned her head just so. At the end of sixty seconds of conversation, Beatriz would have had him hanging on her every word.

But Daisy wasn't her younger sister, she thought as she carried the meal outside to the garden of Three Oaks, with its long pine table and mason jars hanging in the trees, filled with solar-powered candles already beginning to spark to life in the gathering dusk.

She wasn't her sister by a long shot.

Don't miss
The Cliff House *by RaeAnne Thayne,*
available April 2019 wherever
HQN books and ebooks are sold.

www.Harlequin.com